I0744998

STARGÅTE

SG·1™

OUROBOROS

MELISSA SCOTT

FANDEMONIUM BOOKS

An original publication of Fandemonium Ltd, produced under license from MGM Consumer Products.

Fandemonium Books
United Kingdom
Visit our website: www.stargatenovels.com

STARGÅTE
SG·1

METRO-GOLDWYN-MAYER Presents
RICHARD DEAN ANDERSON
in
STARGATE SG-1™
AMANDA TAPPING CHRISTOPHER JUDGE
and MICHAEL SHANKS as Daniel Jackson
Executive Producers ROBERT C. COOPER BRAD WRIGHT
MICHAEL GREENBURG RICHARD DEAN ANDERSON
Developed for Television by BRAD WRIGHT & JONATHAN GLASSNER

STARGATE SG-1 is a trademark of Metro-Goldwyn-Mayer Studios Inc. © 1997-2020 MGM Television Entertainment Inc. and MGM Global Holdings Inc. All Rights Reserved. METRO-GOLDWYN-MAYER is a trademark of Metro-Goldwyn-Mayer Lion Corp. © 2020 Metro-Goldwyn-Mayer Studios Inc. All Rights Reserved.
Photography and cover art: Copyright © 2020 Metro-Goldwyn-Mayer Studios Inc. All Rights Reserved.

WWW.MGM.COM

No part of this publication may be reproduced, stored in or introduced into a retrieval system, or transmitted, in any form, or by any means (electronic, mechanical, photocopying, recording or otherwise) without the prior written consent of the publisher. Any person who does any unauthorized act in relation to this publication may be liable to criminal prosecution and civil claims for damages. If you purchase this book without a cover, you should be aware that this book is stolen property. It was reported as "unsold and destroyed" to the publisher and neither the author nor the publisher has received any payment for this "stripped book".

Print ISBN: 978-1-905586-63-9 Ebook ISBN: 978-1-80070-030-7

CHAPTER ONE
Puzzles

"I'M NOT buying it, Daniel."

Daniel Jackson turned away from the monitor, pointer in hand. Currently the screen was filled with a close-up of the carving over the door of the installation SG-1 had found on P2X-260. "Which part, exactly, aren't you buying, Jack?"

"All of it." General Jack O'Neill squinted at him from the end of the briefing table. It still felt strange to have him there instead of General Hammond, to be a team of three instead of a team of four. Not that Jack hadn't earned the promotion, and not that he didn't deserve the chance to get out of the field, but it was just — odd.

Teal'c tilted his head to one side. "That does not follow, O'Neill."

"It's a metaphor."

Daniel hesitated — it was a figure of speech, certainly, but not actually a metaphor — and Sam Carter cleared her throat. "I really think Daniel's onto something here, sir."

"What something?" O'Neill asked. "What I'm hearing is that you found an abandoned lab with about five data crystals left in it and 'don't touch, very dangerous' plastered all over everything in giant letters."

"Yes and no," Daniel said.

O'Neill looked smug. "I heard yes."

"And no," Daniel said firmly. He looked back at the screen. "It's very clear from the artifact we found that this lab used to belong to Janus — the same Janus who built the time device we found on Maybourne's planet."

"Who is settling in very nicely on his new home, by the way," Jack said. "If anybody cares."

"Not particularly," Daniel said. He looked back at the screen, pressed a button to move to a video clip of the lab's exterior. It was a low building with a heavy stone roof, a style of architecture the Goa'uld had copied repeatedly, with varying degrees of success. A trio of children ran through the scene, which was mercifully silent, but Daniel flinched anyway, their infuriating chant running through his head yet again. Not that he'd ever really been able to get rid of it: every game anybody played seemed to be accompanied by the same monotonous nonsense syllables. By the end of their stay, even Teal'c had looked pained when it started up again. "We've had reason before to think that the Ancients weren't happy with some of Janus's experiments, and this seems to confirm it." He touched another button to zoom in on the symbols that formed a band around the single door.

"And those would be the ones you told me mean Very Very Bad Thing Do Not Touch," Jack said.

"Yes. Except in this case it's a little more complicated." Daniel worked the controls again, so that the video shifted, panning slowly across a second line of carving.

"Looks to me like the same thing," Jack said.

"It does," Daniel said. "But if you look more closely, you can see that this carving was done later, overlaying earlier symbols. And if you enhance them—" He adjusted the image again. "You get Janus's name and a further set of characters."

"Which you can't read," Jack said.

Daniel nodded. "Which I can't read *here*. But once we got inside the lab..." He dismissed the exterior video, called up the tapes they'd made inside the installation. "There are some places where whoever closed down the lab wasn't as thorough, and the symbols are legible. They seem to refer to Atlantis."

There was a little silence as all four of them stared at the screen. In the temporary lights they'd set up, the colors and the carving looked washed out, without subtlety, and somehow that emphasized the bareness of the room. Not that there were obvious gaps in a wall of equipment; there were no trailing wires or broken screens. Instead, there were the low platforms that crisscrossed the space — obviously the bases of missing consoles — and the narrow ledge that ran the length of the chamber's wall. And nothing else, no machinery at all.

"Daniel says that the warning signs are directed at Janus as well as at others," Sam said. "And when you couple that with the absence of equipment here… I think he took whatever it was he was working on with him, before the other Ancients tried to shut him down."

"And you think that — something — has to do with Atlantis," Jack said.

"With getting to Atlantis," Sam said. She held out her hand and Daniel passed her the remote. Sam ran quickly through the tape, found the sequence she wanted. "The lab wasn't entirely stripped. We did find four data crystals, and our preliminary analysis suggests that Janus was attempting to build something that would supersede the Stargates. And, not incidentally, make it easier to reach Atlantis."

On the screen, Sam's hands worried at a piece of carved stone that looked fractionally darker than the stones around it. She tugged, twisted, and abruptly the stone slid out of the wall, displaying a rack meant to hold crystals. It was big enough for power crystals, Daniel thought, but instead it held only a handful of the smaller crystals the Ancients used to store information — a last minute hiding place, surely, the crystals stashed and forgotten in a final rush to escape…

"See, that's where I'm not convinced," Jack said. "Yes, I'd like to find a way to reach the Pegasus Galaxy that doesn't require a ZPM — since we don't have one to spare, and it doesn't seem as though Weir and her people have found one so that they can dial us — but I just don't see what good a big empty lab is going to do us."

"There has to be another lab," Sam said. "Sir, it's the only explanation. Janus knew he was in trouble, and had time to remove everything except these last crystals."

Daniel said, "All of this, all the warnings, the carvings, are an attempt to get control of whatever it was Janus was working on, either by finding him themselves, or by having the local human population notify them if he returned. The other Ancients thought this thing would work."

"You're pushing it," Jack said. He looked at Teal'c. "You got anything here?"

"I believe it is worth further consideration," the Jaffa said, slowly.

"Ah," Jack said. "But consideration where? Do we go back to P2X-260? Daniel said he got everything he was going to get."

"I never said that." Except that he might have, after listening to that chant a few times too many.

"You've got the tapes," Jack said. "And you've got the crystals." He pushed back his chair. "Unless something turns up on either of them — like, say, directions, a gate address, engraved invitations? — we've got other places that look more promising."

"I don't really think so," Daniel said. Sam gave him a look, but he plunged on anyway. "This is the most interesting lead we've had — "

"I don't like interesting," Jack said. He shook his head. "Give me something solid, and I'll reconsider."

"Yes, sir," Sam said, and Teal'c tipped his head forward in grave acknowledgement.

Daniel sighed — it wasn't that Jack was *wrong*, precisely, but he didn't have to like it — and nodded. "OK."

"I'm still right," Daniel said. Sam gave him a look of disbelief as she ran her ID through the elevator control, and Daniel sighed. "Well, I'm right about the installation, anyway."

"I believe General O'Neill is correct," Teal'c said. "Our chances of success are far greater if we first find a likely address."

"The question is how," Sam said. "I didn't want to say it, but those crystals weren't in good shape. I'm having trouble getting anything coherent from them."

"Perhaps the inscriptions will prove more helpful," Teal'c said. It was hard to tell, but Daniel thought he looked a little skeptical. He felt a bit skeptical about that himself. The Ancients had done a thorough job of destroying the sense of Janus's carvings — and how likely was it, really, that Janus would have carved the address of his other secret lab on the walls for everyone to see? They were more likely to find some clue in the village that had grown up between the lab and the Stargate, even if it meant having to listen to that infuriating chant again.

"I still think we should go back," he said aloud, and this time he was sure Teal'c winced.

"I do not wish to hear that song again, Daniel Jackson. Not unless it is absolutely necessary."

"Oh, don't remind me!" Sam made a face. "I'd almost managed to get it out of my head. Ticky-tacky-gnat…"

"Tiskla taskla —" Daniel stopped abruptly. That wasn't it, either, but there was something about those syllables… "I'm going to stick around awhile," he said. "I've — I've maybe got an idea."

"Need some help?" Sam asked. The elevator had arrived, and Teal'c absently braced his arm against the door to hold it back.

"No," Daniel said. "No, I'm good. I don't actually know what I'm looking for yet…"

Sam nodded — she'd heard that before — and stepped into the elevator. Teal'c followed, releasing the doors, and they slid shut with an almost human sigh.

Daniel turned back to his office, retracing his steps down the rounded corridors. It was getting quiet again, the day crew pretty much gone, the night watch settled to work, and for a moment he wondered if he should stop for coffee before he got back to work. No, probably not — if there was anything to find, he would probably be there all night, and the coffee would help more later. He unlocked the door, flipped on the lights to reveal the papers and disks still stacked on his work table, and rummaged through them until he found the disk Sam had marked "Handle With Care." He made a face — it was amazing how annoying that chant could be — and stopped abruptly. Amazingly, even improbably annoying, as though someone had deliberately chosen a rhythm and pitch that would stick in a human brain without it really being heard...

He slipped the disk into the machine, wincing in anticipation, and the screen filled with a line of children holding hands. They were chanting, swinging their arms in time with the words, and a single child ran into the frame, charging straight for the linked arms of two stocky girls. At the last possible moment, they let go, and the running child went sprawling, face down on the muddy ground. Not a nice game, Daniel thought, again, and touched keys to isolate the sound. It was a two-word phrase, repeated over and over, and there was something about it, some syllable that sounded familiar. He reached for a pen, began to transcribe what he was hearing into a phonetic alphabet. He studied the result and then, slowly, began to grin.

"Tisklamor taksanat," Daniel said. He was late to the morning briefing, later than usual, and he was glad he'd shaved the day before.

Teal'c raised an eyebrow. Jack looked at him.

"Shouldn't you be naked?"

"What?"

"Running in here shouting in Greek," Jack said. "Aren't you supposed to have jumped out of a bath or something?"

"It's Ancient," Daniel said. "Closer to Latin — and when did you start reading up on classical scientists?"

"Carter told me," Jack said. Sam gave him a look, and Jack matched it with his best smile. "See? Sometimes I pay attention."

"I do not know this story, Daniel Jackson," Teal'c said. It was hard to tell whether that particular lack of expression was annoyed or merely curious.

"Oh. Well. There was a Greek scientist named Archimedes, and legend — which probably isn't true, given the lack of sensitivity of the experiment in question — but anyway, he was working on a problem involving determining the metal content of an object, and supposedly he noticed that there was a relationship between the amount of water he displaced while getting into his bathtub and the mass involved. He was so excited by the discovery that he leaped from his bath and ran down the street shouting 'Eureka,' which means, literally, 'I have found it.'" Daniel felt his voice trail off in the face of Teal'c's stare. "Having forgotten to dress beforehand."

"Indeed."

"You probably had to be there," Jack said, helpfully.

"That's — it's really not the point," Daniel said.

"Then what is the point?" Jack asked.

"The point is, you said you'd let us look for Janus's lab if we had a better idea of where it was."

Jack gave an impatient nod. "Yes. Like a gate address."

Daniel smiled. "And that's exactly what I've got for you. One perfectly good gate address. Tisklamor taksanat."

"That," Jack said, "is not a gate address."

"Actually, sir, it is," Sam said. She looked at Daniel. "You mean to tell us that incredibly annoying chant —"

"Is the address of Janus's next base," Daniel said. "Or, at least, it is a gate address. But why else would anyone have embedded it in a children's nonsense rhyme?"

"An incredibly adhesive nonsense rhyme," Sam said.

"Indeed," Teal'c said.

Sam reached for her laptop and began typing. "Sir, it's a valid address. P6T-847."

"Never heard of it," Jack said.

Sam peered at her screen. "We sent a MALP through a little more than a year ago. No sign of inhabitants, just a huge field of grass as far as the eye — or the camera — could see. But now...

Sir, I think it's worth checking out. If we could find a way to reach Atlantis, to find out what's going on —"

Jack nodded. "All right. Let's see what's out there."

The image in the screen was almost unchanged from the pictures sent back from the first survey. Tall grass, with dark, tightly closed seed heads waved at the edge of the Stargate's platform, and as Walter manipulated the camera, zooming out, there was only more grass, stretching toward the horizon. The sky was streaked with cloud, their edges shell-pink in the planetary dawn, and something fluttered in the middle distance, a bird or a large insect, hopping from seed to seed.

"I'm not seeing any secret lab," Jack said.

"It's going to be hidden," Daniel pointed out.

Sam ignored them both, frowning at the control readouts. "Is there any way we can get the MALP further away from the platform?"

Walter glanced up at her. "Yes, ma'am, I can take it down the steps, but we won't be able to see anything but grass. It's taller than our longest periscope extension."

Sam sighed. She hadn't really expected a better answer. "Leave it there, then," she said, and straightened. "General, there's no reason not to take a quick look."

"Except for there being nothing there," Jack answered.

"Or there might be directions to another location," Daniel said. "That would be like Janus."

"If that's the case," Jack said, "I expect you to come back before following any more mysterious leads."

Daniel looked as though he wanted to protest, but Sam kicked him, none too subtly. "Yes, sir."

"Then you have a go," Jack said.

They walked through the gate into a warm breeze and a low buzzing sound. At first Sam thought it was insects, but after a moment she realized that the air was clear of flying things. The noise came from the grass itself, from the wind playing in the hollows of the seed heads. The MALP hadn't lied. There was nothing but grass as far as she could see, and in every direction. She turned slowly through a full circle, hoping to spot some change, something different in the sea of grass, but there was nothing. The Stargate stood on a stone platform perhaps a meter above the ground, a platform big enough to hold the DHD as well as the gate itself. The sun was well up now, and most of the clouds had burned off, leaving an empty pale blue sky. There was no sound except the buzz of the grass, and the sound of their boots on the stones.

"This has been here a long time, Colonel Carter," Teal'c said, and touched the edge of the platform with the butt of his staff weapon.

"Yeah." The stone was chipped and crumbling, the edges of the platform no longer perfectly even. Steps led down into the grass, and the lowest stair was already half swallowed by new growth, thick strands poking up between the stones. "And nobody's been taking care of it."

Daniel was already ahead of them, head down, following some pattern only he could see. It took him to the DHD, and he stooped to examine it, then crouched beside it.

"Hey! Take a look at this!"

"What have you got?" Sam moved to join him, the sun already hot on her neck.

"Some unusual carvings." Daniel ran his hand over the DHD's pedestal, beneath the overhanging rim of the dialing device itself.

"That seems an unusual place to decorate," Teal'c said.

"Yeah." Sam leaned closer, trying to make out the pattern.

"I don't think it's decorative," Daniel said. "Or not entirely." He reached into his pocket, found a sheet of paper and a pencil. He laid the paper against the stone and began rubbing the pencil lightly over it. "I mean, there's definitely a pattern to it, like, oh, calligraphy, but it also says something—"

He pulled the paper away and sat back on his heels, spreading the paper out so that they all could see.

"Indeed," Teal'c said, and Sam nodded.

"'To look for the stone'?"

"Yeah." Daniel squinted at the pedestal again. "And, wait—yeah, there." He grabbed his pencil again, and a second sheet of paper, began rubbing the graphite over the paper. "I think these are coordinates."

He stood up, holding out the paper, and Sam frowned. It looked more like a stylized flower—except that when you looked closely at each petal, it was an Ancient directional marker. "I see it," she said. "That's the sunrise sign, and that, plus these, would send us—" She swung back to the east, a few points south of the sun. "Approximately there, thirty meters out."

"To look for the stone," Daniel said. "Janus was here."

Sam nodded thoughtfully. "We'd better spread out a little, though. The exact direction of sunrise is going to have changed a little since Janus's day. And we don't know the exact season, either."

"Which argues that it has to be fairly obvious," Daniel said. "Janus must have anticipated this."

"I don't know if that follows," Sam began, but Daniel was already stepping off the platform and wading out into the grass. It reached almost to his shoulders, and Sam sighed at the thought of forcing her way through the thick stems.

"I must agree, Colonel Carter," Teal'c said. "The Ancients were long-lived, but—I do not think even Janus planned this far ahead."

"We'll find out," Sam said, and started into the grass herself. Teal'c moved to her left and did the same.

The hum was louder down in the sea of grass, and the stalks gave off an odd, pleasant scent when they were bruised, something like apples and musk, but neither. She waded through it, turning back at regular intervals to check her progress, and stopped when she thought she'd gone about thirty meters. The grass rose on all sides, the bent stems behind her already straightening to erase her passage. She keyed her radio.

"Daniel? Anything?"

"Not yet."

"Teal'c?"

There was a little pause, and Sam frowned. There had been no sign of life, no evidence that anyone had been here in decades, but it was always possible they'd missed something. She keyed her radio again.

"Come in, Teal'c."

"I believe I have found something," Teal'c said. "It appears to be the stone."

Sam pushed her way through the thick stems of grass, came out at last into a small clearing. It would have been visible from the air, she thought, but of course they hadn't sent a UAV. The stone was a huge rectangular slab, dull gray, its surface spotted here and there with patches of lichen. It rose a little less than the height of her knee, and there was no mistaking it for something natural. The edges were neatly carved, if dulled by weather, and a circle at least a meter wide had been carved more or less in the center of the stone, the lines only slightly blurred. Teal'c knelt at its foot, frowning thoughtfully at a smaller set of carvings. It was a series of shallow depressions arranged in a five by six grid that looked vaguely familiar. Or maybe it had been familiar to Jolinar — the fleeting connection was without context, without detail. She had long ago adjusted to those random flashes of another self, and looked from the grid to the circle. Except it wasn't a circle, she realized. It was an enormous snake, curled into a ring and biting its own tail. The scales had been more lightly carved, were more worn than the rest of the carving, but she could still make out the details. And it was a symbol she had seen before, a symbol for infinity.

There was a thrashing from the grass behind her, and Daniel

joined them, his eyebrows rising as he took in the stone and its markings.

"Ouroboros," he said.

"What?" Sam gave him a wary glance.

"The snake that eats its own tail." Daniel moved further along the side of the stone slab, studying the carving. "It's a symbol for infinity, and also for alchemy, for the transformation of base matter into gold, or matter into energy. And also —" He looked over his shoulder, his smile suddenly mischievous. "In Earth's mythology, it's associated with the god Janus."

"Oh, come on," Sam protested, but it made a certain amount of sense. Everything they'd seen of Janus so far suggested that he was just that arrogant. "If he went to all this trouble to hide his secret lab, why would he carve his name on the front door?"

"It may not be his actual laboratory," Daniel answered. "It may just tell just how to get there — give us the next clue for the puzzle."

"Then you will want to see this, Daniel Jackson." Teal'c covered one of the stone pits with his thumb, and there was a faint, almost musical whistle from the stone. Definitely musical, Sam amended, and she went to one knee beside the Jaffa.

"Do that again."

Teal'c covered the same pit, and this time she was sure she heard a note. He nodded, covering a second hole, and the sound changed.

"Wait, what have you got there?" Daniel crouched beside them.

"I'm not entirely certain," Teal'c said. "But I believe it is intended to create sounds of specific pitch."

"Yeah." Daniel frowned at the grid, shoving his glasses back up onto his nose. "Yes, definitely, that's a formation that we've seen the Ancients use for musical notation. But why here?"

"You said it yourself," Sam answered. "A puzzle?"

"Yes, but —" Daniel stopped abruptly, his frown deepening, and covered the pit in the lower left corner of the grid, cock-ing his head as though he was trying to memorize the sound. "Although, if it's a puzzle —" He shrugged off his pack, and began covering holes, one after the other. Sam blinked, and then winced as she recognized the pattern. He was playing the children's chant, tisklamor taksanat, and sure enough as the last note sounded, there was a rumble from inside the stone. Sam grabbed her P90 and pushed herself to her feet, and she heard the click as Teal'c armed his staff weapon. Daniel didn't move, still crouching in the dirt at the base of the stone, still didn't move as the stone split above the musical grid, two thin slabs sliding apart to reveal a pattern inlaid with gold. Nothing else happened, and Sam slowly lowered her weapon.

"Ancient numbers?" she asked.

"Yeah." Daniel ran a careful hand across the carved surface. "It looks like some kind of sequence, but I can't figure out the intent. There's a gap here, see? And one here."

"It's another puzzle," Sam said. She unfastened her P90, and went to one knee beside Daniel.

"OK, I'll buy that," Daniel said. "But —"

"You've seen them before," Sam said. "You're supposed to guess the next number in the sequence — figure out what the formula is." She narrowed her eyes at the stone. "Give me your notebook."

Daniel handed it over, and she transcribed the carving into Arabic numerals, considered the result. No, it didn't make sense, not completely.

"That's a nine," Daniel said, pointing, and she corrected the number.

"Got it," she said, and looked at the stone. "So how do we enter it? Just — write it in?"

"I think we need gold," Daniel said. "To match the other numbers."

"Great." Sam sat back on her heels. "I don't suppose you've got a class ring or something?"

"Not with me," Daniel answered.

"Perhaps this will suffice," Teal'c said. He held out a cylinder about the size of his thumb, and Daniel took it warily.

"Trade gold," Teal'c said. "I believe it is soft enough to mark the stone."

Daniel tested it on the rock beside the musical grid and, after a couple of tries, was able to leave a more or less solid line. "OK," he said. "So what's the answer?"

Sam looked back at the notebook. "Well, assuming I've worked out the formula correctly, the first missing number is 58, and the last one is 172."

Daniel took the notebook from her, transcribed the numbers into Ancient characters. "OK," he said again. "Here we go."

He leaned forward, stretching to reach the first gap in the sequence, and carefully wrote in the first number. Teal'c had risen to his feet again, and his staff weapon was primed and ready. Sam grabbed her P90 as Daniel inscribed the second number, bracing herself for whatever happened next.

Nothing happened, not for long enough that she was starting to rethink her calculations, and then something beneath the stone gave a deep groan, and the slab split neatly down the middle. The two sides pivoted apart, stone grating on stone, to reveal a set of steps leading down into darkness.

"Well, we've got something," she said, and flicked on the light attached to her weapon. Daniel produced a flashlight, and shone it ahead of them as well.

The steps stretched down for at least ten, maybe twelve feet, ending in a bare stone floor that seemed to match the material of the slab. The air smelled dry and dusty, but not foul. Clearly the chamber had had some ventilation over the years. "Cover us, Teal'c," she said, and started down the stairs, Daniel on her heels.

At the bottom of the steps she stopped, swinging the P90 to cover the room, its light playing across what looked like control consoles, running parallel to the side walls. Light bounced back from the end of the room: a wall of glass, no, a huge window, stood between the consoles and something at the far end of the underground room. Otherwise the place was empty except for a thin drift of dust, and she relaxed a little, moving toward the glass wall. Daniel came with her, tilting his light so that the reflection was minimized.

The space beyond the glass was smaller, a narrow room narrowed further by what looked like some kind of capacitor system. There was a platform in the center, and on the wall above it was carved another ouroboros, this one filled with gold.

"Well," Daniel said. "I guess we've found the secret lab."

"Yeah." Sam turned her back on the ouroboros, swung her light around the other room. It had to be the control room for whatever it was the inner room did, and as her light flicked over the consoles, she thought she recognized some of the systems. "I think we've got it. I think — it looks to me as though this is what Janus was working on, his system that was going to supersede the Stargates. And that means —"

Daniel nodded. "Atlantis."

CHAPTER TWO
Testing

JACK SETTLED his body armor more comfortably on his shoulders, and tried to pretend he was completely unaware of the paperwork still piled on his desk. It'll get done, he told himself, just as he'd told Davis, and wished he believed it any more than Davis did. Still, this was an important discovery, the biggest Ancient lab since they'd opened up Antarctica, and they had definitely needed people with the ATA gene to help initialize the systems. And he had the ATA gene, even if Sergeant Ito of SG-12 had already done the human light switch thing, and he needed to take a look at the place: two birds with one stone.

He accepted his P90 from the hovering sergeant, and made his way into the gateroom. Dr. Lee was there already, along with SG-7 — and he was pleased to see that Major Perry had only issued Lee a sidearm. That was iffy enough, on past performance, but a lot better than giving him a submachine gun.

Perry came to attention at his entrance. "Ready to go, sir."

Jack returned the salute, letting his eyes roam around the gateroom one last time. There was a pallet of equipment waiting, too, lights and a generator recognizable among the unmarked boxes. "Got everything you need?"

"Dr. Lee says we do," Perry answered, and Lee gave him a preoccupied smile.

"Yes. I mean, assuming that we've read the situation correctly—"

"I'm sure you have," Jack said, and turned to look up at the control room window. "You can go ahead and dial, Sergeant."

"Initiating dialing sequence." The voice echoed from the loudspeakers, and Lee took a quick step back, making sure he was far enough away from the gate. The ring turned, the chevrons lit and locked, and the wormhole opened with a kawhoosh. It fell back, steadied to a gently rippling pool, and Jack looked up at the window again.

"Keep the lights on, Sergeant," he called, and looked at Perry. "All right, Major. You have a go."

It had been a while since he'd been through the gate, long enough that the sensation was strange instead of completely familiar. He paused at the edge of the gate platform, letting the feelings settle, scanned the area over the top of his sunglasses. Sure enough, there was a lot of the tall grass, but SG-1 and SG-12 had cut a path through it, and Perry's team was already manhandling the pallet toward that gap. Lee was standing frankly open-mouthed, staring up into the pale sky, and Jack clapped him on the shoulder.

"You need to get out more, Doc," he said, and started toward the lab.

The two halves of the stone slab had folded back like the lid of a sarcophagus — not a happy image, that, and he was glad to hear the sound of voices from the base of the steps and hear the familiar whine of a generator. The lab itself was huge, large enough that the lights didn't reach to all the corners, and the air was cool, but the main thing, the thing you couldn't miss, was the giant gold snake on the back wall. There were more lights set up there, and a door had been opened in the barrier, power cords snaking through.

"General O'Neill!"

That was Carter, coming up with a grin and a neat salute. There was dust in her hair and smeared across her black tee shirt, and she looked intensely pleased with herself.

"Colonel Carter," Jack said. "What have you got for me?"

"One almost intact Ancient installation," Carter answered. "Pretty much as advertised, sir."

"I don't know." Jack looked around. "It didn't come with one of those face-grabber things."

"Which is probably a good thing." That was Daniel, coming

to join them with his notebook in his hand. "They never seem to work out very well in the long run."

That was true enough, so Jack ignored it. "Any idea what it was meant to do?"

The other two exchanged glances, and for a moment Jack was very aware that he was on the outside. They were SG-1, and he was in command of the SGC, and — he shoved the thought aside, made himself concentrate on Carter's response.

"We're getting an idea, sir," she began. "I'm pretty sure it's one of Janus's installations, and I think he was trying to build at least the next generation of Stargates, and maybe something that would make them obsolete altogether."

"And, you know, I think I'm entitled to a quick 'I told you so,'" Daniel added.

"Maybe," Jack said. He waved at the gold snake on the back wall. "And that's it?"

"We think so, sir." Carter looked as though she wanted to open her laptop and start showing him formulae, and Jack shook his head.

"Bottom line, Carter."

"Sergeant Ito got all the consoles initialized," she said, "so we've got everything running on stand-by right now. Everything you see in here is to control and power the devices behind the wall — which isn't glass, by the way, but an ultra-pure form of carbon. Almost like a wall of diamond, in fact. Most of what's in here is either stuff we've seen before, or very similar to things we've seen, either in Antarctica or the other installations. It's power control devices, computers, systems to monitor and record results. But all of this is ancillary to the main device, and there — we're still not sure what it does."

"We do know what it's meant to do," Daniel said. There was an edge to his voice that suggested there was still some disagreement about that. "I've been able to pull records from the computers and translate the crucial ones, and it's just what Sam said. Janus was trying to build a — well, I guess you'd call it a super Stargate system, one that could dial Atlantis and possibly other extra-galactic addresses. It looks as though there are placeholders in the programming for eight and even nine-symbol gate addresses."

"Yes, but it's also clear that he wasn't successful in making the transport part work," Carter said.

"That's actually debatable," Daniel said. "The latest entries strongly suggest that he'd made a breakthrough."

"So why didn't he follow it up?" Jack asked.

"It looks as though the other Ancients shut him down," Daniel said. "Or he had to abandon the place to avoid being shut down, because it looks like he was planning to come back."

"That's not actually the most interesting thing, sir," Carter said

Daniel started to say more, but someone called his name. He hurried to answer, and Jack lifted an eyebrow at Carter.

"Oh?"

"No, sir. You see, the problem with dialing addresses outside the galaxy is the amount of power it requires — we needed a ZPM to dial Atlantis, and it's pretty clear that the expedition hasn't had any luck finding a power source for the gate on their side."

Or they were all dead, Jack thought. There were too many things that could have gone wrong, too many possible disasters, too many dangers that could not have been foreseen. He'd known when he'd approved the mission that it was potentially a one-way trip, and just because everyone who'd gone had agreed to it didn't make him feel any better. If they were lost, it was on his watch, and there was nothing he could do about it. Except maybe until now.

Carter was hurrying on as though she'd guessed his thought. "Janus was trying to solve the same problem, sir, and it looks like he made a good start. That's why I asked for Dr. Lee to come here, to confirm my calculations, because if I'm right… Sir, I think Janus has figured out how to tap vacuum energy directly, without having to create a separate region of sub-space/time to draw from."

"Carter…"

"Look, sir, a ZPM is essentially a container for a cut-off region of subspace, from which we can draw not quite infinite power, but something very close to that. What Janus seems to have done is, well, hard-wired this new device directly into the fabric of subspace. If we could figure out how he did it, we'd never have to worry about needing a ZPM or anything like it ever again."

Jack glanced toward the wall of diamond, clamping down hard on his enthusiasm. "It doesn't look like it's doing much right now, Carter."

"No, sir." She looked at her laptop again, but resisted the urge to unfold it. "But as far as I can tell, sir, it's all on-line and ready to go. All we need is to inject a small amount of energy — a hundredth of what a naquadah generator is capable of producing — and we can start it up. That's what I want Dr. Lee to check out."

Jack looked at the golden snake, gleaming in their lights, and then past Carter's shoulder to the teams busy at the consoles. "How likely is it that we can figure out how to use this new power system safely?" he asked, and Carter grinned.

"Honestly, sir? I think the odds are fifty-fifty. But — if Daniel's right, this thing was meant to take people to Atlantis. If we can get it working, we can at least find out what's happening with the expedition."

And that was the kicker, as she'd known it would be. Jack nodded. "All right, Colonel, you can carry on. But you're not to turn it on without direct authorization. Clear?"

She nodded briskly. "Yes, sir."

"Right," Jack said. He looked toward the snake again, the plain platform beneath it. It was so tempting, it looked so easy, just turn it on and go. They could find out what was happening in the Pegasus galaxy, maybe even figure out a way to power up all the Antarctic systems, and for once have solid protection for the entire planet against whatever else was out there. Except — it was Janus. Never, not once in the history of the Stargate program, had anything gone right when Janus was involved. He wished he could believe this would be an exception.

It took another three days for Lee and his team to confirm Carter's theory, and the best part of another week for them to work out a way to turn on the power without starting up the device in the inner chamber. Jack sat patiently through the briefing, repressing the urge to ask either smart-ass or annoyingly stupid questions, listening less to the technical explanations than to the tone of Carter's voice. It wasn't that she ever sounded less than confident — if she didn't think something was going to work, she wouldn't let it get this far — but he'd long ago learned to hear the difference between certainty and general enthusiasm. He heard certainty this time, and that was good enough for him.

"OK," he said, breaking up one last squabble between two of the junior scientists. "Carter. Let me get this straight. The plan is to turn on the power but not activate the device itself."

"Yes, sir."

"So how are you going to know you've got the power working?"

"The system was designed with two stages, a power-up stage, and then turning on the actual device. We're just going to do the power up."

"And you're sure that's all you're going to do?"

"As sure as I can be, sir," she answered. "And if I'm wrong, we've got breakers in place that should shut down the entire system."

Jack hadn't missed the difference between *should* and *will*, but he also knew that this was about the best he could reasonably expect. If he had to choose, he'd take Carter's 'should' over anybody else's 'will'. "OK," he said again. "Let's see what we've got."

"Thank you, sir," Carter said.

"Oh, Colonel?" Jack said, before she could turn away. "I'd like to sit in. If you don't mind."

Her smile widened, just for an instant. "Of course not, sir."

He was just looking for an excuse to avoid the paperwork. That was what he told himself, and what he told Davis, who was starting to look a bit harried. But it was an important discovery, this potential replacement for ZPMs, and he wanted to see it in action himself.

It was all an excuse, and he admitted as much to himself as he shaved, making sure he looked like what he was, the man in charge, head of the SGC, a man who could sleep every night in his own bed and wouldn't show up unshaven for anything short of an act of God and maybe not then. The face in the mirror smirked back at him. He just wanted to walk through the gate one more time, each chance precious because it might be the last. This was as good an excuse as he was likely to get.

Janus's lab was brighter than before, the lights he'd seen on the travel pallet now set up to banish the last of the shadows. For the first time, he realized that the walls had been painted an odd terracotta color. It matched the nail polish one of the civilian technicians was wearing, busy entering data into a laptop, and he wondered if she'd picked it on purpose.

Carter and Lee were in the inner room, and Jack moved to join them, stepping over the cables that still ran through the doorway. He hadn't actually been inside before, and somehow it wasn't quite what he'd expected. For starters, it was a lot taller than it was wide, with a ceiling that rose a good eight or nine feet higher than the one in the other room. Which had to mean that there was only a thin layer of dirt overhead, though probably Janus had put some solid shell in place. He craned his neck to see, but couldn't make out either reinforcements or any signs that the building had degraded. The walls were painted pure white — or maybe it wasn't paint, but some kind of thick insulation. The golden snake looked more like it had been inlaid than painted on the rough surface.

"General!" Carter broke off her conversation with Lee, and came to join him. "We're just about ready."

"Except for the back-up generator," Lee said. "And the cut-out switch."

"That's installed now," Carter said, patiently.

"Yes, but — there's still that one circuit that we haven't identified."

"Colonel?" Jack tipped his head to one side.

"There is still one set of connections that doesn't have any apparent purpose," Carter said. She still seemed briskly confident. "In fact, I'm not sure it ever did anything, it looks as though it might be completely redundant, but —" She shrugged. "To be safe, we've pulled the crystals that connect it to the main part of the system. In any case, we're not trying to turn on the device. We're just seeing if we can tap the power source."

"OK," Jack said. "So where's the — generator?"

"I think we're standing in it, sir," Carter said. "Although it doesn't really exist in our area of space/time."

"The walls are coated with a special material, of which we haven't been able to identify all the compounds," Lee said. "And there is a bank of capacitors beneath the platform that seem designed to accept the power once it starts flowing."

"Wait a minute." Jack looked around. Yes, that was definitely what looked like a control panel beside the platform, and he pointed to it. "If this is the generator —"

Carter nodded, looking pleased. "Exactly, sir. The device is definitely intended to be controlled from that console, so, while this chamber seems to function as a reinforcement to the subspace field, the actual power generated goes straight into the capacitors. It's not only potentially a lot of power, it's really clean."

Jack nodded back. Even he could see what that could mean, the power of a ZPM ready for the taking, without any of the problems of nuclear power, or oil, or coal, or the instability of things like wind and sun. If they could figure out how to attach this device, or build these chambers themselves — He curbed his thoughts sharply. First they'd better see if the thing worked at all. "All right," he said. "Ready when you are, Colonel."

"Yes, sir. We're just about there, so if you wouldn't mind —"

"Getting out of the line of fire?" Jack asked. "Not a problem, Colonel."

He retreated to the main chamber and settled in behind Lee, who was typing frantically into his laptop. Beyond the wall of diamond, Carter and a couple of technicians were setting up a naquadah generator, running a cord from it to what looked like a port beneath the platform.

"Wait a minute," Jack said. "If this thing is so powerful, how come you need the most powerful generator we have short of the ZPM?"

"We have to open the connection between this universe and subspace," Lee answered. "That takes a lot of power initially, but once it's open, the connection should be self-sustaining."

Somehow that didn't sound as reassuring as it did when Carter said it. Still, it was too late to back out now. Jack folded his arms, doing his best to look impassive, and Teal'c came to stand behind him.

"Is this not impressive, O'Neill?"

"Yeah." Jack slanted a glance at him. "You're not having any bad feelings about this, right? No funny feelings, no sense of impending doom, nothing like that?"

Teal'c smiled. "I do not. And if I did, it would mean very little."

"Maybe, maybe not."

Beyond the wall of diamond, Daniel had joined Carter and the technicians and was apparently checking translations, bending close over the console's screen. Carter straightened then and waved to Lee.

"OK. We're going to close up now."

A technician hauled back the last of the cables and pushed

the almost invisible door into place. It took all her strength to move it and the door sealed itself with a dull hiss. In the chamber, Carter touched her radio.

"Are you receiving me, Dr. Lee?"

"We're hearing you just fine," Lee answered. "I'm pulling the cut-outs and running the current test. And — everything's fine. You're good to go, Colonel."

"Confirmed," Carter said. "We're starting the naquadah generator."

One of the technicians did something to it and there was a faint low rumble, settling instantly to a hum that was barely a vibration in the soles of Jack's feet. He braced himself, waiting for — well, he wasn't exactly sure for what, but for something to happen. Beyond the diamond glass, Daniel said something and the second technician made an adjustment.

"I'm getting subspace ripples," one of the technicians on their side of the glass said, and Lee touched his radio.

"Colonel Carter, we're seeing a response on the subspace monitors. We're getting Marston ripples."

"We're seeing that, too," Carter answered. "I'm increasing power to damp them out."

She did something to the generator controls and Jack felt something snap. There was a weird flicker, as though the chamber itself had blinked, and Lee looked up sharply.

"Colonel! We've opened the connection!"

"Holding steady," Carter said. "Still holding..."

On the wall behind her, the snake's eye began to glow.

Sam looked from the Ancient console to the attached laptops and back again, watching the power build in the capacitors. So far, everything was working exactly as predicted. The pulse of power from the naquadah generator was just enough to open the connection and, as she'd expected, the connection, once opened, was self-sustaining. The air felt thick, electric, and she could feel her hair lifting away from her scalp. That was only to be expected and she checked the readings again. Still steady, the capacitors building slowly, and she touched her radio. It crackled, distorted by the field, and behind the diamond glass she saw Lee frown.

"I think we've got a good result," she said. "I'm going to begin shutting down."

Lee's voice was equally distorted, but the words were clear enough. "Ok, Colonel, go ahead."

Sam checked her screen again, then looked at the technicians. "Get ready to begin our shut-down procedure. Pereira, what's the transfer rate?"

"We're holding at seventy percent, ma'am."

"Dial it back to fifty," Sam said.

"Yes, ma'am," Pereira said. "Fifty percent."

There was a whoop of an alarm from Daniel's end of the console, and a flashing light.

"Oh, that's not good," Daniel said, his hands racing over the controls. "Um, Sam, this says — it looks like it's saying there's turbulence in the system. Backflow?"

Sam could see the same pattern emerging on the laptop screens, coils of yellow and orange flickering to life in the middle of the steady blue that was the representation of the power flow. "I see it. Pereira. Open back up to sixty percent."

"Yes, ma'am." Pereira did as he was told and the other technician looked up sharply.

"Colonel, I'm getting an instability in the capacitors — it's like they're trying to feed the power back out again."

If the capacitors failed, if they refused to accept the incoming power… Sam tried not to think about the size of the resulting explosion. "Seventy percent, Pereira."

"Back to seventy percent, ma'am."

"It's not enough," Daniel said. "I'm still showing the backflow and now it's telling me that it's time to turn on the device."

That was presumably just an automated warning, Sam thought, part of the normal sequence for activating the machine.

"Seventy-five percent, Pereira."

"Yes, ma'am." There was a pause and then she saw his shoulders sag with relief. "We're steady."

"Carter?" That was Jack's voice, distorted by the crackling radio.

Sam checked the readouts again, decided they really were stable, and turned back to face the diamond glass. "Sorry, sir. When we started to shut down, we ran into a little problem."

"How little?"

"Not big, sir." I hope, she added silently. "We'll try our secondary procedure."

"OK," Jack said, and she saw him take a step back again.

"Ma'am," the second technician said. "I'm getting containment warnings on the capacitors."

Crap. Sam leaned over her shoulder to check the readings. The capacitor was nowhere near what should be its limits, but those were definitely containment warnings. "See if you can dial back again, Pereira."

Another alarm sounded from Daniel's end of the console. "Sam, it's saying we have to turn the device on now."

"Or else?" Sam asked.

"It doesn't say, but I don't think it's good." Daniel was busy with his keyboard, trying to access further information.

"Pereira?" Sam could see the answer before he spoke: the turbulence was back in the display, the swirls now orange tinged with red.

"No luck." He touched keys again, shaking his head. "Every time I try to decrease the flow, it just makes it worse."

"Yasmin, try to damp down the capacitors' containment field, see if you can't bottle it up until we get the backflow sorted out." Sam turned back to the wall. "Dr. Lee, I think you should evacuate non-essential personnel."

"On it," Lee answered, and behind him Jack stepped forward again.

"Carter?"

"We're working on it, sir." She turned back to the console, but not before she saw him begin ordering people away from their stations.

She put that aside, touched keys to call up a schematic of the system. The weird blind circuit was flashing orange — which didn't exactly make sense, because there was no way it could affect anything, but she keyed her radio again. "Bill. I need the crystals we took out of that blind circuit."

"What?" She couldn't spare the time to look, but she could hear the confusion. "But that can't possibly be —"

"That's what the device is telling me," Sam said. "I need them now."

"Yeah, OK —"

"On their way," Jack said.

Sam nodded, all her attention on the readings. The backflow was getting worse, even after Pereira raised the power to eighty percent, and then to eighty-five; at eighty-eight percent the system was barely stable, but at least she had a few seconds' breathing room.

"Got your crystals, Carter," Jack said. "Where do you want them?"

"Thank you, sir," she said, and snatched them out of his hand. Access to that circuit was through the side of the platform. She dropped to her knees beside it, prying open the cover, and tugged the tray out. She gave it a quick once-over — no cracks, no chips, nothing out of normal — and slotted the last two crystals into place. They lit, and she snatched her hands back, swearing at the shock. The tray slid closed without her intervention, and she hauled herself to her feet, tucking her stinging hands into her armpits. One of the alarms cut out, but the other one kept sounding.

"Colonel, the containment is expanding," Yasmin said, and Pereira spoke in the same moment.

"Backflow's getting worse."

"Go to full power," Sam said. She glanced at the control

room, saw only Lee and his assistant at the main consoles. Teal'c was inside the chamber as well, bracing himself to hold the door open.

"Full power, yes, ma'am," Pereira echoed. "Stable, but I don't think it's going to last."

"We have to turn the device on," Daniel said. "That's what this is telling me. The power has to go somewhere."

Sam came to look over his shoulder, hoping against hope that for once he'd gotten it wrong, but the symbols were unmistakable. Why can't we turn it off? The feedback loop should accept interruption, that was the first thing she'd thought of — unless that was what the blind circuit did, somehow prevented the system from being turned off until the device was used? She shoved the thought away, looked at the technicians. "Pereira, Yasmin, get out of here. You, too, Daniel."

"Not likely." Daniel didn't move from his place, still typing frantically.

"Go," Sam said, and the technicians went, reluctantly, squeezing out past Teal'c.

"What's the plan, Carter?" Jack's voice was weirdly calm.

"We're going to have to let the device activate," Sam answered, "or else this whole place is going to explode." She looked at the diamond wall. "Or something. I'm not actually sure what subspace power will do to living beings, but I don't think we should find out. I think we'll be safe behind the wall." She stepped into Pereira's place, leaning down to adjust the flow. "It'll take about a minute for the device to come on line, so we should just have time to get out once I've activated it."

Daniel pushed himself to his feet, though his attention was still on his screens. "Better hurry, Sam."

Sam took a breath. The switch was obvious, a plain gold button set apart from the rest of the controls, its surface marked with the same ouroboros. "Go," she said, and pressed it.

The entire chamber shuddered as she turned, and the door slipped from Teal'c's clutching hands, closing solidly behind him and sealing them in the chamber.

"Well, crap," Jack said. "Carter—"

"It'll be worse if we turn it off, sir," she said. "Subspace energy—"

"Is bad, yeah, I got that." Jack's face was drawn into an unhappy grimace. "But this device—is it any better?"

"It's a transport device, like the Stargate," Daniel said. His tone was less confident than his words. "It should just open, not—anything else."

"Stand by the console," Sam said. She was suddenly consumed by the memory of the prison planet, a pair of smoking shoes that was all that was left after a man was caught in the outflow of the opening wormhole. "Quick, move."

They scrambled into its doubtful shelter. On the wall above them, the ouroboros was glowing, the light traveling from the head around the circle of the body. It was almost white-hot at the head, and golden at the leading edge, brilliant and strangely without heat. The light was almost at the serpent's mouth, almost touching itself, and even as she thought it, the light joined into a solid ring. There was a flash, a blow like the sound of thunder, and then nothing.

CHAPTER THREE
Lost City

TEAL'C opened his eyes slowly, assessing the odd, dry smell of the air and the taste of blood on his tongue. His body hurt, a dozen spots bruised and sore, but even as he took his first full breath he could tell that there was nothing seriously wrong. The worst was the cut on the inside of his lip, where presumably he'd hit his jaw as he fell. He tested his joints carefully anyway, moving cautiously until he could confirm that he was no more than bruised, and sat up slowly.

The light was different, cooler, and the ouroboros looked as though the power channeled through it had damaged it. Except that this was not the chamber they had been in before. Teal'c pushed himself to his feet, reaching for a staff weapon that wasn't there. But of course he had been unarmed in the laboratory, safe among friends. He braced himself against the wall, and even that was different, slick, polished pearl-gray stone rather than the tough white coating. Nor was there a wall of glass and a darkened control room beyond. Instead, there was only blank stone and the ouroboros carved into the wall above the low platform. The others were sprawled beside it, as though they had been thrown from some considerable distance. Teal'c could see their chests moving and assumed from his own condition that they weren't seriously harmed, but nonetheless it was reassuring to feel their heartbeats beneath his fingertips. They would recover quickly, and in the meantime they seemed to be in no immediate danger. Although there was no telling how long that would last.

There was only a single narrow door, set close into a corner. It was edged by bands of decorative carving only a little darker than the walls themselves. The designs looked Ancient, but there was no writing, nor, when he examined it, could he find either lock or latch.

The lack of his staff weapon was a sharp pain. Colonel Carter almost certainly had some C4 somewhere about her person, but he would have felt better if he were armed. Still, blowing open the door had to be a last resort, particularly when they had no idea what was on the other side. He went back to the others and began methodically to try to rouse them.

O'Neill came to first, as usual, sat up with a groan and a muttered curse, his eyes flicking from side to side as he assessed the situation.

"Well, crap."

Teal'c bent his head in agreement. "Indeed."

"Looks like we're not in Kansas any more." O'Neill hauled himself to his feet, wincing.

Teal'c refrained from pointing out that they had not been in Kansas in the first place. "I believe that Janus's transport device was still capable of function."

"Yeah, but where did it transport us to?" O'Neill rubbed the back of his neck. "Sam and Daniel?"

"Evidently unharmed," Teal'c answered. "Or no more so than are we."

"Your definition of 'unharmed' is a lot different from mine," O'Neill said. Daniel was starting to stir, and O'Neill bent down to shake him gently. "Come on, Danny, rise and shine."

Carter sat up in the same moment, her face crumpling in pain. "Where —? Ow."

"I was going to ask you that," O'Neill said.

"I'm sorry, sir," Carter said. "I have no idea."

"Well, if the whole system was supposed to take people to Atlantis," Daniel began, and Carter shook her head, wincing.

"This doesn't look like anything we saw from the MALP," she said. She looked at O'Neill. "I'm sorry, sir. That shouldn't have happened."

"Yet here we are," O'Neill said.

"There aren't any controls in here," Daniel said. "What kind of transport system doesn't have some way to enter a destination?"

"A one-way one," O'Neill said, and Teal'c felt the chill of memory. They had been imprisoned once by the Taldur, who believed that their Stargate opened only to their prison world, and only went one way. But it had been an ordinary gate, and in the end they had found a way to open it. They would do so again.

Daniel was already pacing the length of the room. "This door's locked," he said. "But these are Ancient markings."

"OK," O'Neill said, and came warily to join him. There was a dull click and the door split open, sliding back to reveal a darkened hall. Lights came on as O'Neill peered out, and Teal'c allowed himself to relax a little. At least this was an Ancient installation, not Goa'uld.

More lights came on as they moved into the hall, and O'Neill looked at Daniel.

"Any idea which way to go?"

"Sorry, no." Daniel squinted at the walls and shrugged. "I'd guess up, when we get that choice, but until then…"

"Not exactly one of our options," O'Neill said. "Fine. We'll go — left."

Teal'c took him at his word and started off down the corridor. They moved in a bubble of light, the curved fixtures coming on as O'Neill approached, flicking off again once he was past. The corridor seemed to curve, so slightly that at first he wasn't sure it was actually happening. The lack of steady light didn't help, either, making it impossible to see the full length of the corridor, but after a while Teal'c began to suspect that they were moving in a circle. Perhaps it was just the shape of the installation, he thought, hopefully, rather than that they were being taken back to their starting point. If there were other rooms, or even doors, they were well-hidden. The corridor remained empty and unmarked and seemingly infinite.

Then, quite suddenly, the corridor ended, blocked by a massive pair of doors. Daniel, in the lead, let his flashlight's beam play across the enormous slabs of bronze, carved like the chamber door in some unfamiliar pattern.

"These look like pressure doors," he said. "Jack?"

O'Neill came toward them and an orange circle began to glow at the point where the doors met. O'Neill placed his hand against it and the doors slid ponderously open, the metal groaning softly.

Beyond was a circular chamber with a square central console, and two more doors lay beyond that, one open onto what looked like stairs, and the other closed.

"Finally," Daniel said, and started toward the console before he remembered. "Um, Jack?"

"General Lightswitch O'Neill, that's me." O'Neill laid a hand on the console and, to no one's surprise, the screen lit. Daniel made a noise of satisfaction and began touching keys.

"Any luck?" O'Neill asked, after what Teal'c thought was an unreasonably short amount of time.

"Not — well, some," Daniel answered. "It's only the emergency stand-by systems that are running, and I can't get anything else to come on line. But as far as I can tell, that door —" He pointed to the closed one. " — will take us to the control room."

"That's helpful," O'Neill said. He advanced on the door and it slid obediently open. Behind it was a small room, lights fading reluctantly on to reveal ruddy walls and bronze fittings. There were neither controls nor a further door to be seen.

"OK," O'Neill said, after a moment. "That's not funny."

"Wait a minute, sir." Carter was leaning over Daniel's shoulder. "It's a — transfer chamber, I supposed you'd call it. If we all step in there — and if you, sir, think about the control room — it should take us there."

For just an instant, Teal'c thought that O'Neill was going to remind them that this was how they'd gotten into this situation in the first place, but instead the General just nodded. "OK," he said. "You people better get in first, in case I set it off."

That was logical and Teal'c turned toward the open door.

Still, the situation was uncertain enough that he couldn't help saying, "I would be more comfortable, O'Neill, if we were better armed."

"You and me both," O'Neill said. "But…"

He shrugged. Teal'c nodded, and followed Carter and Daniel into the chamber. O'Neill squeezed in after them, but for a long moment nothing happened.

"Oh, for —" O'Neill began, and the door slid closed. There was an odd flicker from the light and the door opened again to reveal an entirely different room.

A familiar room, Teal'c thought. He had seen it in the images transmitted by the MALP, seen it again and again as the SGC's scientists analyzed the footage frame by frame, waiting for the expedition to make contact and tell them more. They had found Atlantis's gate room, though it stood empty and shadowed, filled with grayed light.

"Whoa," Daniel said. "This — Janus's device worked."

"But if this is Atlantis," Carter said, "where is everyone?"

They filed out into the echoing space. The Stargate loomed to their left, filling one end of the room, walls of colored stone or glass behind it. Opposite it was a broad staircase that led to what appeared to be a control room, tucked into a mezzanine that overlooked the gate room. The consoles were dark, the silence like a weight, without even the sound of moving air. Teal'c turned in a slow circle, scanning the room. It was undeniably beautiful, with its soaring walls and elaborate carvings, but it was also uninhabited, and looked to have been so for some time.

There was something lying at the base of one of the columns, small and dark enough to be overlooked at first glance. Teal'c crouched beside it, turned it over carefully, as though that might change what he had found.

"O'Neill."

The general turned, surprise changing to recognition as he saw the stash bag unfolded in Teal'c's hand.

"The expedition was here," Tealc said.

O'Neill nodded. "Yeah. But where are they now?"

Once they looked, there were more signs of the expedition's presence: a bundle of MRE wrappers, another empty bag, an unfired shell. But no note, no marker, nothing to see where they were or why they'd gone. Jack looked up at the control room and started up the stairs.

The consoles came on at his approach, offering lights and soft chimes. As far as he could tell, things were normal, or at least nothing was seriously wrong, and he stepped back to let Carter take a seat before the controls. She studied the screens for a moment, then began to poke at the controls, searching through a series of displays.

"Jack!" Daniel waved at him from the floor at the gateroom, and Jack came forward to the rail.

"You got something?"

Daniel held up a bottle. Jack recognized it with a chill as the champagne he'd sent through the gate just before it closed.

"There's a message in it," Daniel called. "I'm going to have to break it to get it open."

Jack nodded. "Go ahead."

The sound of shattering glass was loud in the dull air. Jack flinched in spite of himself, Carter looked up from the console, and even Teal'c looked momentarily startled. Daniel poked cautiously among the shards of glass, and came up with a sheet of paper rolled into a narrow tube.

"It's a gate address," he called.

"Anything else?"

"No." Daniel held up the sheet of paper. Someone had scrawled the symbols across it in thick red marker.

Croatoan. Jack felt the hairs rise on the back of his neck. That story had given him the willies when he was a kid: the Roanoke colonists vanishing into the forest, leaving nothing but a single word carved into a tree to say where they had gone, what had happened to them…

"Sir!" Carter's voice was sharp and he spun on his heel.

"Sir, we've got a problem." Her hands were busy on the console's controls, her eyes darting from screen to screen. "I don't know where they've gone, but I think I know why. Power levels are dropping rapidly everywhere in the city."

"What?" Jack came to stand behind her. He didn't know what every display meant, but he couldn't misunderstand the flashing lights and warning symbols that filled one screen and spilled over into another.

"It looks as though the city's ZPM is very nearly depleted," Carter said, frowning at the displays. "We turned on a bunch of systems getting up here, and that's causing problems. I'm shutting them down as fast as I can, but —" She touched more controls, her frown deepening at the result. "There's one big drain, it says it's a shield surrounding the city —"

"O'Neill!"

That was Teal'c voice, and Jack turned back to the rail. "Yeah?"

"The city is underwater." Teal'c's face was impassive, but Jack thought he heard the first notes of concern in the Jaffa's voice. "There is some kind of force field protecting the city."

"Damn it!" Jack turned back to Carter. "You hear that?"

"Yes, sir." She gave him a wry smile. "I guess I can't reduce any power to the shield."

"I don't think that's a good plan," Jack answered. "Shut down everything else, see if you can stabilize things."

Carter nodded. "I'm almost there."

Daniel came to join them, the slip of paper still rolled in one hand. He seated himself at the console next to Carter's, and called up a second screen. She nodded again, approval and agreement this time, and they both worked in silence for what seemed a very long time.

"Ok," Carter said at last, and Daniel shook his head.

"It's not enough."

"It'll hold for now," Carter said. She looked up. "But Daniel's right, sir, this isn't a permanent solution. What I've been able to do is turn off everything that we've turned on, but just being here is still drawing too much power."

"Is there any chance of dialing Earth?" Jack asked, without much hope, and wasn't surprised when Carter shook her head,

"No, sir. There's not nearly enough power left for that."

"We go where they went," Daniel said. He flourished the roll of paper. "The expedition left this for anyone who came after them — they must have arrived here, figured out the power problem just like we did, and found a safe world to dial out to."

"Or they just dialed blind," Jack said.

Carter was already touching keys, frowning at the screens that appeared. "No, Daniel's right, I think. It looks as though someone was searching the databanks quite recently, checking gate addresses, and I'm guessing that was our people."

Jack looked over his shoulder at the empty gateroom, the soaring glass and the immense ring of the Stargate itself. There was nothing here — they'd seen nothing in the halls they'd passed on their way to the gateroom, and it was unlikely they'd find anything more even if they took the time to search. The smart money was to follow the expedition. They'd obviously been confident enough in their choice of world that they felt safe telling the next expedition to follow them, but he hated jumping blind. Blind and unarmed, except for sidearms, and even then he'd bet none of the others had more than a single spare clip, if that. He shook the thought away. That was just another reason to go find his people. They'd get food and supplies and then they'd find a way home.

"Teal'c!" He went to the rail a final time. "You find anything salvageable down there?"

"No, O'Neill." Teal'c looked up at him from the base of the stairs. "The Atlantis expedition left nothing behind."

"Right." Jack squared his shoulder. "OK, Carter. Dial the gate."

The last chevron locked as Jack came down the gateroom stairs, and the wormhole opened with a whoosh of blue. It steadied, stabilized, and he looked over his shoulders.

"Ready, Carter?"

"Almost there, sir." She was still bent over the console, locking down the last systems. Daniel came down the stairs, folding the expedition's message into a tiny packet. He took a tin from his pocket, emptied the mints into his hand, and stuck the folded paper into the tin, pressing hard to seal it. He saw Jack looking, and shoved the handful of mints into a pocket.

"We need to be sure somebody knows where we've gone."

"If anyone is stupid enough to try that thing after what happened to us," Jack began, and shook his head. The SGC probably would make some kind of rescue attempt once it became clear they weren't going to come back, and that was another reason to get moving, to figure out some way back before anyone else was put at risk.

Daniel set the tin carefully on the steps below the Stargate, and looked up at the control room. "Sam?"

"Coming," she called, and hurried down the stairs.

Teal'c moved closer. "I will go first, O'Neill."

Jack nodded. "I'll take six." He paused. "Ok, people, let's move."

They came through the gate into a damp field flooded with golden light and long shadows. Early morning or late afternoon, Jack thought, shading his eyes. He hoped it was morning: more time to get their bearings before night magnified any dangers. Trees ringed the field, tall and dark, looking like any dozen worlds they'd visited in the Milky Way. The others were already moving forward, and Jack followed them, his hand resting lightly on his sidearm. The grass was damp underfoot, heavy dew or light rain, and the air smelled of a pine-like resin. Only the symbols on the DHD said he wasn't in the Milky Way.

"Anything?" he said quietly to Teal'c, who was scanning the surrounding woods, and the Jaffa shook his head.

"I see no sign of habitation, O'Neill."

Daniel surveyed the meadow, then headed out into the long grass. Jack started to call him back, and stopped himself. They wouldn't gain anything by being overcautious, either.

"The gate's in use," Carter said, bending over the DHD. "It's been dialed from Atlantis, and it's dialed Atlantis twice, though there are maybe a dozen addresses in between. Mostly different, though one repeats—"

They all heard it then, the heavy snick of P90s being armed, and Jack dove for cover beside the DHD, grabbing for his pistol. Carter and Teal'c were right beside him, and Daniel flattened himself into the grass of the clearing. But it was definitely a P90 they'd heard, and there was only one group of people in the Pegasus Galaxy who should be carrying those — unless, of course, Weir's people had managed to lose them already, but he wasn't going to think like that.

"Identify yourself!" he shouted, and there was a rustle from the tree line.

"General O'Neill?"

The voice was familiar, one of the young Marine lieutenants, but Jack couldn't come up with the name. "Yes. Who's that?"

"Come out where I can see you. Sir."

Carter stirred at that. "They ought to recognize you, sir."

"Yeah." Jack peered around the edge of the DHD, trying to make out the shapes in the forest. It was evening, no doubt about it now, the light fading fast. "You first, lieutenant!"

There was more movement in the trees, barely a shift of shadows, and then, slowly, a young Marine emerged from between the trees, his P90 braced and ready. Jack knew the face, the high-planed cheeks, and dredged his memory for the name.

"Ford?" He stood just as slowly, showing his hands empty. "Sir!"

Ford moved out onto the grass, weapons still ready, and Jack came cautiously toward him, his hands well away from his body. Something had definitely gone wrong here, more than just the problem with Atlantis itself, some kind of external threat, and there was no point pushing anything until he had a better idea what was going on. He passed Daniel, still flattened in the grass, and got a definite *are-you-crazy* glare as he went past. He was tempted to drop him his pistol, but knew Ford would see the movement. Instead, he kept walking, stopped when he and Ford were about fifteen feet from each other in the gathering dusk. He saw Ford's shoulders sag, sheer relief, and the Marine brought his P90 to port-arms.

"Sorry, sir, we've had some problems." He paused. "Does this mean we've got a new ZPM?"

Jack kept his face expressionless. "Not yet, I'm afraid. We were testing a new system and it — activated prematurely."

Ford grimaced, got himself under control immediately. "Look, sir, we need to get back to the city before full dark."

"City?"

"Yes, sir." For an instant, Ford's face was relaxed, almost eager. "We found another Ancient city."

Jack waved for the others to join him, and the rest of Ford's team eased out of the woods. They were in full armor, with stun grenades at their belts, and Jack looked curiously at Ford. "Problems, Lieutenant?"

"Yes, sir." Ford's voice was grim. "There's an alien species in Pegasus, a hostile, it can make you see things that aren't there — that's why we didn't rush out all at once, just in case it was another trick. And the locals don't much like us, either. Colonel Sumner doesn't want us to offer them any temptation by being out after dark."

That made sense, and Jack nodded. "What's the problem with the locals?"

Ford had started off toward the edge of the forest, obviously eager to get them moving, but that made him glance warily over his shoulder. "You should probably talk to Colonel Sumner about that, sir."

Out of the corner of his eye, Jack saw Daniel's face tighten — he'd never liked Sumner — but this wasn't the place to have that argument. For a miracle, Daniel seemed to realize it, and said nothing, trailing along in the Marines' wake. They were nervy, Jack thought, not precisely jumpy, but definitely on edge, watching the trees as though they expected an ambush. It was contagious, and he found himself scanning the shadows himself, watching for a flicker of movement, anything that shouldn't be there.

"O'Neill." Teal'c had drifted to his shoulder, spoke quietly enough that they were unlikely to be overheard. "I have seen no sign of these locals, nor any sign of technology that could match our own."

"Yeah, me neither." And that made him wonder all the more, storing up questions to ask Sumner once they reached this city.

They had joined a wider path, but there was still no sign of a human presence. The underbrush could as easily have been beaten down by animals as by human feet. And then, quite suddenly, they came around a gentle curve and the path opened up to reveal a lake and the ruins of a towered city beyond it. Lights glowed in the ruin, familiar floodlights and strings of bulbs, and tarps had been spread to make roofs and walls.

Ford fell back a little, an easy grin on his face now that they were in sight of safety. "There it is, sir, Atlantis base." He added, "The locals call it Emege."

Daniel let himself fall back toward the rear of the group, scanning the woods for signs of the locals. Maybe it was just that he didn't like Sumner, but he had a feeling that there might be a reason for the hostility. He tried to strike up a conversation with the nearest Marine, but the young man answered in monosyllables, his eyes roving the shadows. Daniel had learned enough to know that was a bad sign and so shut up, matching their pace, but keeping an eye on the ground around them. Once or twice he thought he saw signs of a campsite — a spot where a firepit had been hastily filled in, a suspiciously regular pattern of potholes that might have come from tent pegs — but nothing more.

The path ended at a lake, where another trio of Marines were waiting with a rubber boat. "Lieutenant!" one of them called. "We were just about to pull up the drawbridge."

He stopped, seeing Jack, and Ford said, "Radio base, Spence. Tell them we've got four more for dinner."

"Yes, sir." The Marine — his name badge read "Spencer" — stepped out of earshot, speaking into his shoulder-mounted radio. And that was odd, Daniel thought. He'd thought the expedition had been equipped with the newer earpieces, but maybe there was some reason they were using the older equipment.

"All aboard," another Marine called, and they filed down to the boat, the crew already knee deep in the lake to launch it.

The oldest of the Marines gave him a smile as they climbed aboard. "Glad to see you're doing better, Doc."

"Thanks," Daniel said. He wasn't exactly sure what the man meant, but before he could ask, they were underway.

The lake wasn't large, and the boat's little motor sped them across the calm surface. The city swelled ahead of them, a central gate, its walls gently curved, the only thing that seemed mostly intact. Beyond it the buildings were in ruins, broken stone that still show the marks of burning, and the expedition's lights looked feeble against the desolation.

"Someone really wanted to be sure this place — what's it called? — was completely destroyed," he said, and Ford looked over his shoulder.

"The Wraith — they're the alien hostiles, that's what the locals call them, anyway — they do that to anyone who gets too technologically advanced. That's why the locals don't like us living in the city."

"Uh-huh." Daniel scanned the ruins again, trying to match that with the people who'd left almost no sign of their campsites. OK, maybe these aliens, the Wraith, had pounded the locals back to a more primitive existence, but the ruins looked old, really old. And if it was an Ancient city… The pieces didn't fit.

They reached the opposite shore, under the shadow of the tower, and climbed out onto the rocky shingle. The Marines quickly broke down the boat, carried it with them past the barrier that blocked the entrance to the settlement. The city was definitely Ancient, Daniel thought, and the few surviving decorations were similar to ones they'd seen on Atlantis, but there were other buildings, newer ones, that looked as though they'd been repaired and then destroyed again. More than once, possibly; and each time the city had been leveled, the locals had been less able to rebuild. He could see the signs of that, place where metal fittings had been reused, forced to fit because the locals couldn't make new ones, here and there replaced entirely with wood and leather that had been burned away to be replaced again.

The expedition had set up tents inside the shells of the least damaged buildings, and here and there people had begun to shore up and mend walls and roofs. The building the expedition had chosen for its headquarters wasn't much more than a shell of stone walls and curious bits of silver filigree that had somehow survived the fires that had blackened the pale stone, but the walls, at least, were mostly intact, and a solid wooden roof had been slung across the gaps. It was obviously also the mess hall, a thread of smoke rising from an improvised chimney, and civilian and military personnel alike were heading toward it, only to stop short on seeing Jack and SG-1.

"Ford! Hey, Ford!" That voice was all too familiar, Rodney McKay's imperious bleat, and Daniel braced himself to intervene if the man resumed his ill-advised pursuit of Sam. McKay skidded to a stop in front of the group, mouth falling open.

"General O'Neill? You're here? Does this mean we've finally got a link back to the Milky Way?" He turned to Ford. "Why wasn't I informed?"

And why would you be informed? Daniel thought. You're only Head of Sciences, not the expedition leader. In fact, Jack had gone to some lengths to make sure that McKay was in direct charge of as few people as possible.

"We only just made contact, Dr. McKay," Ford said. "And I think Colonel Sumner needs to hear this first."

"Then I'm coming with you," McKay said.

Something was very wrong. Daniel felt a chill run down his spine, but Jack beat him to the question.

"Out of curiosity, Lieutenant — where's Dr. Weir?"

There was a moment of silence, the familiar shock, embarrassed and miserable, that meant no one wanted to give bad news, and that answered the question before Ford spoke again.

"I'm sorry, General. She was killed by the Wraith."

CHAPTER FOUR
Explanations

SUMNER had set up his quarters in the back of the headquarters building, behind the section used as the mess hall. The building itself was the most defensible spot in the ruined city, Jack noted, without much surprise, and this inner section had been made into a secondary stronghold within the main building. They'd rigged a naquadah generator to give them lights, and the room, outer office and a sleeping area behind a canvas partition, looked like pretty much every other front line commander's quarters Jack had ever seen.

There weren't enough chairs to go around, also par for the course. There was a certain amount of jostling as junior officers produced a couple of storage crates, and a carved wooden stool that looked as though it came apart for travel, and in the confusion Jack heard at least two people say that they were glad to see Daniel after all. When everything settled, Ford, McKay, and Daniel were left standing. A young airman, her hair cut close to her scalp, appeared with a thermos and mugs, and Ford handed around the coffee in silence. Sumner looked like hell, Jack thought. This was not going to be good.

"It's good to see you, sir," Sumner said, with a forced smile. "Even if Ford tells me this isn't a relief force."

Jack shook his head. "Afraid not." You knew the score, he wanted to say, but that wasn't really the way it worked. The SGC didn't leave its people behind, not if there was the slightest chance. That had been Hammond's policy from the start, and he wasn't about to change it now. "Dr. Jackson found an Ancient installation that seemed to be designed to reach Atlantis. Since you hadn't reestablished contact, and we couldn't spare the ZPM, it seemed worth checking out." He ran through the outline of the failed experiment and their arrival on Atlantis, not giving Carter a chance to offer a technical explanation. "So we found your message with this address, and dialed the gate."

"Then you see our problem," McKay began, and Sumner glared at him.

"Dr. McKay!"

McKay glared right back. "That's our fundamental problem, and you know it. If we hadn't had to abandon Atlantis, none of this would have happened."

Jack cleared his throat. "Colonel. How about you fill me in on what's happened here?"

"Yes, sir." Sumner's expression didn't change, but his voice was grim.

It wasn't a pretty story. Things had seemed normal on Atlantis at first, but once they'd begun exploring the city, turning on systems, they'd discovered the power problem. The shield was the biggest drain on the city's only remaining ZPM, but it couldn't be deactivated without drowning the city, so in desperation, Dr. Weir had ordered the expedition to evacuate to Athos. The local population was primitive, a nomadic culture that seemed to follow the crop cycle, but there were definite signs that the Ancients had once lived there as well, and the scientists had hoped that they would find either a working ZPM or some other way to get back in contact with the Milky Way.

Everyone had been ecstatic when they saw the ruined city — except for the nomads. They refused to go near it, and warned the expedition away as well: too much interest in the Ancients, in any technology, drew the attention of the Wraith, a species of hostile aliens who fed on the life-force of humans, and who dropped from the sky without warning. Dr. Weir had negotiated with the Athosians' leaders, Halling, who seemed to be the chief of the tribe, and their chief trader, Teyla Emmagan, and obtained their reluctant consent to the expedition's sending small teams to investigate the ruins.

And then the Wraith appeared. It wasn't clear whether this was a routine hunting mission, a Culling, as the Athosians called it, or if they'd known about the expedition in the ruins, but the Stargate had opened and four fast, needle-nosed fighters had come through. They were armed with some kind of transporter beam that they used to capture humans, and swooped down on the joint campsite. The Athosians had fled, but the expedition's Marines stood their ground and succeeded in driving them off, and even shot down one of the Darts. There hadn't been much left of the pilot, but the medical team had been able to confirm the Athosians' story: the Wraith were fast, deadly, and very hard to kill. And they fed on humans.

The first problems with the Athosians had appeared in the aftermath of the attack. Sumner had urged Weir to move to the city, where it would be easier to set up a defensive perimeter, but the Athosians had opposed the idea, and Weir, in an attempt to keep up good relations, had postponed her decision. Halling and Emmagan told them that the Wraith would be back in force — the Wraith destroyed any human society that developed beyond a certain level of technology, which was one of the reasons the Athosians stayed away from the city, and traded for the little technology they used, rather than making their own. They urged the expedition to move away from the Stargate and the city, warning that the Wraith would be back, and Halling sent the elders and children away to traditional hiding places, even though it would mean a lean winter for his people, without every hand to gather the crops for harvest. Weir had declined to leave, but volunteered the expedition's help with the harvest — and then the Wraith had come again.

This time, the Darts had come not to hunt but to fight, and instead of scooping humans up in their beams they'd dropped dozens of masked fighters. The Marines had engaged, and in the fight they'd seen the truth of everything the Athosians had told them. The Wraith were almost impossible to kill, taking multiple head and body shots to put them down, and if they weren't killed outright, their wounds healed with terrifying speed. The expedition lost twenty people before they learned to be sure the Wraith were dead, and still more were taken by the Darts once the Wraith realized they weren't going to win.

But by then it was too late. The expedition had lost nearly fifty people, and among them was Weir herself. They had found her body, shriveled and unrecognizable, among a group of Athosians that had been trapped against a cliff. They had only known her by her hair and her uniform jacket.

Sumner shrugged. "At that point, sir, I took command, as ranking officer. We were clearly in a combat situation and expedition safety was the first priority. I ordered the expedition to relocate to the city, and — here we are."

Here we are indeed, Jack thought. He didn't like the way this had gone down — didn't like anything about it, but the way Sumner had gotten on the wrong side of the locals after Weir was killed was pretty much the icing on the cake. Unfortunately, there wasn't much he could say about it now.

"All that is really beside the point," McKay said. "The point is that we need to figure out some way to get back to Atlantis. And that was why I was really hoping Colonel Carter here had brought a solution to the Gerbrandt equations."

The name wasn't familiar to Jack, but Carter looked up sharply. "We rejected those before you left."

"We did not." McKay glared back at her. "Gordon and Schenk had a partial solution that looked promising, but there wasn't time to finish the work. And, quite frankly, while I imagine I will eventually solve the problem, I've been otherwise occupied ever since we left Atlantis."

"You solved the equations before you left Earth," Carter repeated. "Gerbrandt's theorum turned out to be irrelevant to the ZPM problem."

"I did not!" McKay's voice scaled up, and Sumner scowled.

"Colonel, I don't see what's to be gained by calling Dr. McKay a liar."

Carter shook her head. "I don't mean to be. But —"

"Wait a minute," Daniel said. "Before we get any further — why have people been saying they're glad I'm here? I was never supposed to be on this mission."

No thanks to me, Jack thought. That was still a sore point, though he knew he was right.

Sumner's frown deepened. "You didn't come because you had emergency surgery for appendicitis. What's the point of saying otherwise? Or is this some kind of test?"

He fixed Jack with an accusing stare, and Jack shook his head. "Sorry, Colonel, Daniel's right. He was never attached to the Atlantis project. I made sure of that."

"Wait a minute." Carter had that look again, half satisfied and half embarrassed, the one that meant she'd figured out the situation and it wasn't bad, it was worse. "General, I think — there's a possibility that Janus's device didn't just displace us in space, but possibly also in quantum continuity."

"Oh, boy," Daniel said. "You know, that might explain what Janus was talking about with the side effects —"

"Hold it," Jack said. He fixed Carter with a look. "Words of one syllable, Carter."

"Sorry, sir." The abashed look didn't change. "It's just — I'm beginning to think that Janus's device didn't just transport us to Atlantis. I think it may have taken us to a different Atlantis, one that belongs to an alternate reality."

"An alternate reality," Jack repeated, as if denying it might make the problem go away.

"Yes, sir," Carter said. "According to the latest theories, our reality is only one of an infinite number of possibilities, each branching off from decisions made within each universe."

"I know what an alternate reality is," Jack said, "and I really wish I couldn't say that. But — this is like that damned quantum mirror thing, right?"

"I would say so." Carter gave an apologetic smile.

"Wait, wait, wait," McKay said. He looked at Carter. "He's not our O'Neill? Because he sounds exactly like him. And he sounds just like Dr. Jackson. Though I suppose if the universes hadn't branched much, there wouldn't be a good way to tell them apart, except by largely trivial differences —"

"Like Daniel having been supposed to come on the mission." Carter nodded. "And our having solved the Gerbrandt equations when you didn't."

"Not that we couldn't," McKay said.

Sumner scowled. "Dr. McKay…"

"Well, we could have. Only apparently it's not as important as we thought—"

"McKay!"

The scientist subsided, pursing his lips, and Sumner looked at Jack.

"Under the circumstances, General, I can't see my way clear to cede command. You're not actually part of my chain of command—you're not my general. Sir."

"It certainly looks as though we've come through something like the quantum mirror," Jack said carefully. "You do have one of those, right?"

"We had one," Sumner answered. "General Hammond had it destroyed."

Carter shifted uneasily. "It's more that Janus's device functioned like the quantum mirror, sir."

"Which makes me wonder if the quantum mirror was one of his toys," Daniel said.

"Be that as it may," Jack said loudly. They both looked at him, startled, and he took a breath, focusing again on Sumner. "Under the circumstances, Colonel, I take your point. There may be subtle differences between our universes that turn out to be significant. But by the same token, I expect to be able to offer suggestions and advice."

"I'd welcome that, sir," Sumner answered.

"Excellent," Jack answered. And why, he wondered, do I think Sumner's relieved? He glanced at Teal'c, but the Jaffa's expression was as impassive as ever.

"And I would really appreciate Colonel Carter's help," McKay said. There was an odd note of challenge in his voice. "And Dr. Jackson's, for that matter. There's so much here that we haven't been able to explore properly, any extra staff will make a difference."

"I'm sure Colonel Carter and Dr. Jackson will be more than willing to help," Jack said.

For just an instant, Sumner looked murderous, but the expression vanished almost quickly enough that Jack could pretend he hadn't seen it. "We can discuss whether it's safe to explore any further tomorrow," he said. "First, General O'Neill and his party need a place to sleep. Lieutenant Ford, you'll see to that."

"Yes, sir." The young Marine snapped a salute.

"And then you can bring them along to the mess tent." Sumner pushed himself to his feet, and held out his hand. "General, I'm sorry you're here under these circumstances, but you're more than welcome."

"Thanks, Colonel," Jack answered. "We'll try not to get in your hair too much. But we're going to figure out a way to get back to our own timeline."

"Absolutely, sir," Sumner said.

Ford led them down what had once been a major street, offering them the choice of three different buildings that could be made perfectly sound with the addition of a tarp. "We can put up a real roof as soon as you're settled," he said, "but for tonight, it'll have to be tents."

"Not a problem, Lieutenant," Jack said. He looked over his options, chose the one that seemed to have a back door out of sight of the expedition's perimeter guards. He saw Teal'c's eyebrow tick up at that, but ignored him. Ford sent over a couple of airmen with the tarp, and another group arrived with cots and sleeping bags and a portable stove. They had lanterns, too, and promised to run power to the building in the morning.

"All the comforts of home," Jack said, and let them go. It was fully dark now and Carter lit the lanterns in silence, holding one high to examine the space. They had a shallow front room and two bedrooms with a connecting door, and the back door that opened onto an alley that ran between two relatively intact buildings.

Teal'c's eyebrow rose even higher. "That is not an entirely defensible position, O'Neill."

"We can rig a bar across the back door," Jack answered. He shook his head. "Let's just say I'd like to have another way out."

"You don't like this either," Daniel said.

"No, I don't," Jack said. "Ok, maybe it's just this is a different time line, and, yeah, they've been having bad problems, but — something's off. And while we're on that note — Teal'c, you'll share with Carter. Daniel, you're with me."

That had always been the arrangement when they had to split up in hostile territory, and Carter nodded.

"Yes, sir. Sir, these hostiles, the Wraith — they sound a little too bad to be true, if you know what I mean."

"Oh, I don't know," Jack said. "Life-sucking unkillable vampires who can make you see things that aren't there — it's kind of par for the course, Carter."

She grinned, but the smile faded. "You know what I mean, sir."

"Sam's right," Daniel said. "It's like something out of somebody's horror novel."

"Yet Dr. Weir is dead," Teal'c said. "Along with other expedition members. The Wraith are clearly real."

"And the locals think Sumner is pissing them off by camping here," Daniel said. "I'd like to know more about that."

"So would I," Jack said. "I'm guessing Major Sheppard must have been killed along with her, since he wasn't at the meeting, but — somehow I've got a feeling there's a lot we haven't heard."

"I agree," Teal'c said. "And the men are agitated. Either there is more danger than they have told us, or —" He shook his head. "I do not know what the alternative would be."

"Well, kids, that's what we have to find out," Jack said. "We're invited to dinner —" He checked his watch. "Any minute now, so let's see if we can't have a few quiet conversations, draw some people out. I'd like to know what's really going on here."

The young lieutenant — Ford — returned shortly to escort them to the mess area. It was in the central building where Sumner had his quarters, and where it seemed as though most of the Marines slept as well. That was reasonable, Teal'c thought, given that the expedition had been subject to irregular and violent attacks, just as it was reasonable for conversations to be subdued and for the food served from the steam tables to be carefully measured. And closely watched: there was a Marine at the only door whose job seemed to be to ensure that no one took food with them. It made some sense to be certain that no one was hoarding what must be limited supplies — particularly if their relations with the locals were strained — but he could not remember ever seeing a similar precaution on any other Tau'ri base.

Nor had he seen such a strong division between military and civilian personnel. Of course there was always a certain rivalry between the two groups, an inevitable outcome of different function and goal, but usually Teal'c had seen it sublimated into jokes and harmless posturing. The bonds of the team were generally more important than caste loyalties. But here… Perhaps it was just that the situation meant that the formation of exploration teams had been suspended, but all across the room scientists sat with scientists and soldiers with soldiers.

He realized his tray had been filled without his asking and he turned to follow Carter toward an empty table, frowning at his plate. Stew, two slices of bread, half of something that looked like a nepti fruit: as a whole it was nutritious enough, he was sure, but neither ample nor particularly appealing.

"Are you thinking what I'm thinking?" O'Neill said quietly, from just behind him.

"Indeed." Teal'c did not look back. "It seems things are — less orderly—than Colonel Sumner wishes to acknowledge."

"Yeah." O'Neill broke off as Ford came to join them, and they settled themselves at the table Daniel had chosen.

The archeologist gave Ford a sharp look. "What's with the rationing?"

"We've had some trouble with the locals," Ford answered. "Colonel Sumner had the cooks work out a sustainable menu until we can be sure we can get supplies locally."

Teal'c took a careful bite of the fruit. It was indeed a nepti, which did not surprise him. They grew wild on many worlds the Ancients had seeded, and were surprisingly nutritious for something that tasted good.

"Yeah, you keep saying 'trouble with the locals,'" Daniel said. "What kind of trouble are you talking about? Arguments, harsh words, shooting people?"

Teal'c slanted a glance at O'Neill, but he was busy spooning up more of his stew. Once again he was letting Daniel ask the awkward questions, all of them falling back into their roles just as if O'Neill had never left the team.

Ford scowled. "You heard what Colonel Sumner said. They're a nomadic people, call themselves Athosians. We were getting along ok with them at first, after we came through from Atlantis, I mean. We made a deal with their chief trader to trade medical services and medicines for food, and that seemed to be working out. Even after Colonel Sumner took control of the Stargate, it looked as though we could keep things friendly. But once we started exploring the city, that's when they got all hinky about it."

"What's wrong with the city?" Daniel asked. "I mean, it's obvious it was built by the Ancients, and it's equally obvious no one's lived here in a very long time. Presumably there wasn't anything left to salvage?"

"The Athosians believe that the Wraith destroy any people who show too much command of technology," Ford answered. "They stay out of the city so that the Wraith won't notice them, and they believe we've drawn too much attention by being here."

"Seems like they're not entirely wrong," O'Neill observed.

Ford looked at his plate. "Maybe so, sir, but Dr. McKay thinks there may be a ZPM here, or at least information that'll tell us where to find one. We can't just leave it alone because the Athosians are scared of the Wraith."

"Tell me about these Wraith," Teal'c said. "I have never heard of their like, not even from the oldest Jaffa."

"They must be native to the Pegasus Galaxy," Ford said. He paused, as though he were trying to come up with the words. "They're seriously scary-looking — tall, gray-green skin, long white hair, fangs and claws. They look a lot like that guy in the vampire movies, Nosferatu. And they're mean and they're fast, and you can't be sure they're dead unless you put a lot of bullets into them or cut their heads off."

"And they eat people," O'Neill said.

"Sort of, sir. I mean, you end up dead, but — the Athosians said they consume the life-force. It's not like they're, you know, cannibals." Ford looked faintly spooked at the memory. "They've got this feeding organ in the palm of the hand, and if they get their claws in you, it'll suck the life right out of you. The first of our guys they killed, they looked like they'd been mummified. There wasn't much left of them but skin and hair."

"Sounds pretty alarming," Daniel said, through a mouthful of nepti fruit.

"Oh, they're alarming, all right." That was Sumner, sliding up behind them. "May I join you, General?"

O'Neill nodded. "Absolutely, Colonel."

Ford shot to his feet, picking up his tray. "If you'll excuse me, sirs, I'm on duty in twenty."

Sumner nodded, and the younger man hurried away. Teal'c watched him go, careful to keep his face expressionless. He didn't like the sound of the Wraith, but he also didn't like the sense that there was so much going on beneath the surface. He let his gaze slide across the mess area, searching for faces he remembered from the expedition's preparations. A few he recognized — McKay, certainly, Sergeant Bates, a young Asian scientist — but there were more that he expected who were not present, Major Sheppard being most notable. He glanced at O'Neill again, saw him give the colonel a measuring stare.

"From what Lieutenant Ford was telling us, you've had your hands full," O'Neill said. His voice was deceptively mild. "If the Wraith are that hard to kill, how are you handling them?"

"They are damn hard to kill," Sumner said. "But we've got three things going for us. First, we're well supplied. We managed to get all the arms and ammo out of Atlantis, so we're ready for the long haul. Second, the Wraith come in two flavors, masked warriors who frankly aren't very bright, and regular Wraith who are in charge of them. We figured out pretty quick that you kill the unmasked ones first, and the drones can't handle it. But mostly —" He bared teeth in a smile. "Dr. Beckett figured out a drug that gives my men a limited immunity to the enzyme that triggers the Wraith feeding process. It's not foolproof, but it gives a man a chance to break free before he's really hurt."

"That's quite an advantage," Daniel said. "I would think that would help improve things with the Athosians. It must be worth a lot to them, if they're that afraid of the Wraith."

An expression that was almost a sneer flickered across Sumner's face. "We're not really prepared to do that. You see, the enzyme drug also improves reflexes, strength, and endurance, and in some men it enhances both sight and hearing. The last thing we want is to give that to the locals."

"Pity," Daniel said, not quite under his breath.

"I never yet met a wonder drug that didn't have its down side," O'Neill said. "What's the bad news?"

"It burns energy faster than usual," Sumner said. "Which is one of the reasons we monitor our food supplies so carefully. And Dr. Beckett says it will create dependency if used continuously, so we rotate the men on and off it on a carefully planned schedule. But other than that — not bad at all, General."

"That's a pleasant surprise," O'Neill said. Teal'c didn't think he believed it, either. O'Neill looked around the mess hall, which was starting to empty out as the food line closed down. "Tell me, Colonel, where's Major Sheppard?"

Sumner froze for an instant. "I'm afraid I have bad news."

"Dead?" O'Neill's expression didn't change.

"Worse," Sumner said. "He's gone AWOL. And with all due respect, sir, I warned you that he wasn't a good fit for the expedition. His record in Afghanistan proved he was unreliable, and—" He stopped abruptly. "The other you. Sir."

"But—" Carter began, and subsided at a look from O'Neill.

"That's ok," O'Neill said. "I'm sure there are unexpected and subtle differences between our — counterparts."

Teal'c lifted an eyebrow at that, and didn't think Sumner bought it, either.

"Anyway." O'Neill pushed himself back from the table. "It's been a long, weird day, Colonel, and I think we should turn in. What do you say, kids?"

Carter pushed back her own chair. "Yes, sir."

"Whatever you say, Jack," Daniel muttered, but he, too, reached for his tray.

"Sergeant Bates!" Sumner waved the man over. "He'll show you back to your quarters, sir."

"Thanks," O'Neill said, without much attempt at sincerity.

"Indeed," Teal'c said.

Bates brought them back to the battered building — now roofed with a city-camouflage tarp — and waited to be sure they stayed, on the pretense of being sure they had all the necessities. O'Neill assured him that they did, and dismissed him, while Daniel switched on the battery-powered lamps they'd been given.

"You know, Jack, I never liked that guy."

"Colonel Sumner's a fine officer," O'Neill said, and motioned for Daniel to keep talking.

The archeologist's jaw dropped, but he picked up gamely. "Well, if you say so. I'm not sure I really understand what's going on with the Athosians, or, for that matter, with the Wraith —"

Teal'c nodded, recognizing O'Neill's intent, and began to search the main room. He found the first bug within minutes, tucked inside the empty packing crate that was serving as a table, but he didn't stop until he had finished his half of the room and the bedroom. O'Neill held up a second bug. Teal'c nodded again, and pointed to the front door. Behind them, Daniel was still talking, running on about the Ancients and vampire myths. O'Neill leaned out the door, then held out his hand. Teal'c handed him the bug, and O'Neill disappeared into the dark. He returned a moment later, dusting off his hands.

"I defy them to hear anything interesting from there."

"You didn't," Carter said.

O'Neill nodded. "Just don't talk about anything important when you visit the latrine."

Daniel grimaced, and O'Neill shrugged.

"What? They'll pull them out as soon as they realize we found them — and that I'm not going to put up with eavesdropping."

"Is it a good idea to show your hand so soon, sir?" Carter asked.

"What are they going to do, complain that I moved the bug they weren't exactly supposed to plant on me in the first place?" O'Neill shook his head. "Don't worry, Carter."

"I do not believe that matters are well here, O'Neill," Teal'c said.

"No kidding," Daniel said.

"Sir, you can't really believe Sheppard just went AWOL," Carter said.

"He might," Daniel said, reluctantly. "I mean, these people all look like the people we know, but they come from a different timeline. There may well be subtle differences in their behavior. Look at McKay, he's not —" He stopped abruptly, flushing, and Carter gave a wry smile.

"He's acting like he's never seen me before. And I'm not complaining."

"I don't think Sheppard would desert," O'Neill said. "That's too much of a change. And I also don't think it was going to be a good idea to talk about it in public. Sumner's clearly touchy about his authority, and there's no point setting him off yet."

"And at the moment we're stuck here on the far side of a lake with no way to confirm anything he's telling us," Daniel said. "You never dated him, did you, Sam?"

"God, no."

Teal'c remembered all too clearly that at least one of her former lovers had tried to set himself up as a god. He felt his eyebrow rise.

"No, really!" Carter said.

"Kids." Just for a moment, O'Neill looked painfully weary.

Teal'c straightened. "Colonel Carter. There has been no chance to consider the matter before now, but — is there any possibility that we will suffer side effects from the ouroboros device?"

Carter sighed. "I really don't know, Teal'c. I'd assume that we'd have seen them already if there were going to be any, but…" Her voice trailed off, and she spread her hands. "I just don't know."

"Well, that's one good excuse for talking to Dr. Beckett," O'Neill said. "Because I'd like to know a lot more about this anti-Wraith drug of Sumner's."

"Me, too," Daniel said. "It sounds like it could be a spectacularly bad idea."

"Or it could work exactly as advertised," O'Neill said. He shook his head. "Ok. All of this isn't actually our problem, assuming that Carter's right and this isn't our own timeline. Our first priority has to be getting home."

"I don't think we're going to be able to do much without help from the expedition," Carter said. "Including McKay."

"Sorry about that," O'Neill said.

"I don't know if we're going to have the option of not getting involved, either," Daniel said. "We're stuck in the middle of what's starting to look like Sumner's own private war, and — Jack, I'd really like to talk to the Athosians and find out their side of the story."

"That's going to have to wait," O'Neill said. "All right. Tomorrow, Carter, I want you and Daniel to start working on a way to get us back to our own reality."

Daniel started to say something, and O'Neill held up his hand.

"And if that means finding out more of what's going on, I don't exactly have a problem with that. Just — prioritize."

"Yeah, ok." Daniel nodded.

"And in the meantime," O'Neill went on, "Teal'c, you and I should probably have a word with Dr. Beckett."

"Indeed." Teal'c dipped his head in acknowledgement. He had met Carson Beckett at the SGC, had found him a pleasant, mild-mannered man — not the sort of person who seemed likely to develop drugs with such complex side effects. He was also incapable of keeping a secret. Yes, a conversation with him was likely to prove enlightening.

CHAPTER FIVE
Interlude

THE QUEEN reclined in her chair of bone, long limbs comfortably sprawled, scarlet hair caught up in a style as complex as any of her blades'. The lords of her zenana, her private household within the hive, moved in cautious orbit, none quite willing to break the spell with the unfortunate news from Athos. The Master of Sciences Physical lifted his head, caught the Consort's eye, and subsided into silence. The Consort rested his hands on the wing of the Queen's chair, and she looked up at him, smiling faintly. He seemed about to speak, the star tattooed around his left eye very dark in the pleasant light, then dipped his head, conceding defeat. At that, the Master of Sciences Biological turned sharply, the skirts of his long leather coat brushing game pieces from their table, but he ignored their clattering fall.

We cannot go on pretending nothing has happened. His mental voice was a sweep of light, seeking through the dark.

I could, the Master of Sciences Physical murmured, his tone the blue snap of electricity.

It wasn't your men who died. That was the Hivemaster, and they all jumped a little at the touch of his mind. He was the queen's full brother, and it was not entirely malice that proclaimed his birthright was to be mostly invisible.

The Queen straightened, the amusement vanishing from her face. *Tell me what happened, then.*

Seldom Seen spread his hands. *You've seen my report. I sent men to Athos to Cull, as the feeding cells are growing empty — experienced hunters, all of them — and instead of the nomads we expected, we were met by sophisticated weapons and humans determined to fight back.*

You said they didn't have energy weapons, Spark said.

They didn't, Seldom Seen agreed. *But they had gunpowder weapons that fired at a previously unknown rate of fire, enough to overwhelm our drones when the Young Queen's Pallax sent men to retaliate.*

An unwise choice, the Queen said. She had not yet resigned herself to her daughter's favorite.

I beg to differ, Seeker said. He picked up the game pieces one by one, set them into a new pattern on the board. The Consort raised his brow ridges at the sight. *It was perfectly reasonable, given the available evidence.*

Nonetheless, you would have done differently? Spark examined impeccably tended claws.

Irrelevant, as I wasn't there.

I agree with Seeker, Seldom Seen said. *It was what any blade would have done, in his position.*

It's what we're trained to do, the Consort said. He looked down at the Queen, her hair redder than human blood in the warm shiplight. *Shall I take a larger force, see what's there?*

The Queen lifted her hand. *Athos. We have not Culled there since we woke from hibernation, and that's, what, at least half of one of their generations?*

A full generation, maybe more, Seeker answered. *So if you were thinking it was some plot of your sisters' to keep us longer in hibernation the next time, I do not believe it likely.* He paused. *Though it is possible they withheld information.*

It's been known to happen, the Queen agreed. She pushed herself out of her chair, her gown of midnight silk swirling about her. *Perhaps we will go to Athos. I'm curious about these new humans.*

She swept from the zenana, and behind her back the lords exchanged wary glances. The curiosity of a queen was always a deadly thing.

CHAPTER SIX

Morning on Athos

THE NEXT morning dawned chill and damp, though by the time Sam finished her uninspiring breakfast the fog had burned off the lake and the sun had risen above the trees. Sergeant Bates was barking orders at the team of Marines readying the boat to cross the narrow water, and a group of scientists was huddling outside the mess tent peering at the images on someone's laptop. Daniel had joined them, head tilted to one side as he craned to see the screen, and Sam started toward them.

"Colonel Carter!"

Sam barely stopped herself from rolling her eyes as she turned to face McKay. He'd been perfectly well behaved the whole time they'd been here, but it was hard not to expect him to start hitting on her again. The lack of appropriate circumstances hadn't stopped him before. Although — this was an alternate universe. Maybe for once that was working in her favor. "Dr. McKay?"

"Colonel Sumner — and General O'Neill — said I could have you for the day. We've been working in what I think was the main power generating station for the city, and I'd like you to take a look at the ZPM."

"You found a ZPM?" Sam stared at him.

"We found a dead ZPM." McKay pronounced it 'zed pee em,' Canadian style. "But there's something peculiar about the way it's hooked into the city, and I'd appreciate another pair of eyes on the problem."

"Sure," Sam said. "Just let me grab Daniel."

"Fine. Bring him along. The more the merrier." McKay brushed past her and disappeared into the mess hall brandishing a travel mug.

"Sam?" Daniel looked at her over the top of his glasses.

"Dr. McKay wants me to take a look at the city's power plant," Sam answered. "It seems there was a ZPM, but it's depleted."

"No surprise there," Daniel said. "You want me to stick close?"

Sam hesitated. "I think I'm fine with him—maybe in this reality he isn't interested—but I'd like you to come anyway. McKay said something about the installation being unusual."

"You're hoping it's Janus," Daniel said.

Sam nodded. "This was an Ancient city almost as large as Atlantis, at least from the look of it, and the gate address is the one that came up first when I was in Atlantis's database. I can hope."

"I'd like to take a look around just in general," Daniel said. "But, sure, I'll tag along for now."

Sam lowered her voice. "And General O'Neill?"

"He and Teal'c were going to try to have a word with Dr. Beckett."

"Colonel Carter!" McKay was glaring at them and Sam gave him a wide smile.

"Coming."

McKay had assembled his team, but didn't bother to introduce them, striking out instead along what had once been a broad avenue leading into the center of the city. Sam trailed behind him, and by the time they'd reached the narrow square where most of the work seemed to be being done, she'd sorted most of them out. Kusanagi was the deferential Asian woman, Grodin—*call me Peter*—was the Englishman, and the sunburnt redhead was Campbell. Airman Salawi was a technical specialist who'd worked in the gateroom at the SGC, but McKay treated her as an unwanted spy. And to be fair, Carter thought, she wouldn't exactly put it past Sumner to expect Salawi to spy on the scientists.

To her surprise, there was a guard post at the end of the street, where the wreckage of a house had been rearranged to create a defensible machine gun nest, and one of the Marines lifted his hand in greeting as the group approached.

"Morning, Doc."

"Good morning," McKay snapped. "Have you seen any Wraith, or is this another pointless exercise?"

"If we see 'em, Doc, you'll be the first to know." There was a note of genial contempt in the Marine's voice that made Sam glance quickly at Daniel. It wasn't unusual for there to be some tension between the civilian scientists and the military personnel, but this was the worst she'd seen. Daniel shook his head slightly, a warning that they'd discuss it later, and she let McKay lead them into the ruins.

The upper floors of the building had long ago collapsed onto the foundations, and McKay and his people had shored up the entrance with timber and stone salvaged from the wreckage. Sam gave the improvised supports a wary look, and Peter Grodin grinned at her.

"Don't worry, Colonel, Dr. Zelenka set up the whole thing."

Zelenka was an excellent engineer, and Sam nodded. "Where is Dr. Zelenka, anyway?"

Grodin's face closed. "I have no idea," he said, and gave Salawi a significant glance.

Sam raised an eyebrow at that, but knew better than to ask directly. Instead, she ducked under the low lintel, and came out into the ruin of what must have been the city's main power station. It had been beautiful once, she thought, long and narrow and low-ceilinged, yes, but the walls had been carved with a pattern of stylized trees and — yes, those were dancers, male and female, weaving hand in hand through the forest so that their chains of two and three became part of the design. Daniel whistled softly and moved closer, tracing what looked like a ribbon trailing from the nearest dancer's hand.

"Emege," he said. "For the peoples of Emege — the children of the Ancestors of Emege?"

"Apparently that's the name of the place," McKay said. "Emege. Not that I see where that gets us."

"You might be surprised," Daniel said, with deceptive mildness, and Sam stepped in hastily.

"And that's the ZPM station."

"Yes." McKay refrained from pointing out that she'd just stated the obvious. "Only the ZPM's completely drained."

Sam picked it up carefully, noting that the contacts were still clean, the surface smooth and undamaged despite the object's apparent fragility.

"They had three ZPMs here originally," McKay went on, pointing to the sockets set at the points of the triangular central console. "And presumably the power was transmitted through a series of overhead conduits, all of which are smashed."

Sam looked up. There had apparently been some sort of dropped ceiling, because some of the grid that had held it still dangled from the cracked and uneven surface, but now there was just a mess of broken stone and jagged metal. "What's holding all this up?"

Grodin overheard the question and came to join them, opening his laptop. "When the tower fell, most of an intermediate floor came down in one piece. That caught most of the rubble and preserved this chamber intact." He turned the screen to show a schematic. "And we've put in jacks in the back there where things looked a little dicey."

Sam looked from the screen to the heavy metal props that braced the ceiling at the edge of the lighted area and back again. Salawi was out of earshot, so she risked what she hoped was a safe question. "More of Dr. Zelenka's work?"

"Yes —"

"Contrary to what you might think, the state of the ceiling, and the hundreds of tonnes of rubble directly overhead, isn't actually the most interesting thing here," McKay said. "Here's the really interesting part."

Sam followed obediently to a second console set apart from the others. She recognized the controls and most of the markings, and frowned. "That's a weapons console."

"Uh-huh. It runs both a shield, like the one on Atlantis that's keeping the water out, and a series of weapons emplacements around the perimeter of the city. Probably firing drones like the ones in Antarctica, but also maybe including beam weapons." McKay paused. "We haven't found any sign of a chair, though. And since the Wraith attacks, Sumner isn't letting us go too far outside his secure perimeter."

Daniel had drifted over to join them, was studying the lines of elegant script carved into the side of the console. It formed what looked to Sam like a decorative band, but Daniel ran his fingers over it and looked up at McKay. "Have you tried to read this?"

"Of course. It says something like, *this is a weapons console, no unauthorized access.* The Ancients liked to put labels on things when it was spectacularly unhelpful."

"Yeah, but…" Daniel crouched, tracing a line of writing around to the back of the console. "Why would you label something like this? And in such an inconvenient place? This is one of the more recent forms of Ancient, too."

"That we did figure out," McKay said. "This console, the whole weapons-and-shield thing, it's a lot newer than the rest of the city. And one thing we did find out from the Athosians before — before things got awkward — was that the Ancients and the Wraith fought a long war, but the city was much older than that. I'm guessing this was all part of the defensive systems installed to fight the Wraith."

"Ok, that makes sense," Sam said. She took a step back, tracing where the power inputs must have run, where the connections to the ZPM console must have been. "Wait a minute. I don't — That console can't pull nearly enough power to run a shield like the one on Atlantis."

McKay gave her a tight little smile. "Precisely. Except somehow it did."

"But not from the ZPMs," Sam said. "I don't know of anything else that could provide that kind of power —" She stopped abruptly. Except the power source for Janus's ouroboros device.

"I don't either," McKay said. "And I hate not knowing. But there was something here, and I'm going to figure it out."

"Janus," Daniel said, and Sam glared at him. This was not the time to start talking about Janus's mysterious devices, at least not until they had a better idea of what was going on. He pointed to a string of Ancient characters. "See? Janus was here."

Sam took a breath. Sure enough, under his finger an 'o' resolved to a snake eating its tail. And that meant — what? Janus was here, certainly, just as Daniel said, but it also meant that there was a chance that Janus had either tried to use the 'hard-wired' subspace tap or maybe even tried to work on his super-Stargate here in Emege. Daniel nodded as though he'd read her thought and pushed himself to his feet.

"I'd like to take a look around the ruins, see what else I can find."

"Those goons on the guard tower aren't going to let you," McKay said. "Not without permission from Colonel Sumner."

"Then I'm going to try to get permission," Daniel said, and looked at Sam. "You'll stay here?"

Sam nodded. "I'll see if Dr. McKay and I can't trace where the other power source was."

"Please," McKay said. "You think I haven't tried it?"

Sam looked at him, and he threw up his hands.

"Fine! We'll do it again."

"Thank you, Doctor," she said, firmly, and moved to the back of the console. McKay had managed to pry off the first protective layer and she recognized many of the basic components, but there was a deeper layer protected behind what looked like tinted glass. More of the pure carbon that had formed the shield on P6T-847? If so, then the connection to Janus's new power source was probably inside.

"You know something," McKay said abruptly. "You've seen something like this before."

"Maybe." They were out of earshot of the rest of the team, she thought, and she spoke before he could go any further. "Look,

Doctor, I've got questions for you first. What's happened to the rest of the expedition?"

"Rodney," he said. "Call me Rodney."

Sam ignored the offer. "Come on. What happened?"

McKay ran a hand over his face. "You mean like Zelenka? And Sheppard?"

"Yes."

He glanced over his shoulder. "Look, Colonel Sumner is not being entirely honest with you. He and Dr. Weir had some major disagreements even before the Wraith showed up — she wanted to respect the locals' feelings, not interfere with their traffic through the Stargate, not settle in the city and all that, which seems in the long run to have been a better idea, since Halling — he's the Athosian leader — Halling says our being in the city is why the Wraith keep coming."

Sam blinked, not sure she was making sense of it all. "So where are your missing people?"

"Well, some of them are dead," McKay answered. She'd forgotten how maddeningly thorough he could be. "I think we must have lost, oh, forty-five, maybe fifty people to the Wraith, either dead or — Well, presumably dead by now, taken and fed on later. But after Dr. Weir was killed, a bunch of us, particularly medical staff and technicians, were living with the Athosians, and when Sumner ordered everybody to evacuate to Emege — not everybody did. Halling says he doesn't know where they are, but Sumner doesn't believe him. And, frankly, neither do I."

"Zelenka's one of them," Sam said slowly.

"And Keller, Beckett's number two. Dumais, Peterson, a bunch of others."

"Major Sheppard?"

McKay nodded. "And Sheppard."

Sam stood silent for a moment. That was disobeying a direct order, best case, and worst case — worst case, she didn't really want to think about. Jack had said enough that she knew there was already a black mark on Sheppard's file, disobeying orders in Afghanistan, and this was not going to help matters at all. Assuming they made it back to Earth, of course, but even if they didn't — what could Sheppard do without the rest of the expedition?

"Look, I know what you're thinking," McKay said. "But Sheppard's doing the right thing. Sumner — he's going to get a lot more people killed if we're not careful."

"If you think that," Sam said, "why aren't you off in the woods with the rest of them?"

"Because somebody has to figure out how to get us back to Atlantis," McKay answered. "That's the only smart answer. We find a power source, we juice up Atlantis's shield, and we move back there so that we're not putting the Athosians in danger. It's the only answer."

Sam nodded slowly. "I think you're right, McKay. Let's see if we can make some sense of this."

Jack leaned against the sun-warmed wall outside the mess area, sipping, apparently idly, at his cup of coffee. Carter and Daniel were already off with the scientists, and that was a good start to the day; for now, he watched Bates' team paddle their unsteady inflatable boats back across the lake. They left one boat on the far shore under guard, and a couple of Marines began rowing the second boat back toward the city while Bates formed up his men and began giving orders. It was too far to hear, of course, but Jack could guess what the sergeant was saying. There would be a detail left to guard the boat, and the large party would head out to secure the Stargate. It seemed a little weird that Sumner wouldn't try to keep the gate under guard over night, but maybe the risk was just too great. It would be too easy to get cut off, even if the locals didn't much like to be out at night.

"O'Neill." Teal'c ducked under the low lintel, carrying a cup of coffee. He held it out and Jack took it gratefully. Teal'c accepted O'Neill's almost empty cup in return. "I have been looking for Dr Beckett, but I have not seen him."

"Nor have I," Jack said. He squinted at the group across the lake. "Correct me if I'm wrong, but wasn't one of the things the Athosians were complaining about access to the Stargate?"

"I believe you are correct, O'Neill."

"And yet we're not guarding it overnight," Jack said. "So presumably the Athosians could use it at night if they wanted to."

"Unless the Wraith are more likely to attack at night," Teal'c said. "Or indeed if there are other dangers in the forests that they would prefer to avoid."

"We haven't heard of any," Jack said. "And you'd think, if they needed off-world supplies so much, they'd be willing to take the risk. Nope, no matter how you slice it, it's not adding up."

"Indeed."

Across the lake there was a sudden swirl of movement and Jack straightened. A tall man with red hair stepped out of the trees, hands spread to show himself unarmed. Bates's men relaxed, and Bates conferred for a moment with the redhead before sending three men off with him and sending the larger group off toward the Stargate.

"For that matter," Jack said, "why not station people at the gate overnight? You'd think it would be worth the risk to get advance warning of a Wraith attack."

"I do not know," Teal'c said. "Unless the Athosians are more hostile than Colonel Sumner has indicated."

"Yeah." Jack drained the last of his coffee, wishing there was more. The mess crew had been very firm about it, though: one cup per person, and even then the supplies weren't going to last a whole lot longer. "Did you see Beckett at breakfast?"

"I did not."

"I'd really like to have a chat with him," Jack said. He straightened, gave the party on the far side of the lake a final glance — Bates' main party was just entering the trees — and ducked back in the mess hall to place his cup in the rack of dishes to be washed. The sergeant in charge of the mess line gave him a grateful glance and Jack squinted at the man's name tag.

"Sergeant Pollard," he said. "Can you tell me where I'd find Dr. Beckett?"

"The infirmary's three buildings to the west," Pollard answered promptly. "It's the one with the white tarp for a roof." He paused. "Is everything all right, sir?"

"Oh, yeah, fine," Jack said. "I'd just like a word with the doctor."

"Yes, sir," Pollard answered, and chivvied his crew back to work.

Jack ducked back out into the rising sunshine and Teal'c fell into step at his side. The expedition had made a considerable effort to make the ruins in the immediate area of the landing habitable, or at least resembling something from a high-class safari, but as they made their way toward the infirmary, as conspicuous as promised with its white roof, Jack couldn't help noticing that the rebuilt area was chosen so that Sumner could cover it from the central building they were using as a mess hall. Protection, he wondered, or keeping the civilians under control?

Beckett had slung a length of tarp to serve as a door, but it was pulled back to let in the morning sun. Jack looked into the outer room, empty except for a row of packing-crate chairs and another curtain across an inner door, then stepped inside, Teal'c still at his heels.

"Knock knock."

"Yes?" The inner curtain was swept back with a brisk rattle of rings, and a young woman in scrubs looked from one to the other. "Oh. General O'Neill. It really is you."

"Well, sort of," Jack answered. He hated these kinds of explanations. "I mean, I am O'Neill, I'm just not the General O'Neill from your timeline. We think."

"Really?" She ducked her head, blushing. "Sorry. Of course you wouldn't say it if it wasn't true. I'm Marie Wu, by the way."

"Wu," Jack said, and Teal'c made a polite half bow. "We were looking for Dr. Beckett."

"Oh. He's not here."

"Indeed?" Teal'c cocked his head to one side.

"No. I guess Colonel Sumner called him early, there's a note saying for me to take the morning appointments, not that we have any."

The sense of something wrong was growing again. Everything about her body language said she wanted to run, from her stretched uneasy smile to her hands closed in tight fists. Jack tried a gentler smile of his own. "Maybe you could answer some of my questions. About this anti-Wraith drug of Dr. Beckett's?"

"Oh, no, I couldn't do that." Wu shook her head for emphasis. "I'm really not involved in that."

"Well, is Doctor—" Jack tried to remember the name of Beckett's number two. "Dr. Keller. Is she here?"

Wu's expression closed down even further. "No. Sir. General."

"Where is she?"

He saw her face change before the shadow blocked the door, and turned without haste to smile at Sumner. "Good morning, Colonel."

"Sir." Sumner nodded to Wu. "Thanks, Marie, that'll be all."

"Yes, Colonel," she said, and slipped back into the inner room, rattling the curtain closed behind her.

"I was looking to talk to Dr. Beckett," Jack said, "but now I'm curious. What's happened to Dr. Keller?"

"She's one of the missing," Sumner answered. "The last we heard, she was with the Athosians, but—as you know—we've had trouble keeping in contact with them."

"So she could be dead, as far as you know." Jack meant the words to sting, but Sumner shrugged them off.

"Yes, sir, she could. I can't risk the people I have to find out, on the off chance that the Athosians are feeling cooperative. Or that the ones who like us are in charge that day." He paused.

"Maybe we should go back to my office?"

There wasn't any point in staying here, Jack thought. He'd learned everything he was going to. "Sure."

"The thing about the Athosians," Sumner said, as they started back toward the main building, "is that they don't really have a government, at least not one as we understand it. They've got a batch of what I'd guess you'd call tribal elders, plus some younger people who seem to represent various constituencies, and I'm damned — sorry, sir. I can't tell who's in charge of what from one day to the next. There's an old woman, Charin, who's kind of on our side, and then there's a guy called Nedellin who wants us out of the city yesterday. And then Halling, who seems to be as close to a leader as the younger people have, he's been willing to work with us, but their trade person, Teyla, she just wants us dead."

"That seems extreme," Jack said. They were back at the main building now, and Sumner gestured for them to precede him into the room he was using as an office.

"She's hot-headed," Sumner said. "If anything's happened to our people, Teyla's behind it."

"So what did happen?" Jack asked. "How'd you end up with people stuck in the Athosian — village? Camp?"

"Could be either," Sumner said. "I mean, there is a village site, and we know people are there — that's where Dr. Beckett is. Halling sent word this morning that one of the kids hurt his leg, needed our medicine. Of course Beckett said he'd go." He paused. "I asked him to keep an eye out for any of our missing people, and anything else he can find out."

"Ok," Jack said. "That's probably a good plan. But can we get back to how your people got stuck in the first place?"

"Sir." Sumner folded his hands as though that would help him control his temper. "Before Dr. Weir was killed, there was a difference of opinion on how best to deal with the locals' resistance to the idea of our exploring the city. We all agreed that we needed to either find a ZPM or confirm that there wasn't one, and once Dr. McKay began examining the ruins it was pretty clear we were going to find some useful things. Dr. Weir thought we should stay in the forest with the Athosians, and search the city in daylight. Dr. McKay felt that this was wasting time, and I felt that we would be in a much more defensible position if we set up camp in the ruins. I was overruled, and we remained with the locals. When the Wraith attacked, we were scattered, us and the locals both. After it was over, I withdrew to the city to establish a more solid defense. Military personnel were under orders, and — for the most part — followed them. Not all the civilians complied, and — honestly, sir, we didn't try very hard to get them back, not then. Once we had a decent perimeter established, I sent Ford back for them, but Teyla wouldn't let him talk to them. And that's why I don't know the status of all the civilian personnel. Sir."

Jack nodded, and risked a guess of his own. "And this would be when you lost Sheppard?"

"Yes, sir." Sumner's fists were closed tight, but he was keeping control of his anger. "He went AWOL — I have reason to believe that he was fraternizing with the locals, particularly with Teyla. I believe her influence is the reason he didn't return to the unit."

That didn't sound much like the John Sheppard Jack had met in Antarctica, the man he'd talked into joining the Atlantis expedition, and not just because of his ATA gene. He said only, "A messy situation, Colonel."

Sumner straightened his spine. "Yes, sir."

"I still want to talk to Beckett when he gets back from the village," Jack said. "In the meantime — you don't mind if we look around?"

Sumner shook his head. "Not at all, sir. But — for your own safety, I'd recommend you stay inside the perimeter."

"I just want to look around the ruins," Jack said.

He suited his actions to his words, tracing a meandering path through the ruined walls and heaps of rubble until he was sure that they weren't being followed. Even so, he climbed to the top of one of the piles of broken stone, turning as though he were trying to get a good view of Sumner's camp. The man had done a good job making it secure, he had to admit, with strong fire points protecting the main building and clear lines of sight along the perimeter and covering the boat landing. Of course, it didn't look as though they'd done more than search a quarter of the city, and the area in which they were camping was even smaller, but — it was getting the job done.

"O'Neill," Teal'c said. "I do not believe that Colonel Sumner was telling us the entire truth about Dr. Beckett."

"You noticed that too?" Jack said.

Teal'c dipped his head. "Indeed. We saw the first patrol leave the city this morning, and Dr. Beckett was not among them. Nor was he with the Athosian who met them at the landing."

"I imagine Sumner would say the call came in the middle of the night, and they sent Beckett across as a matter of mercy."

"Except that we would have heard the disturbance," Teal'c pointed out, and Jack nodded.

"Yeah. Let's let him think we believe him, at least for the moment." Jack squinted at the sun, gauging its height. "In the meantime, let's you and me just wander around and see what turns up."

"General Hammond would approve," Teal'c said. "It will be interesting to see what Colonel Carter and Daniel Jackson discover."

"Won't it just?" Jack began carefully descending the pile of stones. "Come on, let's see what kind of trouble we can not get into."

CHAPTER SEVEN
Guerilla Archeology

DANIEL made his way through the ruins, following a track that might, by a generous interpretation, bring him back to the main camp. He went slowly, stopping often to look at broken inscriptions, automatically fitting them into the picture he was beginning to build of the city's history. Emege was old, that was the main thing. He counted at least four different styles of Ancient inscription so far, and even assuming a somewhat different development in the Pegasus Galaxy, that put the founding of Emege close to the arrival of the Ancients. If that was the case, this might be one of their first settlement points, one of the first place humans were seeded.

He glanced casually over his shoulder. Still in the line of sight from the guard post, though the marines seemed to have gotten used to his presence. He eased himself to his feet and followed the line of a fallen column, craning his head to read the words that spiraled around it. They were mostly proper names, and the column ended in a shattered stub before he found anything to indicate what sort of memorial had been intended.

But at least he was now completely out of sight of the guard post. He paused, scanning the ruins. The center of the city was where he expected to find the sort of information he needed, confirmation that Janus had in fact worked here, rather than just leaving his name on some of the equipment. He didn't really think the latter was likely — it wasn't Janus's style, exactly — but he didn't think it was going to be easy. Not only was Emege old, but it had been destroyed a very long time ago. The ground had risen around and over it, thousands of years of dust and shifting stones slowly covering the wreckage; he guessed that what he was seeing, the bone-white shards of stone and metal, was only the top of the most prominent of the city's original buildings. There would be far more beneath the surface, and if Janus had had a laboratory here, they'd need to dig for it.

First, though, find if there was one. If there was anything left of the Ancients' usual archive, it was going to be buried too deeply for him to find it today. That left looking for the most likely place for a lab, and that was somewhere along the perimeter — possibly there, where the dull red walls marked out what was left of an eight-sided tower. There were towers like that on M3R-273 and on P2Y-229, and, in both cases, they'd been the formal entrance to a scientific installation. It also looked as though it rose a little higher from the beaten ground, a possible indication that it was newer than some of the other ruins. Janus would have been here toward the end of the Ancients' tenure in Emege.

He checked the guard post again, making sure he was still both out of sight and un-missed, then struck out along the line of a grassy ditch that he suspected had once been a major thoroughfare. He was tempted to stop and cut a little way through the turf, see if he couldn't find signs of paving or some other markers, but he knew there wasn't time. His priority had to be finding Janus's work.

The red-walled tower was a mess, the roof and walls fallen in on themselves to create a miniature mountain within the octagon, slabs of stone overgrown with patchy grass and clumps of tiny blue-white flowers. There were dark gaps between the stones, and Daniel pulled out his flashlight, lying prone to shine the light into the largest openings. There was definitely some space under the rubble, but none of the breaks were big enough to let him crawl through.

He was going to have to come back with shovels or, better still, heavy equipment to get through there, and he pushed himself to his feet. On M3R-273 there had been a second entrance about fifty meters beyond the tower, and — yes, there were slabs of stone there that looked as though they had been part of the same complex. A little further, the ground had slumped in, possibly after a heavy rain, and a sinkhole opened between two of the larger slabs.

That was promising. He reached for his flashlight again and went to his knees, testing the edge of the opening before trusting his weight to it. The gap wasn't very large, but he could feel air moving through it, a faint cool sigh from under the earth. And that was a good sign, a sign that there was a bigger space and enough air. He lay flat and wormed his way cautiously forward, until head and shoulders were well into the opening, and flicked on his flashlight.

The beam carved into the darkness, sweeping across consoles and bits of equipment that he didn't recognize, picked up glints like metal from a floor about fifteen feet down. Halfway across the room, there was a partition, and the flashlight's beam bounced back from it as though it were glass. The layout was the same, he thought, and brought the light back to sweep across the consoles again. Yes, that was the same pattern, the same way the consoles had been laid out on P6T-847.

He pushed himself back, reaching for his radio, and stopped. Any transmission was going to be overheard by Sumner's men and he wasn't sure he wanted to share this with them just yet, at least not until he'd had a chance to talk things over with Jack. On the other hand, climbing down into a buried ruin by himself, with no one knowing where he'd gone… Even in conventional archeology, that was a recipe for disaster.

But if he did try to go back, tell Sam what he was doing, he'd draw the attention of the guards at the machine gun post, and McKay had been very clear that part of their job was to stop people who wanted to explore the city. Maybe if he could find a way back to the main expedition, he could tell Jack or Teal'c, but that carried the same risk of notice, and would take too much time besides. No, it was worth taking a chance. Methodically, he unrolled the looped rope that would serve as a ladder, staked it securely to the turf. After a moment's thought, he pulled out his bandana and tied it around the nearer stake, letting in flutter in the faint breeze from underground. And, anyway, if he got into trouble, there was a reasonable chance the radio would work. But if this was another of Janus's machines — he had to take the risk. He took a deep breath and lowered himself into the hole.

It was cool in the chamber, but dry, the air smelling only faintly of dirt, and when he turned his light on the hole through which he'd come, he saw the signs of recent slippage. The chamber had only recently become accessible, then; that explained why it was so well-preserved.

It was very nearly identical to the installation on P6T-847, down to the wall of diamond — pure carbon — between the rows of consoles and the inner chamber with the golden ouroboros on the back wall. The door between the two rooms was missing and Daniel stepped cautiously through the opening, letting his light play across the walls and the central console. The ouroboros was the same, gold inlaid into the rough surface of the walls, but the main console was definitely different. He reached for his video camera, switched on its light as well, and began to record the details of the room. It was a pity he had to use the light, it would run down the batteries twice as fast, but he should be able to get a decent set of pictures before they were completely gone.

He saw the movement out of the corner of his eye before he heard the scuffling, made himself keep filming as though there was nothing wrong.

"Dr. Jackson!" That was the young lieutenant, Ford, but Daniel didn't look away from his work. Two more consoles, close-ups of the controls, then one more long shot of the inner chamber —

"I'm in here," he called, not taking the camera from his eye.

"Sir, you shouldn't be here." Ford advanced nervously to the door, the light from his P90 flickering across the consoles.

"Don't do that," Daniel said. "I'm trying to get some decent pictures."

"Dr. Jackson, this area is off limits."

"Why?" Daniel kept filming, moving to the second console to pan slowly across the unfamiliar controls.

"It's for your own safety," Ford said. "You're a long way outside the secure perimeter. If the Wraith were to attack, you'd never get back inside in time."

"Is it really all that likely the Wraith are going to attack in broad daylight?"

"Sir, we don't know why or when they're likely to attack. That's why Colonel Sumner set up the perimeter."

Daniel took a step back, began his last sweeping shots of the entire room. "Ok, point, but look what you missed by not looking just a little further."

"Dr. McKay probably knows all about it," Ford said. "Dr. Jackson, we can't stay here."

"Let me just finish taking these pictures," Daniel said. "This is a really interesting installation —"

"Does it have a ZPM?" Ford asked.

"No."

"Then with all respect, Doctor, it's not that interesting." Ford lifted his P90. "I'm going to have to ask that you come back with me right now."

"Let me just —"

The sound of the bolts going back on three P90s was very loud in the inner chamber.

Daniel turned, lowering the camera, to see all three weapons pointed at him. "You can't be serious."

"Yes, sir. I am." Ford didn't waver. "You need to come back with me now."

"Fine." Daniel made a production of putting away the camera, hid his sigh of relief as the P90s swung away. "But we're wasting an incredible opportunity."

"Sir, if you'd gotten permission and an escort from Colonel

Sumner, I'm sure it would have been fine," Ford said. "But for now — this way, please."

It wasn't the first time Jack had seen Daniel brought back to camp under Marine escort, and he had no real hope of its being the last. Daniel looked more annoyed than anything, so maybe there was some hope it was all a misunderstanding, but somehow Jack doubted it. He pulled himself upright as they got closer.

"Daniel? What's up?"

"Apparently I went out of bounds," Daniel answered.

"I'm sorry, General," Ford said. "Colonel Sumner's orders are for everyone to stay inside the perimeter unless he gives explicit permission otherwise."

"And the problem with that is, there's lots of interesting stuff outside that perimeter," Daniel said. "Except these guys said they'd shoot me if I didn't come back right away." There was a sharp note in his voice that Jack recognized and didn't like: Ford's threat had been serious.

"You have found something, Daniel Jackson," Teal'c said, before Ford could protest again.

"I did." Daniel was holding his camcorder, Jack saw, keeping it low at his side as though he wanted the Marines to forget he had it. "It looks like there's another one of Janus's chambers here. It's not identical to the one we came through, but —"

"You're sure?" Jack couldn't stop his own voice from sharpening. If they'd found another one of the control rooms — well, it was a lot more likely to take them home than anything else they'd come across.

"No, I'm not sure," Daniel snapped. "They didn't give me time enough to examine it properly."

"Colonel Sumner's orders —" Ford began again, and a stocky sergeant ducked out of the nearest building, P90 ready. Two Marines were at his heels, armed and ready, and the hairs rose at the back of Jack's neck.

"Is there a problem, sir?" The sergeant's name tape read Harwood, but Jack didn't remember the man.

"Yes," Daniel said. "Yes, there is —"

"Want me to take care of this, sir?" Harwood said to Ford, his hands moving on the weapon with unmistakable intent.

"Now, wait just a minute," Jack said. "Sergeant!"

"You're not in chain of command," Harwood said. "Sir. Lieutenant?"

Ford hesitated, and Harwood rocked forward on the balls of his feet, an odd little smile curving across his face.

"Stand down, Sergeant!" That was Sumner, coming around the corner of the mess hall in a hurry, and Jack let out the breath he'd been holding.

Harwood relaxed abruptly. "Sir!"

"That'll be all," Sumner said, and the sergeant saluted.

"Yes, sir," he said, and he and his men backed away. They didn't go far, though, Jack saw, just back inside the doorway of the building they'd originally come from, and he willed Daniel to keep his mouth shut for a change.

"What's the problem, Ford?" Sumner went on.

Ford came to attention. "Sir. Dr. Jackson was doing some investigating outside the secure perimeter, and we brought him back. No problem, sir."

Daniel's eyebrows twitched at that, but for once he didn't say anything, and Jack spoke before he could change his mind.

"If I could have a word, Colonel?"

"Of course," Sumner answered. "Dr. Jackson, the perimeter is there to keep everyone safe. I'd appreciate it if you would follow the regulations."

"But —"

Jack made a chopping motion, and Daniel subsided.

"I'm at your disposal, General," Sumner said, and motioned for them to step out of earshot.

"Yeah, about that." Jack paused. "Look, Colonel, it seems to me you might get a little further if you loosened the reins a little. Dr. Jackson managed to find what may be an important installation in just a couple of hours."

"Yeah, and I'm kind of curious as to how he did that, sir," Sumner said.

"It's what I do," Daniel said, joining them without waiting for an invitation. "Look, this could be the key to getting us back to our own timeline."

"It strikes me as suspicious that you could just walk up to this installation when no one else has noticed it," Sumner said. "Unless McKay's been holding out again."

"I've been in any number of ruined Ancient cities," Daniel said. "I know where to look. And if you'd just let us go back there…"

Sumner reached for his radio, no longer seeming to be paying attention, and Jack took the opportunity to glare at Daniel. This was clearly not a good time to push Sumner. Daniel glared back, and Jack wondered if he'd gotten the message at all.

"McKay," Sumner said. "McKay!"

The radio crackled, and a British voice answered. "Grodin here, Colonel. Dr. McKay's — a bit unavailable, sir. Can I relay a message?"

"What do you mean, unavailable?"

"He and Colonel Carter are trying to track some power conduit, and Dr. McKay's halfway down a hole," Grodin said.

"Well, get him out," Sumner began, but Jack spoke first.

"Colonel." It was the tone he'd perfected for junior officers who were getting out of line, and Sumner stopped, flushing to the roots of his hair.

"Sir."

"No harm's been done," Jack said. "Dr. Jackson was a little over-enthusiastic, that's all."

"Jack," Daniel protested.

"Daniel?" Jack fixed him with a stare and Daniel flung up his hands.

"Fine! Be that way." He stalked off, and Jack turned his attention back to Sumner.

Sumner keyed his radio again. "Grodin. Never mind. Just tell Dr. McKay I'll want to talk to him when he gets back."

"I'll let him know, sir," Grodin said.

"I'm sure Dr. Jackson will be happy to wait for an escort before he goes back," Jack said. And the sooner he can get back there, the sooner we can get the hell out of here— He swallowed the words, made himself look as patient and kindly as he could manage.

"We set up that perimeter for a reason," Sumner said. "It's for their own good. We can't protect anything outside it, and there's no telling when the Wraith are going to show up next. Even with men at the Stargate, we've got less than a minute's warning before their Darts are overhead and the attack begins. Anybody who's out in the open is going to die. We found that out the hard way."

"So can we get an escort?" Jack asked. "I'd like to see what he's found."

"Not today." Sumner's face hardened. "I don't have the men to spare."

"What?" Jack barely stopped himself from looking around in disbelief. "Look, Colonel, I don't need more than a couple of men — I'm willing to take the chance and go without anybody, come to that."

"First of all—" Sumner broke off. "With all respect, General, you're not in your own timeline here, and you don't get to give me orders. And you don't know what kind of firepower you need when the Wraith come at you. You have no idea. And that doesn't even begin to cover the locals."

"You didn't mention the locals were actually shooting at you," Jack said. "In fact, seems to me you said the opposite."

"It's just a matter of time," Sumner said. "Right now, they just watch us. And there's damn all we can do about it. They watch, and they report, and one of these days, they're going to try it. We'll be ready for them, but —" He shook his head. "Weir screwed up the situation, making them think we'd jeopardize security over their superstitions, and we're going to pay for it in my men's lives."

Jack studied him for a long moment. He'd been on the ragged edge himself more often than he liked to remember, knew what stress and responsibility and the constant threat of combat could to do a man, but this — this felt different, somehow. "How many attacks have you had to deal with, Colonel?"

Sumner sighed. "Three so far. And they'll be back."

"Because you're in the city," Jack said. He paused. "Doesn't that kind of indicate that the Athosians might be right?"

"It's the most defensible place on the planet," Sumner said. "And it's the only place we're going to find the technology we need to get back to Atlantis. And, anyway, the locals said the Wraith keep coming until they wipe out anyone with higher technology."

"Ok," Jack said. This was not an argument he was going to win. "Look, is Dr. Beckett back from wherever it is he went? Because I'd really like to have a word with him."

"No." Sumner controlled himself again. "Sorry, General, I don't know when he'll be back. Maybe tomorrow." He turned away without waiting for an answer.

"Then I'll want to talk to him tomorrow," Jack said, to his retreating back. "Damn."

"Colonel Sumner does not seem to be a great respecter of rank," Teal'c said, after a moment.

"Yeah. He's made it pretty clear I'm not in his chain of command." Jack shook his head.

"Can he do that?" Daniel asked. "I mean, a general's a general, right?"

"I don't think it's ever come up before," Jack said. "Whether or not you have the obligation to obey someone who outranks you in another timeline. Not that it matters a whole lot, since he's got more guys with guns than we do."

"Yeah, I kind of noticed that," Daniel said.

"Did you have to get caught?" Jack asked. "Whatever happened to being sneaky?"

"I didn't feel like being so sneaky that I got trapped down a hole where no one could find me," Daniel answered. He lowered his voice. "It's very like the ouroboros chamber on P6T-847, but it's not identical. I really think Sam needs to take a look at it."

"You heard Sumner," Jack said.

"Perhaps Colonel Sumner will be in a more reasonable frame of mind tomorrow," Teal'c said. Jack didn't think he believed it, either.

Daniel held up the camcorder he'd been holding cupped in the palm of his hand. "Well, I got some decent footage of the place, we can at least start by looking at that. But, Jack —"

"I know," Jack said. "Let's not push him any further. Not until we have to."

Dinner was served early and McKay herded them back from the installation before the sun had fully set. Sam trailed along behind the main group, glad of a brief moment of quiet to make sense of everything she'd seen. McKay had done a good job tracing the conduit, which did in fact seem to indicate that there was another power source somewhere, but the most promising segment dead-ended in a wall of fallen rubble. They'd either need to get a lot of people in to help clear it — and even then it would need to be shored up, and she wasn't sure the expedition had the equipment to do it — or they would need to find a way to get at the conduit from beyond the blockage. It was possible that there was another ZPM, but at least it was a pure engineering problem. Not like the other issues.

She'd seen hostility between military and civilian personnel before, but nothing like this, and in a weird way she was glad it wasn't happening in her own timeline. Although, given that they'd heard nothing from Atlantis since the expedition walked through the Stargate, this or something even worse could be going on right now…

She pushed that thought aside, made herself nod at Airman Salawi, slogging along at the back of the group, her pack loaded down with the team's spare laptop and several other pieces of equipment. "Why doesn't Dr. McKay leave stuff set up?"

Salawi gave her a wary glance. "Colonel Sumner's orders, ma'am. He doesn't want the Athosians to get their hands on any of our equipment."

"Oh." There was nothing to say to that, Sam thought, or at least nothing she was going to say to Salawi. She just hoped Daniel had found something useful when he wandered off.

Dinner was pretty much the same as they'd been served the previous night, more, if different, stew, bread, a half cup of coffee for those who couldn't be persuaded to take a cup of the local tea. Sam took some, sniffing warily, and decided it didn't go too badly with the stew. It had a faint undertone of something between mint and ginger, and she wasn't surprised to see Jack set his aside.

"Anything?" she said to Daniel, and he shrugged.

"Maybe. I'll show you later."

"Ok."

The divided mess hall was depressing, and neither Jack nor Daniel seemed in the mood to linger. Sam shoveled down her share of the stew and, as soon as they had all finished, Jack shoved back his stool.

"Come on, kids, let's call it a night."

No one tried to stop them — in fact, no one spoke at all — and when Jack and Teal'c searched their quarters for bugs, they came up empty.

"So maybe they took the hint," Daniel said, sitting on the edge of a packing case to take his boots off.

"Maybe," Jack said. He went to the door and looked out, his expression unhappy.

Sam busied herself lighting the lamps. "So what was this 'maybe'?" she said to Daniel, who produced a small camcorder from one of his pockets.

"I think Janus was here, too," he said. "This looks like the installation we came through."

"Yeah." Sam adjusted the picture, slowing it down so that she could examine it frame by frame. "Nice camera work."

"Thanks."

"Dr. Beckett was not at dinner either," Teal'c said.

"You noticed that," Jack said, and Teal'c inclined his head.

"Indeed."

"Yeah, I don't know where he's gone, but I'm beginning to think it's not as simple as 'off helping the locals out of the goodness of his heart.'"

"Do you think he is a prisoner, O'Neill?"

"I don't know." Jack shook his head. "The only thing I do know is that it doesn't make a hell of a lot of sense."

Sam tuned them out, focusing her attention on the installation, and after a moment Daniel came to look over her shoulder. It was, as he had said, a close match to the installation on P6T-847, though the consoles in the outer room were laid out in a different pattern. It looked as though Janus had divided power monitoring from the control functions, and there was more redundancy in the controls — two separate positions that seemed to expect someone to enter a destination. She looked up.

"Can you tell if this is older or newer than the one we saw before?"

"I'm not sure," Daniel said. "That's one of the things that would be easier if we could just go back and take another look —"

"Just a guess."

"I think it's older. Although a large part of that is based on knowing that the Ancients abandoned Pegasus when they did."

"It would really nice to know," Sam said. "If this is an older unit, then we can assume that the changes Janus made were improvements — well, that Janus thought they were improvements, anyway."

"Yeah, Janus's ideas of 'new and improved' can be a little — unorthodox. But I take your point."

Sam let the images spool forward, slowed them again as Daniel entered the inner chamber. "The lack of a door does seem to suggest that this one's earlier."

"That might have been removed later," Daniel said. "I didn't really look that hard."

"Mm." Sam let the images run, sliding past consoles and instrument panels that she'd seen before. The equipment in the inner chamber looked less finished, the ouroboros wider and less detailed, and the central console was definitely different. There were fewer displays, and on at least one the readings were given in an entirely different scale. Less sensitive? More sensitive? She closed her eyes for a moment, making the conversion. This was less sensitive than the one on P6T-847, which argued that it was indeed older, before Janus had worked out how closely he needed to control the energy build-up. But the main console… It was entirely different, and she froze the image for a long time before she was able to identify the various pieces. They all seemed to be there after all, except…

"That's weird," she said, squinting at the little screen. "It looks like — yeah. That redundant circuit, the one we had all the trouble with…"

"The one that caused the problem?" Daniel looked at her over the top of his glasses.

"We don't know that," Sam said. "But, yeah. That one. I'm pretty sure it's missing."

"That's… interesting."

Sam nodded. "Except that since I still don't know what it was supposed to do, it makes it hard to figure out what it means that it's missing."

"We need to go back there," Daniel said. "Jack!"

Jack looked over at them. "Don't say it."

"I'm afraid Daniel's right," Sam said. "It's definitely another version of the installation that brought us here, but there are enough differences that I'd need to go over it in detail before I could figure out if I could repair it enough to get us home." She looked back at the camcorder's screen, touched buttons to move the pictures back and then forward again. "I bet the Ancients were trying to run their shields and everything off the power source originally designed for this device. McKay and I agreed that there wasn't enough power in the ZPMs to do it, not the way the power room was configured. I wonder if the conduits we were tracing don't ultimately lead right back here."

"It may do — that." Jack waved his hand to encompass physics and other sciences. "But I'm not sure just how cooperative Colonel Sumner is feeling."

Sam turned off the camcorder to save the battery. "Sir, that doesn't make sense. I would think that the best way to deal with us — with the problem that we represent — is to let us figure out how to get back where we belong so he can go on running things the way he wants."

"You'd think," Jack said. "He says he's just trying to keep everybody safe — and maybe he is. We've been here less than thirty-six hours and we don't know anything about these Wraith. But I'm damned sure he's not going to let us go explore that installation on our own."

"So what he doesn't know won't hurt him," Daniel said.

"I don't think that'll work," Sam said, with regret. "If we're not in sight, he's going to know exactly where we've gone."

"We could sneak off from McKay," Daniel suggested. "He'd cover for you."

"Daniel," Jack said. "I'm not ready to cause that kind of trouble yet. The situation just isn't clear enough."

"One thing that's clear is that you out-rank him," Daniel said.

"Not in this world. Carter. Is there any problem with your examining the installation with, say, Lieutenant Ford for an escort?"

Sam paused. "I don't — I don't think so, but I don't know.

Though I'll be the first to say I don't understand everything it does."

"No kidding," Jack murmured. "Is there any reason we don't want Sumner to get his hands on it?"

"It's one of Janus's devices," Daniel said.

Sam winced. "Daniel has a point, sir. If either the colonel or the situation are unstable —"

"If?" Jack made quotes in the air.

"Yes, sir. Then maybe we don't really want him to have access to one of Janus's machines. Particularly one whose limits are unknown."

"But, Colonel Carter," Teal'c said. "If we do not investigate this device, are we not ignoring our best way to return to our own time?"

"Not ignoring," Jack said. "We're just — delaying a bit. Carter. You're with McKay tomorrow again, right?"

"Yes, sir." Sam nodded. "He asked me to help finish tracing that conduit — which is likely to lead us to the new installation, by the way."

"See if you can't find something else for him to look at," Jack said. "Daniel, go with her, do what you can to help."

Daniel nodded.

"We'll do what Sumner wants tomorrow," Jack said, "be nice and cooperative, and then we'll see. And I still want to talk to Dr. Beckett."

CHAPTER EIGHT
Attack

TEAL'C rolled upright at the first clatter of the alarm. It sounded like someone beating pots together, and as he stuck his head out the door of their shelter he saw that was exactly what it was. Sergeant Pollard was standing in the door of the mess hall banging on a pot with a metal ladle, and behind him one of the airmen was slamming two pots together. The air was filled with a thin, rising whine, growing ever louder and coming from the direction of the Stargate.

"Everybody to the mess hall!" someone was shouting, and flashlights split the pre-dawn darkness as Sumner's Marines rushed for what were obviously well-prepared positions.

"We're out of here," O'Neill said, at his shoulder, and Teal'c looked back to see the others up and ready, O'Neill and Carter with their pistols drawn, Daniel with the rest of their gear slung over his shoulder. Not for the first time, Teal'c wished he had his staff weapon.

If wishes were deeds, all men would be First Prime. The old proverb flitted through his brain, and he shook it away, drawing his own pistol. "Indeed."

The whine had become a shriek, a scream of tortured air, and Teal'c looked up to see a sleek aircraft with a needle nose flash past against the thin clouds.

"Those must be the Wraith," Daniel said.

"You think?" O'Neill caught his shoulder, shoved him toward the mess hall. "Come on, move!"

They dashed across the open space, the Marines opening the perimeter at their approach, and ducked inside just as a new sound came from behind them. Teal'c glanced over his shoulder to see a shimmer and then the shape of a dozen men appeared out of thin air. Most of them were armored, their faces hidden behind bizarrely organic masks, coarse white hair straggling lank to their shoulders. The skin of their bared arms and hands was the pale green-white of corpse-light. The Marines opened fire at once, two or three men firing on each of the masked warriors. The first one staggered, bullet holes blooming on his chest, but kept coming for far too long before it fell. One Marine kept pumping bullets into it, while his teammates switched to a new target.

"Teal'c!"

Teal'c turned, taking the P90 O'Neill held out to him.

"Bates says they'll try beaming drones inside next."

Teal'c glanced around the hall, saw the way the civilian scientists and the rest of the Marines had toppled tables to create makeshift fire points, backs to the wall, leaving the main room empty. Carter and Daniel had already done the same, and Carter had also acquired a P90, while Daniel was hastily checking what looked like O'Neill's pistol. Teal'c moved to join them. "Drones, O'Neill?"

"The ones with the face-things." O'Neill mimed putting on a mask, his expression unhappy. "Apparently they're controlled from somewhere else —"

The air shimmered again and Teal'c dropped to one knee behind the table.

"Here we go," O'Neill said, and cocked his weapon.

The Marines fired first, careless of crossfire, and Teal'c ducked into the table's dubious shelter. Daniel yelped as a splinter tore past them, and O'Neill swore. Teal'c took more careful aim, aware that O'Neill was doing the same at his side, and held down the trigger. The first masked Wraith staggered, snarling like an animal; behind it a second masked Wraith leveled its long staff-like weapon. Teal'c ducked again, and blue fire crackled past him, struck the wall and clung for a moment, writhing, before it vanished. O'Neill kept firing and finally the first Wraith fell, but the second one kept coming, roaring its rage. Teal'c aimed more carefully, stitched another line of bullets across its chest and through its legs, and finally it, too, fell.

Behind them, one of the scientists screamed. Teal'c jerked around to see the man held off the ground, a Wraith's hand fastened at the base of his neck. The scientist screamed again, and shrank, withering to a mummy, a corpse left too long in the sun, dead before the Wraith could cast him aside. Two of the Marines fired then, and the Wraith turned toward them, roaring, fighting through the hail of bullets for three more steps before it finally collapsed.

That was the last of them, at least for the moment. Teal'c cocked his head to listen for the distinct whine of the attacking aircraft, but there was only relative silence, the harsh breathing of the humans, the soft whimper of someone wounded. Someone's radio crackled.

"Darts have cleared to the west."

Sergeant Bates triggered his radio. "Not back to the gate?"

"No, sir. They headed straight west and took off like we had missiles."

"Copy that." Bates touched his radio again. "Colonel Sumner, Bates here. Permission to stand down?"

There was a moment's pause before Sumner answered. "Go ahead. But keep the civilians under cover just in case they decide to come back."

"You heard the man," Bates called. "Stand down. Civilians are to remain —"

"We need a medic here!" That was McKay, his voice high and strained. "Where's Beckett?"

"On my way," a woman's voice answered — Dr. Beckett's assistant Marie Wu. She scrambled across the open space, lugging a pack marked with a large red cross, and dropped to her knees beside the table.

Teal'c looked around again. None of the Marines seemed to be injured, and there was only the one casualty, the scientist who had been attacked by the drone. The mess hall door opened then, and two Marines came in, dragging a third between them. They dumped him unceremoniously against the wall and went back out again, to return for a second man. Neither one showed any signs of obvious injury, but they lay sprawled as though dead.

"Wu!" That was Bates again. "Marines down!"

The woman's head appeared over the top of the table. "Unless they're bleeding, Sergeant, Dr. Parrish has priority."

O'Neill's eyes narrowed. "What's wrong with them?" he said, to no one in particular, but one of the younger Marines gave him a quick glance.

"Stunned, sir. They should be ok. The Wraith only carry non-lethal."

Teal'c lifted his eyebrows at that, but Daniel nodded.

"Ok, that makes sense, in an unpleasant kind of way. If we're a food source, they're not going to want to waste resources just killing us out of hand."

"That is indeed an unpleasant thought, Daniel Jackson." Teal'c eyed the wall where the blue fire had crawled. It did make sense, though, and he had seen one Wraith feed.

Daniel gave O'Neill's pistol a rueful glance. "And, you know, I don't think this would have been very effective."

Teal'c put his head to one side, considering the matter. "I believe you would need to empty the entire clip in rapid succession. And even then…"

"Those things heal fast," Carter said.

"Indeed."

O'Neill climbed out from behind the table, moved toward McKay, who was still standing hands on hips, glaring at everyone. Teal'c followed, curious, and saw one of the other scientists propped up on somebody's pack, clutching at a bloody field dressing high on his left thigh. He was a tall, skinny man with a long face that might have been attractive by Tau'ri standards if it hadn't been screwed up in pain. That was definitely not from a Wraith weapon, and McKay bared teeth in a savage smile, as though he'd read Teal'c's thought.

"Yes, this is the sort of thing that keeps happening, and if Parrish gets an infection and dies, we'll have lost our senior biologist —"

"Oh, thanks. That makes me feel a whole lot better," Parrish said, and winced again as Marie Wu tightened the dressing. "Ow."

"If you've got him squared away, Dr. Wu, we could use your help over here," Bates said.

"Yes, I'm coming." Wu pushed herself to her feet, stripping off a set of latex gloves. "Dr. McKay, can you get him back to the infirmary?"

"I suppose —"

"We'll help," Carter said quickly, and Daniel nodded. Teal'c watched long enough to be certain that McKay was not going to impede them, and turned his attention back to O'Neill.

The general was watching Bates with an expression that most of his men had learned meant trouble. "Seems like there's an awful lot of collateral damage, Sergeant."

Bates gave him a fulminating stare. "You saw what the Wraith are like. It's only volume of fire that puts them down for good."

"I saw that," O'Neill said, still in that same deceptively mild tone. "And given that you don't exactly have an unlimited supply of ammunition, I'm thinking that more disciplined fire is warranted."

Indeed. Teal'c swallowed the word, though he had been wanting to make the same point, and Bates' face darkened further.

"With all respect, General —"

"Yeah, I know," O'Neill said. "I'm not from your timeline, and you don't have to take orders from me. But I wouldn't think I'd need to order you not to shoot your own people."

He stalked away without waiting for an answer, following Carter and the others from the mess hall. Bates glared after him, fingers twitching, and Teal'c readied himself to intervene.

But then the sergeant seemed to master himself, and waved to the nearest Marines.

"All right, get these bodies out of here. You know the drill."

Something in his tone seemed odd, Teal'c thought, though he could not quite define it. Of course there would be a procedure for dealing with the dead Wraith, it was only logical — necessary, to keep disease from spreading in the camp, and also a matter of honor, or at least it would have been in his own universe. He allowed himself to drift toward one of the groups hoisting bodies under Ford's supervision, and spoke quietly.

"Do you need assistance, Lieutenant?"

The young man stopped as though the idea startled him. "Um. No, no thank you," he said. "We'll manage."

And that was even more odd. A burial detail, even of the enemy, was never something that couldn't be lightened by more hands. Teal'c stepped back, watching as the Marines hauled the bodies away. Behind him, Pollard and his crew were putting the mess hall back to rights, talking quietly among themselves, while the rest of the scientists picked up their gear. Teal'c caught references to breakfast, to the normal routine of the day's work, now starting earlier than planned, and slipped through the door before anyone could notice what he was doing.

It was light out now, the eastern sky as pale pink as the inside of a shell, a white spot between the trees showing where the sun would rise, but there was no sign of the Marines. Teal'c glanced at the trampled ground, but it offered no useful sign. Instead, he tipped his head to the side, listening, and thought he could pick out the sound of equipment and a mutter of voices toward the edge of the camp. He moved toward the sounds, careful to stay in cover, and finally eased between two broken walls to look out onto the burial ground.

Only it was not just a burial ground. Teal'c lifted his eyebrows as he watched two of the Marines hoist a Wraith body up onto an improvised table, adjusting it so that its right arm lay palm down. Ford examined it, then drew a long-bladed knife and cut carefully into the skin along the top of the forearm. It was hard to be certain, but he seemed to be following the line of a dark vein that ran up the Wraith's arm. Dark green blood welled sluggishly from the cut, and Teal'c tensed, wondering if the creature could still be alive. But, no, it did not stir, and surely if it were living it would protest this dissection. Ford stopped the cut a little below the elbow and made a second incision perpendicular to the first. From within it, he drew out a dark green sac the size of a child's fist. It was attached by several thick veins, and one of the other Marines tied them off before Ford cut the sac free. A third man produced a plastic box, the sort used for collecting plant specimens, and Ford set it carefully inside before nodding for the Marines to remove the first body. They took it to a pit that Teal'c had not noticed before and dropped it in, while two more Marines hoisted the next Wraith body onto the table. Ford examined its arm, and began again to cut.

Teal'c watched, his expression impassive, as Ford removed the same organ from each of the dead Wraith. There were more than a dozen, and the collecting box was stuffed full of the sacs by the time they were done. Ford closed the box carefully and started back toward the camp, leaving the others to finish burying the bodies, and Teal'c drew further into the shadow of the ruins until he had passed.

The action made no sense. It was clearly not random desecration: the Marines were targeting a specific thing, some part of the Wraith feeding system, perhaps, since it was attached to the feeding hand. But what they could possibly want with such things… Teal'c shook his head and started back toward the mess hall. They would need to investigate thoroughly, beginning with the expedition doctors. But he was certain of one thing: O'Neill would not approve.

Jack followed McKay's people through the rising light toward the infirmary, trying to get a grip on his temper. Bates's handling of the firefight in the mess hall had been criminally stupid, and it was just luck that more people hadn't been killed or injured. He wanted nothing more than to put Bates on report, and add some trenchant comments to both his and Sumner's permanent files — hell, if he had his way, he'd bring Bates up on charges, recklessly endangering the civilians he was supposed to be protecting. In the back of his mind, he could almost hear George Hammond expostulating — *what are you going to do about it, Jack?* — but practically there was nothing he could do. Sumner had made his position very clear, and he had the men to back it up. For now, Jack promised himself. He wasn't about to let this ride much longer.

It was hot and crowded in the infirmary, Dr. Wu still working on Dr. Parrish's leg while several of her own staff and a Marine corpsman tended a string of minor cuts and abrasions. The corpsman was working mostly on Marines, Jack noted, while the civilian staff took care of scientists and Air Force personnel. That was not a good sign, and his frown deepened as he noticed that the corpsman finished the treatment of each Marine with an injection into their upper arms. Neither the civilians nor the airmen received those shots, and Dr. Wu seemed to go out of her way not to see them given.

"How's Parrish doing?" he asked quietly, and Wu looked up, seeming almost grateful for the question.

"He got off lucky," she said. "The bullet went through the fleshy part of his thigh, missed the bone and the big blood vessels, and it may even have been a ricochet. I was afraid it might have broken his femur."

"You and me both," Parrish muttered. "It hurts like hell, Marie. Is there any chance of something stronger than ibuprofen?"

"Absolutely." Wu unlocked one of the storage chests and took out a bottle of tablets. She counted out six and wrapped them in a twist of paper. "Sorry I don't have any nice bottles for you, but this is what I've got. Take one every 8 hours for pain, and stay off the leg for at least 24 hours. Then I'll give you crutches and we'll see."

"Like crutches are going to do me any good on this terrain," Parrish said, but took the paper. "Thanks, Marie."

One of the other biologists helped him to his feet and a dark-haired man came to support him on the other side.

"I mean stay off your feet," Wu said, and the botanist nodded.

"Believe me, I'd like nothing better."

The curtain fell closed behind him, and Wu turned to Daniel. "Let me take a look at that."

Jack gave him a sharp look, and Daniel held up his left wrist. "It's — and I say this with all due appreciation of the irony of the comment — it really is just a scratch."

"No reason not to clean it properly," Wu said, and reached for a bottle of alcohol.

"Ow! When it hurts like that — yeah, that's a reason." Daniel contrived to look hurt, but Jack could see that it wasn't anything more than a shallow graze along the back of his arm, not really large enough to need a bandage.

"What's with the shots?" Jack asked, and nodded toward the corpsman, who was packing his gear back into his kit. "Don't tell me your guys aren't up-to-date on tetanus."

Wu's face changed. "That's — it's Dr. Beckett's anti-Wraith drug. It needs to be taken regularly to maintain the effect."

"Speaking of which," Jack said. "Where is Dr. Beckett? I'd expect him to be here helping."

"I don't know, sir." Wu's face and voice were wooden, and she wouldn't meet his eyes.

"Dr. Beckett was on his way back from the Athosian village when the attack happened," the corpsman volunteered. "He fell and hit his head. Colonel Sumner said to take him to his quarters and let him recover there."

"You know, I'd really like a word with him," Jack said.

"He's under sedation, sir. I'm sorry." The corpsman fitted the last of the vials into his kit and stood up quickly.

"I'm sure Colonel Sumner will let you know as soon as he's fit to talk." He ducked through the curtain without waiting to be dismissed.

"Sir," Carter said.

"Yeah, I know." Jack looked at Wu. "Tell me, Doctor, do you usually sedate somebody who's suffered a head injury?"

"Not generally, no." She still wouldn't meet his eyes.

"You want to tell me what's really going on?" Jack pitched his voice low enough that the last of the Marines wouldn't hear.

"Not right now." Wu took a deep breath. "Come back after breakfast, we can talk then. Bring Dr. Jackson back and I'll find a bandage for him."

Jack nodded. "Ok. Carter, Daniel — let's go."

Breakfast was about as bad as Jack had expected: some weird local egg that tasted just as bad as the powdered version, and the dregs of the coffee pot. He made himself eat anyway, knowing he'd want the calories later, though Daniel pushed his plate away unhappily.

"Colonel Carter."

And that was McKay, just in time to make the morning perfect. Jack squinted up at him, trying to look unwelcoming, and Carter said, "Yes?"

"Can I borrow you again today? I've got an idea about patching a naquadah generator into what's left of the city's defense system. Since that's likely to be a little less dangerous to random bystanders than our current system."

"But —" Carter stopped, swallowed a quick mouthful of coffee. "Yes, of course. Unless General O'Neill needs me here?"

Jack shook his head. "Go ahead. I'll just take Daniel back to the infirmary. Keep in radio contact."

"They didn't shoot you, too," McKay said, to Daniel, who shook his head.

"Just a scratch. From a splinter or something."

McKay sniffed, but forbore further comment as Carter scrambled to her feet.

"I'll stay in touch, sir," she said, and followed McKay from the mess hall.

Daniel poked at the last of his eggs, and put his fork down. "Are we done here?"

Jack managed not to look over his shoulder to see how many Marines were left in the room, glanced instead at his watch. "Yeah. I'd say so."

They walked slowly back toward the infirmary building, Jack doing his best to project 'aimless wandering' rather than purposeful progress. No one seemed to be paying attention, most of the scientists busy with their projects, the military either on duty or sleeping after the morning's excitement, but nonetheless Jack kept and eye out for any unwanted attention. They had turned the final corner when Teal'c stepped out of the shadows.

"O'Neill. I hoped I would catch you here."

"You might give a person some warning."

"I will bear that in mind," Teal'c said, without sincerity. "I have seen something profoundly disturbing. The Marines are harvesting organs from the dead Wraith."

"Organs?"

Jack was glad Daniel had said it, as it spared him from sounding equally queasy.

"Indeed. A sac or gland on the arm that bears their — feeding hand, I have heard it called." Teal'c looked perhaps a hair less impassive than usual. "I believe the Marines removed that organ from every Wraith killed this morning."

"We're on our way to Dr. Wu," Jack said, after a moment. "Since Dr. Beckett still isn't available. I'm betting she has the answer."

"If she'll tell us," Daniel said.

"I think she wants to," Jack answered, and ducked under the infirmary curtain. "Dr. Wu?"

"Here." She stepped out from the inner room, looking more relaxed than she had any other time Jack had seen her. She held up a roll of adhesive tape and a pack of gauze. "It looks as though I did have some bandages to spare after all."

"Is that really necessary?" Jack asked.

This time, Wu met his gaze directly. "I'd like to have an excuse for talking to you, General. You may be getting out of here and back to your own time, but I'm in it for the long haul."

"That bad?" Daniel said. He seated himself on the edge of the table and began rolling up his sleeve.

"At the moment."

"Tell me about this drug of Beckett's," Jack said.

"You saw how the Wraith kill," Wu said. "It's important you understand that, understand why."

Jack nodded. He'd seen the scientist they dragged away, withered to a caricature of a human being.

"The thing about the Wraith is that they're — Dr. Beckett called them 'obligate animavores'. They feed on what I supposed you'd describe as the vitality, the life force, of intelligent beings, and nothing else. When they feed they drain the body of that force, and it's horribly painful and debilitating. In fact, even a partial feeding is usually fatal in the long run. That happened to one of the Marines, after the first attack. His buddies got the Wraith off him before it killed him, but he slipped into a coma and died anyway. That's when we, Dr. Beckett and I, figured out about the enzyme."

Teal'c lifted his head. "This would be why I saw organs taken from the dead?"

Wu nodded. "Being fed upon is a horrible strain on the body, so the Wraith have evolved to secrete an enzyme that mitigates some of the effects. They inject it into the body through one of the claws on the feeding hand, and it slows the physical degeneration. Dr. Beckett believes that it allows the Wraith to take more 'food' from an individual human, because we don't die so quickly when we're attacked."

"Lovely," Daniel said.

"The thing is, once we realized how the enzyme worked,

Dr. Beckett saw a way to use it to increase resistance to the Wraith feeding process. We tweaked the chemical structure slightly, so that the actual Wraith enzyme is blocked, and we tailored it so it's not so hard on the human body." Wu gave an odd sad smile. "It even had some positive side effects — the people who tested it found that their reaction times increased, they were stronger, faster, didn't tire as quickly. It seemed like a real breakthrough."

"But?" Jack asked, when she seemed unwilling to go on.

"But it also has other, cumulative problems," Wu said. "The body builds up a resistance to its effects — we did anticipate that, and I think we could have controlled for it, but it is a problem. And it seems to have psychological effects as well."

"Why am I not surprised?" Daniel murmured.

"Psychological effect such as — ?" Jack prompted.

"Obsessive thoughts of various kinds. Including what one might diagnose as paranoia."

"Wonderful." Jack couldn't say he was entirely surprised. It fit with Sumner's barely leashed temper, with the way Bates's men acted as though they were looking for a fight. "So what's really happened to Dr. Beckett?"

"Colonel Sumner has him working to stockpile as much of the drug as possible," Wu answered. "The Colonel set him up in a laboratory beneath one of the Ancient buildings, one that's hidden from the Wraith. I expect — if Mr. Teal'c saw them harvesting the enzyme sacs, I expect Dr. Beckett is working on them now. The enzyme has to be extracted while the sacs are still relatively fresh."

She shook herself and reached for the tape and gauze, began mechanically to bandage Daniel's arm.

"So the whole story about helping the Athosians was just more bull," Jack said.

"Not entirely." Wu cut strips of tape and hung them on the side of the metal tray. "Halling — he's the Athosians' other leader, their internal leader, we think. Halling does ask for him when they have medical problems, especially since Colonel Sumner isn't letting them go through the Stargate to do their usual trading."

"Great," Daniel said. He flexed his newly bandaged arm. "And — thanks, that's a lot better."

Yeah, Jack thought. Just dandy. A paranoid colonel leading a pack of trigger-happy Marines who looked like they were on the verge of forgetting that they were here to protect the civilian part of the expedition — yeah, that was exactly what he wanted to deal with. "Do you see Dr. Beckett?"

"Sometimes," Wu answered. She closed the lid of the medical cabinet with a sharp click.

"If you can," Jack said. "Will you tell him that I want to talk to him?"

"Of course." She nodded. "But, General? Be careful."

"Believe me," Jack answered, "I intend to be."

CHAPTER NINE

Interlude

THIS WAS entirely unnecessary, the Queen said. The lords of her zenana were making themselves small, even the Consort standing carefully out of her direct line of sight. Only the Young Queen faced her, scowling, her heavy bone-white hair framing her delicate face.

With respect, it was exactly the opposite, she said. *It's vital that we show the humans that we are their masters, and especially in a case like this one, where they've suddenly acquired new technology.*

And yet what you have done is lost a dozen of my best drones, the Queen answered. *Nor do we have any better idea where the Athosians came by this technology.*

What does it matter? Were the Young Queen not nearly of an age to command her own hive, one would have said she was pouting. *We will destroy them.*

Will we? You have not managed it so far.

Give me another chance.

At the cost of how many more drones, and the blades to lead them? The Queen glared at her daughter. *Nor has the one you would call pallax acquitted himself as I would wish, were I his mistress.*

It is not his fault. The Young Queen matched her glare for glare. *The tactics were my own.*

They were ill-chosen.

They didn't work. The Young Queen dropped her gaze at last, shrugging her shoulders angrily. *We should have been able to kill or capture far more of them than we did, and it's not just the advantage their weapons gave them. I don't understand it.*

Against the far wall, Seeker shifted his weight uneasily, his beautifully dressed hair slithering across the shoulders of his coat. The

Queen bared teeth, silencing anything he might have said, and looked back at her daughter. *Why do you think this might be so?*

I don't know. The Young Queen made another shrugging movement. *If I knew, I wouldn't have let it happen this way.*

There were weapons that we did not expect, the Queen said, *and then greater strength and resistance. What does that tell you?*

The Young Queen took a breath, controlling her fury. *That they got their weapons elsewhere. The Athosians are traders, that's how they get that which they cannot make or harvest themselves.* She stopped, allowing the puzzle to wash through her. *And yet these are weapons beyond any I have seen or heard of. Neither the Satedans nor the humans of Hoff have such. Nor did the Genii, before we put them down.*

Just so, the Queen said softly. *What else?*

I don't know of any human world that has such, the Young Queen said, after a moment's thought. *Nor can I think of any Queen of our lineage or any other who would permit humans to develop so far without a check. Unless there were a world unclaimed, a hunting ground unknown?* She shook her head. *I cannot believe that.*

Seeker shifted again, drawing the Queen's eye, and this time she nodded. *I believe the Master of Sciences Biological has a suggestion.*

Seeker bowed, the gesture graceful and formal at once. *There have been humans in the past who have developed their own compounds to counteract the effects of the feeding process. Usually it is derived from our own mitigating enzyme. The description of these humans' behavior suggests that such a drug is in use among them.*

The Young Queen turned, her head tilting sharply to one side. *Aren't there eventual — deadly — side effects?*

There are, Seeker answered. *Or there have been in the past. I do not think a human population has used such a drug since before we last slept.*

So why now? The Young Queen shook her head. *It doesn't make sense.*

If they were unaware of the consequences, the Queen said.

How could they be? the Young Queen answered. *Any group with the sophistication to build such a drug would trade off-world, and so would come to know of the problems. Unless they believed they had solved them?*

I am sure everyone who tries it believes that, Seeker said. *But it has never been true.*

And yet, the Young Queen went on as though he hadn't spoken, *Athos is a trading world, they make no weapons or drugs of their own, so presumably they are playing host to another group? One that doesn't know...* Her mental voice trailed off as she considered the problem.

The Queen nodded. *The Athosians, if they are separate as it seems they must be — they have not told these strangers all they know.* She looked at Seeker. *They trade with Hoff, do they not?*

Seeker bowed again. *They do. And the Hoffans were the last to make a version of the drug. It depopulated three cities before they ceased to slaughter each other.*

So we have a group of humans with weapons beyond anything we've seen who do not know the dangers of the enzyme drug, the Queen said. *What does that suggest to you, Daughter?*

The Young Queen frowned. *That they come from some world that we have not discovered and that has been out of touch with other humans for some time. But I don't see how that can be. I mean, if they were on a world where the Ring was buried, or where it hung in orbit — though I don't see how they could reach it, so that doesn't work — and that still doesn't explain why we don't know about them.*

Just so, the Queen said again. She leaned back in her chair, taking in the rest of her zenana with a glance. *I would give a great deal to question one of these strangers.*

That can always be arranged, Seeker said.

I think I need to see for myself, the Queen said, and pushed herself to her feet. "Hivemaster! Set us a course for Athos, please."

As my queen commands. Seldom Seen bowed deeply, and backed from the zenana.

You and I, Daughter, will make our own plans. The Queen vanished into her own quarters, the Young Queen at her heels, and there was silence in the zenana for a long moment.

Well, the Master of Sciences Physical said at last. *The Young Queen has found an iratus nest, and now we're going to prod it with short sticks.*

The Consort gave him a narrow stare. *I would have thought you'd find it fascinating.*

I do. Spark put his hands on his hips, matching him stare for stare. *And only your get would want to spoil it.*

Careful, the Consort said.

I am careful, Spark said. *I am always careful.*

That drew a snarl of disbelief from Seeker, but the other cleverman ignored him.

It makes no sense. Not only do we have no idea where these strangers spring from, or how they've put their hands on this technology, but they've moved themselves into a city of the Ancients. We don't know what they may find there, or whether they might even be able to use it.

You're not seriously suggesting they're a nest of Ancients, the Consort said.

We can't actually rule it out, Seeker said, and that silenced them again. *So if we are going to poke this nest of iratus — the Queen is right, we need to question one of them first. Preferably more than one, and not quickly, either.*

If they are Ancients... the Consort began, then shook his head. *They cannot be. We defeated them ten thousand years ago.*

We were there, Seeker agreed. *You and I saw the cities fall — saw Emege fall, and the towers of Atlantis vanish beneath the waves. But the Ancients were strong and clever. It is possible their descendants may still have survived in some hidden place.*

I don't believe it, Spark said. *The Ancients are dead, their cities fallen, there is nothing left of their culture but broken writing on shattered walls.*

And yet, Seeker said.

The Consort paused. *And is there any way that we could prove whether or not they are Ancients? That would also seem to be a crucial point.*

Seeker smiled. *As it happens…*

Spark snarled. *You cannot.*

But I can. Seeker's smile was definitely smug. *The Ancients built many of their devices so that they could only be used by one of their own blood, one whose molecular makeup bears certain markers. I have one of those devices. We can use it to test any human we take, even without its knowledge.*

An excellent notion, the Consort said.

And if they prove to be Ancients… Seeker's smile vanished. *Then we must destroy them all.*

CHAPTER TEN

Patrol

SAM JOINED the group of scientists heading back to the power control room, very aware of the weight of the borrowed P90 on its clip against her chest. Spare ammo was heavy in her pockets, and she was glad of it. It took significant weight of fire to bring down a Wraith, and that was far more disconcerting than she felt it ought to be. The rest of the group seemed just as shaken by the morning's attack, and there was little conversation as they threaded their way through the ruins. The Marines on duty at the guard post were morose and silent, and the scientists climbed down into the power control room as though they were glad to get under cover.

"Get the lights hooked up," McKay ordered. "Dr. Grodin, see if you can get that tracer program to run better than it did yesterday. Colonel Carter, if I might have a word?"

He drew her away from the others without waiting for an answer. Sam followed warily, stopping well before they reached the shadows.

"I thought the weapons console was that one over there."

"It is, but it's too close to that airman. I don't want her to hear us."

Salawi's fine. The words died before Sam could articulate them, not least because she wasn't sure where anyone's loyalties lay. "So what did you want?" she asked instead, and McKay glared at her.

"What happened this morning — if we weren't in the city, it wouldn't keep happening."

Sam nodded once. "Or at least that's what the Athosians told you."

"Don't tell me you think they're lying, too!"

"I don't think anything," Sam said. "I don't know enough

to have an opinion. But I do wonder if getting out of the city would be enough to stop the Wraith, particularly if their goal is to keep any human civilization from posing a challenge."

"Well, yes, I admit I had wondered that," McKay answered. "But it would be a start."

"I don't think General O'Neill is going to be able to persuade the colonel to anything," Sam answered. "What is it you want us to do?"

"I want General O'Neill to tell Sumner to get his head unwedged," McKay said. "But since that doesn't seem to be about to happen — and, yes, I do understand why it's not happening, wrong chain of command and all that." He stopped, and went on more soberly, "Not to mention a company of Marines with better weapons and hyped-up reflexes, both of which would make a total mess of the rest of us."

Sam looked up sharply. "What do you mean by that?"

"It's the drug they take, the one Beckett developed. It makes them crazy, too."

"I thought Colonel Sumner told General O'Neill there weren't any serious side effects."

"And if you believe that…"

Sam nodded. "Ok, yeah."

"But, anyway, my point is that I'd like to find an answer that doesn't involve people getting shot." McKay glanced over his shoulder again, then pointed to something on the rocky wall beside him. Sam made a production of looking, but saw only a knob of rock that looked at bit like a melted Pac-Man.

"I don't think anybody likes what's happening," she said. "What do you have in mind?"

"Major Sheppard wants to talk to the general," McKay said. "What? You think Sumner's guys have a monopoly on smart and stealthy? Sheppard sneaks in and out of camp like he was some kind of Robin Hood. That's the real reason Sumner won't let us leave anything set up. He's afraid Sheppard will get hold of it and give it to the Athosians."

"Sheppard doesn't think he's Robin Hood," Sam said.

"No. No, he doesn't, that's my metaphor," McKay answered. "Not that it doesn't apply, but that's not Sheppard's style."

Sam decided that was a tangent better left unexplored. "And Sheppard wants to talk to General O'Neill."

"Uh-huh." McKay nodded. "Now, the first thought was to keep it simple, just let Sheppard slip in under cover of night—"

"How was he going to get across the lake?" Sam asked.

"The Athosians have boats," McKay said. "And it's a lot narrower on the other side of the city, not that Sumner knows that because he hasn't bothered to look. But it doesn't matter because after this morning every single Marine is going to be jumping out of his skin for days. O'Neill's going to have to go to him."

Sam gave him a long look. "And how do you expect that to happen?"

McKay waved his hands. "Look, all O'Neill has to do is find a way to leave the city. Sheppard will contact him."

"No," Sam said. "I'm not buying it. You haven't had time to set this up—"

"Will you give me a little credit?" McKay demanded. "That's the fallback plan. I've already signaled that Sheppard shouldn't enter the city, so now we go to the fallback. All O'Neill has to do is get out of the city—join one of the patrols or something, I don't know, but Sheppard will find him."

"I'll pass the word," Sam said. She didn't think it was a trap—McKay's hostility was too genuine, too unrelieved for that—but she couldn't help feeling there was something more going on.

"And in the meantime," McKay said, "how about helping me attach a naquadah generator to the weapons platform and see if we can't do something about the Wraith?"

It was a clever idea, Sam thought, and almost successful. If only part of the crystal array hadn't cracked under the strain, it would have worked, and McKay was certain he could find more of the crystals elsewhere in the city. Still, it was a disappointing result, and conversation lagged again as they collected the equipment to carry it back to the main camp. To her relief, McKay chose another table in the mess hall and Sam was able to settle into place next to Teal'c, who was eating the evening stew as though it were actually tasty. Sam took a careful bite, decided it tasted enough like any other beans-and-rice meal that she wasn't going to have to worry about, say, random bits that tasted like chocolate, and began methodically to eat.

"Did you have a good day, Carter?" Jack looked at her over the rim of his cup. He'd finished most of his stew already, and the nepti fruit that was served as dessert.

"Yes, sir." Carter carefully didn't look around. "Though we weren't able to hook up the generator the way we hoped. And you?"

"Interesting," Jack said. His voice was pitched low, and she trusted that he could see that there was no one in earshot behind her.

"Indeed," Teal'c said.

"It turns out Sumner's men are using an anti-Wraith drug that slows down the effects of the Wraith feeding enzyme," Daniel said, "and ramps up their reflexes. Unfortunately, it seems to have side effects."

"McKay said something about that," Sam said. They ran through the details quickly while she ate, and when they were done, she shook her head again. "Sir, Dr. McKay has a message for you."

Jack nodded. "Ok."

"He says Major Sheppard wants to meet with you."

"Oh, he does, does he?" Jack's eyes narrowed. "Did he say what he wanted?"

"Not exactly," Sam admitted. "McKay—"

"I know, talking to McKay is like drinking from a firehose," Jack said. "But he must have said something."

"McKay wants you to take command," Sam said. "And before you say anything, he does see the problems inherent in the idea. From what I gather, Sheppard's worried about the people who are still here."

"I'm worried about them," Daniel said. "For that matter, I'm worried about us."

"How's he want to meet?" Jack's expression was inscrutable.

"From what McKay said, Sheppard manages to come and go pretty freely," Sam answered. "But with this latest Wraith attack — he said if you can get out of the city, he'll contact you."

"I do not believe that is wise, O'Neill." Teal'c's protest sounded heartfelt.

"Probably not." Jack gave a crooked smile. "Since when did that stop us?"

"We could wait until it's safe for Sheppard to enter the city again," Sam said.

"Who knows how long that's going to take?" Daniel asked. "Especially if this drug is making everybody paranoid. I'd like to talk to the Athosians, myself. There's a lot they can probably tell us about the Wraith that I expect Colonel Sumner hasn't bothered to listen to."

"Yeah." Jack nodded. "All right, Carter, you can tell McKay I'll do it."

"Yes, sir." Sam looked at her plate, decided she really didn't want another plate of stew. She could stand another cup of tea, however, and she pushed herself to her feet. For all that McKay hadn't hit on her once since they'd arrived on Athos, she still felt awkward as she approached the table where he was eating with Grodin, Campbell, and an open laptop.

"Dr. McKay?"

"Call me Rodney."

Sam flinched, but at least he didn't follow up on it. "Look, I just wanted to say — that thing we talked about earlier. I think it will work."

"Thing?" McKay blinked. "Oh. Oh, that thing! Ok, yeah — wait. You *think* it will work?"

"It'll work," Sam said, and hoped she wasn't blushing. Neither she nor McKay was particularly good at spycraft. "Just the way you said it would."

McKay nodded hard, twice. "Yeah. Yes, all right, we'll do that. Thank you, Colonel."

"You're welcome," Sam said, and was pleased she remembered to refill her glass of tea before she returned to her own table.

"I take it that was a yes?" Jack asked.

"Yes, sir." Sam took a sip of the tea, barely tasting it. "At least I hope so."

Jack lay awake for some time after they turned out the lights, too aware of the lump of his pistol settled in easy reach, listening to Daniel's heavy breathing in the other cot. It wasn't going to be easy, getting Sumner's permission to leave the camp in the ruined city. If he just asked to leave, Sumner was going to say no, or, at best, send him with an escort that Sheppard or SG-1 would have to deal with, and that would mean tipping their hand before he was ready. He didn't want to make an enemy of Sumner, not while the man controlled access to both the Stargate and whatever Ancient technology remained in the city. Maybe he could use Daniel as a stalking horse, offer him as a way to undermine this Teyla Emmagan's influence on the Athosians. Daniel wouldn't like it, but he'd play along. Or maybe, if Beckett was 'recovered' — maybe he could ask to see the relief work Beckett had been doing among the Athosians? No, that was likely to get Sumner worrying about protecting the source of his drug, and that was more likely to make him keep everybody tied up in the city. No, probably the best bet was to see what he could do with Daniel.

He rolled over, determined to sleep, but he couldn't help thinking about the drowned city, Atlantis floating beneath a failing shield. Was that what their own expedition had found — was that what he'd sent them through to find? It was too easy to imagine, his own private disaster movie compounded of equal parts news video and Hollywood: the shields failing and the water crashing in, splintering those soaring walls of glass, bodies washed away in a tangle of blood and metal. Maybe they got out before it happened, like this expedition had done. They might be stranded on some unanticipated world, but at least they'd be alive. Even if they were being hunted by life-sucking aliens, though maybe the Wraith were specific to this universe. Jack smiled in the dark. In his experience, though, things like life-sucking aliens tended to be pretty evenly distributed across worlds.

And maybe none of it had happened. Maybe in his own universe, Elizabeth Weir was alive and well, maybe the expedition was settling happily into a city that had never fallen below the sea, and maybe all they needed was to find a ZPM so that they could dial home again. He knew perfectly well that the better outcome was just as likely as the worse, no matter how much it felt otherwise. He turned over again, settling himself more comfortably on the thin mattress. Until he had proof, he was going to assume that they were all alive.

"How'd you like to talk to the Athosians?" he said to Daniel as they walked toward the mess hall the next morning, and Daniel gave him a predictably dubious look.

"You know I'd like to. What exactly do you have in mind?"

"I was thinking we might see if you couldn't persuade the Athosians to think more kindly of Colonel Sumner," Jack said.

Daniel snorted. "Yeah, somehow I don't think they're going to buy it, and I'm not really sure I'm the guy to sell it to them, either."

"You're the one who said how badly you wanted to talk to the Athosians."

"Yeah, but I don't want Sumner's goons breathing down my neck while I do it."

And that was the problem, Jack thought. They needed to get out of the city without an escort, and the chances of that happening were slim to none.

Sumner was still in the mess hall when they arrived, sitting at a table set a little apart from the others, looking at a laptop while Bates explained something to him and Ford and another officer hovered nervously. Jack slowed his steps as he passed within earshot and heard Ford say, " — not enough for both patrols, sir."

"Smaller groups, maybe," the other officer said, and Bates shook his head.

"With respect, sir, it'd be better to cover more ground and keep more men together."

It was a gift Jack hadn't hoped for, and he set his tray on the table beside Carter's. She looked up, frowning as she realized he wasn't going to sit down, and he gave them all his most rakish grin. "I'm going to have a word with the colonel," he said, and turned away.

Sumner looked up at his approach, frowning but not actually hostile, and Jack did his best to seem relaxed and cooperative. "Excuse me, Colonel, if I might have a word?"

The two younger officers had gone, though Bates still fussed over something on the laptop, and Sumner pushed the nearest chair away from the table. "Of course, sir."

Jack seated himself and rested his elbows on the table. "I couldn't help overhearing." He kept his own voice low enough that it was clear he wasn't challenging Sumner's judgment. "If you're short-handed — we'd be willing to help out."

"We're short of men for patrols," Sumner said. His voice was neutral.

"We've done patrols," Jack said. "We're not exactly busy here."

Sumner paused. "We need Colonel Carter here in the city. McKay says she's been very helpful. And I can't see that Dr. Jackson is really ideal for the job."

"He's been with SG-1 for eight years," Jack said.

"With all respect, you and Teal'c are the only real soldiers on the team," Sumner said.

Jack lifted his head. "I'm really glad Colonel Carter didn't hear you say that. And that I'm not actually in your chain of command so I'd have to notice it. But I'd suggest you look over her record before you say anything that stupid again."

"Sorry, sir." Sumner had the grace to look abashed, rubbing his eyes as though they pained him. "What I mean to say is, she and Jackson are more use here. But if you and Teal'c would like to join a patrol — we are short-handed, and it would be helpful."

Jack paused in turn. He hated splitting the team, but if he pushed any harder there was a good chance Sumner would refuse him altogether. "We'll do that, then, Colonel."

"Thank you, sir." For a moment, Sumner looked genuinely relieved. He glanced down at his laptop. "If you'd be willing to join Lieutenant Ford's team? He leaves at 0840."

"We'll be there," Jack said, and pushed himself away from the table. It was a risk, he thought, but he was betting this was the best chance they'd have to contact Sheppard.

Neither Daniel Jackson nor Colonel Carter were pleased with O'Neill's plan, but both of them were quick to realize he was right. This was their best chance to allow Major Sheppard to contact them. Teal'c kept his face impassive as he and O'Neill walked to the landing where the young Marine lieutenant was collecting his patrol. They had been lucky there, Teal'c thought: Ford was still young enough to be overawed by a general, and no one was better than O'Neill at exploiting such things. The Marines had brought spare weapons for them, P90s that showed signs of field repair. Teal'c took his without comment, but O'Neill examined his carefully.

"You're sure these work, Lieutenant?"

"Yes, sir."

"So what's the plan?"

"Sir!" Ford drew himself up automatically. "Colonel Sumner wants us to check the road — well, it's really more of a path — that leads through the edge of the woods to the hills. We're to find out if the locals have been using it lately."

"Using it for what?" O'Neill grabbed a handhold on the gunwale of the inflatable boat. Teal'c did the same and the entire team ran it forward into the water, the Marines scrambling easily aboard. Ford didn't answer until they were well underway, but then he glanced over his shoulder.

"The colonel's worried they're spying on us, sir. And there's reason to believe that the bulk of the population has gone to ground up in the hills, until either the Wraith give up or we're all killed. We'd like to confirm that."

"You know," O'Neill said, "that's one of those things maybe you don't want to find out."

"Sir?"

"You don't want the Athosians to think you're hunting for their women and children," O'Neill said. "Not unless you mean to threaten them."

Ford hesitated, and O'Neill lifted his hands.

"Just saying! I know you have your orders."

They pulled the boat up onto the far shore, secured it to the bank under the watchful eye of another of Sumner's patrols. There were only two of them, and Teal'c glanced curiously back at the city. Sure enough, he could just make out a mortar in the guard post on the far side of the water. Anyone who tried to steal the boats or rush the crossing was in for an unpleasant surprise.

There were several paths in evidence, one that led directly away from the lake and into the trees — the one that led to the Stargate, Teal'c thought — another, not much used, that skirted the shore, and a third that curved into the woods at an oblique angle, threading through the outer edges of the forest. It was that path that Ford chose, waving for them to spread out as though they were in hostile country.

Teal'c fell easily into one of the flanking positions and O'Neill slid into place beside him, P90 resting almost lazily in his hands. "See anything?"

"I do not. Unless you are referring to the trees."

O'Neill gave him a suspicious look. "Careful, T, that was

almost a joke."

Teal'c dipped his head in acknowledgement.

"It doesn't look to me as though anybody's been coming this way too often," O'Neill went on.

They were far enough from the others that a quiet conversation could not be overheard, at least not as more than the murmur of voices. "I agree," Teal'c said. "But it was once in considerable use."

"Yeah." O'Neill glanced to their right, where the water of the lake could just be seen through the trees. "Of course, if the Athosians try to stay away from the city—"

"Then they would avoid this road," Teal'c said. "Except that once it was much used. I wish Daniel Jackson were here."

Ford had stopped ahead of them, talking quietly into his radio, and he turned as they came up. "I wish he was, too. Not having somebody who could talk to the locals—that's been our biggest problem since we got here."

"Well, maybe next time," O'Neill said easily. "Who was acting as your liaison?"

"Dr. Weir at first, sir," Ford answered. "And Major Sheppard. Everything was going fine until we told them we wanted to move into the city."

"If it mattered that much to the Athosians, why didn't you compromise, stay out of the city except to try to find a ZPM?"

Teal'c thought O'Neill already knew the answer, but he, too, was curious as to the young lieutenant's version of the story.

Ford grimaced. "That's what we were doing when Dr. Weir was killed. We had a camp in the woods, right by where the Athosians were camped, and only a dozen people in the city. They were supposed to be lying low, not using unnecessary power, all that stuff. If we'd all been in the city, there's a good chance Dr. Weir wouldn't have been killed. It's a lot easier to defend ourselves from inside all that stone."

"Indeed," Teal'c said, when it seemed that O'Neill wasn't going to respond. He could see both sides of the problem, the need to establish a defensible position opposed to the need to stay on good terms with the locals, and he found he could not entirely blame Colonel Sumner for his first choice. He was less sure about decision to develop the anti-enzyme drug, or its consequences.

"And the Wraith only attack the city?" O'Neill asked.

"They attack us wherever they can catch us, sir," Ford said. "What you saw the other morning, that's just the tip of the iceberg. They send those Darts of theirs through the gate, try to pick off any working parties — not just in the city but in the woods and by the Stargate itself."

"Are they leaving the Athosians alone?"

Ford shrugged. "I don't know, sir. I'm not sure they'd tell us either way. And I'm not sure they're not doing some kind of deal with the Wraith — you know, let the Wraith have us and maybe they won't bother the locals for a while."

One of the other Marines nodded in agreement, but spoke to Ford. "Sir, looks like we've got some fresh tracks off to the north."

"Check it out," Ford said. "Stay in sight if you can, and keep in radio contact."

"Yes, sir." The Marine moved away, waving for one of the others to join him.

"We'll take six," O'Neill said.

Teal'c thought Ford wanted to protest, but couldn't quite figure out how. "Yes, sir."

"What kind of weapons do these Athosians have?" Teal'c asked.

"Everything from bows and arrows to bolt-action rifles." Ford lengthened his stride to catch up with the rest of the party, but O'Neill gestured for them to stay back. Teal'c nodded his understanding, and went to one knee to adjust the fastening of his boot. The rest of the party moved ahead, following the new trail, uniforms blending with the trees.

"Ok," O'Neill said. "We'll just — mosey along."

"Mosey?" Teal'c had heard the word from General Hammond,

but had never received a satisfactory definition.

"Wander. Slowly. Without purpose." O'Neill waved one hand vaguely. "Mosey."

"Indeed."

The Marines were almost out of sight — Lieutenant Ford was out of sight, hurrying after his point men — and Teal'c was newly aware of the soft sounds of the forest. Such sounds were different on every world, depending on the nature of the vegetation, the animal and bird life, the season of the year, and yet fundamentally similar enough that it was possible to recognize a break in the pattern. He tipped his head to listen. Yes, there had been a distant whistle, a bird, perhaps, or an insect, that was no longer present, and the sound of the leaves was different.

"O'Neill," he said, and in that moment, a slight, pretty woman stepped out from between the trees. She was smiling, but Teal'c could not believe it to be entirely friendly.

"Gentlemen," she said. "If you would step this way quickly and quietly."

"And why would we want to do that?" O'Neill asked, though he kept his voice down and made no move to raise his P90.

"You said you wanted to talk to me."

Teal'c had not heard the newcomer approach, and whirled, just managing to keep from bringing his P90 up as he recognized the Atlantis uniform.

"Major Sheppard," O'Neill said. "You've got some explaining to do."

Sheppard gave an unhappy little smile. "Yes, sir. But if you don't mind, I'd rather not do it here."

"Lead on," O'Neill said, but it was the woman who answered.

"Quickly, then. This way."

CHAPTER ELEVEN
Prisoners

THE SMALL woman led them quickly through the trees at a sharp angle to the main path, following a trail that seemed no bigger than a deer's track. She had to be the woman Sumner had complained about, Jack thought, the Athosian's head trader Teyla Emmagan. She didn't seem precisely hostile, though she was intently focused, and Sheppard seemed neither to defer to her nor to give her orders. There was one moment when a second path split off from the trail they were following when the two of them spoke quietly, but Jack couldn't tell which of them made the final decision. And that — if Sumner was right, and she was part of the problem, then they were in serious trouble. She was good.

They were going uphill now, the slope rising steeply enough underfoot that Jack had to watch his footing carefully. At last the ground leveled a little, and they came out of the trees onto a rocky slope. A cliff rose sheer above them, and there were dark openings in the rock that looked like the mouths of caves. Several figures stepped out of the woods, three Athosians and a stocky woman in the Atlantis uniform, and Sheppard gave another of his wincing smiles.

"Easy, folks. It's General O'Neill, and Teal'c, just like I told you."

"What's that on his forehead?" That was a teenage boy at the mouth of the closest cave, his breaking voice louder than he'd meant, and Teyla gave him a stern look.

"Jinto. Did your father send you?"

The boy nodded, flushing to the roots of his hair. "I brought salt and a message."

"Take the salt to Farres," Teyla said. "And then you can bring me the message." She took a breath, looking back at Sheppard.

"Let us go inside."

Sheppard nodded. "Good idea. If you'll come this way, General?"

He led them further along the cliff to a somewhat larger opening partially obscured by what looked like vines but proved to be a netting woven with leaves. Inside the cave it was dry and warm, light provided equally by familiar battery-powered lanterns with the Atlantis logo and by candles as big around as Jack's arm. There were a few chairs, and what looked like a disassembled trestle table stacked against the wall, but most of the furniture seemed to be pillows and boxes and heavy rugs. At the back of the cave a fire was burning in a wide metal brazier that looked as though it had come from a museum. An old man sat beside it, a heavy woolen wrap pulled tight across his shoulders, tending a pot nestled in the embers.

"Perhaps you would like a cup of tea," Teyla said.

Jack had played that game before and he met her smile with one of his own. "Thank you. It was a long walk."

"We prefer not to come too close to the city," she answered. "But I'm sure you've been told that already."

"I'd heard." Jack accepted a pottery cup from the old man, and let Teyla steer them to a set of chairs and pillows that were set a little bit apart from the rest of the room. His knees weren't up for the pillows and he settled himself carefully on one of the wood and canvas stools. Teal'c seated himself gracefully on the pillows, as did Sheppard, and Teyla took the other chair. "I've heard quite a lot of things."

"Yeah. I bet you have." Sheppard took a gulp of his tea.

"I have, Major, and I'm waiting for an explanation." Jack meant the words to sting, and Sheppard flinched, but Teyla merely smiled.

"Sir." Sheppard straightened in spite of himself. "I imagine you've heard most of it already."

"Why don't you tell me everything?" Jack asked. "We've got the time."

"Yes, sir." Sheppard took a breath, marshaling his thoughts. "After we got through to Altantis, everything was fine for a while. We didn't have the power to dial the Milky Way again and we were running down the ZPM that was left, but as long as we were careful, McKay figured we had about eighty hours before we'd have to abandon the city, and that would still leave a decent reserve in the ZPM for when we came back. And we were planning to come back. We combed the Ancient database, found a series of addresses, sent teams through — Athos was the most promising. We made a deal with Halling — he's the leader of these people, sir —"

"Not Ms. Emmagan?" Jack asked.

Teyla's smile widened, though it was no more sincere. "I am a trader, General O'Neill."

"But not without influence among your people," Jack said.

She nodded. "That is also true."

Dangerous, she was dangerous, and Jack hoped they could find a way to end up on the same side. "Go on, Major."

The rest of the story was basically the same as the one Sumner had told, but with a few crucial differences. Weir had brokered a deal with Halling, promising to respect their concerns about too much activity in the city and offering medical help as well as encouraging expedition members to volunteer to help with the Athosians' gathering.

"Something that we appreciated," Teyla interjected, "as this is our high trading season, and we are always short-handed then."

Jack nodded. He'd seen enough of the rhythms of nomadic peoples in the Milky Way to have some idea of the pattern and the work involved.

"But then the Wraith showed up." Sheppard's face was bleak. Jack slanted a look at Teyla; her expression was unreadable. But then, the Wraith were a normal hazard of life in Pegasus. "Elizabeth — Dr. Weir was killed, along with two other expedition members and three of Teyla's people. A dozen more, our people and Athosians, vanished and are presumed dead, taken by the Wraith to be fed on later. As a result, Colonel Sumner decided, over the objections of Halling, Charrin, and other Athosian leaders, that the expedition needed to move into the city so that we could defend ourselves."

"I gather you objected, too?" Jack asked.

Sheppard met his eyes squarely. "I did, sir. And was overruled. We relocated to the city, and — as we'd been warned — the Wraith came back. We suffered more casualties before we were able to beat them back, and they came again four days later. I believed, and said to Colonel Sumner, that we were being targeted because we were in the city, and that the Wraith were trying to destroy us rather than to collect… food. I recommended that we withdraw to the Athosian settlement, but Colonel Sumner rejected that idea."

"Uh-huh."

"Colonel Sumner then proposed that we take control of the Stargate, in hopes of preventing further Wraith attack. He also proposed interdicting the Athosians' normal gate travel so as to ensure that they weren't — inadvertently or otherwise — giving away our location to the Wraith." Sheppard took a deep breath, his back rigid. "This meant that the Athosians' trading season was effectively halted, which meant they were unable to import a number of products, Satedan medicines, ammunition for their own weapons, everything they don't make themselves, all of which they need if they're going to get through the winter. I couldn't go along with that, not when no other provision was being made to alleviate the hardship we were causing. Some others agreed, and — Teyla took us in."

Jack was silent for a long moment. This was desertion, at best, and pretty much what he should have expected from the man who stole a helicopter to go after his missing squadron-mate. Sheppard had gone against direct orders then, too. And also for good reason. "I'm not going to tell you how much trouble you're in, because I figure you know that."

"Yes, sir."

"If the Wraith only show up because people are in the city, why did they attack you the first time?"

"We think it was a routine Culling," Sheppard said.

Teyla leaned forward. "The Wraith attack every world now and again. Usually, if they find no resistance and no sign that humans are trying to develop technology that might allow us to stand against them, they Cull to fill their feeding pens and then do not return for some time. Had they not seen Colonel Sumner's activities in the city, I do not think they would have returned at all, and had the city been abandoned on their return, they certainly would not have come a third time. But now Colonel Sumner has challenged them, and made clear that he has the weapons with which to do so, and the Wraith will not rest until he is destroyed."

Jack took a sip of his cooling tea, buying time. "What's your alternative?"

"I do not think there is a good one," Teyla answered. "And I fear that as much for my own people as for yours."

Sheppard grimaced. "Actually, sir… If we were to withdraw from the city, abandon the camp and maybe even dial a few outgoing addresses, we might be able to convince the Wraith that we've given up and left this planet. But it needs to happen now, before the Wraith are any more deeply engaged. I was hoping that you might be able to help persuade Colonel Sumner to see reason."

Teal'c tipped his head to one side. "That may be more complicated than it seems, Major Sheppard."

"Yeah." Jack sighed. "You see, part of my problem is that we — SG-1 — are not from your particular timeline. When Janus's experimental device — went off — it not only transported us to Atlantis but took us to a different Atlantis."

Sheppard bit his lip. "You're sure, sir?"

"The evidence is incontrovertible," Teal'c said.

"Then we will have to try something else," Teyla said firmly. She gave Sheppard a look that smacked distinctly of *I-told-*

you-so, and rose to her feet. "In the meantime, General O'Neill, and Teal'c, I regret to say that you must remain here for the conceivable future."

Crap. Jack looked from her to Sheppard. "Are you telling me we're prisoners, Major?"

"No, sir," Sheppard said, with a shifty smile, "not at all—"

"I am sorry, but yes," Teyla said. "I trust you will behave accordingly. And I must ask that you hand over your weapons."

From the cave mouth, Jack heard the click of bolts being thrown, and looked over his shoulder to see two big men covering them with rifles. "Ok…"

"Please place your weapons on the ground and then you will step back from them," Teyla said. "And your radios."

And that ruined their only chance to jump her and get away. Jack nodded and laid his P90 on the ground, then unclipped his radio and set it beside the weapon. Teal'c copied him and they both stepped back three paces. Teyla still didn't move, but a third man slipped forward to collect them.

"This is not what we agreed," Sheppard said, fiercely.

"They are not what you promised," Teyla answered. "And they are no good to me."

"Hey," Jack said. "I'm sure we can work something out."

"I hope so," Teyla said. "For all our sakes."

It had been a less than profitable day working in the power control center, and Daniel was having to make an effort to keep from snapping at sweet Dr. Kusanagi, trying so hard to see the bright side of everything. No, he wanted to say, no, we haven't actually accomplished a damn thing, especially when you consider that the answer to a whole bunch of our problems is about a thousand yards away. But that wasn't kind, or even fair, and he ran his hand through his hair, trying to wipe away the frustration.

Ahead of him, Sam and McKay were discussing whether or not it made sense to try to get the city's weapons working again, and he lengthened his stride. "You know, Sam, we should really talk some more to the Athosians before we go making exactly the kinds of changes that they tell us will bring more Wraith —"

"Actually, we had thought of that," McKay said. "Believe it or not. And this is more of a last ditch effort to keep us alive if we fail to make any kind of deal, which so far we have signally failed to do —"

Daniel raised his hands in surrender. "Ok, ok."

"I don't think a naquadah generator's going to be enough though," Sam said.

For a moment, McKay looked beaten, but then he shook his head. "We'll find a way," he said, and turned off to his improvised hut.

Daniel and Sam walked on toward the mess hut, Daniel frowning as they got closer. There was Ford, looking nervous, but there was no sign of Jack or Teal'c. "Sam..."

"I see." Her hands tightened on the stock of the borrowed P90, but relaxed again. They weren't going to get anywhere fighting, Daniel thought. And maybe it wouldn't come to that.

"Colonel Carter!" Sumner stepped out of the main building, the setting sun throwing his shadow almost the length of the street. Like a cheap effect in a bad Western, Daniel thought, and forced himself to stay silent.

"Colonel?" Sam stopped well out of reach, frowning as though she was puzzled.

"I don't suppose you've seen General O'Neill." Sumner's voice was taunting.

"He didn't come back with Ford?" Sam put just the right note of surprise into her voice. "What happened? Do we need to send someone out after them?"

"O'Neill didn't come back with Ford, no," Sumner said. "In fact, he deserted the patrol —"

"Deserted!" Sam sounded genuinely shocked. "General O'Neill would never —"

"He did." Sumner cut her off without hesitation. "And since

there's every possibility he's gone over to the locals, I'll have to ask you for your weapons."

"Wait a minute," Daniel said.

"That was an order, Dr. Jackson."

Daniel spread his hands, let Ford pluck the pistol from his holster.

Bates reached for Sam's P90 and she didn't resist, only the set of her mouth betraying her anger. "You're making a mistake, Colonel."

"I doubt it."

"Wait," Daniel said again. "How do you know they deserted? You said yourself that the Athosians are dangerous. What makes you so sure they haven't been taken prisoner?"

"They were both fully armed and they're well-trained. No native is going to take them by surprise."

"But—" Daniel caught Sam's look and closed his mouth over the rest of what he'd been going to say.

"While I don't have any reason yet to doubt your loyalty," Sumner went on, "I also have no choice but to secure this camp. Sergeant Bates, take them to the cells."

"Oh, so you've got cells," Daniel said, and jerked away from Bates's hand on his shoulder.

"Unless you want to go in handcuffs, Dr. Jackson," Sumner said.

"Fine," Daniel said. "Fine, I'm going. But if I were you I'd start looking for O'Neill…"

Sumner ignored him, turning away.

"Colonel," Sam began, and Bates blocked her way.

"I'm sorry, Colonel. This way."

The cells were exactly that, a remnant of some Ancient lock-up that had survived the destruction of the city. Sumner's men had cleared the steps that led down to the four surviving cells as well as a single, well-barred ventilator shaft, and set up a lantern in the center of the corridor between the cells. Too far to be reached from inside the cells, Daniel noted automatically, not unless you had a fishing rod or something like that. Beyond the last cell, the wall had crumbled and the floor had fallen in, leaving a black gap between the stones.

"Are you sure this is solid?" Daniel asked, but the Marine escorting him didn't answer, just hauled back the barred door of the first empty cell.

"Don't do any tap-dancing," Bates answered, from the top of the stairs. "No, don't put the Colonel in with him."

Damn. Daniel kept his face impassive as Sam was shoved into the cell across the corridor, and the Marines dragged the door back into place, securing each one with a modern combination lock. At least the machines that had created the force fields were long gone, Daniel thought. He could see the six evenly spaced holes where the projectors had been. Unfortunately, he had no idea how to pick a combination lock, either — unless… He waited until the last of the Marines had pounded up the stairs. They pulled the door closed behind them, leaving only the lantern for light, and Daniel grabbed the bars of his cell door.

"I don't suppose you know how to pick a lock?"

"No. And I don't have any C4, either."

"Damn." Daniel turned, surveying the narrow space. Sumner had left them each a cot and blankets, plus a covered bucket in the back corner. There was a bottle by the door, and when he investigated, it was full of slightly stale water. "Looks like he uses these on a regular basis."

"Yeah." Carter came to her own door. "Do you really think Jack's a prisoner?"

"I think he'd have come back if he wasn't," Daniel answered. "He'd have known Sumner was likely to do exactly this if he didn't show up."

Something moved in the cell next to Daniel's, a shape moving out of the shadows that resolved into a tall man with a beard and long locks held back in a neat tail. He was taller than Teal'c, Daniel thought, though not quite as big, but that didn't make him any less impressive… He was dressed in plain pants and a white shirt under an oddly asymmetrical vest and a well-cut leather coat: not the clothes of a nomad, Daniel thought, his attention sharpening even further.

"So what'd you do?" the stranger asked, and rested his arms on the bars between his cell and Daniel's.

"I'm not entirely sure," Daniel answered. "I'm Daniel Jackson."

"Specialist Ronon Dex."

"Military?"

Dex nodded. "Off duty, though. Or I was supposed to be. Step through the Stargate, find out whether the Athosians were going to trade with us or not this autumn, their autumn, and — wham. Here I am. How about you?"

"Our commanding officer is missing," Sam said. "Colonel Sumner thinks he deserted."

"Did he?" Dex sounded only idly curious.

"He might be a prisoner," Daniel said. "That's Colonel Carter, by the way."

Dex nodded again. "Colonel. Either you don't rank him, or he's gone rogue."

"It's — complicated," Sam said.

"I got time."

"Well, yes, we seem to have potentially quite a lot of that," Daniel said. "But —"

Dex ignored him, his eyes fixed on Sam. "Well?"

"We're not actually in his chain of command," she said.

"Uh-huh."

Sam lifted her chin. "No more than you are, Specialist Dex."

Dex looked away. "Ok, point. But the man's a nut case."

"You won't get any disagreement from me," Daniel said. "Where are you from, anyway?"

"Sateda."

Daniel nodded, trying to pretend the word meant something, but the stranger's eyebrows rose.

"How about you? Where are you from?"

"We're from another galaxy," Sam said quietly. "Almost certainly from another timeline than yours. We're trying to get back there."

Dex let out a long breath in a sound that wasn't quite a laugh. "That explains a lot."

"Such as?" The sudden sharp stare made Sam look almost like she was channeling Jack.

"Why that Colonel of yours is being an idiot."

"What do you mean?" Daniel asked.

"Messing around with the Wraith enzyme. Everybody knows that never ends well." Dex jammed his hands in his pockets.

"Actually, we don't," Daniel said. "Not that we weren't beginning to suspect, but — tell me what's wrong with it."

The Satedan gave him a suspicious stare. "It makes people crazy."

"Colonel Sumner says it protects them from Wraith attacks," Sam observed.

"Well, yeah. At first. And it makes you stronger and faster, too," Dex said. "But the longer you use it, the more of it you need, and the more crazy it makes you. First you start thinking everybody's out to get you, and eventually you start seeing Wraith everywhere. But most people don't last long enough for that to be a problem."

"Great," Daniel said. "And everybody knows this? The Athosians, too?"

"Sure," Dex said. "People keep trying it. They keep thinking they've found a way to, I don't know, remove the problem by changing the chemical makeup or something. But in the end, everybody ends up dead."

"Everybody?" Daniel felt a chill that had nothing to do with the stone around him.

"Yeah." Dex looked distinctly unhappy. "Usually they — the units that take the enzyme — kill off all the civilians around them before they turn on each other. That's what happened on Hoff. Three cities burned to the ground before the government got things under control."

"Wonderful." Daniel looked at Sam, seeing the same unease in her expression. "We've got to get out of here."

Sam nodded. "But how? And — then what?"

"I wish I knew," Daniel said.

The bars and stone walls were uncompromisingly solid. Daniel worked his way methodically around the edges of his cell, feeling his way as the light faded further, but found no weak spots in stone or metal. The floor was solid, too, stone fitted so closely he could barely see the edges of the blocks; the frame of the cot was flimsy enough that he could probably break it apart, but that meant it wasn't going to be strong enough to do much to the stone. In the cell opposite, Sam emptied her pockets onto her cot, and shook her head.

"Flashlight, half a power bar, multi-tool, granola bar, circuit tester. Ok, it's one I adapted for Ancient crystals, but I don't think that helps us much here. And the flashlight's not much help. I could maybe start a fire with the batteries, if I had some steel wool, but I don't think's going to help, either."

"No," Daniel said. In the other cell, Dex had returned to his cot, stretched out with his hands behind his head and was apparently asleep. Daniel wasn't sure he believed him, but he also wasn't sure it mattered. "Damn it. We have to get out of here."

Sam nodded and came to the front of her cell. Daniel did the same and they stood for a moment looking at each other.

"Ok," he said. "We're not digging our way out, and we're not cutting the bars."

Sam shrugged. "I'll try to remember to pack some thermite next time."

"Next time we're stupid enough to meddle with one of Janus's devices?" Daniel asked. "Yeah, good plan." He paused. "Maybe when the guards bring supper?"

"If they bring supper."

Daniel looked over his shoulder. "Dex? They do feed us, right?"

The big man didn't open his eyes. "Yeah."

"At a regular time?"

"You're not going to be able to jump them," Dex said. "There's too many of them."

Unfortunately, Dex was right. Sergeant Pollard brought three covered trays after the regular meal time had ended, but he was escorted by three Marines, one of whom remained at the top of the stairs to give himself a clear field of fire in case of trouble.

"I'll collect the trays in the morning," Pollard said. "When I bring breakfast."

"Thank you, Sergeant," Sam said, and earned an embarrassed look.

When they had gone, Daniel settled himself on the edge of his cot and poked idly at the tray. The covered bowl held yet more stew, probably the last left after everyone else had eaten, but he made himself finish it and the rather tasteless slab of doughy bread. Dex inhaled his, wiping the bowl clean with his bread, and looked rather wistfully at Sam's plate until she finished. Daniel piled his dishes together and set them by the door, keeping the spoon out of some vague idea that it might come in handy. According to his watch it was almost nine by the expedition's clock, and he glanced at the lantern.

"Do they leave that on all night?"

"Yeah." Dex sprawled on his cot again, the metal creaking under his weight.

Daniel leaned against the bars, scowling. The problem was, if Jack had managed to make contact with Sheppard — well, first Sheppard obviously wasn't being cooperative, or Jack and Teal'c would be back. And that left him and Sam as potential hostages for Jack's good behavior, which could get unpleasant really fast if they weren't careful. Of course, it was also possible that all his calculations were completely wrong and Jack and Teal'c had been snatched up by the Wraith. The thought was enough to start him pacing again. But surely they would have heard if more Wraith had come through the Stargate, and surely the Wraith would have gone for a better target than two well-armed men — unless they'd gone after the Athosians as an easier target? Daniel shook his head. No, Jack and Teal'c were with Sheppard and the Athosians; the trick now was to figure out how to join them before Sumner tried to make use of them.

And to that end — It wouldn't do anybody any good for him to keep pacing like this. He made himself stretch out on the cot, conserving his strength until he could figure out what to do. The lantern cast odd, unmoving shadows across the cells, and he left his glasses on so he'd be ready to move in an instant.

He hadn't expected to sleep, but something woke him, and he held himself still and quiet as he opened his eyes. Yes, there it was again, a soft scraping noise, and he looked instinctively toward the stairs. Nothing was moving there, but he saw Sam sit up, too. Dex was on his feet, very silent for such a big man, staring at the gap where the floor had collapsed. Something was moving in the dark, motion that resolved to a dirty, human hand groping for purchase on the stone floor. Sam had her multi-tool ready, stubby blade unfolded.

The seeking hand found a grip, and a man heaved himself into sight. He was small and disheveled, his Atlantis uniform jacket smudged with dirt, but he moved with quick purpose, dragging a knapsack out of the hole behind him and scrambling to his feet.

"Hello, Ronon," he said, softly, and stopped, seeing the others.

Daniel blinked — he had no idea who the man was — but Sam's jaw dropped. "Dr. Zelenka?"

"Colonel Carter? Does this mean we have a ZPM?"

Sam winced. "Sorry, no. We're not even properly from this timeline."

"Oh, so Rodney had it right after all? I am surprised."

In spite of everything, Daniel grinned. "I don't suppose you have a way out of here."

"But yes." Zelenka held up an object a little longer than his hand. "In fact — perhaps you could translate the inscription? I have been using it without benefit of an operating manual."

He held it so that Daniel could see the lines of Ancient writing, though he didn't let it out of his hands. It was some kind of cutting tool, Daniel thought, but it was hard to tell what its original purpose might have been. "It says, 'don't look into the aperture'," he said, and Zelenka gave a wry smile.

"I had already deduced that much, thanks. Rodney is right, most things are not labeled in what one might call a useful fashion. But that is not to the point." He adjusted the device, frowning over the tops of his glasses, then turned so that his body shielded the lock on Dex's cell from the stairs. There was a soft hiss and a flash of light, mostly obscured, and Zelenka stepped back, freeing the lock. Dex eased the door back and slipped forward to watch the stairs while Zelenka moved on to Sam's cell. He cut that lock as quickly and then turned to Daniel's door.

"Let us hope," he said. "This is rechargeable and sometimes the charge fades quickly—"

"Now you tell me," Daniel said, and heard the nervousness in his own voice.

The device hissed, producing a single point of blinding white light. Daniel looked away, shielding his eyes, and heard Zelenka's sigh of relief.

"Ok. That's got it. Now, let's get out of here."

"I don't mean to look a gift horse in the mouth," Daniel began, and Sam gave him a look.

"Then don't."

"It would be nice to know where we were going."

"Out of here," Zelenka said, and Sam nodded.

"That's good enough for me."

The hole Zelenka had come through was narrow and twisted awkwardly, so that Daniel had to push himself down the rocky slope and then under a slab of stone, and there was a bad moment before Dex figured out how to get through the gap. Daniel held out a hand to steady him and Dex took it, breathing hard.

"Thanks."

"Tight squeeze."

The Satedan nodded. "I'm not really fond of narrow spaces."

Zelenka produced a pair of flashlights and handed one to Dex.

"I'm sorry," he said. "I was only expecting one of you."

"I have one," Sam said, producing it, and Daniel hid a sigh.

"Is this part of the city's tunnel system?" he asked.

Zelenka nodded. "We think so. I think it's mostly for maintenance. It seems to connect primarily things like the power control room and what I think was the waterworks and the old transport system hub."

"Wait a minute," Daniel said. "Do you know —? Does it connect to a building, an installation with a big gold snake on the wall?"

"Yes," Zelenka said. "And you would know what that is?"

"It's one of Janus's devices," Daniel answered, "or at least it was in our world. If you have a Janus?"

"The Ancient scientist? The one who's creations are always trouble?" Zelenka nodded. "I am familiar with his work."

"One of his devices got us here. Sam, if we can get to that without having to go above ground, without Sumner's goons seeing us—"

"That would definitely be a good thing," Sam said. "But that may not be our best plan at the moment. Dr. Zelenka."

"Yes?"

"We were told you had deserted to the Athosians."

"Those would be Sumner's words, I'm sure," Zelenka said. "But, yes, I did not like the way things were going in the city, and thought I would be better off with Major Sheppard. Because I was the one who found the tunnels, and was mapping them when the Wraith first came, I offered to carry messages back and forth between Sheppard and the friends he still has here. When I found Ronon in the cells, I thought it would be best to get him out of there. We don't want to make enemies of Sateda as well as the Wraith."

"Or the Athosians," Dex said.

"Yes, well, I hope we are mending that," Zelenka answered. He swung his flashlight as they approached a junction, the beam picking out bursts of faded color and fragments of what had once been elegant carving. "The transport system," he said. "It was like the chambers on Atlantis — did you go to the city first?"

Daniel nodded. "The rooms that beam you across the city?"

"Yes, just like on Star Trek." Zelenka held up his hand. "Be careful now, the floor collapsed into a deeper tunnel. I have shored up this side, here, but we should take it one at a time. And, Ronon, you go last."

Dex nodded.

Sam swung the beam of her flashlight, holding it steady on a ledge maybe eighteen inches wide that ran along the base of a pockmarked wall. Zelenka had rigged a rope handhold, but the whole thing looked precarious, and the gap, when Daniel leaned cautiously to look, seemed very deep indeed. Zelenka scrambled across easily enough, and then Sam followed, first handing her light to Daniel. Daniel grabbed the rope in one hand, careful not to let the flashlight's beam fall too far into the emptiness beneath, and came across in a rush, grateful to feel solid ground underfoot. Dex hesitated for a moment, but then took the rope in a death grip and picked his way along the ledge.

"It is easier from here," Zelenka said. "But it is more than an hour's walk to where the tunnels leave the city. We should be able to contact the Athosians there, but only if we arrive well before sunrise. Otherwise we will have to wait until dark again."

Daniel glanced at his watch. They should just make it, assuming there were no unexpected delays, no cave-ins or collapsed tunnels, but Zelenka seemed confident of the direction. And once they were back in contact with the rest of SG-1 — it was still hard not to think of Jack as part of the team — then they could see what they could do in Janus's installation.

CHAPTER TWELVE
Interlude

THE HIVE came out of hyperspace precisely on target, slipped easily into orbit over Athos without additional expenditure of energy. In the privacy of his laboratory, Seeker studied the sensor displays, life form readings superimposed on a planetary map, and tapped the controls to bring the ruined city of Emege into closer focus. There were humans there, though the sensors were finding it hard to come up with a solid number. The Ancients had designed their buildings to conceal their numbers, and even their ruins provided some measure of protection. That was the central nest, though, he was sure of it.

He tapped the controls again, shifting north and west, searching the areas where the Athosians had been known to hide in the past. There were life signs there, certainly, but not as many as he would have expected, and he pulled back, touching controls to run a global scan. Yes, there were others, widely scattered, none large enough to be worth Culling in any normal circumstance — not that they would Cull twice in a generation in any case, or not if it could be avoided — and he brought the focus back to Emege.

A familiar shadow moved to join him, looming over his shoulder to study the screen, and he did not need to look up to recognize the Consort.

Guide.

What have you found?

About what we expected. Here in his own place, Seeker did not bother to guard his thoughts as closely. He and the Consort had come to the queen's hive together, cousins and lovers, cleverman and blade come to try their fortune with the new queen of a new hive like the young men in a hero-tale. The queen had favored them both, admitted them both to the zenana, though Seeker had not yet been permitted to sire a child. He shoved away that feeling, jealousy and sorrow mixed, and Guide rested a hand on his shoulder.

They're guarding the Ring as well?

Seeker nodded. *As though they only expect us to attack through it.* He touched controls, bringing up a closer scan of the field where the Stargate stood. *You see how they are deployed, in the edges of the forest.*

It doesn't make sense, the Consort said, and Seeker nodded again.

And that is why I wish to question some of them. Preferably more than one.

You still think they might be Ancients.

They are not normal humans, Seeker said. *That's obvious. Their technology has leapt beyond anything I have ever seen a human produce, and I cannot see our own kin producing such weapons, never mind allowing humans access to them.*

We tend to settle our difference with greater subtlety, the Consort agreed.

Well, I certainly see nothing to be gained in allowing the kine to slaughter each other, Seeker said. *Particularly if we get nothing from it. Nor do I like the notion of these new weapons being turned on us.*

No, that would indeed be… regrettable.

If they were Ancients, Seeker said, *they would know what we are and how to fight us. If they were ordinary humans, they wouldn't have the weapons or the courage to use them. Everything indicates that they are humans who have never known the Wraith, but how that could be — I have no answer. Therefore, we must question them.*

Snow agrees. Between themselves, they used the Queen's name, the memory of her mind's touch, shared and secret intimacy.

I thought she would.

The Consort dipped his head in agreement. *However, she has set conditions.*

Again, I thought she would.

The Consort showed teeth in a smile. *She doesn't want to lose any more blades, and would prefer not to lose drones, either.*

I daresay.

She's serious.

I don't doubt it. Seeker looked up from the maps, frowning slightly. *I'm just not sure it's possible. The Young Queen has stirred the nest, and they will be on their guard.*

Perhaps a diversion?

Would be useful, yes, but I cannot promise it would be safe.

The Consort grinned at that. *Well, no, there are no guarantees in the business.* He paused. *The Young Queen's Pallax has volunteered to assist us.*

Because he did such a brilliant job the first time? Seeker's smile was sardonic.

I think he wants to make amends, yes, the Consort answered, *and he wishes to impress his lady. And he is not utterly a fool.*

No. Seeker turned back to his displays, touched keys to set the data cascading down the screen again, a rain of green and gold that resolved into a new set of images, the life sign readings overlaid on a map of Emege and the area around the Stargate. *I'll grant that he has promise.* And considerable courage, to attach himself to the Young Queen when the Queen herself was still young and strong enough to consider all service her due, but that was another matter entirely. *I agree that a diversion would be our best choice. If we send Darts to harass the humans at the gate field, perhaps they will take that as the main attack, and send out reinforcements from the city. Another Dart, or perhaps a pair, could take them then with little risk of loss.*

In the screen, shapes moved, sketching the plan, and the

Consort nodded slowly. *Are you planning to land drones by the Ring?*

I would expect it to be necessary, Seeker answered. *But I will leave that decision to the Pallax.*

The Consort gave him a considering look. *And which of them would you like to see fail, I wonder, the Pallax — or my daughter?*

They were close enough to touch without effort, close enough to set feeding hands in an instant's thought, but Seeker did not step away. *She is your daughter. I do not forget it.*

The Consort relaxed slowly. *I didn't think you would.*

It was as close to an apology as he was likely to come, and Seeker nodded. *We should do this soon — tonight, if possible. The sooner we can determine the nature of these humans, the easier it will be to deal with them.*

I agree. The Consort paused. *You think we're going to have to kill them.*

I'm very much afraid so, Seeker answered, and bent to his work again.

CHAPTER THIRTEEN
Taken

IT WAS surprisingly comfortable in the Athosian caverns, or at least it would have been if it hadn't been for the three large men with guns who were watching the only entrance. And the pair who sat at the entrance to the cavern, shotguns resting on their laps. At least there was light — not from one of the expedition's lanterns, though there were half a dozen of those scattered about the main room, but something that looked a lot like an oil-fashioned oil lamp and burned a thick purple liquid that smelled faintly of balsam. Jack had eyed it thoughtfully when they'd been escorted to the cave, but there was no structure to burn down, just the beds and bedding and the folding stools, and even if he could figure out something they'd gain by setting them on fire, there were too many people watching them. He saw Teal'c's shoulders relax as the Jaffa came to the same conclusion, and Jack lowered himself carefully to one of the folding stools.

"Might as well take it easy," he said, for all that it was the last thing he wanted to do.

"Indeed." Teal'c gave the stool a thoughtful glance, and seated himself cross-legged on the woven matting that covered the floor. It looked like it was made from some kind of grass, Jack thought, and certainly it cut the worst of the chill from the dirt and stone. One of the women had brought a padded jar and two cups, and he pried the top off, sniffing carefully.

"More tea," he said, and poured them each some. He lowered his voice as he handed one of the cups to Teal'c. "Any sign of a back door?"

"No, O'Neill." Teal'c accepted the cup, his expression unchanged. "I cannot look more closely without drawing suspicion, but I see no other exit."

"Yeah, I didn't, either." Jack sipped at the tea, barely tasting it. He didn't see any way of fighting his way past the guards, either, though maybe once it was fully dark they'd have more of a chance. The Athosians didn't look like the sort of people who got careless very often.

Ford would have missed them hours ago, had probably searched the forest until it started getting dark, and then headed back to the city to warn Sumner. At least, that was what Jack would have done, and he didn't think Ford was stupid. Sumner... Well, it all depended on what Ford told Sumner, and what Sumner believed. If Dr. Wu was right, and the anti-Wraith drug was making him increasingly paranoid... No, Jack thought, I don't really want to go there. Not if I don't have to.

He pushed himself to his feet, strolled as casually as he could toward the mouth of the cave. The nearest guard leveled his rifle, and Jack spread his hands.

"Hey, I'm harmless. Not causing any trouble at all. Is there any chance I could talk to Major Sheppard?"

The Athosian considered him for a moment, then shrugged one shoulder. "I'll see if he wants to talk to you."

"Thanks." For a moment, Jack thought he was going to carry the message himself, and out of the corner of his eye saw Teal'c's attention focus, but then the Athosian beckoned to one of the kids hanging around the central fire.

"Go find Major Sheppard, tell him General O'Neill wants to talk to him."

"He's gone down to the lower caves with Teyla," the kid answered.

"So go get him," the guard said, and looked at Jack. "He'll come or he won't. Now, step back, please."

Jack retreated, newly aware that the sun was down and the air inside the cave was getting distinctly cooler. More kids, younger ones now, ten or eleven or twelve, appeared in the cave mouth, carrying bundles of brush and wood, and an older woman began to build up the central fire. The same man who had been tending the tea began to scrape embers together around the base of an enormous iron kettle, while a younger woman brought baskets from somewhere out of Jack's line of sight. A couple of people in Atlantis's civilian uniforms ducked into the cave together, talking animatedly, but vanished into a side cavern before Jack could decide whether they'd seen him.

"I am concerned about Colonel Carter," Teal'c said. "And Daniel Jackson. I am not entirely sure Colonel Sumner will believe that we are captives."

"Yeah, I thought of that." Jack jammed his hands in his pockets, wishing it was just the cold that made his skin crawl.

"I do not see any good way to break out of here," Teal'c said. "And yet—"

A familiar figure appeared in the cave mouth, and Jack looked up sharply. Yes, it was Sheppard, and alone for once. He drew breath to shout, but the major was already coming toward them, and Jack made himself relax.

"Firrel said you wanted to talk to me," Sheppard said.

"Yeah." Jack eyed him thoughtfully, wondering if there was any chance of using him as a hostage. Behind him, Teal'c rose to his feet, visibly contemplating the same question. "I'd like a little privacy."

"Sorry, sir." Sheppard shook his head. "But if you keep your voice down, no one can overhear you."

The guard was too close to try to jump him, and, anyway, it was more than possible that the Athosians wouldn't care all that much about Sheppard's continued health. Jack said, "I'm worried about the rest of my people. Colonel Carter and Dr. Jackson. They're still in the city, and I'm concerned that Colonel Sumner will blame them for our absence."

Sheppard bit his lip. "I've passed word to—friends in the city—to find out what's happened to them. But that's all I can do."

"You're not exactly saying they're not in danger," Jack

pointed out.

"No, sir." Sheppard's voice was steady. "I don't know either way. I'll let you know what I find out, though."

"Great." Jack broke off as he spotted Teyla Emmagan hurrying through the gathering crowd, and Sheppard turned to see what he was looking at.

"Ah, John, there you are," she said. "I would like a word with you."

There was a tension in her stance that Jack didn't like, a suggestion of some new threat, and Jack narrowed his eyes. "If this has anything to do with my people—"

She hesitated for the merest fraction of a second, and then inclined her head. "It has to do with you, General O'Neill. But I tell you now, it can change nothing."

"What's happened?" Jack clenched his fists, then forced himself to relax.

Teyla looked from him to John and back again. "We have been monitoring the radios we took from you. Colonel Sumner has been trying to contact you. Needless to say, we have not answered, but— He has been acting as though he is sure you are listening, and also as though he is sure you have joined us willingly. As I have said, I do not believe he is acting entirely from rational consideration."

"I have two people left in the city," Jack said, his voice tight. "They're at risk. Let me talk to Sumner."

"No." Teyla's voice was flat.

"We came to you in good faith, you're the one who broke the deal," Jack snapped. "You owe me the chance to protect them."

"I've already asked our people in the city to find out what—if anything—has happened to them," Sheppard said. "We don't know there's anything wrong."

Teyla grimaced. "But I believe there will be. General O'Neill, I will bring the radios to you, but I will not, I cannot, let you speak."

"He's arrested them, hasn't he?" Jack asked, but the Athosian woman had already turned away. "Damn it! If anything happens to them, Sheppard—"

He broke off, shaking his head. Carter and Daniel were good, he told himself. The best. They'd be all right. Teal'c came to stand beside him, frowning slightly.

"They'll be fine," Jack said, and Teal'c nodded.

"Of course they will."

It didn't take long for Teyla to reappear, a radio concealed in a woven basket, crackling with static and half-intelligible words. She brought it into the cavern, careful not to block the guards' field of fire, and lifted the basket's lid. Sheppard moved in behind her, though Jack couldn't tell if it was to hear better or to protect her.

"O'Neill! I know you can hear me." Sumner's voice was tinny and small, distorted by the speakers, but the words were clear. "I know you're there." There was a pause, static singing on the open channel. "O'Neill!"

"Let me talk to him," Jack said.

Teyla shook her head. "That would be unwise."

"How long has he been calling like this?" Teal'c asked.

"Some hours," Teyla said. "Since sunset."

The radio was silent in the basket. Jack looked from Teyla to Sheppard, who wouldn't meet his eyes, and back again. "My people are in danger—"

"And so are mine." Teyla's face was grave.

"O'Neill!" Sumner's voice cracked from the radio. "O'Neill, I know you're out there. Carter and Jackson are under arrest and, if you don't respond, I will have them shot. Do you hear me?" There was another pause, as though Sumner was getting himself under control. "You have twenty-four hours, O'Neill. If you don't give yourself up, you and Teal'c, I will have them shot."

Jack grabbed for the radio, but Teyla jerked it out of his reach. The guards took a step forward, bolts clicking as they readied their weapons.

"Whoa, hold it!" Sheppard put himself between the first

guard and O'Neill, his eyes on Teyla. "This changes things."

"It does not." Teyla's voice was less certain than her words, and Jack took a deep breath, struggling for the right words.

"He will do it," he said. "Sumner will shoot them."

"I am sorry, General," Teyla said, "but they are not my people. I will not risk lives for them."

"And if we don't stop him now, this is just the beginning," Jack answered. "That's what everybody's been telling me about this drug he's taking, that they're all taking. He'll kill my team, and, yeah, ok, that's not your problem. But next he's going to decide that your people are the threat, and he'll come after you. Again, maybe he won't be good enough to hunt you out, I'll give you that, but he's going to do his best, and some of your people are going to die. If you guess wrong, lots of your people are going to die. And maybe he'll take himself out of the running before he hunts you down, but that's not a gamble I'd like to take. Are you sure you want to?"

There was a long pause, the silence stretching out between them. If only Daniel was there, Jack thought, or even Carter. One of them would have the words that would tip the balance. Sheppard shifted his weight from one foot to the other, but said nothing. At last Teyla said, "Granting that this is true, still I do not see a useful alternative. We cannot defeat your Marines in a firefight — as you know well."

"That's true," Jack said. God, he wanted Daniel there to do the talking. "But if we stop them now, while there are still people in the city who don't agree with him — and you know there are people, you're in contact with them — then there's a better chance. A much better chance."

"And still the Wraith will come," Teyla said.

"But maybe fewer innocent people will be dead." Jack glared at her, wishing he had the right words, something that would get through.

Sheppard cleared his throat. "I think General O'Neill's right."

"Oh?" Teyla lifted her eyebrows. "And what exactly are you

proposing, either of you, that stands the slightest chance of saving any of our peoples?"

"We start by breaking out Carter and Daniel," Jack said. He was making it up on the fly, and hoped she couldn't tell. "That buys us time. Then we get as many other people out as we can."

"Then we leave Sumner and anyone who's stayed with him to the Wraith," Sheppard said. His face was grim. "I don't like it, but — two birds with one stone. It gets rid of Sumner and with any luck the Wraith think they've killed off their problem humans. We all lie low for a while, and then we start looking for another way back to Atlantis."

"You're going to leave your own people to the Wraith?" Jack said, and this time Sheppard did meet his eyes.

"Yes, sir, if we have to. And I think we'll have to, I don't think he's going to back down."

Jack nodded slowly. Yeah, there were times when you had to make those choices, when somebody stepped over the line — they'd hit that at the very beginning of the program, and he'd never regretted what had happened to Hanson.

Teyla said, "Do you have a plan for rescuing your friends?"

"Not yet." Jack heard Teal'c stir beside him and added quickly, "But we will."

"We do not know where they are held or how they are guarded," Teal'c pointed out. "We cannot make plans until we know those things."

"Teyla," Sheppard said.

She gave him a harried look. "This is not a decision I can make on my own. As you know. General O'Neill, you have been given a full day's grace, and I must beg some of that from you. I must speak with the others who hold authority among our people. I will have an answer for you in the morning." She turned away without waiting for an answer.

"Can you at least see if you can find out where our people are being held?" Jack called after her, but it was Sheppard who responded.

"I'll see what we can do."

Jack watched them walk away, and shook his head. "We need plan B."

"I believe that Teyla Emmagan wishes to cooperate with us," Teal'c said. "Major Sheppard certainly does."

"Yeah, but how many other people does she have to convince?"

"It is her job to be persuasive, O'Neill."

"Yeah." Jack shook his head again. "I'm just saying, if she doesn't persuade them, we're going to need an alternative."

"We will find one." Teal'c's voice was serenely certain, but Jack had known him long enough to recognize the concern beneath the grave tones.

"We'd better," he said, and this time Teal'c did not contradict him.

The central fire had been allowed to die to embers, and the rest of the main cavern was in semi-darkness, lit only by a mix of oil lamps and a handful of lanterns brought by the Atlantis expedition. Teal'c lay on his side on the narrow cot, aware that their single lamp did as much to conceal his movements as to reveal them, but he could see no way to turn that to an advantage. Even if they could rush the closest guards, there were three more on watch at the cavern's entrance, and certainly more out of sight elsewhere in the system of caves. There was nothing sensible to do but wait, though it took all his willpower to lie motionless, waiting for sleep to come. He could hear O'Neill's breathing, and guessed he was also awake in the dark.

"Hey, Teal'c." O'Neill's voice was pitched low, barely above a whisper.

"O'Neill?"

"How're you doing?"

For a moment, Teal'c didn't know what he meant, but then realized. "I am well. My supply of tretonin will last some weeks yet."

"Good. Though I hope we don't need that much of it."

"As do I, O'Neill." In spite of himself, Teal'c shifted so that he could slip his hand into his pocket, curl his fingers around the cylinder of the injector. That was his secret nightmare, the thing he could not bring himself to say even to O'Neill. If they were trapped here forever in the Pegasus Galaxy — in a Pegasus Galaxy that was not his own — eventually he would run out of tretonin. And without tretonin he would die, slowly, painfully, and pointlessly.

He made himself release his grip, take his hand out of his pocket and rest his forearm over his eyes. It would not come to that. In the first place, they would find a way back to their own galaxy. Colonel Carter was unquestionably the most brilliant practical physicist he had ever known, and she would solve the riddle of Janus's ouroboros device. And, if by some incredible misfortune, it took more than a month to solve the problem, it wasn't as though they were completely cut off from the SGC's technology, even if they couldn't reach the SGC. It was remotely possible that the Atlantis expedition had brought some tretonin with them, and, even if they hadn't, the medical staff would know how to make it. They had created this monstrous enzyme drug; certainly they could make tretonin for him. He would not be left to die of some opportunistic infection or a wound that even an ordinary human's biology should have healed. Bra'tac would scold him for his concern.

And that was a good thing to bear in mind, his old teacher's lifted eyebrows, the tart reminder that there were things far more important than one Jaffa's life. Even now that they were free, it was still true, though he trusted O'Neill and the rest of SG-1 to save him if it was at all possible. And, most important of all, he had time to spare. In a month, entire solar systems could be won and lost: surely they would find their way home.

And, at the very worst, he would die free.

He did not know how long he had slept, but the sound of hushed voices from the cavern entrance brought him instantly awake, lying still in the dark as he assessed the situation. Not an immediate threat, he thought, the voices were too quiet for that, but definitely something unexpected, and he turned his head to see. A young woman in a hooded coat stood beside the remains of the fire, stripping off her gloves and holding out her hands as another Athosian stirred up the embers, releasing a spray of sparks. Teyla came hurrying from some other cavern, dressed but not entirely tidy, and a few moments later Sheppard appeared as well, unshaven and with his hair sticking out in wild directions. Two more Athosians joined them, and a man in a mix of expedition gear and Athosian dress, and the group conferred by the rebuilt fire, the young woman tracing patterns in the air as she spoke.

The guards were watching, too, aware but not afraid, and Teal'c rolled slowly out of his bed. One looked back instantly, but did not cock his weapon. Teal'c moved closer, careful not to seem alarming. "What is wrong?"

The first guard hesitated, but the other shrugged. "The Wraith. They've attacked again. Through the Ring of the Ancestors and again in the city."

"Crap." O'Neill had risen so quietly that Teal'c hadn't heard him approach. "How bad is it?"

"I don't know," the guard began, but Sheppard had seen them and turned away from the group by the fire.

"What's going on?" O'Neill asked.

"Looks like the Wraith came through the gate again," Sheppard answered. "They dropped drones in the field by the Stargate, but they also sent Darts over Emege. That's all I know right now."

O'Neill grimaced. "Look, Sheppard, this is exactly why we have to act *now*."

"Yes, sir," Sheppard said. "But, with respect — it's not going to help to push."

It wouldn't, Teal'c thought, and laid a careful hand on O'Neill's shoulder. "We will wait patiently," he said, and O'Neill gave him an unhappy look.

"Yeah, fine."

"Thanks," Sheppard said, and turned back to the group around the fire.

"I don't like it," O'Neill said, but he kept his voice down.

No more do I. Teal'c swallowed the words as unproductive, said instead, "If Colonel Sumner is holding Colonel Carter and Daniel Jackson in a secure place, then they are more than likely safe. And after this, it will be easier to persuade the Athosians and Major Sheppard to help us."

O'Neill's expression eased a little. "Yeah. I hope you're right."

Teal'c dipped his head. "Indeed."

Zelenka had said it would take about an hour to get from Sumner's improvised jail to the place where they would rendezvous with the Athosians, but at this rate, Sam thought, it was going to be more like three hours. She pressed herself back into the shelter of the Ancient building as flashlight beams swung past, and heard Zelenka swear in Czech under his breath.

"They must have spotted we were gone," Daniel said softly behind her.

"No, I don't think so," Zelenka said. "They would have raised the alarm, and I do mean there would have been an alarm. Something else has gotten the colonel upset enough to turn out his men."

"General O'Neill," Sam said, and heard Daniel give a soft huff of laughter.

"Well, that would be like Jack, all right."

"Possible," Zelenka said. "But extremely inconvenient." He swore again as the lights swung closer. "Back."

They retraced their steps into the depths of the building, Zelenka in the lead, Dex holding on to the back of his jacket. Sam felt her way along the left-hand wall, feeling for the band of smooth tile Zelenka had showed them earlier, swallowed a curse herself as she nearly ran into Dex. Daniel did run into her then, and muttered something unhappy under his breath.

"A little further," Zelenka said, "and we can risk the light again."

The floor sloped steeply away underfoot, and Sam had to slow down to keep her balance. He breath caught, hearing the others moving away, and then Dex said, "Wait. Hold hands."

"Ah. Yes." Zelenka stopped, and Sam groped her way forward, hand colliding at least with Dex's shoulder. Behind her she could hear Daniel's breathing, and reached back, swinging her left arm until she struck his chest.

"Ow," Daniel said, but his grip on her hand was almost painfully tight.

"Ready?" Zelenka asked, and they started off again.

It was truly dark in the narrow space, only a faintly lighter patch behind them to show where they'd been. The ground steepened further, and Sam heard Dex grunt as he nearly tripped over something.

"Just a little more," Zelenka said. "Ok, stop."

They stumbled to a halt in the dark and Sam heard the click of a switch. Light flared, not directly in front of them but around a corner where it would be hidden from the entrance, and Zelenka said, "This way. I'll tell you when you can turn on your lights."

"Where are we going?" Sam asked, but followed obediently. Zelenka's flashlight picked out broken paving, fragments of tan and red and blue among the pale rubble. It was another broad corridor — another part of the service areas, maybe? There was no machinery left to give her any clue.

"We'll try another way," Zelenka said. "Sumner's men are between us and the city's edge, we'll need to go around and under, which — we'll need to hurry if we're going to make it in time."

The corridor ended in a sprawl of rubble, stone dust spread across the tiles. Zelenka pointed them to a crude ladder leading to another tunnel, and produced a knot of rags on a stick that he used to obliterate their footprints. Sam lowered herself into the deeper dark — it smelled of mud and old iron — and Zelenka scrambled down behind her.

"All right," he said. "You can turn on your lights now."

"We're back in the transport tunnels?" Daniel asked, casting his light around.

"I think so," Zelenka answered. "The subway, more or less."

The beam of Daniel's light caught a long oval plaque set into the wall, embossed with Ancient characters, and Sam moved hers to join it. "That's pretty. What does it say?"

Daniel let his light fall again. "Do not throw trash in conduits."

"Oh."

"That's disappointing," Zelenka said.

"The Ancestors' stuff usually is," Dex muttered.

Zelenka led them to the end of what seemed to have been a platform and then down another newly-built ladder to the floor of a square tunnel. Curved rails hung from each of the corners, their surfaces still black and glossy. Sam shone her light on the nearest one, and it struck glittering iridescence from the dustless material. Curious now, she crouched to touch it, felt her fingers glide across it as though it were oiled ice. She tried again, pressing harder, but there was no way to get any purchase on the gleaming substance.

"Frictionless material?" she said. That would explain why no dust gathered on it. And placed in the corners like that, it could certainly allow a vehicle to slide effortlessly along its track.

Zelenka looked over his shoulder, his glasses catching the light. "Yes, or very nearly so. Rodney would like to get his hands on enough to run some proper tests, but he can't without having to explain where it comes from."

"That must be frustrating," Daniel said, without much sympathy.

The tunnel curved gently, making it hard to judge how far they'd come. Once they had to climb over piles of rubble where a cross tunnel had partially collapsed, but in general the tunnels seemed reasonably intact. At last they reached another 'station,' where a modern ladder led up a slope of debris. At the top, a hole showed paler gray against the black and Sam automatically covered her light. Zelenka switched off his own and climbed up, pausing at the top to peer slowly around, but then beckoned for them to follow.

They emerged in the shell of a building, roof and windows long gone, but all four walls still mostly intact. The sky was lighter overhead, and Dex made a face. "How far north did we come?"

"Yes, we're cutting it close," Zelenka answered. "If we hurry…"

His voice trailed off as though he didn't quite believe it himself, and started for what had been the main door. Sam switched off her light and followed, the others at her heels. She was starting to feel the effects of only a few hours' sleep and the climb through the ruins, and she wasn't at all sure she was going to be able to keep up the pace. But if the alternative was hiding all day — she'd give it her best shot.

It was lighter outside, the sky to the east starting to grow pale, the stars fading. In the distance, she could see a string of lights that had to be the campsite, but there was a vast swath of darkness between them and it, and no sign of Sumner's men. Ahead, between the buildings, she could just make out the edge of the lake.

"So where exactly are we going?" Daniel asked.

"Back toward the camp, I'm afraid," Zelenka answered. "And hope Sumner has called off whatever was going on."

Sam suppressed a sigh. At least they wouldn't be climbing through tunnels. Presumably it would be easier on the surface.

A thin whine sounded in the distance, rising sharply. Dex reached for his hip as though he was still carrying a weapon, then pointed instead.

"Wraith!"

Sam turned to see lights above the lake, coming rapidly closer and resolving to weird needle-nosed fighters. Two swooped toward the camp, turning on a dime — I wouldn't like to follow them in a 302, she thought — but a third came straight on as though it was homing in on them.

"Cover!" Dex yelled, all caution vanished. "Get under cover!"

The building they'd just left was roofless, no protection there. Dex was waving them on, pointing toward another building that seemed to be more intact, and Sam dashed for it as the scream of the Wraith ship grew louder. Daniel was at her heels, stumbling as he tried to watch where he was going and get a look at the ships; ahead of them, Zelenka dove through the doorway just as a beam of blue light dropped from the belly of the fighter. It swept along the ground, carried with the ship, and Dex grabbed her arm, jerking her off her feet. She rolled and came up swearing. Daniel leaped after her, but the beam caught him, and he vanished. Sam flung herself after him, but Dex dragged her back.

"Daniel!"

The fighter streaked away, pulling up sharply to vanish into the night. Sam stared after it, her heart racing.

"Oh, God, Daniel."

"I'm sorry," Dex said.

Sam turned on him. "What the hell do you think you were doing? I could have gone after him —"

"You'd be dead." Dex stared down at her, his expression bleak. "Just like he is."

"No."

"That was a Culling beam," Dex said. "That's how they hunt. They've taken him back to their ship, and — I'm sorry."

Oh, God. Sam realized she was shaking, stiffened her shoulders. "We've got to go after them —"

"Inside," Dex said, and Sam let herself be pulled into the shelter of the nearest building. The whine was sounding again, rising to a scream, and another of the Wraith ships swooped by overhead, low enough that if she'd only had a P90 she could have done some serious damage. Gunfire sounded from the camp, and the Wraith ship rolled into a looping turn and headed to join the fight.

"They're distracted," Sam said. "We've got to get to General O'Neill—"

Zelenka shook his head. "We must stay here," he said. "The Athosians will not be waiting for us, not with Darts in the air, and even if it weren't foolish to take the chance, I cannot take us to their camp on my own."

"But—" Sam stopped, knowing he was right.

"We will wait for a better chance," Zelenka said. "Which will probably not be until nightfall. I am sorry, Colonel."

So am I. Sam swallowed the words along with the lump in her throat. "There has to be a way to get him back."

"No one's ever escaped from a hiveship," Dex said.

"Then we'll rescue him."

"That's—" Dex stopped, silenced by her glare.

"We'll rescue him," she said again, as though the repetition could make it true, and let herself slide down to sit at the base of the nearest wall. *Somehow.*

CHAPTER FOURTEEN

Kine

DANIEL regained consciousness upright and immobilized, his cheek resting against something that felt like a thick vine. The rest of his face was exposed, the air cool and faintly damp. He could hear a distant jumble of sounds, but couldn't make sense of them — were they machinery, voices, something else entirely? They weren't nearby, however, and he risked opening his eyes.

It was dark, but not so dark that he couldn't make out the shapes around him. He hung suspended in a shallow niche, wrapped securely in an organic-feeling net, cords and membranes holding him immobilized. There was another niche directly opposite him, perhaps three meters away; it was empty, the cords withered and slack, the membranes desiccated and in tatters, but the shape of the empty space was unpleasantly like a coffin. The Wraith — he'd been taken by the Wraith, caught in a flash of light that had to have been some kind of transport beam, and now he was — where? The net was too tight to allow him to turn his head and the angle didn't allow him to see either the floor of the corridor or its ceiling. A Wraith ship, probably, he thought, and closed his eyes to listen. Yes, those could be the common sounds of a ship in space, ventilators, machinery, but he couldn't be sure.

Still, that was the most probable answer, and one he didn't like at all. He was on a Wraith ship — a hive, one of the scientists had called it, taking the word from the Athosians, and there was something nastily insectile about the web that held him. The rest of the corridor looked organic, too, as though he were inside the body of some enormous animal. He filed that for later consideration — maybe it would prove some kind of advantage — and tried to lift his arms.

There was no give at all in the webbing, not even when he exerted his full strength. It was no better when he tried to move his legs and, finally, he had to admit that he couldn't really move at all. Well, he could move the forefinger and thumb of his left hand, but that didn't seem to get him anywhere. He let himself hang for a few minutes, listening while he got his breath back, then pressed himself forward against the web.

"Hello? Is anyone out there?"

There was no answer, just the distant sound of machines — or possibly, he thought, if the ship was in some sense alive, then perhaps what he was hearing was the sound of its internal organs, breathing, circulation, digestion. That wasn't a particularly pleasant thought, either, and he rocked forward again.

"Hello?"

There was a sound, soft and directionless, something between a sob and an indrawn breath. He froze, straining to hear, but it was not repeated.

"Hello! If you're out there —" He stopped, the sentence dying unfinished. *Talk to me and we can help each other,* he would have said, but the words were hollow. There was nothing he could do for himself in this position, never mind helping anyone else, and from the look of the cell opposite, anyone else in here with him would be in exactly the same position. In fact — In fact, given everything he'd heard about the Wraith so far, there was every chance that this was the ship's larder, and that he and any other humans were simply stored here until some Wraith was hungry enough to feed.

That thought was enough to get him straining against the web again, with the same lack of result, and he stopped, panting. Clearly, he wasn't going to break free using brute force — Teal'c might have been able to do it, but not him. Ok, what was he carrying in the way of gear? A flashlight, unless he'd dropped it — he couldn't feel it in his pocket, though he could feel the webbing pressing his pocketknife against his thigh. The pocketknife! Though what use a three-inch blade was going to be against the heavy cords even if he could figure out how to get at it…

There was a new sound from the corridor to his left, only a bit louder than the ambient noise, but unmistakably footsteps. Someone, more than one, was coming. He rocked forward again, straining against the web, but could see nothing until the footsteps were almost opposite him. There were three of them, a female with two males hovering deferentially behind her, and Daniel swallowed hard. He'd only gotten a brief look at the Wraith during the fighting and its aftermath, and then most of them had been the faceless drones. These were far closer to human, disconcertingly so despite the pale green skin and the pointed teeth, so sharp and so many of them, the clawed hands and the grooves beside their noses, secondary organs that looked like a snake's sensory pits. The female was paler than the others, veins showing green beneath her marble skin, and her heavy white hair hung in a luminous curtain; she seemed to be in charge, too, and Daniel tried what he hoped was a plausible smile.

"Hey, hi. Could we maybe talk about this whole prisoner thing?"

The female had been looking away, but when he spoke her head whipped around faster than he would have believed possible, eyes green as a cat's fixing on his. Her clawed hand flashed past his face, releasing the strands that held his head immobile and drawing a thin line of blood from his cheek. He was suddenly, painfully aware of her presence, a pressure against his mind, worse than the Replicators, worse even than the Ancients, and he fumbled for the barriers he had taught himself.

"Whoa, don't — That's not a good idea." Even as he spoke, he'd found the right countermeasure, like tuning in to a radio frequency, and shoved back hard. He caught a momentary jumble of her thoughts — shock, anger — and then the tumbling warnings of the two males, urging her to caution. She snarled, her right hand coming up, claws flexed, the mouth that crossed its palm gaping wide, and Daniel flinched in spite of himself.

The two males started forward themselves, their thoughts a clamor of warning and concern.

* — must not endanger yourself —*

That was the taller and tidier of the pair, the one whose silver hair was drawn up in a complicated tail; the other, short and wild-haired, was blunter:

* — Queen will *kill* you if —*

And then he'd lost the thread, shook his head hard. The female snarled like a tiger. "What are you?" Her voice was low and throaty, slit-pupiled eyes almost glowing in the dark.

"Um, human?" Daniel's mouth was dry. "Just a traveler passing through —"

"Liar." She cocked her head to one side. "My mother will destroy you utterly, you and all your kind."

"That really isn't necessary," Daniel began.

She spun around, though Daniel hadn't heard anyone else approach, and the other males made hasty bows. Daniel strained forward to see the newcomer. It was another male, even more elegant than the others, with silver hair pulled up and back into an elaborate fall that framed a narrow, long-boned face. He wore the same long leather coat as the others, but his seemed to be embossed with delicate patterns, and the tuft of beard at the tip of his chin had been divided into two points, each one tipped with a tiny silver bead. The female glared at him, visibly unimpressed — most of their communication was telepathic, Daniel thought, but he couldn't seem to find the way to tune in again. The newcomer bowed.

"But the Queen has given him to me," he said aloud. "For my research."

"I will not quarrel with her," the female said. "Or with you. But it's a mistake."

The scruffy Wraith — his hair was a mass of matted dreadlocks and a dark green tattoo spiraled over cheek and jaw and down his neck — said, "If it's what she wants —"

"Then we'll certainly oblige," the other male said firmly.

"Excellent." The newcomer fixed his eyes on Daniel. They were darker green than the female's, the pupils narrowed as though the light was stronger than it was. Which must mean that the hives weren't dark to them, Daniel thought. No wonder they attacked so often at night. "What's your name?"

"Jackson. Daniel Jackson."

The newcomer nodded. "So. Daniel Jackson, our queen has given you to me. If you cooperate, you may be allowed to live a little longer, and so may your kin on Athos. Resist, and there will be no reason so spare any of you."

Daniel licked his lips. "I understand."

"Excellent." The newcomer did something to the web, and it sagged away. Daniel hadn't been expecting that, and stumbled forward, almost into the arms of the female. She made a noise between annoyance and disgust and shoved him away. The scruffy Wraith caught him, set him upright again.

Now that he was in the corridor, he could see that there were dozens of cells on either side, lining the walls from the more brightly-lit hatch twenty yards to his left and disappearing into the shadows to his right. Most of them seemed to contain a human being, though most of them appeared unconscious — a mercy for them, maybe, but deeply disconcerting all the same. A trio of the masked drones was waiting, weapons in hand. The newcomer nodded to them and they took up positions on either side of Daniel, moving with that same eerie quickness that the female had shown.

"You will come with me," the newcomer said.

There was no point in resisting, and Daniel nodded. "Ok — do you have a name? I mean, you know who I am, but what am I supposed to call you?"

The Wraith considered him for a long moment, his expression unreadable. "You may call me Seeker."

Seeker and the drones brought him out of the cells and into a broad main corridor filled with Wraith. Some of them stared as he passed, and once or twice Daniel felt the pressure of a mind against his, but always it slipped away. Certainly the hive seemed well-manned, full of Wraith in their dark leather, shadows against the grim organic walls. All of them were male, or drones, but Daniel was beginning to pick out at least two different types among the males. There were the long-coated, long-haired males, usually with tattoos on their hands and faces, and then there were ones with shorter, paler coats and a variety of different hairstyles. The latter seemed to acknowledge Seeker more than the others, but that was all Daniel could make of it. Once, as they passed a cross-corridor, his eye was caught by brighter light, and he glanced toward it just as shadow crossed between it and him. It looked almost human, but it was gone before he could be sure. And that seemed at best unlikely, if not impossible: what human would be allowed to move freely on a Wraith hive?

They left the main corridor for a maze of smaller passages, with brighter, mottled walls that curved in on each other, as though they spiraled into the heart of the hive. There were obvious compartments here, hatches braced with ribbing that looked grown from bone and tendon, and Seeker stopped at one, waving his feeding hand at a sensor plate growing from the wall. The hatch rolled back, revealing a long narrow space lined with consoles and screens. A lab, Daniel guessed, and one of the drones shoved him toward a low chair.

"Sit," Seeker said, and turned to examine one of the screens.

Daniel did as he was told, though the chair itself felt more like bone than wood. It was knobby like bone, too, and he suppressed a shudder. "So, um, Seeker. What exactly do you want from me? I mean, up to a point, I'd be glad to cooperate —"

The Wraith swung around again, almost too fast to follow, and tossed a small ovoid at Daniel's chest. He caught it, awkwardly, and realized it was an Ancient device shaped something like one of the communications stones. He felt writing under his fingers, and turned it over gingerly.

"Do not use without full supply of — I'm not sure what poteras means in this context, but you shouldn't use this without it."

"Interesting," Seeker said. He held out his hand and Daniel handed him back the device. "You are not of the Ancestors' blood."

"No. No, I'm not."

"Then what are you? You are most certainly not any ordinary sort of human."

"Um." Daniel had no idea how he ought to answer that question. "We're travelers, from far away —"

Seeker pressed two clawed fingers into his neck below the point of his jaw, forcing his head up and back. "You're no more a Traveler than I am."

"If 'traveler' refers to some ethnic group, no, I'm not," Daniel said. It took all his willpower not to push himself further back into the chair. "I simply mean that we travel. A long way."

Seeker hissed softly, but released him. "And yet you do not know who the Travelers are — or, I think, the Wraith. I would have been willing to swear that there were no humans left in the galaxy who did not know us." He paused, and Daniel felt the pressure of his mind again. "Tell me, Daniel Jackson, where are you from?"

Daniel shook his head. "I really can't do that."

"Of course you can."

The pressure increased, subtle but definite, seeking a glimpse of night sky, some image of Daniel's home world, some clue to its location. Daniel parried as best he could, blocking each probe only to feel the pressure resume elsewhere. This was nothing like the Replicator Carter's attack, a single illusion backed by endless brutal strength. This was fluid, deadly, as strong in its way as the Ancients' mental powers, but not without limits. He allowed Seeker a glimpse of Cheyenne Mountain — contextless, it should tell him nothing more than he'd already guessed — and in the same moment reached out himself, grasping for control. Seeker snarled and flung him back into the chair, but not before Daniel had caught a glimpse of a scarlet-haired female — Seeker's queen — surrounded by other Wraith that Seeker saw as old and well-loved rivals.

"You seem determined to make me kill you," Seeker said, after a moment.

"You're going to feed on me anyway," Daniel answered.

"That is not inevitable."

"In that case…" Daniel paused, but couldn't see any harm in trying. "There are people back on Athos who would be willing to ransom me."

Seeker gave him a skeptical look. "And how many lives do you believe you're worth?"

"Maybe we could think of something else to trade," Daniel answered.

"There's nothing else you have that we want," Seeker said. He turned away, pacing the length of his laboratory and back again, the skirts of his long coat hissing at his ankles. If there was only one queen, Daniel thought, unable not to make the connections, or only a few dominant females per hive, then display must be vitally important for the males, to earn and keep a queen's attention. "A human who does not carry the Ancestors' blood, who knows nothing of the Wraith, and whose people carry weapons far in advance of anything we permit… You are a puzzle, Daniel Jackson."

"All we want is to return home," Daniel said. "We'll go, leave you in peace —"

"Go where?"

Daniel shook his head and Seeker smiled, showing a mouthful of very sharp teeth.

"And that is the answer I will have from you. Make no mistake. I will have answers." He turned away before Daniel could speak, and touched a control buried in one of the consoles. "Dekaas!"

A moment later, an inner door slid open, one that Daniel hadn't noticed in the dim light. A figure in a short coat appeared, short coat and short hair — not a Wraith at all, Daniel realized, but a human, an ordinary-looking man with graying hair and a wary expression.

"Lord?"

"Take Daniel Jackson to my quarters and keep him there. See that he is fed and sleeps and that you explain how it would benefit him to cooperate." Seeker picked up the Ancient device, bounced it thoughtfully in his hand, and turned away. "I'll return later." The laboratory door rolled shut again behind him.

"Very well," Dekaas answered, and beckoned to the drones. "This way."

"You're really on his side?" Daniel asked, and the other man stared at him for a moment before a wry smile curved his mouth.

"Better to serve the Wraith than to be their dinner. Now, move."

By dint of concentrated effort, Jack drifted back to sleep before dawn, and woke again to the bustle of breakfast being prepared in the main cavern. Teal'c was awake already, talking quietly to one of the guards — a new one, presumably the morning relief. Jack rolled out of his cot, running his hands through his hair, and moved to join them.

"Morning. Any news?"

"Good morning, O'Neill," Teal'c said. "Apparently the attack on the city was not as bad as feared."

"That's good news," Jack said. "Any word on Carter and Daniel?"

"Regrettably, no." Teal'c gave the guard a faintly reproachful look, and the young man blushed.

"With the attack, we could hardly make contact with our people in the city," he protested.

"Indeed."

"No, we couldn't," Sheppard said. He'd come up quietly enough that Jack glared at him. "We'll send someone back tonight, make contact then."

"That will be too late," Jack began.

"Teyla says the radio's been quiet," Sheppard offered. "No more threats. It's possible Sumner's calmed down."

"But hardly likely, Major!" Jack glared at him.

Sheppard bit his lip, but before he could answer, a stocky woman in an Atlantis uniform hurried up to him carrying a laptop.

"Major Sheppard! You need to see this."

"What's up, Anderson?"

She angled the screen toward him. "You remember I brought the portable telescope array with me when I left?"

Sheppard nodded. "Teyla said you could set it up on the ridge if you hid it properly."

"Yeah." Anderson nodded back. "Last night — I think I'm picking up a ship in orbit. A big one."

"Crap," Sheppard said.

"The Wraith?" Jack didn't dare move closer, not with the guards frowning unhappily. "Dr. Anderson, do you have any idea when the ship arrived?"

It was a gamble, he knew, but she didn't seem bothered by his assumption of authority. "Early last night, it looks like," she said, poking at the laptop. "I first picked it up around — at 2210 last night."

"How does that fit with the Dart attack?" Jack asked.

"Already there, General," Sheppard answered, with the ghost of a grin. "Halling says the first attack on the gate started after one this morning, and another wave came through the gate about three. That's the one that hit Emege."

"This changes everything," Jack said. "We've got no idea what Sumner's going to do now. We have to get Carter and Jackson out of there."

Sheppard looked over his shoulder, and Jack saw Teyla walking toward them, her long brown coat flowing back from her shoulders.

"Jinto said you wanted to see me, Dr. Anderson?"

The scientist nodded. "Yes. There's a large ship in orbit, and I think it's probably the Wraith."

For a moment, Teyla's face was old and bleak, but then she'd shaken herself back to order. "You are sure of this?"

"As sure as I can be." Anderson offered the laptop screen again, and Teyla bent her head to it, but Jack guessed she didn't know what she was looking at any more than he did. "There's definitely something in orbit that wasn't there yesterday, which implies a ship, and — who else could it be?"

"There are others in the galaxy who use starships rather than the Stargates," Teyla said. "But, no, if it were any of them, they would have tried to contact me or Halling." She frowned at the screen. "This is a worrying development, Major."

"I need to get my people out of the city," Jack said.

"We need to get all our people out of there," Sheppard said. "Everyone who'll come."

"Which is hardly everyone," Teyla answered, "and to attempt it puts us all in danger."

"The Wraith must be planning a big attack," Sheppard said. "What else could they possibly be doing here? You said yourself we were too advanced for the Wraith to let us live. They've come to wipe us out, just like you said they did to the Genii."

"I wish it were not so," Teyla said, "but, yes, it seems the most likely answer. I must inform Halling and the rest of the council."

"Our people," Sheppard said again, and she stopped, taking a deep breath.

"I know. Yes, we must do what we can for them, though what that will be —" She shook herself. "John, I must warn Halling and the rest of my people. Then, yes, we will discuss this."

She turned without waiting for his answer, and Sheppard looked at Jack. "She'll be back shortly, sir. In the meantime, I'd welcome any suggestions you have."

"It might be easier if you let us out of here," Jack said, and Sheppard bit his lip again.

"I can't do that, sir. But if you'd care to join me for breakfast, we could talk."

Jack's stomach growled at the thought, and Teal'c cocked his head to one side. "That would be welcome, Major Sheppard."

Breakfast did mean being let out of the cave, though Jack thought it probably wouldn't do him any favors to mention it. They were still under guard, though the skinny Athosian boy didn't look old enough to shave, and the old man who filled their bowls with a savory-smelling stew gave them an uncertain glance. Sheppard returned a wincing smile that was unlikely to reassure anyone, and motioned them to a group of stools set to one side of the central fire. Jack wolfed down about half the bowl — a lot like the grits he'd had at bases in the south, if grits were flavored with smoke and salami — and then pointed his spoon at Sheppard.

"Major. How many people have you got in the city?"

"It depends on what you mean by people," Sheppard answered. "Most of the civilian staff isn't happy with the current state of affairs. Most of the Air Force personnel would follow me — or you, sir — but the Marines are Sumner's picked men. And they're all on the drug."

"Which I'm guessing is addictive," Jack said.

"Dr. Beckett says it creates a dependence, but it should be easy to wean them off," Sheppard answered. "Teyla disagrees."

Jack nodded. He wasn't going to argue with Teyla about that one. "So the civilians and the Air Force personnel — are the latter armed?"

"They were. I don't know if they are now."

"And presumably Colonel Sumner has Colonel Carter and Daniel Jackson under guard," Teal'c said.

"That may not be our biggest problem," Sheppard said. "If we catch a break — Zelenka may be able to get to them."

"Zelenka?" The name was vaguely familiar, but Jack couldn't attach a face.

"One of the science team, Dr. McKay's second-in-command," Sheppard said. "There's a tunnel system under the city, Zelenka was exploring it when the Wraith first came. Dr. Weir talked about moving part of the expedition down there while they explored the city, but there wasn't space enough for everyone, so Colonel Sumner vetoed the idea."

"That figures." Jack closed his eyes, trying to visualize the layout of the camp. "The problem is, we're operating on a deadline."

"We're not going to be able to do anything before dark," Sheppard said.

Jack shook his head. "That's cutting it too close, Major. Let me and Teal'c go in after them. If your guy, Zelenka, can take us in through those tunnels, that would be ideal. We can release our people, and maybe that will distract Sumner enough for you to get your people out."

"It's an idea," Sheppard began, and Teyla came to join them, breathing as though she'd been running.

"What is an idea?"

"General O'Neill has a suggestion," Sheppard said, and ran through the idea. With a few additions of his own, Jack admitted, and not bad ones, either.

Teyla nodded slowly. "Yes, that could work, and I believe the council will agree. But we cannot make the attempt in daylight. If General O'Neill will make his attempt in the mid-afternoon, and if he is willing to lead them off — then we can move as soon as the sun is down."

"You're putting all the risks on us," Jack pointed out. "Can we get some support before sunset?"

"We cannot fight Colonel Sumner's men," Teyla answered. "Our goal is to help our friends, Major Sheppard's people, escape before the Wraith can destroy them all. That is all we can do."

"Great." Jack rocked back on his stool. The odds weren't wonderful — were pretty crappy, in fact — but it was the best chance they had of saving Carter and Daniel. "All right. We'll do it. But your guy, Zelenka, he'd better be waiting for us."

"I'm sure he will be," Teyla said, with a smile that left him with no confidence whatsoever.

"Can we have our weapons back?"

"As soon as we are ready to leave," Teyla answered serenely, and Jack rocked back on the stool again. At least they had a fighting chance of rescuing Daniel and Carter before Sumner did something they'd all regret.

CHAPTER FIFTEEN
Ouroboros

THE SUN was fully up now, shafts of light streaming down through the broken ceiling — floor, really, Sam thought, the floor of the half-collapsed building above them. Zelenka had done his best to shore up the area where they were, but she couldn't help eyeing the farther walls uneasily. The stone was cracked and fragile-looking, brittle as bone left too long in the fire. Zelenka saw her looking, and gave a little shrug.

"Yes, well, I would not go too far in that direction. Whatever the Wraith used to destroy the city, it leached the strongest minerals from the stone."

"Like they draw the life from humans," Dex muttered. He was sitting on the ground at the foot of their improvised ladder, back against the wall. "Is there any way we can get weapons? We're too vulnerable like this."

"Only by going back toward the camp," Zelenka said. "I'm reluctant to make the attempt."

Sam moved cautiously toward the nearest piece of broken stone, wishing she had one of the Ancient sampling devices or even a geologist's test kit. She went to one knee, probing the stone floor, and when she was sure it was going to hold her, turned her attention to the crumbling wall. It looked like limestone or some other form of calcium carbonate, which might explain how the Wraith had damaged it. If they had created some sort of blast weapon that disrupted the same chemical bonds that were dissolved by water and mild acid — yes, there were tiny pits in the stone, though not the large holes that flowing water would have made. She touched it, lightly at first, then pressing harder, and jumped as the stone fell away under her touch, opening another hole in the floor. She winced at the noise, and Zelenka gave the ladder a nervous glance.

"We should be out of earshot," he said, but his tone didn't carry much conviction.

"Sorry," Sam said.

"We should move on." Dex was already on his feet.

Zelenka hesitated for a moment, then nodded. "Yes, it would probably be wise. And we need water and food."

Sam nodded. Her mouth was painfully dry — she was hungry, too, but water was the pressing need.

"We will have to go back toward the camp," Zelenka went on, "but if we are careful, I do not think we will be discovered."

He led them back through the maze of tunnels, though by this point Sam had been through so many caverns and sections of old transit system that she could no longer tell if they'd walked through those areas before. Nor could she tell how far they'd come, except that her boots were a weight on her ankles and she was starting to doze off any time they stopped. They'd been walking for perhaps forty minutes when Dex lifted his head sharply and Sam felt a breath of damp air on her face. She could hear water, too, the faint musical sound of water running over stone, and a few minutes later they ducked through a triangular gap in one wall to emerge in a larger chamber where the sound of the water was suddenly very loud.

Zelenka fumbled in the dark, and then a match flared for an instant before he got the lamp lit. It was Athosian, Sam guessed, another of the oil lamps that the scientist had collected, and the warm light revealed a hole high in the opposite wall. Water flowed from it, a steady stream, spilling over irregular debris to pool in what looked like a shallow basin carved from the stone. Sam licked her lips at the sight, and Zelenka nodded.

"It's clean. Perfectly safe to drink."

Sam didn't need another invitation. She scooped it up in both hands, not caring that she spilled some down the front of her shirt, swallowed four or five mouthfuls before she made herself step away and give Dex and Zelenka their turns. While they drank, she glanced at her watch, pressing the bezel to light the numbers so that she could see clearly. A little past one in the afternoon: surely Sumner would be searching for them now, and she hoped McKay and his people weren't in any trouble. Another four hours to sunset, five hours to full dark, so an hour or two after that before they could link up with Jack and Teal'c and start figuring out how to rescue Daniel…

Her eyes stung at the thought, tears she couldn't afford and that she told herself fiercely were uncalled for. This was Daniel they were talking about. He'd have managed to talk his way out of being fed on, was surely already plotting his own escape.

"There is also — yes." Zelenka reached up into a niche carved into the wall and produced a box that seemed to be made of thin strips of wood woven together. "There is not much, but it's high energy, like a concentrate bar. We can each have two."

He held out the box to reveal bricks the sized of dominos stacked on a waxy-looking leaf. Sam took two, slightly sticky to the touch and looking like pressed tobacco, but Dex grabbed his with visible relish.

"Trail bricks."

"Something like that, I think," Zelenka agreed. "The Athosians call them way-loaves."

Sam sniffed. It was a pungent sweetness, like raisins or molasses, and when she nibbled off a corner it had the same heavy flavor. There was an undertone of salt, a pleasing contrast, and she finished them more quickly than she'd meant, then went to rinse her fingers in the pool and take another long drink of water.

"Not ours," Dex said, and turned his remaining bar over. "No government stamp."

"I believe Teyla said these were made here," Zelenka answered, "not traded for."

Daniel would know what to make of that, Sam thought, her eyes prickling again. Just like he'd know how to analyze the different names, and know what questions to ask Dex about his government. She cleared her throat. "Look, if we could take down one of those — what did you call them, Darts?"

"That's what they're called," Dex said.

"If we could capture one — has anyone every tried flying one back into a hive?" There were plenty of problems with the idea, Sam knew, starting with the inherent problems of flying an unfamiliar aircraft, but it was at least a place to start.

"Nobody's been that crazy," Dex said bluntly.

"Somebody must have tried."

Dex shook his head. "Not that I ever heard."

Zelenka gave her a sharp look. "If one were to somehow steal a Dart, one would have to fly it onto the hive, find the person, and then fly the same or another Dart back out again. This is not the Milky Way, there are no people here who are capable of powered flight. The Wraith have destroyed them all."

Sam closed her mouth tight over her automatic protest. He was right, that was the problem — except that there had to be a way. She wasn't prepared to surrender.

"I was on a wrecked hiveship once," Dex said. "Not here, on a world called Tarrengh. Nobody knew what had happened to it, but it was empty — you'd think it was just another big hill until you got around to the eastern side and could see there were openings that were too regular to be caves. My unit did some exploring there when I was first in training. What was left of it was enormous, and that was maybe half the ship — the bow half, the regimental engineer thought, because there weren't any engines. It looked like it was made of bone and metal, and there were two long halls that were just niches that were the ship's larder, where they stored the humans they Culled." He shook his head. "One door at each end and a hundred cells on each side. Even if you could get there, it would be a death trap."

"There has to be a way," Sam said. "We can't leave him."

Dex's voice was flat. "If you don't, you'll just die, too."

"No." Sam glared at him.

"Be that as it may," Zelenka said firmly. "We can do nothing until dark. This is as good a place as any, we'll rest here for a few hours and then move on."

Sam controlled herself, nodding. It wasn't Dex's fault — well, except that he'd kept her from going after Daniel. But she was not going to give up yet. Not until she had to.

Seeker's quarters were a suite of rooms not too far from the laboratory. They were dark and cool, mist coiling from the corners and around the pillars that divided the largest room into several separate areas. The furniture was low and sprawling, curved and placed as though it had been grown from the fabric of the ship itself. Daniel would have like to examine it more closely, particularly the display globe that grew from a thick stalk, cradled in vine-like fingers, and table set with what looked like some sort of game board, but Dekaas hurried him on toward a corner where the furniture was more shaped to human bodies. Well, more like a lobe than a corner, Daniel thought, or like the curve of a leaf. The interior in general was as rounded as the inside of a seashell, if seashells came in shades of green and gray — one more reason to think that the ships were in some sense organic.

Dekaas sent a drone for food, and waved his hand over a sensor shaped like a flower to bring up a stronger light. "Let me take a look at your face," he said.

"Why bother?" Daniel asked. "If I'm just going to be fed upon, it seems like a waste."

"He might not feed on you." Daniel couldn't tell if that was irony in Dekaas's voice or if the other man was utterly serious. "And if he doesn't you don't want to die of preventable infection."

"True enough." Daniel sat motionless as Dekaas examined the long scratch, and then sprayed it with something that stung and smelled like cotton candy. The drone returned with a tray that held half a dozen covered dishes, and Dekaas waved for it to stand further off. It was still too close for him to try attacking Dekaas, Daniel thought, and relaxed again as the other human uncovered the plates. "What is all this?"

"Food."

Daniel sighed. "Ok, I'd gotten that far. What is it? And, more importantly, why feed us?"

"There are humans who live among the Wraith," Dekaas answered. "It would be pointless to starve us."

"Yes, ok, but why?" Daniel studied the plates, newly aware that he hadn't eaten for almost a day.

"Because starving humans are hardly satisfying." Dekaas chose a round object that looked like it had been wrapped in a leaf and popped it into his mouth.

"That wasn't what I meant." Daniel took one of the leaf-wrapped spheres and bit cautiously into it. It contained some sort of grain wrapped around a soft, cheesy center. He thought for an instant that Dekaas smiled, but then the other man's expression hardened.

"I was born with the Taint — I can hear the Wraith, feel their presence and their thoughts. I tried to hide it, but eventually I was found out. I was included in the next draft sent to the Culling grounds. Fortunately, there were others there who knew what it meant to carry the Taint and, before the Wraith came, they taught the rest of us the rudiments of the mind speech. The Queen took us into her service."

"But you — serve — Seeker, I thought." Daniel chose another of the bite-sized wraps, careful to sound unchallenging.

"I do."

"So what is he, exactly?"

"He is a chief cleverman, Master of Sciences Biological." There was a note in Dekaas's voice that suggested he was translating literally. "He is also one of the Queen's favorites, lord of her council."

And also a note of pride, Daniel thought. Dekaas cared that Seeker was an important man on the hive. "Was that the queen I saw earlier?" he asked, though he was already fairly sure it wasn't. Or at least not the person Seeker considered to be the queen. "White hair, really quick with her claws?" He touched his cheek below the scratch.

This time he was sure Dekaas smiled. "That was the Young Queen," he said.

"The Queen's daughter?"

"Yes." Dekaas considered him. "You are very curious."

"I'm hoping it's a survival mechanism," Daniel said.

"Perhaps. Or perhaps not."

That wasn't particularly encouraging. Daniel chose another couple of bite-sized pieces from the tray — sweet and spicy, sort of like barbecued chicken — and ate them while he considered his next move. "Look, all I and my people want is to go back where we came from. We were not expecting to find anything as — fearsome as the Wraith, and honestly I think our leaders will just want to stay home and stay out of your way."

"I have never yet met a human who did not know of the Wraith," Dekaas said thoughtfully. "Where are you from, I wonder?"

"Obviously, I can't tell you that."

"But that is the question." The door of the suite had opened so silently that Daniel hadn't heard, and he looked up to see Seeker striding toward them. "The question of the hour, I fear. Dekaas, you may go."

"Yes, lord." Dekaas rose gracefully, collected the tray, and disappeared into the inner room.

Daniel came to his feet as well. "I was just saying to Dekaas that all we, me and my people, all we want to is to go back where we came from. You're definitely not people we want to mess with, and frankly I think we'd all be happy if we didn't have anything to do with you ever again."

"An interesting offer." Seeker tipped his head to one side, and waved his hand at the sensor to dim the lights again. "Had we met under other circumstances, it might have been acceptable. However, too many men have been killed for that to work."

"We've lost people, too," Daniel said. "We'd both have to

accept that."

"Just so, and the Queen does not wish to do so," Seeker answered. "And I wish to know where you are from."

Too late, Daniel realized that Seeker's mental attack had already begun, winding delicately around his thoughts as they spoke. He caught his breath, struggling to find mental purchase — it felt as though he were standing on ice, with no way to hold his ground, no way to push back against the pressure that was slowly driving him toward the answer it sought. A name, a glimpse of the cloudless sky at night, a map, the path he'd taken to come to Athos, all that and more Seeker demanded, a thousand questions like a thousand cuts nibbling at the edges of his mind. Daniel took a stumbling step backward, shaking his head as though that could clear his mind. There was Cheyenne Mountain, and the gate room, and Seeker pressed him further, toward the outside, toward the parking lot and the empty night sky over Colorado —

"No!"

Daniel shoved back against the question, clumsy and fumbling, but strong enough to make some progress. Instantly the pressure faded, reappearing in another place, probing for how he'd come to Athos. And that he really couldn't answer, didn't dare answer. The Wraith disliked light, and he dredged up the memory of desert suns, of Egypt and Abydos and a dozen other worlds, flung that blinding brilliance into Seeker's mind. He flinched back, hissing sharply, and Daniel pressed his advantage, groping for secrets behind Seeker's mental barriers. He caught the briefest glimpse, a cascade of jumbled images too swift, too complex to understand, and then Seeker slammed him against the wall, claws flexed and ready. Daniel cried out as they pierced his skin, delivering a jolt of pain and something else that sent his heart racing. He felt the hand-mouth opening against his skin, felt the skin parting, a terrible suction tugging at heart and lungs and life, all the more painful for being utterly unnatural.

Seeker drank, teeth bared, one long pull like a man draining a water bottle on a hot day. Daniel hung suspended, shriveling under Seeker's touch, fire running like water along every nerve. And then, as suddenly as it had begun, it stopped. Daniel could feel himself shaking, shivering as though he were freezing, every nerve on edge and empty. He tried to raise his hand, sure that he'd see the skin wrinkled and spotted with age, but he couldn't find the strength. And still Seeker stared at him, the green eyes unreadable, contemplating something Daniel could not begin to see.

Abruptly he was falling again, cool water pouring through him, quenching the pains and filling out the shriveled spaces. He caught his breath, his head falling back, unable to believe that he was alive again, whole again, and Seeker released him. He wasn't quite quick enough to respond, slithering halfway down the wall before he could command his legs again, but he managed to straighten before he fell.

"So." Seeker's voice was very soft, silky smooth. "You have had a taste of what I can do. And believe me, that was nothing more than a taste. I can drain your life entirely, Daniel Jackson, leave you dead, and then restore you — but how far? Shall I leave you as you are, a young man, or shall I make you old before your time? Or shall I leave you crippled, just alive enough to know what I have done and will do to your kin on Athos?" He smiled, showing teeth. "Yes, that has merit. I will ask these questions again, and I trust you will have rethought your answers."

The suite door slid shut behind Seeker, and Daniel let himself sink slowly to the floor, not sure how much longer his legs would have held him. It was no wonder the people of Pegasus were terrified of the Wraith, he thought, struggling for some kind of objectivity, anything to hold back the memory of his life being drawn inexorably from his body. The pain was agonizing, but worst was the knowledge, the absolute certainty of impending death.

And yet he hadn't died. He spread his hands in the dim light, remotely pleased to see that they weren't trembling. He wasn't even visibly aged, not withered the way the corpses had been on Athos. Which meant that somehow the Wraith had returned what he'd taken, the life force or whatever it was that they actually fed upon. None of the expedition members had even mentioned that as a possibility—though perhaps the Athosians knew? If only he'd been able to talk to them before he'd been taken, found out what they knew about the Wraith...

How long he sat there he didn't know. The drones had disappeared, though he didn't remember their departure, and there was a pitcher of what proved to be water sitting on the floor by his foot. He was painfully thirsty, he realized, probably a side effect of being fed on and restored, but he still sniffed cautiously at it before he drank. Not that there was much he could do to tell if the water was drugged, or much he could do if he guessed wrong. Still, he made himself stop and wait after the first few mouthfuls just in case.

Nothing happened. He drained the rest of the pitcher more slowly, considering what this meant. Certainly the Wraith seemed entirely confident of themselves in their dealings with humans. And well they might: they were stronger, faster, and they had a monopoly on any technology more advanced than, say, the early twentieth century. But they were not indestructible. It took a lot of bullets, but any Wraith could be killed. They were no different from the Goa'uld in that.

He pushed himself to his feet, swaying for a moment before he regained his balance. A side effect of the feeding, he thought, not some drug, and he rested his hand on the wall until he was steady. Dekaas was nowhere in sight, either—another indication of the Wraith's general confidence—and Daniel moved quickly to the main door. It was locked, of course, and the controls refused to respond to his touch. He searched his pockets, came up with the pocketknife, and began to pry at the cover. The thick spongy material gave under pressure, but the blade made no real impression, and he abandoned that for the moment to search the room instead.

It was large, even allowing for the size of the ship, and he guessed it reflected Seeker's status among the Wraith. The furnishings were elaborately made, organic shapes spiraling up out of the floor or slumping down the walls; the covering of mottled hide and twined cords — tendons? — was hardly to his taste, but he had to admit it was a coherent aesthetic. The center of the room was dominated by the display globe on its stalk, and there were buttons marked with odd characters hidden in the leaves around its rim, but nothing Daniel did could make it function. He glared at it for a moment and moved on.

The other end of the room held more furniture, a set of low couches around the table with the game board. They looked a little bit like dining furniture in classical Greece, if the Ancient Greeks had grown their couches from giant gourds. The board was hexagonal, and divided into unequal sections; the polished surface was covered with counters of stone or bone, pale against dark wood. They were clearly laid out in a pattern, but Daniel couldn't tell whether he was looking at an interrupted game or some sort of problem set out to be solved. He thought it might be designed for three players, but that was as far as he could get.

Beyond the table was an irregular niche in the wall, banded with tiny crystals like the inside of a broken geode. A hidden light came on as he approached it, revealing a dozen or more objects settled among the crystals. They looked like artifact, he thought, all sorts of artifacts, human-made and Wraith and animal jumbled together like some weird cabinet of curiosities. There was a cylinder that looked like an enormous rifle shell, except that the tip was a quartz-like stone that flashed green as he turned it in the light. A pale green plaque of something that felt like shell or ivory, carved with a stylized, striding man carrying what looked like a shop sign under his arm; a coil of what felt like well-cured leather cord, thick as his hand at one end, tapering to an odd metal connector at the other; a sharply pointed metal rod with a teardrop black stone at one end—and an Ancient crystal, chipped and broken, but still unmistakable.

He snatched it up, squinting in the dim light. He couldn't quite read the eroded markings on its surface, but it was shaped like the crystals he'd seen inside the DHD. And there were more of them, he realized. Three, no, five of them, the dim light rendering them almost invisible against the tiny bands of crystal that held them. He picked them up one by one, turning them over to try to make sense of why Seeker had collected them. Two of them were completely undamaged, three were unusable, and the fourth had a single chip in its leading edge. That one was of a shape he didn't recognize, and he held it closer to the light to examine its markings. Sam would know what it was—she'd know what they all were, he thought, and then he saw the mark in the center of the long shaft. It was a snake eating its own tail.

Janus's mark. He checked the others, but they were ordinary, unmarked, and mostly styles he recognized. But this one... He slipped it into his pocket, wishing he had something to wrap it in, something to protect it from further damage. Ok, maybe there wasn't much point, but if somehow he managed to escape—

There was a noise at the door, and he took two quick steps away from the niche and its jumble of treasures as the door slid open. Seeker smiled at him, showing very sharp teeth.

"So, Daniel Jackson. I hope you have reconsidered."

"I thought maybe you might have changed your mind." Daniel took another step backward, but there was no place to run. "Really, you don't want to pursue this. It's just going to end with everyone killing each other."

"Which you could prevent."

"So could you." But he couldn't, Daniel realized. Not if the Wraith lived on human lives, if they only lived on human lives.

"Look, the last thing we wanted was to start a war. Just let us go, and we will not bother you again."

"You cannot seriously expect me to believe that." Seeker turned toward the gaming table, and it took all Daniel's self-control not to reach for the ouroboros crystal in his pocket. Seeker didn't seem to pay any attention to the niches, however, his gaze focused instead on the stones scattered on the table. He moved one, and then another, studying the result for a long moment. "Still. There is no harm in… conversation."

Daniel felt the first delicate pressure of Seeker's thoughts against his own mind, and braced himself to resist. "No harm at all."

CHAPTER SIXTEEN

Interlude

THE ZENANA was in an uproar, the Queen on her feet, glaring, while her favorites dodged her glance. Only the Consort seemed unmoved, but his rivals noted that he had been caught with his back to the wall, no other place to be without seeming to surrender. The Young Queen and her court, all the rest of the lesser courtiers, had been banished from this meeting; this was only the Queen and her closest men.

How many men are dead? she asked, dangerously calm.

One blade, the Consort answered. *A dozen drones.*

A dozen!

Drones. The Consort met her snarl without flinching.

Drones cost me something, though you may not think it!

And we achieved our goal, Seeker said. He was always willing to draw her fire when the Consort was concerned, and both Spark and Seldom Seen bared teeth. *I found one useful mind among them.*

Only one? Spark examined his claws.

Only one survived interrogation, Seeker answered. *The other knew nothing, anyway. Ill-informed and highly disciplined — more independence than I would have seen had I questioned one of our own drones, but no more knowledge.*

And this other one. That was Seldom Seen, not looking at his sister. *You've proved he's no Ancient?*

Yes.

As best you can, Spark pointed out.

Seeker controlled himself with a palpable effort. *The Ancient device did not respond to him, as it would to anyone who carries the Ancients' genetic heritage. And there are other reasons to believe he is no Ancient.*

The Queen took a deep breath and returned to her chair, though she did not fully relax. *Go on.*

If they were Ancients returned, they would know what we are and how to fight us, Seeker said. *Daniel Jackson knows only the most basic information about us, and there are gaps that are shocking. He is not an Ancient, and I do not believe he is from any world that has ever known our kind.*

There aren't many of those, Seldom Seen said.

No, indeed, the Queen agreed. *Have you found this unknown world?*

Not yet. Seeker faced her unflinching. *He is strong, and he has some form of the Gift — he is aware of some of my probes, and is able to parry them.*

*Are you sure he's not an Ancient?" the Consort asked.

Absolutely.

Spark uncoiled himself from the pillar where he had been leaning, and tossed his long braid back over his shoulder. *Be that as it may, I see no reason not to wipe them out entirely. They have proved themselves dangerous, their weapons are too far advanced, and nothing good can come of leaving them alive.*

It would be a waste, Seeker snapped.

Putting aside your predilections, it's the only sensible thing to do, Spark answered. *While you have been busy — questioning — I have been monitoring what is happening on Athos, and all is not well. I believe they are joining forces with the Athosians, and that means the contagion is spreading.*

You believe, Seeker said.

I have tracked their movements, the ones who are outside the city, Spark said. *Parties have gone into the mountains where we have always had trouble hunting them, and the rest have joined into two bands. They are waiting for the right moment to join the ones in Emege.*

Or they are waiting to attack them, Seeker said. *We have no reason to believe that they are allies.*

*Most humans would ally with their worst enemies against

us,* Seldom Seen said. *I've looked over the readings and I agree with Spark.*

Ridiculous. Seeker framed the words as a thought escaped involuntarily, but the Queen fixed him with a look.

And what, then, do you propose we do?

Cull deep and often, he answered promptly. *Take and question as many of the feral humans as we may, until we find where they have come from. That is the world we should destroy, not Athos.* He paused. *I have seen some glimpses of its location, images of its night skies, but I cannot yet identify it. There is a possibility it is not a world within this galaxy.*

All the more reason to destroy them now, Seldom Seen exclaimed, and Spark turned sharply, his coats flaring.

What proof do you have of that extraordinary statement?

More than you have of an alliance. Seeker framed the image of the sky he had cut from the human's mind, presented it carefully. *I cannot match those patterns, not myself nor through the calculators. I do not say I have exhausted all other options — it could still be some world exceedingly distant from our usual haunts — but I must admit it to be possible."

How could they get here? the Queen asked.

I don't know, Seeker said. *Not through the Rings, certainly, and there's no sign of a starship. It's a puzzle we need to solve.*

It's a puzzle that we can solve without leaving too many of them alive, Spark said. *We cannot allow their technology to spread.*

The Queen tapped her claws on the arm of her chair, frowning slightly. *I agree with Spark,* she said at last. *You may keep your choice of those we Cull, Seeker, but we must destroy this infection before it spreads.*

They can be contained and controlled, Seeker protested. He looked at the Consort, but Guide shook his head.

Spark is right, he said. *The danger's too great.*

It's wasteful — Seeker stopped himself, made an abrupt bow. *As the Queen wishes, then.*

We'll attack tonight, the Queen said. *In case Spark is right and the groups are planning to join forces.* She looked over her shoulder at the Consort. *I want them utterly destroyed.*

The Consort bowed, graceful and deadly. *As the Queen commands.*

CHAPTER SEVENTEEN
Into the City

TEYLA proved to be as good as her word, returning their P90s and offering a couple of the younger Athosians as guides to take them as far as the lake's edge. To Teal'c's surprise, Sheppard accompanied them as well, carrying one of the expedition radios tuned to a tertiary frequency.

"There's no guarantee Sumner won't be monitoring it," he told O'Neill, "but this way we can yell if there's an emergency. At least Teyla and Halling will know what went wrong."

"I'm not really reassured by that, Major," O'Neill said.

"Me, neither, General," Sheppard answered, and they moved off into the forest.

The young Athosians brought them east along the ridge where the caves lay and then down an easier slope where the trees reached almost to the edge of the lake. Teal'c frowned — it seemed an obvious place for Sumner to expect an attempt to cross the lake, particularly as it narrowed here — but then he saw how far they had come around the curve of the lake. They were several miles from the encampment, further if the straight line through the city was blocked by fallen debris.

"As far as we know, nobody from the expedition has reconnoitered this far," Sheppard said. "Or at least none of Colonel Sumner's men have." He looked at the Athosians. "You'll stay here."

"You will need our help, Major," the taller one protested.

"I've got to say I agree with him," O'Neill said. "Three of us just aren't quite enough to take on the expedition's entire Marine contingent."

"Five of us wouldn't be much better, sir," Sheppard said. "If we can't sneak them out, we're not going to be able to break them out."

"Indeed," Teal'c said. He was beginning to believe that Sheppard was more reliable than he had first thought.

O'Neill made a face, but didn't say anything. Sheppard rooted in the underbrush and dragged out a wooden boat. It was Athosian, by the look of it, long and narrow with a flat bottom. Teal'c eyed it warily — he had had unfortunate experiences with small watercraft when he was in Apophis's service — but helped the Tau'ri run it down to the water's edge.

"Timar, you'll wait on the bank across from the rendezvous site. If we're not back, or if we haven't signaled, by the time the sun hits the tops of the trees, get on back to the caves and tell Teyla," Sheppard said. He looked at O'Neill. "If we can't make it back, she knows we'll rendezvous with them in the city."

"Ok," O'Neill said. He squinted across the water. "You're sure Sumner's not looking in this direction?"

"He never has before," Sheppard answered, and shoved the boat into the water.

"I will help paddle, Major Sheppard," Teal'c said firmly, and climbed aboard.

They made it across without mishap, though there was less freeboard than Teal'c would have liked. Sheppard dragged the boat into a space hollowed out between the stub of a wall and an intimidatingly thorny bush, then turned, squinting into the declining sun.

"You see that stubby building, the one that looks like someone poured purple paint down it?"

Teal'c shaded his eyes. "I do."

O'Neill nodded.

"That's our fallback — the general one, I mean. If we get separated, or if there's some other problem, that's where we'll meet. Where we're going is to its right, that lumpy dome like an igloo."

Teal'c frowned at that, but O'Neill nodded again. "That one?" he asked, pointing, and Sheppard nodded back.

Teal'c identified the dome then, and nodded in turn.

"Zelenka should be there," Sheppard said. "He'll know where

your people are."

They picked their way carefully through the ruins as the sun sank toward the Stargate, moving in near-silence through the rubble. There were no birds, Teal'c realized, none of the small animal life that he generally expected in a place that had been abandoned as long as this. Here and there, an insect droned, or hovered for a moment in a shaft of sunlight, but he saw nothing larger. Emege had been empty for a long time, but it seemed nothing dared shelter in its remnants.

They had come perhaps two miles when Sheppard raised his fist, then motioned them into the shelter of a standing wall. Teal'c flattened himself against the shadowed stone, cool against his back, his P90 ready in his hands.

"Major?" O'Neill said, after a moment, and Sheppard dropped back to join them.

"Sorry. False alarm. I thought I saw somebody moving in the cross street up ahead."

"You're sure you didn't?" O'Neill asked.

"As sure as I can be." Sheppard shrugged. "We go underground from here, anyway."

"Underground," Teal'c said.

"Yeah." Sheppard peered around the end of the wall. "There's a network of tunnels under the city, and it's mostly intact. Zelenka says he thinks it was some kind of transit system."

"I knew I should have brought my spelunking gear," O'Neill said.

Sheppard led them across a wide space that seemed to have been some kind of open square. Teal'c surveyed their surroundings as they crossed, but saw no movement, no sign that there was anyone else in the ruins. On the far side, what seemed to be a rubble-choked doorway proved to have a gap just big enough for Teal'c to slip between the piled debris and the remaining wall. He found himself in a circular room, unfurnished and roofless, but with a wooden ladder leading down through the floor. Sheppard rummaged in a wall niche, and pulled out a pair of flashlights, produced a third from his pockets. He handed each of them a flashlight, then swung himself down into the hole. O'Neill eyes him dubiously, but Teal'c merely switched his light on and off again to be sure it worked, and climbed down after him. He thought he heard O'Neill swear, but it was soft enough that he didn't have to notice.

The next short tunnel was punishingly narrow, so that Teal'c had to go sideways, and by the time it widened again, his shoulders were burning from holding himself from touching the walls. Sheppard led them down another hold, scrambling down a slope of rubble, and they emerged into a much larger tube, its walls covered with faded paint in unfamiliar geometric designs. Daniel Jackson would know what they meant, Teal'c thought, but he himself certainly did not.

They followed that tunnel for perhaps half a mile, until it was blocked by more chunks of stone and concrete. Teal'c swung his light to examine the walls and ceiling, but saw no sign that further collapse was likely. Even so, he stepped lightly as Sheppard led them around the obstruction and into a smaller tunnel. This one was lined with battered tiles, streaked here and there with stains that looked as though they had come from flowing water. Where the tiles were intact, they were unexpectedly slippery, and Teal'c was glad when they returned to one of the larger tunnels.

At last a faint light showed ahead, and Teal'c wasn't surprised when Sheppard waved for them to stop.

"Up ahead's the rendezvous point," he said softly. "I'll go first."

Teal'c moved to cover him as he swung himself up the ladder, head cocked for the slightest sound of trouble from above. There was nothing, no voices, no sounds at all, and then Sheppard leaned over the opening, his face grim.

"Come on up. Zelenka's not here."

"Crap." O'Neill re-slung his P90 and climbed up, Teal'c on his heels. They emerged in a room that looked little different from the other ruined buildings — except, Teal'c realized, that there was slightly less dust on the floor. There was also a rag by the mouth of the tunnel, ready to brush away unwanted footprints, and he nodded his approval.

"So where is he?" O'Neill demanded.

"I don't know." Sheppard was pulling stones out of the wall, reaching into a narrow space as though searching for something. He pulled out a piece of white stone marked with "thirty-seven" in what looked like red crayon, and bit his lip. "And he hasn't been here since yesterday."

O'Neill gave the stone a jaundiced glare. "So what does that mean, Major?"

"I don't know." Sheppard looked around the room again, then went to peer out the narrow window. They were closer to the lake again, Teal'c saw, and closer still to Sumner's encampment. "I imagine that with all the trouble last night he hasn't been able to get back here."

"Or maybe he got caught," O'Neill said.

"Or maybe he got taken by the Wraith," Sheppard answered. "If you want to be really negative about it. But probably he didn't and probably he's just gone to ground somewhere else. He's got a lot of hidey holes in the city."

"That doesn't help my people much," O'Neill said. "I take it you know where they're being held?"

Sheppard looked out the window again. "Probably. But I'm not the expert in these tunnels."

"I think it would be in everyone's interest if you took us there, Major Sheppard," Teal'c said.

"Yeah." Sheppard didn't look particularly happy at the idea, but he nodded. "This way."

Sheppard's knowledge of the tunnels proved adequate, though they did have to retrace their steps once after an apparently promising tunnel ended in an abrupt dead end, where water flowed from broken pipes into a hole too wide to jump. Teal'c shone his light into the depths, but could not see the bottom, just the sparkle of the water falling away into the dark.

Sheppard stood silent for a moment, brow furrowed in concentration, then led them back through a series of corridors until they reached the base of another steep slope of rubble. Sheppard gestured for them to turn off their lights, and leaned close.

"Up there are the old cells. That's where I'm guessing Sumner's got your people."

Teal'c nodded and eyed the climb. It wouldn't be that difficult, except for the need for silence. "There is a grave risk of dislodging stones," he said.

Sheppard nodded. "So we go slow and quiet."

"Right," O'Neill muttered. He looked at Teal'c. "Go ahead. I'll cover you both."

Teal'c slung his P90 and studied the approach for a moment, then heaved himself up the unstable rock. A few stones crumbled away beneath his boots, rock slithering on rock, but there were no loud crashes. He paused just below the opening, setting feet and hands more securely, then slowly raised his head until he could see over the edge.

It was a cell block, all right, though the space was dark and the cells were empty and there was no indication that the force fields that should seal the doors were working. An expedition lantern was overturned at the base of the stairs that led presumably toward the surface, but there was no other sign that the area was in use.

Stones shifted beside him, and Sheppard eased himself up. "Crap."

Teal'c ignored him, frowning. Surely there was something wrong with the cell door — surely they should not all have been left sagging open like that. He pulled himself up, put one knee on the edge and hoisted himself out of the hole. Another stone slipped away, and he froze, but there was no movement from the stairs.

He darted across, peered up to see only empty space, cloudy sky and a patch of dirt, and stepped back to examine the cells. The doors had been held by padlocks, but they had been taken off and left in the dirt — no, he thought, they'd been cut, and by some sort of energy beam. He risked putting his flashlight on the lowest setting, and examined the corners of the nearest cell. Dirt and stones, the detritus of centuries, and then a bright flash of color that resolved to the wrapper of an energy bar. It was not positive proof, of course — the expedition had probably also stocked chocolate chip flavored granola bars — but certainly it was a strong indication that Colonel Carter had been here.

He returned to the hole and let himself back down the slope, Sheppard at his heels, but said nothing until they had retreated around the sharp corner that blocked both light and sound.

"They're not there?" O'Neill glared. "Damn it, we have to find where Sumner's got them —"

"I do not think they are prisoners any longer, O'Neill," Teal'c said. "They were there, yes — or at least Colonel Carter was there, and as the other cells were in use, I think we can say that Daniel Jackson was there also. But the locks were cut, by a beam weapon or perhaps some Ancient device, and that surely indicated that it was not Colonel Sumner's men who released them."

"Unless it was the Wraith," O'Neill said.

"The Wraith don't do things quietly," Sheppard said. "That would explain why Teyla didn't hear any more threats from Sumner overnight."

"If it had been the Wraith," Teal'c said, "I believe there would have been more signs of a struggle. I do not believe Colonel Carter would have allowed them to take her without a fight."

"Zelenka must have gotten them out," Sheppard said.

"Then why wasn't he at the rendezvous?" O'Neill demanded.

Sheppard shrugged. "I don't know. Probably they got stuck somewhere when the Wraith attacked. But that means we need to get back there ourselves."

O'Neill looked as though he wanted to object, and Teal'c could hardly blame him. He, too, would rather be doing something active, either searching for their teammates or taking action against Sumner and his men. But Sheppard was right, their first priority was to reconnect with the others, and the most efficient way — the only sure way — of doing that was to wait patiently at the rendezvous point.

"Let us go," he said, and fell into step at Sheppard's back.

O'Neill gave the steep slope a last unhappy look. "I hope to hell you're right, Major."

"So do I," Sheppard said.

Teal'c was right, of course, Jack told himself, but it didn't do much to ease the nagging sense of frustration. They had made it back to the rendezvous point without incident, were sitting now in its shadows, nibbling energy bars and the Athosian equivalent that looked and tasted like pressed and salted dates. They couldn't do anything until Zelenka showed up, and there were good reasons he wouldn't move until dark; the only good thing was that they weren't expected to provide a diversion. Sheppard had passed that message across the river, pinpoint light winking from between the trees, and now all they could do was wait.

That was easier said than done. Jack extended his leg, easing his knee, and looked up through the broken roof. It was late afternoon, the sky hazed with pale cloud, thickening toward the west. Rain toward morning, Sheppard had said, grimacing, and Jack had to admit he didn't like the idea of trying to get a pack of civilians back through the forest in the rain. Assuming that was Teyla's plan: Sheppard had been pretty evasive all along. Jack couldn't entirely blame him for that, but it wasn't helping anything.

Something flickered in the pale sky, a streak like a shadow, so fast it was more motion than object. Jack sat up quickly. Too fast for a bird, even if there were any birds living in the city, and he reached for his P90.

"Sheppard! Did you see that?"

"See what?" Sheppard looked over his shoulder, frowning.

"I saw nothing, O'Neill," Teal'c reported, and Jack settled himself against the cold stone, still frowning at the sky. He had seen something, he was sure of it, but it had been too fast and too high to get any sense of what it might be. Except that if it was real, it was probably Wraith, and he hauled himself to his feet.

"It could have been one of those pointy-nosed fighters — what-do-you-call-them? Darts."

"You can generally hear those coming," Sheppard said, but he bit his lip nervously.

"Not if it was high enough," Jack said.

"They don't usually do that," Sheppard said. "They do their scouting from orbit."

"There," Teal'c said, and pointed. Jack caught the tail of the movement, less even than before.

"I still don't see it," Sheppard said.

"If the Wraith are scouting from altitude, then presumably they are planning another attack," Teal'c said.

"Or they're trying to get a better read on numbers and locations," Jack said, "since things didn't exactly go so well for them last time."

Sheppard was chewing on his lip again. "If there are Wraith around, I need to warn the Athosians — Teyla can sense them, usually, but these guys are a long way up — and maybe Sumner, damn it. If he'll listen."

"He'll listen to me," Jack said, with more confidence than he felt. "Go on, signal your people."

Sheppard slipped out of the ruin, crouching low, and Jack looked at Teal'c. "What do you think? Attack or scouting?"

"I would scout from orbit, O'Neill, as Major Sheppard said. I think an attack is coming."

"Waiting for dark?"

"Perhaps."

"Where the hell is Zelenka?" Jack burst out. "I need to know what's happened to Carter and Daniel — we can't do a damn thing until we know where they are."

"Indeed —" Teal'c broke off as Sheppard ducked back into their shelter.

"Message received across the water. Now the question is, how do we warn Colonel Sumner?"

"How 'bout the radio?" Jack said.

"I don't want him tracking me down," Sheppard answered. "And I don't want to give up this hide." He shook his head. "But, yeah, we have to let him know."

"Surely he has already seen the scouts, as we have done," Teal'c said.

It was tempting, Jack thought, but he couldn't be sure enough. Crazy or not, Sumner was one of theirs, and he had too many people under him to let it slide. "We call up once on the general frequency, tell him that there are Wraith sniffing around — that has the advantage of warning the rest of your people, too, Sheppard — and then we switch the thing off and leave it alone. They can't track us that quickly."

"Yeah, that should work." Sheppard still didn't sound happy, but he reached for the radio and adjusted the frequency. "Ok, that's the main band."

"Thanks." Jack picked up the microphone, considering his message, then keyed the transmitter. "Sumner, this is O'Neill. You're being scouted by Wraith from high altitude. Take precautions."

He released the button, and Sheppard switched off the radio entirely.

"Now we can be sure they can't track us."

You hope, Jack thought, but he knew how the system worked. "What about trying to find Zelenka?"

"He could be anywhere," Sheppard began, and grabbed for his P90 as something made a noise in the tunnel entrance.

"But I am here," a tired voice said, and a little rumpled man in expedition uniform pulled himself out of the space. He was followed by a much taller man with long dreadlocks pulled back in a sort of ponytail—not an expedition member, he wasn't in uniform, but his clothes didn't look Athosian—and then by Carter, looking worn and grim.

"Carter!" Jack stopped. "Daniel?"

"The Wraith took him, sir," Carter answered. "One of their fighters scooped him up last night."

Jack swore under his breath. "Where have they taken him?"

Carter shook her head, and Sheppard said, "Probably to the hive." He saw Carter's questioning look, and said, "There's a hive ship in orbit since sometime last night. It looks like they're planning to wipe out the settlement."

"But if Daniel's on the ship," Carter began. "Sir, if we can get there ourselves, there's a chance we can get him out."

"Are you out of your minds?" That was the big man, shaking his head so that the tail of dreadlocks swung heavily across his shoulders.

"This is Specialist Ronon Dex," Zelenka said. "He's from Sateda. He came through the Stargate with a message for Halling, and Colonel Sumner locked him up as a spy. When I went to release him, I found Colonel Carter and Dr. Jackson as well. We were on our way back here when the Wraith attacked."

Sheppard nodded.

Jack said, "Ok, somebody must have tried to rescue people from a hive ship before."

"It's in orbit," Dex said.

"They—we—don't have anything that will get us to it," Sheppard said.

Zelenka added, "The Wraith kill off any people who develop technology more advanced than, say, what we had on Earth in the early twentieth century. Like—what were their names, the people you were telling me about, Ronon?"

"The Genii." The Satedan looked grim. "They hid what they were doing in underground caves, pretended to be just another agricultural people, but the Wraith found out. Six hives came to their homeworld, razed the villages to the ground, burned out the tunnels, and killed everyone they didn't keep to feed on. They even left the land in ruins." He looked up as though he could see the Wraith ship through the thin haze. "They're probably still feeding on Genii up there."

Jack tried to ignore the chill that ran down his spine. He said, "What if we were able to steal one of those Dart things?"

Teal'c tipped his head to one side. "Indeed."

"As long as it's not keyed to specific Wraith DNA, like the ATA gene," Carter said, "and if we could figure out the controls."

"We'd have to shoot one down," Jack said. "That means repairing damage."

Carter shrugged. "I can try, sir."

"You really think you can just sit down in a Dart and fly it?" Dex asked.

"We've done harder," Jack said.

Teal'c lifted an eyebrow. "I am not entirely sure of that, O'Neill."

"Sure we have." Jack matched him stare for stare.

"Someone is signaling," Zelenka said, from the doorway, and ducked past Sheppard, who frowned nervously.

"I told your friends, I was on a hive ship once," Dex said. "It was huge, as big as a city. You'd never find your friend."

"We have to try," Carter said.

Zelenka slipped in again, spoke quietly to Sheppard. Jack caught only "Athosians" and "moving up" but Sheppard nodded, looking relieved.

"Teyla says she can sense the Wraith, and they are gathering. She's sending her people across the lake now, and we'll try to get as many of our people away as we can."

"What about Sumner?" Carter asked.

Sheppard gave a little shrug. "Let's hope he's being paranoid in the opposite direction."

Jack paced the length of the underground room and back again, unable to sit still. As the shadows lengthened, Sheppard had led them back into the city, joining forces with Teyla and the rest of the Athosians, who had laid out an escape route that would take people back to the lake and across to the shelter of the forest. The lake crossing would be the most dangerous part, and Teyla was concentrating her people there, along with the two other airmen who'd joined the Athosians. A couple of P90s would be a help, Jack thought, but if the Wraith spotted them, it wasn't going to be enough. *They will concentrate on Sumner and his men as the true threat*, Teyla had said, her voice serene, but Jack couldn't say he was all that happy with that idea, either.

"Hey, Carter."

"Sir?"

"If I get you one of those Darts, slightly used — you think you can make it fly again?"

"Absolutely, sir." She tightened the strap of her P90, and nodded at something Zelenka was saying. "Excuse me, sir, I'm heading out —"

"Go ahead, Carter," Jack said.

Carter would never say anything else, but it was still good to hear it, as though saying it would make it true. Shoot down a Dart, repair it, fly it back to the hive… Maybe he didn't want to think too closely about it after all. Maybe he could bring down a Dart without messing it up too badly, skip the repairs.

"Dex."

"Yeah?" The Satedan was fiddling with his wrist bracer, and didn't look up.

"Don't the Wraith have some way of getting down to the planet quickly? Some variation on the Stargate or the transport beams, something like that?"

"No." Dex did look up at that. "Sometimes they bring regiments of drones in the buffer they use for storing the people they Cull, but — no, there's nothing like that."

"Crap." So much for Plan B.

"We've had word from Jinto," Sheppard said quietly, coming

up beside him. "The first group of civilians is on its way out."

"That was quick."

Sheppard shrugged. "We've had a contingency plan in place for a while. McKay and Zelenka designated people to pass the word quickly and quietly and – it works."

"Good." Jack made himself focus on the business at hand. It was getting dark outside, the sun dropping below the tops of the distant trees. Sumner would be tightening up his perimeter, readying himself for the night. "How many people?"

"About thirty all told. They're the ones Sumner's least likely to miss."

"Good," Jack said again. The hard part would be getting the Air Force personnel out, and the support staff in particular, the ones who were handling logistics for the expedition, but they'd cross that bridge when they got there.

Something sounded in the distance, a faint high whine that swelled in an instant to the scream of a Dart. Of more than one Dart, Jack thought, squinting into the sky, and sure enough he could make out four, no, five of them, streaking from the Stargate toward the expedition's camp.

"Crap," Sheppard said, and grabbed for the radio. "Colonel Sumner! You're under attack!" He shifted frequencies. "Teyla, Zelenka, McKay, go to Plan X. I repeat, Plan X."

He didn't wait for answers, but grabbed his P90.

"Plan X?" Jack asked.

"Get as many people out of the city as we can."

Sam heard the shriek of the Darts as she helped an older woman scientist down the steep slope into one of Zelenka's tunnels, saw the sudden fear in her eyes as she looked over her shoulder before starting after the rest of her group. The Darts were answered by the discordant clanging of bells, and she risked a look back toward the center of the camp. The Marines were taking up their positions along the well-planned perimeter, the chain of mutually supporting fire points; some of the civilians were running for the shelter of the mess hall—the only shelter left to them, she guessed—but there seemed to be fewer than she remembered, and she hoped that meant that the rest had escaped to the tunnels below.

The air shimmered and a dozen drones materialized in the broken streets. Sumner's men fired at once, sending the first wave staggering backward, but another dozen appeared, and then another, breaking up the carefully planned defenses. Toward the lake, another party landed, and this one, she thought, had fewer drones and more of the dark-coated warriors.

"Colonel!" Zelenka waved to her from the bottom of the slope.

"That's everyone," she called back, and he nodded sharply. He said something to someone he couldn't see, probably one of the other scientists, and then scrambled up to join her.

"Can you see any sign of McKay?"

Sam shook her head. "Was he coming?"

"He is supposed to be in the next party." Zelenka ducked as a pair of Darts swept overhead, energy weapons blasting the ruins. "Oh, that is not good."

"Will the tunnels hold?" Sam asked.

Zelenka shrugged. "Let us hope so." He broke off abruptly, swearing in Czech. "There."

Sam looked where he was pointing. McKay and a group of scientists were huddled in the door of one of the shattered buildings. None of them seemed to be armed, and even as she watched another half dozen drones appeared on the streets in front of them. She held her breath, hoping they wouldn't notice the cowering humans, but sure enough one of them turned his head sharply, and the others copied him, raising their stunners. Sam took a deep breath and stepped out into the street, switching her P90 to automatic fire. She pulled the trigger, the drones jerking and staggering for a moment before one managed to turn his stunner toward her, and she ducked as blue fire crackled past her head. She was up and firing in an instant, and the drones staggered back again, first one and then the rest collapsing under the weight of fire.

"McKay!"

He waved in answer, and she saw him shove Kusanagi forward. "Go, go!"

Kusanagi darted across the open space, and Zelenka caught her hand, pulling her to shelter. "Down the slope and into the tunnel. There are lights, follow them."

She nodded, mute, but did as she was told, disappearing just as two more scientists stumbled into the shelter. Zelenka dispatched them as well, and reached to grab another stumbling man, hauling him to his feet. A Dart shrieked overhead, energy weapons firing. Sam flattened herself against the stones, flinching at the weight of the blasts, but the Dart soared past without dropping more drones.

"McKay!" she called again. "Come on!"

The last of them came in a rush, Grodin and another man supporting Dr. Campbell, who seemed conscious, but unable to move one leg.

"A stunner caught me," she said, almost in tears. "Leave me, I'll just slow you down."

"Nonsense," Grodin said, and he and the other man lowered her bodily down the slope.

"Well?" McKay demanded, slithering into place beside her, and Sam blinked.

"We're trying to get everyone out and safely to the Athosians," she said. "And I need volunteers to stay with me and cover the route."

"Yes, I know that. Did you bring me a gun?"

"I've got one P90 to spare," Sam said. "Are you sure you can handle it?"

McKay glared at her. "Despite what some people think, I have been trained, and I do know how to use automatic weapons."

"Except for the friendly fire incident," Zelenka said briskly.

"That wasn't friendly fire!" McKay said. "That was a ricochet."

"Great," Sam said, weakly, but handed over the P90.

Grodin looked up at her form the bottom of the slope. "I'd like to stay, too, Colonel Carter."

"I don't have a weapon for you," Sam answered. "I'm sorry, Dr. Grodin."

"Get them out of here, Peter," Zelenka said. "You know the tunnels better than McKay does."

Grodin nodded and turned away.

Sam looked at McKay. "This can't be everyone. Where's the rest of your people?"

"Coming, I hope," McKay answered. He looked over his shoulder as though he expected to see them there. "It was all planned."

"Except for the Wraith attacking," Zelenka said.

"We could hardly plan on that," McKay snapped.

"We'll wait," Sam said firmly, riding over whatever else McKay might have said.

CHAPTER EIGHTEEN
Finders Keepers

TEAL'C crouched in the underbrush beside the lake, watching the Darts wheel and dive over the expedition's camp, energy beams flaring blue against the purpling sky. A part of him wanted fiercely to be back there, with O'Neill or Carter, but he knew that this crossing was the most dangerous part of the escape. The lake was at its narrowest here, with brush and broken walls that came down almost to the water's edge, but even so there was a thirty-yard span of open water, far too visible from above, and utterly vulnerable to a Dart's attack. And the Athosian boat was small and unstable — larger than the one they had crossed in, but still not enough to hold all of the escaping scientists.

He turned his head as Ronon Dex slipped through the brush to kneel at his side. "Halling says the first party's in sight."

"That is good." Halling was the Athosians' other leader, Teal'c remembered, the one who had been reluctant to involve himself until now. Teal'c suspected Teyla had something to do with that; she seemed to have a gift for persuasion.

"Damn it." Dex shook his head unhappily. "They're getting pasted in the city."

"Indeed." Teal'c didn't really want to think about that, about they way they were using Colonel Sumner to cover their retreat. Even if the man had become deranged, it was a bad end.

He turned at the sound of footsteps behind them, to see Halling and the first group of refugees emerging from the ruins. Teal'c lifted his hand in salute, received the same acknowledgement, and turned his attention back to the weaving Darts. He heard splashing as the boat was launched, the soft mumble of warning and advice as the passengers climbed aboard, and then the steady splash of paddles as the boat began to cross.

"It's too light," Dex said, under his breath. "The Wraith will see them."

"Hopefully they will be concentrating on the city," Teal'c said. "The lights there should be deceiving." He glanced over his shoulder, saw the boat halfway across. "They are making good progress."

"Yeah." Dex's hands tightened on his P90, and he relaxed them with an obvious effort. "It's just — the first thing we were taught was never to get bunched up."

Teal'c nodded, accepting the logic of that advice. The Wraith Culling beam would all too easily sweep up any group on the ground; far better to spread out, so that the Wraith could only attack one person at a time, and all the rest could cover them. And yet in this case… "There is no choice," he said, and saw Dex nod.

Jack followed Sheppard around the corner of the building the expedition had been using as its infirmary, stopped dead as Sheppard raised his fist. Jack repeated the gesture, and heard Teyla and the others freeze in place. They'd made a wide circuit around the edge of the fighting, hoping to come in behind the Wraith and Sumner's men, somehow open up an escape for the handful of civilians and Air Force personnel who were still trapped in the mess hall. Jack had thought from the start that it was a long shot, and he hadn't seen anything yet to change his mind. In the distance he could hear the chatter of P90s, see the blue flash of the Wraith weapons, centered on the mess hall area. At least nobody seemed to know they were here, at least not yet…

Sheppard slipped back and waved the rest of the team off to his left, circling further around the camp site. "Wraith overhead," he said softly, and everyone froze as another Dart screamed past.

Another followed, and a third, slowing to release another

of the wide blue-white beams. Drones materialized where it hit, half a dozen of them, plus two of the long-coated leaders. Their plan was obvious: they were behind Sumner's position, had a fighting chance of taking him by surprise.

"Crap," Sheppard said, and Jack nodded.

"Yeah. We'd better take them, Major."

"That will give away our position," Teyla said, cool as ever.

"So we take them out and run," Jack answered.

To his surprise, she smiled. "Very well, then."

The long-coated males were conferring, white heads together, gleaming in the dark, while the drones stood slack, their attention elsewhere.

"Now," Sheppard said, and stepped out of the shadows, P90 blazing. Jack joined him, bracing himself against the recoil, and Teyla opened fire beside him.

"The leaders first!" she called.

Jack had already targeted the long-coat on the left, saw him fling up his arms and stagger forward. He tried to turn, but Jack caught him with a second long burst, and the Wraith went sprawling. The second long-coat fell beside him, but the drones had seen them. They charged, stunners firing, and Jack jumped back behind the nearest wall, ducking as blue fire shot over his head to hang writhing against the stones. He fired back, a long burst that sent the nearest drone tumbling into his neighbor. The other Wraith were down, unmoving, and Teyla raised her hand.

"Quickly, this way!"

Already another Dart was winging back their way. Jack raised his P90, fired at the leading wing. He didn't think he did any damage, but the Dart wheeled away as though any attack was unprecedented. It wasn't going to be easy to take one of them out that way.

"Come on," Sheppard called, and Jack scrambled after him. "What now?"

"Work our way a little further west, and try again."

From the look on his face, Sheppard didn't really think it would work, either, but Jack nodded. They had to try.

The boat had made it back to the city side of the lake, ready for the next load of civilians. Teal'c knelt behind the remnants of a low wall, his eyes still on the fighting in the city. Darts spun through the air over the expedition's camp, and the sound of gunfire was almost constant, punctuated by the snap of the Wraith stun weapons. For a moment, Teal'c allowed himself to wish for a staff weapon, then put the thought aside as purposeless. Things were as they were: there was no point in wishing them otherwise.

"The next group is ready," a woman's voice said — not Teyla's — and a man's voice rode over hers.

"No, I am not going with them. I'll wait here, for the rest of my people."

"Dr. McKay," Halling began, and Teal'c looked over to see McKay shaking his head vigorously.

"No arguments! I'm not going."

"Fine, then," Dex said, and held out his hand to an older man, steadying him into the boat.

"Go, and don't stop," Halling said, and shoved the boat free of the shore. It slid out into the dark water, and the sound of paddles began again.

Movement over the camp caught Teal'c eye, and he looked back in time to see one of the Darts break off from the fighting, wings tipped to vertical as it turned toward the lake. Dex cursed, and raised his P90, then lowered it again.

"Everyone under cover!"

Halling echoed the order, but there was no hiding the boat still struggling toward the opposite bank. The paddlers had given up on trying to be discreet, were pulling with all their strength, throwing up fans of spray. The Dart was still coming, dropping lower, black against the lights and flashes of the fighting behind it. It would have them, Teal'c knew. The

Culling beam couldn't miss them, not at that height, and the boat was too unwieldy to attempt evasive action.

He stood in a single quick movement, tucking his weapon against his chest, and took quick but careful aim. The P90 kicked in his hands, all his shots on target, and beside him Dex rose up shouting, his own weapon blazing. The Dart seemed to stagger, then came on, dropping lower. Teal'c kept firing, saw the tiny canopy shatter. The Dart pitched up, rolled over, and came down hard in the lake a dozen yards beyond the expedition members huddling in the boat. The wave from the crash swamped them, but they were almost across, in water that was barely chest deep. The bulk of the party struggled ashore, the taller ones helping the smaller, and a handful of Athosians broke cover to help them out of the water. Several more plunged into the water and joined the group attempting to refloat the long boat.

"Nice shooting," Dex said.

Teal'c dipped his head. "As was yours."

"We'd better make sure it's dead," Dex said, and waded into the water. Teal'c followed, newly wary, the water creeping cold up his thighs.

The Dart had crashed wing down, and either the wing was broken off under the water, or it had wedged deep into the soft mud of the lakebed. The canopy was shattered, the pilot unmistakably dead, half his head missing, and Teal'c saw Dex draw a sigh of relief.

"Ok, he's not going to be yelling for help."

"Indeed not." Teal'c examined the cockpit, found what he hoped was the canopy release, and pulled it. The frame lifted away, shedding the last fragments of canopy, and both he and Dex ducked away from the shower of sharp shards. "Help me get him out of here."

"You're not seriously going to try to fly this," Dex said, but reached for the body. Together they dragged it out of the cockpit and half onto the shore, heaving it most of the way out of the water.

"If we are to rescue Daniel Jackson, this may be our only chance," Teal'c said, and waded back out to the Dart. He leaned into the cockpit, his heart sinking at the amount of water already filling it, at the controls that looked nothing like Goa'uld or Ancient technology, and Halling called from the shore.

"Teal'c! We need you here."

"I am on my way," he answered, and splashed back to his position. Already another group of scientists had appeared, stumbling out of the ruins, and the Athosians were swapping paddlers for the next trip across. If it could be done, Colonel Carter would do it. He would have to trust in that.

The last of the civilian scientists were into the tunnels along with a handful of airmen; the rest of the Air Force personnel, the ones who'd managed to get away armed, perhaps ten of them, were clustered in the dubious shelter of the building. A few of them had minor cuts and bruises from scrambling through the ruins, but no one had been more seriously hurt. That was one good thing about the Wraith stun weapons, Sam thought. You were either stunned or not, and a stunned person could apparently make a full recovery.

She looked at Sergeant Florian, who seemed to be the ranking person there: a big man, big enough that the P90 looked small against his chest. "What's the situation, Sergeant?"

A rattle of gunfire punctuated her question and she saw Airman Salawi wince. The young woman had managed to grab a tac vest that was too big for her, but she looked ready to go.

"Not good, Colonel," Florian answered. "The Wraith were driving them back onto the mess hall. If they can't break out, they'll be trapped."

Sam peered around the edge of the building, trying to make sense of what she was seeing. If Sumner was in trouble, they ought to go back for him — she couldn't leave him or his men to be eaten by the Wraith, no matter how stupidly they'd behaved.

If they came around from the north, taking cover in the buildings that ran up the side of the broad street where their quarters had been, they could get almost to the mess hall without too much chance of being seen. And, just as important, they'd have a decent chance of getting back underground without being seen.

"All right," she said. "We're going in."

It didn't take long to outline the plan, and she led them along the edge of the ruins, keeping to the deepest shadows. The Wraith's attention was focused on the mess hall, and as they drew closer, she could see that the perimeter was shrinking. Sumner's men were being driven back on the mess hall itself, and there were too many bodies on the ground between the edge of the camp and the buildings. The Wraith were massing, two groups of them assembling in shelter, and there were more of the unmasked warriors among the drones. And she'd brought them out perfectly, in position to take the nearer group under solid fire.

She waved for her men to split, sending one group further along the ruins where they could take cover behind a set of fallen columns. Florian signaled that he was in position, and a moment later Sam saw her people were set as well.

"Now!"

She fired as she spoke, the first blast of her P90 sending a drone staggering. The rest of her unit fired as well, long blasts that knocked the drones back and pinned them until they ceased moving. They got two of the warriors in the first salvo, but the rest got themselves into makeshift cover, and the drones ducked for cover as well. The warriors had to be controlling the drones, Sam thought. That was the only explanation for their behavior.

"Target the ones in the long coats!" she shouted, and the lines of fire converged.

Sumner's men had seen their chance and rose from their positions to counterattack, dropping seven or eight drones. Overhead, a Dart turned and wheeled, and the broad blue beam flashed from its belly, dropping another dozen Wraith, drones and warriors together.

Sam shifted to cover them, felt her magazine empty itself, and slammed a new one home. She had three more; two more for this, she thought, and one to get us out of here. She picked a warrior out of the melee, brought him down with three quick bursts.

"Colonel! Incoming!" Florian pointed to the sky just as another Dart flashed past. More drones materialized, closer to their position and clearly focused on it.

"Crap," Carter said, and waved for her people to retreat. Ok, Sumner, she thought. We did what we could.

Jack lifted his hand at the sound of gunfire from a new point — from the far side of the camp, near where Sumner had put their quarters — and his half of the party froze in place. A moment later, Sheppard slipped into cover beside him.

"Your people?"

"Or some of yours that got away," Jack answered. But he'd bet it was Carter, that was the kind of thing she'd do, come back for Sumner once she'd gotten the civilians out of harm's way…

"It does not matter," Teyla said. "They are the diversion we need."

She was right, and Jack nodded sharply. Only a little further, and they could come in almost on the Wraith's rear, and he lifted his hand, waving his people forward.

"Go!" Teyla said, and they opened fire. Jack aimed for the line of drones that was stalking toward a knot of Marines in bad cover. Two of the Marines were already down, stunned, he hoped, and the stones behind them crawled with blue fire. A Dart screamed overhead, cannons firing, but they were too well sheltered between the standing walls for the blasts to touch them. Another line of drones materialized, and Sheppard yelled something, urging the Athosians to bring them down. The locals might not manufacture the technology themselves,

Jack thought, but they'd certainly learned how to use it fast enough. Though they'd seen that in the Milky Way, too — the Stargates meant that no culture was ever entirely isolated. And a damn good thing, too, at a time like this.

He fired again, emptying his clip, ducked back into shelter to change the magazine. As long as the Wraith weren't willing to spend too many drones, as long as they could be made to give up — He killed that thought. Of course they'd withdraw. Even the Wraith couldn't afford to waste too many of their men. He slammed the fresh magazine into place, popped up again to begin firing. Drone bodies littered the ground, and still they kept coming, another half dozen materializing out of thin air even as he watched. He turned his P90 on them, and saw them stagger and fall. If the Wraith were trying to run them out of ammunition — yeah, that would be really bad. But surely they'd give up — they were taking too many casualties.

"Get the ones in the long coats," Sheppard yelled. "They're the officers, get them."

Most of the Athosians turned their guns on the unmasked Wraith, who scrambled for cover. Jack kept firing at the drones, all too aware that the volume of fire from Sumner's men was dropping drastically. Either they were running out of ammunition or they'd taken too many casualties, but they weren't holding the drones off the way they needed to. Teyla dropped to one knee beside him, wrestling a fresh magazine into place, and turned her fire on the drones as well. Together they brought down another four before one of their officers got them back into shelter.

Gunfire sounded again from the far side of the camp, Carter's people or Sheppard's coming back at the Wraith there. That was good, kept the warriors from finding good cover. Sheppard seemed to see the same thing, waved his people forward. Jack shifted to give them covering fire, and the little group reached the next firing point without taking casualties.

There seemed to be fewer Darts overhead, but the ones that remained pressed their attack fiercely. Two dove at the mess hall, cannons firing bolts of energy. Jack aimed a couple of blasts at the canopies as they swept in, but stopped quickly, not wanting to waste the ammunition. A third Dart came in behind it, lower and slower, the beam emitter glowing in its belly. Teyla shoved him, hard, and they rolled apart just as the beam dropped a trio of drones into their shelter.

"Son of a—" Jack fired a quick burst, taking out the nearest drone with a head shot. At the same moment Teyla fired into their legs, knocking them down, and shifted her aim to finish them off.

The Dart rolled up and over into a turn, came screaming back at them. Jack lifted his P90 almost by reflex, poured a stream of fire into the canopy. The Dart wobbled, steadied, wobbled again, and the blue beam appeared, tumbling bodies into the stones behind them. Then one wing tipped up, and it bored into the ground. Something exploded on contact, knocking Jack to his knees, and he struggled to his feet to see half the newly-landed Wraith scattered on the ground, unconscious or dead.

"John! Behind you!" That was Teyla, her shot blocked.

Jack swung around, fired a short burst at the drone charging Sheppard. One of the Athosians did the same, and Sheppard fired as the drone was falling, leaving it still and definitely dead.

"Thanks." Sheppard's voice wasn't entirely steady.

Jack shrugged. "You get the next one." Along the line of the mess hall, Sumner's men were making progress against the last of the warriors, and Carter's people were moving in from the other side of the camp, ready to finish them off. There were no more Darts, suddenly, the sky empty, and Jack looked toward the crash, the flames already dying to nothing. "Let's make sure there's no one left out here."

"Roger that," Sheppard said, and waved his people into the ruins.

Sam slammed another magazine into her P90, dropping to one knee to catch her breath. It was the next to last, she reminded herself. Time to mop it up or get out of here. Though at the moment…

At the moment, it looked as though they might be mopping up after all. The Darts had vanished after Jack's team had knocked down that one, and the ground between the mess hall and her position was strewn with drone bodies. And the bodies of their commanders, she could count four of them in the long coats, and maybe a fifth in the shadows. Sumner's men had retaken a couple of their forward positions and she heard a last burst of fire from her right.

"Florian?"

"That's the last of them, Colonel," the sergeant answered.

There was a moment of relative silence, and Sam rose slowly to her feet. "Colonel Sumner!"

She could see movement in front of the mess hall, but there was no answer for a long moment.

"Colonel Carter?"

She didn't recognize the voice, but raised her hand anyway, knowing her skin and the movement would show clearly through the dark. "Here."

"Careful, ma'am," Florian said, under his breath.

"Are you clear, ma'am?" the same voice called.

"We're clear on this side," Sam answered, and slowly a figure detached itself from the shadows.

"It's Ford, ma'am. Colonel Sumner's dead. I think I'm senior officer."

"Ok, Lieutenant," Sam said. "We're coming to you."

"Yes, ma'am."

"Florian, stay here," Sam said quickly. "The rest of you, too. Nestor, Saldana, with me."

She picked her way slowly out of shelter, leaving her P90 on its sling against her chest, the airmen following nervously as they picked their way around the Wraith bodies. Ford came to meet them, his face smudged and his uniform smeared with someone's blood, but he seemed otherwise unharmed.

"Colonel Carter? Sumner said you'd gone over to the Athosians."

"General O'Neill wanted the civilians out of harm's way," Sam said. That was the simplest answer. "Then we came back for you. What's your status?"

"Yes, ma'am." Ford took a breath. "We took pretty heavy casualties, but I think most of the civilians here are ok."

Sam nodded. She could see Marine bodies now, withered to mummies, too many of them. The mess hall door swung open, and Marie Wu looked out, peeling latex gloves from her hands. Clean gloves, the Wraith didn't leave a lot of injuries, but there were more bodies behind her, clearly visible in the lantern light. But not withered, Sam saw, with a gasp of relief; they were bonelessly unconscious, but not dead. Behind her, Carson Beckett rose from his knees beside another crumpled shape. This one was withered, and it took a minute before Sam recognized Sergeant Bates.

"Colonel Carter," Beckett said. "It's good to see you."

"And you," Sam answered, repressing the desire to say just how long she'd been waiting to see him.

"Doctor," Ford said. "Should we, you know, harvest?"

"Not right now, Lieutenant," Beckett said, with a guilty glance at Sam. "We've a solid stockpile for the moment."

"But Colonel Sumner said it was important to take them fresh," Ford began, and stopped abruptly, as though he'd just heard what he was saying.

"We're all right for now," Beckett said gently. "Colonel Carter, if I could ask your men to take over the perimeter, I'd like to take a look at the rest of the Marines?"

"Right," Sam answered, and stepped back outside. "Sergeant Florian!"

She gave the necessary orders, then followed the last of the Marines back inside. Sergeant Pollard had gotten his stove working, and a pot of something sweet-smelling was heating on the center burner. Most of the Marines seemed to have cups already, but Sam waved away the offer with a smile. Beckett saw and came to join her.

"Aye, you wouldn't like it. It's heavy glucose, trying to get quick calories back into the men. The enzyme drug takes it out of them, most of them will crash for eight or ten hours if I let them."

"All the locals say that drug is no good," Sam said bluntly.

Beckett nodded. "I don't doubt it. And I'd like a word or three with Charrin, if Teyla will allow it — Charrin's by way of being their medical expert. She may know some other ways to ease the withdrawal. I told Colonel Sumner we had a problem, but he didn't want to listen."

"Can you wean them off it?" Sam asked.

"I can only try." Beckett glanced around the mess hall. "With Sumner dead, and Bates — aye, the rest of them will do as I say."

"That's good." Sam looked around the room, seeing that things were more or less under control. "All right, Doctor, carry on."

Jack picked his way through the ruined buildings, the light from his P90 his only guide. So far, all the Wraith that the last Dart had dropped were dead, or mostly so. He winced at a short burst of fire to his left, but couldn't blame the Athosians for finishing them off. So far, he'd seen no indication that the Wraith were willing to treat humans as anything but a semi-portable food source.

He poked cautiously at another drone, rolled it over to see a jagged hole in its torso. The Wraith were resilient, it seemed, but not that resilient. The wrecked Dart loomed ahead, needle nose crumpled, half buried in the dirt. He trained his P90 on it, letting the light play across the scorched surfaces, and something moved in the shadows.

"Hold it!"

The motion stopped, the shadow resolving to one of the Wraith warriors, sprawled half across the Dart's wing. He slid sideways, half collapse, half purposeful movement, weirdly protective, as though he was putting his body between Jack and — something.

"Move again, and I'll blow your head off," Jack said.

The warrior bared teeth at him, hissing, but did not speak. He didn't move, either, and Jack decided he was going to take that as a hopeful sign. If the Wraith had Daniel, maybe they could trade this guy for him. It was a forlorn hope, he knew, but it was the best option he'd seen so far.

"You better hope you're someone important," he said aloud. "Because otherwise, you're dead."

"General?" That was Sheppard, pounding up behind him, Teyla at his side. She saw the Wraith and made a soft sound of disgust and anger, and the Wraith snarled weakly back at her.

"Kill him, General," she said.

"Now, wait a minute," Jack said. "They've got Daniel, and I want him back. Maybe they'll make a trade."

"The Wraith do not negotiate," Teyla said, her voice flat. "And we cannot keep him prisoner for any length of time. He will starve, and I would not wish that on even a Wraith. Best to kill him now."

Jack looked back at the Wraith. "You heard the lady. Any reason I shouldn't do what she says?"

"The Queen…" The Wraith shook himself, tried again, his rough voice growing stronger. "The Queen will not trade for me. But she will trade for this, if it is not more damaged."

"That Dart?" Jack asked.

The Wraith dipped his head. He looked young, Jack thought, beardless and with fewer of the facial tattoos that he'd seen on the other warriors, and his leather coat was ragged with holes.

"Why?" Sheppard asked.

The Wraith didn't answer, and Jack motioned him away from the Dart. The Wraith bared teeth again, in refusal, Jack thought, and Teyla cocked her P90.

"I have no reason to keep you alive."

"Teyla," Jack said, but she ignored him, her eyes fixed on the Wraith.

"The Young Queen," the Wraith said. He glanced over his shoulder, his face twisted with something that might almost be grief and fear. "She was on board."

The cockpit was empty as far as Jack could see. Sheppard said, "In the Culling buffer?"

"Yes." The Wraith's eyes shone like a cat's as the light hit them. "The Queen will trade for her. For the Dart, intact as it is."

"That's good enough for me," Jack said.

"You cannot do this," Teyla said, fiercely. "You cannot trust them."

"Wait," Sheppard said. "If they'll trade for Dr. Jackson —"

"But they will not," Teyla snapped. "They are Wraith! They do not bargain with their food, any more than you or I would bargain with cattle, or the fish of the river."

"He says they will," Jack pointed out.

"He lies."

"Why would he lie?" Sheppard asked. Teyla opened her mouth to answer, but Sheppard went on before she could speak. "I don't see what he would gain by it."

Teyla took a breath, visibly tamping down her anger. "Very well, I will grant you that point. He gains his life, but only for such a short time as to be of little worth. Injured as he has been, he will need to feed soon. However, he has not said that your Dr. Jackson is still alive."

"Very true." Jack looked at the Wraith. "How 'bout it? Because I'm not interested unless Jackson's alive and well."

"He was when I left the hive," the Wraith answered. "The Queen had taken an interest."

"And if you believe that —" Teyla stopped herself, shaking her head. "This is not a wise course of action, General O'Neill."

"What did you plan to do with him, sir?" Sheppard asked.

"I expect we can find room for him in those cells Sumner was using," Jack answered. "And then he can tell us how to contact his queen."

CHAPTER NINETEEN

Interlude

THE CONSORT stormed into the Dart bay, teeth bared. The Master of the Darts interposed himself, but the Consort slammed him aside.

Where is the luckless fool who has lost the Young Queen?

The straggle of blades just climbed from their Darts gave way before him, ducking heads and making themselves small, but the bravest of them, a tall and willowy blade with a mind edged as a knife, braced himself to answer.

He is dead.

And you live? The Consort seized him by the throat, pinned him against the hangar wall, claws biting through skin and leather.

Not by any particular intent, Knife answered, and his grief was bright and sharp as a scratch in metal. *I do not believe she is dead, she was not among the fallen that we saw —*

But you cannot say she lives. The Consort flung him aside. He hit the hull of a Dart under repair and slid to the floor. Sensibly, he stayed there, a cleverman kneeling nervously beside him, and the Consort turned on his heel. *Darts! I will go after her, I will kill them all, wipe them out completely —* He looked around, teeth bared. *Do you not hear me? Ready a Dart for me.*

The Queen has forbidden it.

Seeker came slowly down the wide aisle between the repair stations, his face impassive. The Consort could feel the cleverman's anger beneath his calm, but snarled nonetheless.

And you would have me leave her there? Trapped the Mothers know where? You're mad to ask it!

If she is not within the buffer, then she is dead, Seeker said. *We must hope she is there, and make plans to recover the Dart intact.*

His mind was cold, hard and brittle as ice, and the Consort wanted nothing more than to shatter that calm. *You would as soon see her dead —*

Seeker moved then, faster than any of the watching blades would have believed possible from a cleverman of his age and stature, his feeding hand fastening on the Consort's chest, his off hand clasping him by the collar. *How dare you?*

The silence stretched between them, terror and fury and love for both mother and daughter roiling between them, carried in the touch of skin, and slowly the Consort looked away. Seeker released him, breathing hard.

It appears her Pallax survived.

Only until I see him. The Consort smiled without humor, and Seeker sighed.

As you will, but let us rescue her first. And that will require the use of the Pallax, I fear.

I can wait.

I'm sure you can. Seeker paused. *The Queen wants you. Now.*

The Consort snarled a final time, but straightened his coat where Seeker had disarranged it. "Very well."

Even the drones, deliberately dulled and insensitive as they were, cowered in the rage that radiated from the queen's chamber. The Consort checked in spite of himself, and Seeker gave a thin smile.

Oh, yes, he said, and nodded for the unhappy blade who supervised the guard to announce them.

The door slid back, as they had known it would, and the Consort lifted his head as he entered. The Queen whirled to face him, her scarlet hair lifting like a banner, feeding hand spread and ready.

How could you allow her to run such a pointless risk?

I did not know she intended to join the battle, the Consort said. *Had I known —*

Had you known, you would have joined her, the Queen

snapped. *Fool and incompetent! You should have known!*

The Young Queen is hard to persuade to any course of action, Seldom Seen pointed out.

That is not helpful, the Queen said. *Be silent, or depart.*

Seldom Seen spread his hands in submission, bowing. Seeker took a breath, but the Consort touched his sleeve. *She is your daughter,* he said, to the Queen. *I am only your consort, when I am that. I am not permitted to give her orders.*

This was an old and tender quarrel, and the Queen snarled aloud. *It is you who taught her such tactics! Your hardheaded folly that has brought us to this.*

And I, as you have often reminded me, am not a queen, to give her orders!

The Consort's teeth were bared, and the Queen turned on him, feeding hand outstretched. *Down!*

There was a moment of utter silence, as though everyone within the zenana held their breath, and then, slowly and not without grace, the Consort knelt, back straight, head up in mute defiance. The Queen caught him by the throat, hand-mouth against his skin, forcing his head up and back. Her claws dented the skin of his cheeks, not quite drawing blood.

The Young Queen is not yet dead. Spark's mental voice cleaved the silence. *And I believe we can still save her.*

The matter hung in the balance for half a heartbeat, and then the Queen released the Consort. She turned slowly, her teeth still showing, and Spark managed a bow that was more graceful then nervous.

If you will permit, of course.

What makes you say she is alive? The Queen's response was mild enough, but Spark was not deceived. He bowed even more deeply.

The blades who returned from the attack say that her Dart was not destroyed. Its pilot attempted to free those held in the buffer before the crash, but was not fully successful. If we can retrieve the Dart, we can save her.

Let me go, the Consort said, still on his knees. *Snow…*

The Queen ignored him. *No one can live forever inside the buffer.*

No, and it also depends on whether or not there is sufficient power to maintain the matrices. Spark spread his hands. *But it's the chance we have.*

We cannot simply take the Dart, she said. *They have proven themselves too strong for that.*

I have not attempted it, the Consort said.

There is another option, Seeker said, before the Queen could speak.

Well?

We have their man, Seeker said. *I believe they will trade for him.*

Bargain with the humans? Seldom Seen asked.

We bargain with humans daily, Seeker said. *Don't deceive yourself.*

I'm impressed with your willingness to sacrifice, Spark murmured.

The Queen glared at him. *Unless you have something constructive to say, you may be silent. Seeker — will they trade?*

As I said, I believe they will. Seeker bowed. *From what I have been able to learn of their culture, loyalty to one another is a primary virtue.*

I still say we can take them, the Consort said.

The Queen took a deep breath, mastering emotion with an effort that made the other shiver. *You, Guide, will determine whether or not we can retrieve the Dart directly. In the meantime — I will speak with this Daniel Jackson.*

Seeker bowed again. *I will fetch him at once.*

CHAPTER TWENTY
Technical Solutions

THE SUN was not quite up as Sam uncoiled herself from the borrowed sleeping bag and made her way out into the mess hall, past the first teams packing up supplies to complete the evacuation of the city. Breakfast was not formally ready yet, but there was an urn of Athosian tea and a platter of something that looked like oatmeal cookies on a side table, and a hurrying airman informed her that she could help herself. She skipped the cookies but drew herself a cup of the tea and stepped out into the open area in front of the hall.

The bodies had been cleared away — presumably not harvested, or at least she hoped Beckett's orders had prevailed — and Jack was sitting on one of the piles of stone that had served as a fire point the night before, staring out at the lake.

"You'd think someone would have tried fishing here already," he said.

Sam shrugged. "Not everyone's an enthusiast, sir?"

"Or a bird-watcher." Jack grinned. "All right, Carter, what have we got?"

Sam squared her shoulders, wishing the tea carried as much kick as a proper cup of coffee. "Major Sheppard and Lieutenant Ford are dealing with the expedition's problems, but it looks as though nine more Marines were killed, plus a couple of airmen."

Jack grimaced.

"On the plus side, Sheppard seems to have taken over command without incident, and Dr. Beckett is ready to start weaning people off the enzyme drug. The plan is to finish withdrawing people and equipment to the Athosian settlement as fast as possible."

"You finally saw Beckett?"

"Yeah. For about five minutes, and then he and Dr. Wu were

trying to get the guys who'd been most affected by the drug to check themselves into the infirmary. Teyla said she'd be in touch this morning about the civilian evacuees, but it looks as though that part of the plan was successful."

"Indeed."

And that was Teal'c, walking up from the lake along with half a dozen Athosians and Teyla, who smiled a greeting, and hurried on toward the mess hall.

"The Wraith concentrated their attack on the encampment," Teal'c went on, stopping with his hands behind his back. "We were able to get everyone across the lake to safety. And we shot down one of the Darts in the process." He gave Sam an almost mischievous look and added, "Though I'm afraid it landed in the water."

"We've got one that's dry," Jack said. "And may contain a Wraith queen."

Teal'c's eyebrows rose. "Indeed."

"Also one live Wraith," Sam said. "Who says the Wraith in orbit will be willing to trade Daniel for him and the queen."

"Before or after she is extracted from the machine?" Teal'c asked.

"Before, I hope," Sam answered. "And, with that in mind, sir — I'd like to take a look at the Dart, see if I can figure out how to contact the hive."

"Go right ahead," Jack answered. "In fact, I'll go with you."

"Yes, sir," Sam said. She refrained from saying she knew perfectly well that he didn't want to be asked to help with the evacuation.

The crashed Dart seemed closer to the camp then it had in the dark. Sam climbed over piles of rubble still marked by the flash fire, stood for a moment examining the long lines of the Wraith fighter. It had gone in almost nose first, she thought, breaking off the long needle only a meter or so short of the cockpit. Nose first and right wing down, she amended; it looked as though the fire had come from that shattered wing — the beam weapon overloading, maybe? — but the stern-mounted engines seemed to be intact.

She walked around it, studying the shape, the materials, trying to get a handle on the Wraith technology. Up close, the surface wasn't smooth, but gently ridged, curves flowing into curves, the tail kicking up like pinfeathers. It didn't look like anything the Goa'uld had, or anything Ancient, for that matter, and she wished again that Daniel was there to interpret. But that was the whole point, to get him back, and she climbed up on the intact left wing to peer into the cockpit.

It was even less familiar than the exterior, even accounting for damage. The pilot's chair was oddly shaped, ridged like a leaf — maybe it was formed to the body of the particular pilot who flew it, she thought, or maybe it reshaped itself to each user. She reached through the broken glass to touch it, grimacing at the weirdly fleshy texture. It wasn't like leather, but like hide over muscle, medium soft and unpleasant. Behind it, a secondary canopy like a spine and ribs covered a device she didn't recognize. The displays were all individually shaped, each piece different from the others, apparently held in place with cords like vines. It was hard to escape the idea that the whole things was somehow organic, an interior grown to fill the sleekly curved metal shell. A few lights flickered weakly, golden characters that she didn't recognize blinking on a side screen, a set of telltales flashing steady yellow, but she'd have to trace the connections to see what they meant.

Not that it would be impossible to do that. She slid back off the wing, and almost collided with Jack. "Oh. Sorry, sir."

"Anything?"

"There's some power," Sam answered. "Which I think is a good thing. And if you give me a few hours, I can probably identify the communications system and figure out how to contact the hive. But before we do that, I'd like to be sure the — what did he call it, the buffer? I'd like to be sure it's still working, and that we actually have this queen alive."

"You want to talk to the Wraith," Jack said.

"Yes, sir." Sam paused. "Actually, I want to bring him here. Along with a laptop."

"You're sure about that?" Jack asked. "The Wraith, I mean, not the laptop."

"Yes, sir. It's the fastest way to get the answers we need."

"Right. I'll see what I can do."

"Thank you, sir," Sam said, and resumed her examination of the Dart's systems.

It was some time before Jack returned, long enough that the sun was high above the ruined city, hot on her back even after she'd shed vest and jacket to work in her tee shirt. She heard footsteps crunching on the stones before Teal'c called her name, and tipped herself upright, squinting into the sun. They'd brought the Wraith, all right, his feeding hand wrapped in a leather sheath beneath the handcuffs, and both Jack and Sheppard had their weapons trained on him, while Teal'c brought up the rear, laptop tucked under one arm. Seen in daylight, the Wraith didn't look any less intimidating, pale green skin, heavy claws, too many sharp teeth that showed as his lips curled in a silent snarl.

"I wouldn't complain too much," Sheppard said. "We could always give you to Teyla."

"Or Specialist Dex," Jack said. He smiled at Sam. "One Wraith, as requested, Colonel."

"Thanks." Sam looked at the Wraith, wishing she could read his expressions. "I want to be sure your — queen, you called her — I want to be sure she's safe before we call your hive."

The Wraith blinked once, but didn't answer.

Sam tried again. "If you help me understand these read-outs, you'll get back to your ship that much faster. Because I can and will figure them out. It's just a matter of how long." The Wraith met her gaze with unnerving calm, the pupils of his eyes contracted to narrow slits in the sunlight. "Look, do you have a name?"

"I've been calling him Will," Sheppard put in, when the Wraith said nothing.

"Will?" Jack asked.

"Yes, sir," Sheppard said. "Doesn't he look like a Will to you?"

"I do not see it," Teal'c said.

The Wraith ignored them all, and Sam frowned. "Come on, either you want to save your queen or you don't."

"And you wish to save your companion," the Wraith said. He took a step closer to the Dart's cockpit. Jack cocked his P90, but the Wraith didn't look back. "Very well."

"What I want to know is whether your queen is still safe," Sam said again.

The Wraith's eyes widened. "The power levels — they are very low."

Sam studied the readouts, and shook her head. "I don't see it."

The Wraith lifted his bound hands, pointing. "There, the left-hand screen, the one in the middle. That is only a third of what it should be, and that is not enough to keep the matrices stable. You must let me divert power to the buffer."

"Not likely," Jack said, and Sam shook her head again.

"Tell me how to do it."

The Wraith bared teeth, but caught himself. "The middle console is the main drive. If you adjust the middle lever to the far right position, that should resolve the problem."

Sam studied the controls. "This one?"

The Wraith nodded.

She reached into the cockpit, slid the lever as far to the right as it would go. The Dart shuddered beneath her, and both Jack and Sheppard raised their weapons. Golden symbols flashed across the main display screen, and she thought the Wraith flinched. "What's wrong?"

"The power is flowing, but — it's not enough. The buffer is failing."

"Can we — retrieve — your queen?" Sam asked.

"Carter, I don't think that's a good idea," Jack said.

"There's not enough power," the Wraith answered. He lifted his hands again, then let them fall. "The Queen will kill you all."

"Wait a minute," Sheppard said, and Jack lifted his P90. "If that's the case, why should we keep you alive?"

"I do not care." The Wraith looked away. "The Queen herself will kill me if you do not."

"Hang on," Sam said. If that console monitored the main power plant, then she thought she could see how the leads ran. She dropped from the Dart's wing and ducked under the tail, reaching up to lever off a half-sprung panel. Yes, that was the main power generation system, she was fairly sure of that, and there were pieces that looked familiar, as though they had been derived from Ancient technology. "Ok, if this is the plant — Will, is this the main input?"

The Wraith gave her an uncomprehending look. "Yes."

"Sheppard, get McKay up here with a naquadah generator." Sam studied the machinery a moment longer, then reached into the cavity and popped loose an internal cover. "Teal'c, can you give me that computer? I think I see how to fix this."

Teal'c handed her the laptop without comment, and Sheppard reached for his radio, not taking his eyes from the Wraith. "McKay!" He relayed the order, and listened for a moment. "He's on his way, Colonel."

"Good." Sam pulled a flashlight from her pocket and examined the network of fleshy cables that disappeared into the depths of the engine. "We may just be able to pull this off."

The warrior and his pack of drones hustled Daniel through the hiveship's corridors, a drone pushing him on every time he tried to slow enough to catch his bearings. He was totally lost, he admitted, unable to match anything he saw to the corridors he'd seen when Seeker brought him from the feeding pens, and he slowed again.

"Hey! Hey, where are we going?"

The warrior ignored him yet again, and the nearest drone

gave him a hard shove that almost knocked him off his feet.

"You know, I'd be more cooperative if you gave me a little information to work with —"

This time, the drone lowered his long weapon, but instead of arming it, he thrust forward, hitting Daniel between the shoulder blades with an end that proved to be painfully pointed.

"Ow." Daniel lifted his hands, picking up his pace. "Ok, I got the message. We're in a hurry."

They turned into a broader corridor, one with high arching ceilings. It looked faintly familiar, Daniel thought. If he hadn't been in this particular passage, he'd been in one very like it. Unfortunately, that didn't help very much.

They stopped at last in front of a set of double doors guarded by drones and a warrior with elaborately-dressed hair. The two warriors exchanged looks — and probably telepathic communication, Daniel thought, though he couldn't grasp it — and the doors slid open. The warrior caught Daniel's shoulder, pushing him on into the room.

It was even more ornate than Seeker's quarters, a long, irregular oval that centered on a throne that seemed to be carved from great fans of bone. There were low benches around the walls, and smaller seats defining areas surrounding tables that held what seemed to be gaming boards, but at the moment all the Wraith were gathered around the throne. He recognized Seeker, standing beside a taller Wraith in a plain leather coat, his hair loose and untidy, a star outlining one eye. A slender Wraith with his hair in a single severe braid stood beside a stockier male who carried some kind of data reader in one hand. In the throne sat the hive's queen. She was paler than most of the males, and unlike the first queen Daniel had seen, her hair flamed scarlet even in the dim light. Unlike the males, her clothes were light and flowing, a long-sleeved gown of a green so pale it was almost white, cut low and tight through the bodice to reveal distinctly mammalian breasts, and she wore a single jewel the color of her hair at the hollow of her throat.

"So you are Daniel Jackson." Her voice was deep and rasping, as though she rarely spoke aloud.

"Yes." Daniel was pleased that his voice didn't waver.

"Daniel Jackson who does not know us — does not know Travelers or the Wraith or any of the ordinary facts of life among our scattered worlds. Daniel Jackson whose people are strangers to us."

"We — my people — are strangers, yes. And we made a terrible mistake coming to Athos," Daniel said. "And, honestly, all we want is to go home again. Surely we can make some kind of bargain."

The Queen rose easily to her feet. She was taller than Daniel had realized, and her skirt was cut shorter in the front, presumably for ease of movement, revealing long and shapely legs. It was disturbingly sexual even if the display wasn't intended for him, and he swallowed hard. "What sort of bargain?"

"Let us go back where we came from, and we will stay there and not bother you ever again. We had no idea what we were going to find when we came here, and I don't think the leaders of my people will want to risk any further encounters with any people as fearsome as yours." It was a mix of truths and half-truths and outright lies, and Daniel did his best to project absolute sincerity. "My people will be glad to have me back —"

"And that," the Queen snapped, "is all that saves you. Your life hangs in the balance, Daniel Jackson, and it is only that my daughter has been taken prisoner that renders you of the slightest worth."

Well done, Jack. Daniel hid his relief. "I'm sure some arrangement can be made —"

Her mental attack slammed him to his knees, her voice cold and angry in his head, freezing his resistance. She was stronger than Seeker had been, and did not bother with subtlety; she reached for images of his home — of Earth, she had the name, and before he could stop her she had an image of the night sky outside Cheyenne Mountain and of the Stargate in its chamber.

No! Daniel gritted his teeth, marshaling everything he had learned from the Ancients and from fighting the Replicators, shoved back hard. She gave way, baring teeth in a snarl, and the pressure abruptly eased. She shook her head hard, the crimson hair flying, and looked at Seeker. He bowed as though in answer to some unspoken thought, and the stocky courtier lifted his head as well. The Queen smiled and looked back at Daniel.

"My clevermen tell me you are not from this galaxy at all. The stars you call home do not exist here, they cannot be seen in those patterns from any known world, or any system that we can identify. And yet you are not of the Ancients."

Crap. Daniel took a careful breath. "We're not Ancients, no."

"And you're not from this galaxy."

Daniel said nothing, and her smile widened.

"You need not bother denying it, I know it to be true. How did you come here, I wonder?"

Too late, Daniel realized her attack had already begun, her thoughts wound with his so that the answer was very nearly surprised from him. He shoved her away, piling clumsy barricades between her and his memories, images of desert and light and flame, anything he could think of that might disconcert her. She retreated, struck again, deft as a fencer, turning his own fires against him so that his nerves were seared with flame. He cried out, flailing, and again she retreated, showing teeth in triumph.

"Through the Stargate!"

"Impossible!" That was the slender Wraith, speaking aloud to be sure he was understood.

"It is the only conclusion that makes sense," Seeker said. "Even if on the face of it, it is impossible."

Daniel pressed his palms to his aching temples. The Queen circled him, her mind brushing his, almost a caress, like fingers brushing his cheek.

"Through the Stargate and from another galaxy."

"We were sent on what might well be a one-way mission,"

Daniel said, his voice tight. More half-truths and lies, he thought, and hoped he could make her believe. "To explore, to see what was here. It is just possible for us to return home — we have one chance to do so. All we want is to return and close the Stargate behind us forever."

The Queen looked at Seeker, who shrugged. The one with the starred face said, "I don't believe him."

"It is not for you to say," the Queen snapped. She stooped, feeding hand flashing out to catch Daniel by the chin. "And they will trade for you."

Her claws were pressed too tightly against his jaw for him to nod. Daniel said, "Yes."

"Bah." She released him abruptly, thumb claw drawing blood. "You had better hope so."

"They will," Daniel said, and hoped Jack really did have someone to trade.

McKay arrived with the naquadah generator just as Sam finished identifying the main power cables. She pushed herself out from under the Dart's fuselage, dragging the laptop with her, and sat up. "Good—"

"I don't see why you want to get a Wraith out of there," McKay said. "And, by the way, how do you know it's only one Wraith? What makes you think there aren't a dozen drones and warriors in there just waiting to feed on us as soon as you press the button?"

Sam looked at him for a long moment. "I've gotten the system monitor up and running. There's only one life-sign in the system."

"Then how do you know it's their queen?"

"I don't," Sam said.

"But we all hope it is, right, Dr. McKay?" Jack strolled over, both hands resting on his P90. "How's it coming, Colonel?"

"Reasonably well," Sam answered. "I've traced the power lines to the buffer circuits and to the — well, let's call it the materializer, for want of a better word. I can see how to hook up the power, and the naquadah generator should be ample."

"So what's the problem?" Jack gave a crooked smile.

"There's a very narrow window of acceptable power," Sam said. "Too little, and the whole process stalls out. Too much, and we blow the system. And it looks to me as though running the materializer is going to set up power fluctuations."

"Let me see that," McKay said. Sam handed him the laptop, and he scowled at the screen. "Ok, no, that's not good."

"I agree, it's not optimum," Sam said. "But it's the best we're going to get. And we're running out of time."

"The power fluctuation is too great," McKay said. He looked up, glaring at the Wraith. "What kind of idiot designed this system, anyway? It's inefficient and it's likely to blow up in your face."

The Wraith snarled. Sam said, "Actually, their power generation system seems to be more sensitive than ours. It's more like a biological feedback loop than the usual power conduit — I wouldn't be entirely surprised if the design wasn't originally taken from a biological model. I've cobbled together a transformer routine that I think will mimic that sensitivity."

McKay touched the laptop's trackpad, scowling even more deeply. "That's not bad, but – let me try something."

"Be my guest." Sam watched his fingers fly across the keyboard, new strings of code appearing as he worked. If he could refine her program – well, it would only help.

"Ok," McKay said at last. "Ok, that might just work. And it won't blow up the generator if it goes wrong."

"Just in case," Sheppard said, "why don't you run some extra-long cords? We can lose the Dart if we have to, but not one of the generators."

"We can do that," Sam said. She climbed back to the cockpit, checking the monitors again. All the lights were steady amber, and she shook her head. "But we need to do it soon."

"Whenever you're ready," Sheppard said, and Jack nodded.

"Do what you have to do, Carter."

She had already traced the cables she could repurpose and borrowed a set of heavy shears from one of the botanists. With Teal'c's help, she worked her way into the Dart's underbelly, found the end that seemed to be plugged into a box she had identified as a sensor unit, and wrestled it free. It came away with a soft pop and a gush of odorless fluid, and she cursed as she wiped it off her face and neck.

"You ok in there, Carter?" Jack called.

"Yeah." The liquid was thick and slimy — alkaline — but it didn't seem to be doing any actual damage. She wiped her face again, and wriggled back down the compartment, dragging the cable free behind her. She pulled out as much as she could get — not quite three meters, which wasn't as much as she'd hoped for, but ought to be enough — and reached for the shears. She was ready for the spurt of liquid this time, and managed to avoid getting it on herself, so that she slid out from under the Dart with a smile of triumph.

"Oh, that is disgusting," McKay exclaimed. "It's dripping!"

Sam examined the cut end of the cable. "Apparently there's a thick alkaline — well, call it a liquid or a gel, it's right between the two — that surrounds the cable core. See if you can splice it onto one of our cables."

"That's like asking me to splice a… a banana into a mainframe," McKay protested. "This isn't a cable, it's a vine."

"If you can't do it, I will," Sam said.

"No! No, no, no, no, I can do it, it's just hardly a physics problem." McKay glared at the offending cable. "These things are more like, I don't know what, some kind of alien monstrosity than an actual device…"

Sam tuned him out, and climbed back up to the cockpit. A new light was blinking on the display, and she looked over her shoulder. "Will! What does this mean?"

Sheppard prodded the Wraith forward. He stretched to see into the cockpit, then recoiled, hissing.

"Well?" Sam put her hands on her hips.

"You are on emergency reserve power," the Wraith said. "There is less than an hour left."

"Crap." Sam slid back off the Dart's wing, ducked around to where McKay was working. "McKay!"

"I heard," McKay answered. "And I really don't think —"

"Just do it," Sam said. "Please."

She turned away without waiting for an answer and began prying off the cover of the materializer. Yes, that was the power input, and it looked as though it was attached with a plug, not hardwired in place. She'd take that, she thought, and began teasing apart the tangle of wires that surrounded a blackened cylinder the size of her little finger. She'd scavenged an apparently identical cylinder from the control servos; the question now was whether she could get it into place before the power ran out.

It took her three tries, but at last she had it in place and seated correctly. "McKay! How's it going with that connection?"

"Well, it's attached." His voice was less peevish than before, and Sam hoped that was a good sign. "And I've got the transformer program running and it looks like it will do the job."

"Right." Sam pulled herself out of the Dart. "Let's run a quick test before we go any further."

"And how do you propose we do that?" McKay demanded. "The only thing that cable connects to is the Dart."

"Got a voltmeter?"

"Of course. Though what good that's going to do —"

"It'll tell us if the current is flowing." Sam held out her hand. "Give."

McKay handed it over without further protest, and Sam walked back to the end of the cable. Attaching the voltmeter was an obvious problem, but she settled for clipping its leads to the edges of the connectors and then took a step back.

"Ok, turn it on!"

McKay waved his hand, and turned to do something with the laptop. There was a blinding flash, blue fire searing Sam's vision, and the voltmeter exploded. The air stank of ozone.

"Turn it off!"

"It's off." McKay came to join her as she bent over the smoking voltmeter. "You know, we don't have a lot of those to spare."

"Sorry." Sam toed it cautiously. "I didn't think it would do that. But we do have power."

"Colonel Carter!" Sheppard called from the other side of the Dart. "Will here is getting kind of antsy."

"What's the problem?" Sam ducked around the back of the Dart.

"There is no more time," the Wraith said. His face was twisted, his teeth bared. "The reserve is failing."

"Crap," Carter said again. "McKay! We're going to have to go for it!"

"No! We're not ready—"

"Get ready!" Carter reached for the cable's end, flicked away the clip from the voltmeter. It showed no signs of scorching, or any other damage, and she fitted it into the input socket. It jammed, and she pulled it back out, swearing. Ok, the configuration was right, three points on the top and two below, but—the bottom two were a hair too close together. She grabbed the multi-tool from her pocket and flipped it to a pair of pliers, pried at the offending tines. One gave, just a little, and she slammed it back into place. This time it went at least partway home, and she waved to McKay. "Start it up!"

"This is very bad idea," he yelled back, but his hands moved on the generator's controls. "Ok, power's on. Transformer's working—"

The smell of ozone rose again, and Sam could see a faint blue haze between the plug and the socket.

"Looks like the power's flowing," McKay called. "All within limits."

Sam scrambled back to the cockpit, dragging herself up onto the wing. The telltales were all brighter gold, and steady rather than flashing, and she looked over her shoulder. "Sheppard!

Teal'c! I'm firing the materializer now."

She pulled the lever before she could change her mind, and a blue beam shot from the belly of the Dart. McKay yelped, his hands busy on the laptop, and there was a small explosion from the rear of the Dart, the cable flapping free. And on the ground, a huddled white-haired shape rolled to its feet, empty hands spread wide.

"Shut it down!" Sam yelled, to McKay, and saw him move to obey.

On the ground, Jack cocked his P90, Teal'c ready at his side. "Don't move," he said. "Or I will blow your head off."

The Wraith froze, her face still contorted in a furious snarl. "How dare you?"

"Let's make it simple," Jack said. "Your queen has one of my people. I want him back. I'm willing to trade you for him."

Sam slid out of the cockpit, grabbing up her own weapon as she came around the Dart's half-buried nose. This was the first female Wraith she'd seen: smaller than the males, and definitely mammalian, dressed like them in black leather coat and high boots, though her coat was shorter and cut to make the most of a slight figure. It had a high collar, framing her pointed chin, and there was a diamond-shaped cutout below the collar, revealing cleavage and the dark spiral of a tattoo across her chest. She was young, Sam thought, a lot younger than she would have expected, and beneath the bravado, Sam thought she was afraid.

The Wraith glared at her. "Tell your blades to let me go,"

"I don't think so," Sam said. "You heard the General."

The young queen tossed her head, her unbound hair flying. "We will feed on you all —"

"Yeah, yeah," Jack said. "But I'd really like to talk to your queen first."

Sam looked over her shoulder. "Will. You want to show us how to contact her?"

The male Wraith bobbed his head. "I will show you."

CHAPTER TWENTY-ONE
Exchange

CARTER worked the Dart controls with somewhat alarming ease — well, maybe 'alarming' wasn't exactly the right word, Jack thought. After all, her ability to pick up the workings of alien machinery had saved their necks more than once already. But that had been Goa'uld technology, or weird Ancient devices, not the disturbingly organic muddle that seemed to be the basis of Wraith science. The *really* alarming thing was seeing the male Wraith that close to her, even with his feeding hand tied up in that leather sheath that the Athosians swore would keep him from using it. Or maybe it was the female Wraith, pacing back and forth under the watchful eyes and guns of Teal'c and Sheppard. She was clearly furious, and clearly in search of any possible advantage, and the best thing they could do was get her back to her queen before she decided to try something stupid. It was a shame they hadn't been able to keep her in the Dart's buffer, but you couldn't worry about technical glitches.

"Hey, Carter! How's it going?"

"Almost there, sir." Her voice was muffled. "I have to re-route a couple of the cables to get power to the communications device, and then it looks like one of the cables I pulled I actually need to make the transmitter work." Carter's head appeared over the edge of the cockpit, followed by the rest of her. "But that's an easy fix." She disappeared around the Dart's stern.

"Whatever you say," Jack muttered. As soon as they got Daniel back — and the male, at least, was convinced that the Wraith queen would be willing to trade — they could go back to trying to figure out what had gone wrong with Janus's ouroboros device, and maybe, just maybe, figure out how to get back to their own timeline. Of course, that meant leaving Sheppard in charge, and in the soup, dealing with the Wraith and the

Athosians. Which was not his problem, Jack told himself, but he wasn't finding himself very convincing.

Carter reappeared, dirt smeared on her forehead, but she was smiling. "The power's all hooked up now, sir, and Will already gave me the frequency. Are you ready to talk to the Wraith queen?"

"Absolutely," Jack said, and climbed onto the wing behind her.

Carter slid into the cockpit, settling herself into the oddly-shaped couch with more ease than he would have expected, then pressed a series of buttons beneath the central screen. It lit, displaying a cascade of golden letters, and Carter looked up at him.

"All set, sir." She hauled herself up onto the edge of the cockpit as he slid down into the couch, squinting at the screen.

"Ok. What does this say, Carter?"

He could hear the shrug in her voice. "I don't really know, sir. I think they're standby messages, and maybe tuning info? But if you press that button all the way to the left, the Dart should call the hiveship."

Jack hesitated for an instant. Pressing buttons because a prisoner told you to was usually a good way to get yourself blown up. But then, Carter would have taken that into account as a matter of course. He reached out and pressed the button.

The letters vanished from the screen, to be replaced by darkness spiked with static. No, there was something moving in the darkness, a shape that resolved itself to another male Wraith, this one with his hair done in dreadlocks. He snarled at the screen and Jack gave him an equally toothy smile in return.

"Hi, there. I want to talk to your queen."

"Human." The Wraith made the word an epithet. "We will destroy you—"

"Whoa, hold on," Jack said. "Let's do a little less destroying here. I've got something—someone—your queen wants, and she's got one of my people. I think we need to talk."

A second Wraith appeared, this one bald, his scalp covered

with tattoos, and the first Wraith backed away, bowing.

"You wish to speak to the Queen?" the second Wraith said.

"That's right. I have someone she's looking for."

There was a long silence, and then the Wraith said, "Wait."

The image in the screen froze, and Jack looked at Carter. "Ok, now what? As long as they're not using this to get a fix on us so they can drop a bomb or something."

Carter glanced up at the sky as though that would tell her something, but she answered seriously enough. "I don't think so. The — Will called her the Young Queen, and I'm getting the impression she might even be the big queen's daughter. She's too important for them to risk."

"You think."

"I wish Daniel were here, too. But — I think she's really young, sir. And if she's the queen's daughter —"

The screen crackled before she could finish, and Jack straightened as a new image swam into focus. It was another Wraith female, scarlet-haired this time, who glared at him from the oval screen.

"Who are you, human, who dares threaten me?"

"My name is Jack O'Neill, General O'Neill, and I wanted to talk to you because I think I have something you want. Or someone — a couple of someones, maybe."

"Prove it to me," the Wraith queen said.

Jack hesitated — he really didn't like the idea of being in the same cockpit as the younger queen, and he didn't like the idea of letting her in it by herself any better — and Carter said, "Here."

She tossed him an egg-shaped object about the size of Teal'c's fist. "Point it at the screen and press the big button on the narrow end. It's like a camcorder, McKay took pictures of Will and the young queen."

"Ok." Jack fumbled with it for a moment, then found the button. "Here you go," he said, and pressed it. The images spilled down the screen, moving like the letters from top to bottom: the young queen snarling at the camera, Will looking miserable. The pictures faded, and the queen snarled at him from the screen.

"So you have her and her worthless blade. Harm her, and I will shred the life from your man whom I hold here."

"About that," Jack said. "I want to see Daniel."

"He is here."

"Before we go any further," Jack began, and abruptly Daniel's face appeared. He looked mostly unhurt — certainly unwithered, though there was a trail of blood along the edge of his jaw — and Jack allowed himself a small sigh of pure relief. "Daniel?"

"I'm ok, Jack." Daniel adjusted his glasses, and someone pulled him away.

The queen took his place, her voice like ice. "As you see, I also have someone you might want."

"Then let's make a deal." Jack spread his hands. "I give you your young queen and this guy, her blade, and you give me Dr. Jackson. And then you go your way, and we go ours."

The queen showed teeth. "I will gladly make the exchange, human, but after that – I make no promises."

"No deal." Jack wanted to cross his fingers, but didn't dare risk a betraying gesture. He let his voice soften just a little. "Look, we're explorers, we just came to see what's here, and we really don't like what we've found. All we want is to go back where we came from and never have to deal with you people again."

This time, Jack was fairly sure the queen's expression was a smile. "You can hardly expect us to allow that. Too many of my people have been killed, we cannot allow you to run free." She paused. "Show us your world, and we will agree to quarantine it. We will not Cull, but we will not allow you to leave it, either."

"I can't do that," Jack said. "Ok, how about this? We make our trade, Dr. Jackson for your people, and then — you give us a grace period. Take your ship out of orbit, go into hyperspace and go somewhere else for — a month. We'll be gone by then, and we won't trouble you anymore."

The queen considered him. "Three days."

"What?"

"You can have three days' grace. I will take my hive elsewhere for seventy-five of your hours, and then I will return. Anyone who remains is fair game, and, make no mistake, we will track down your homeworld, too."

"Three days isn't nearly enough time," Jack said. "Ten days."

"Five." The queen cocked her head. "I will trade you Daniel Jackson and five days' grace for the Young Queen and her blade."

Jack nodded slowly. "It's a deal. We'll meet you in the field by the Stargate in two hours."

"At sundown."

Jack nodded again. "Sundown it is." He reached out and pressed the button again, and to his relief the picture vanished.

"Daniel's all right," Carter said. There was a world of relief in her voice, and Jack reached up to pat her knee.

"Yeah." He hauled himself up out of the uncomfortable pilot's couch. "Come on, Carter, you didn't really think he wouldn't be?"

"I think we were all worried, sir."

"Not me," Jack lied. "Sheppard! I've made a deal with the Wraith queen."

It took some persuasion to get the young queen and the male Wraith safely into separate boats — evidently the Wraith did not travel by water, Teal'c thought — but at last they were settled and a mixed team of Marines and Athosians began paddling across the lake. Neither Teyla nor Halling had been particularly happy about the details of O'Neill's bargain with the Wraith, but both O'Neill and Sheppard had made a solid argument that the Wraith were most concerned with the Atlantis expedition. If they were gone, disappeared through the Stargate to some other world, and the Athosians scattered to the hills as they always did when the Wraith came to Cull, there was a good chance that the Wraith would be more interested in chasing the expedition than in destroying Athos. And we, too, can escape through the Stargate if we must, Teyla had pointed out, though Teal'c didn't think Halling found the idea particularly attractive. But at least it had broken the stalemate, and was going to free Daniel Jackson.

They made their way slowly through the woods, each Wraith the target of at least four weapons at all times, and emerged at last into the grassy field surrounding the gate. The sun had dropped below the tops of the trees, and lay molten on the horizon. The air smelled of sun-warmed resin, and the grasses rippled in the gentle breeze. Teal'c lifted his head, scanning the cloudless sky for any sign of incoming Darts, and O'Neill lifted his hand.

"We'll just wait right here."

'Here' was a few meters into the field, where the trees behind them would make it hard for a Dart to use its Culling beam, or to approach unseen. Teal'c nodded his approval and Sheppard said, "Ford, take a couple of men and set up a perimeter. Make sure we've got a chance to take down any Darts that don't play by the rules."

"Yes, sir," Ford answered, and waved men into position.

He and the surviving Marines seemed to be adjusting well to Sheppard's resumption of command, Teal'c thought. Admittedly, the ones who were most loyal to Sumner's regime had also been the ones to take more of the enzyme drug, and were currently under medical care, but he thought that most of them had begun to have doubts about Sumner's fitness by the end.

The air was split by the thin shriek of an incoming Dart, and Teal'c lifted his P90.

"Hold your fire!" Sheppard yelled, and the Dart swept past a hundred feet above the treetops. It flung itself into a sharp turn, flashed back over the field, and disappeared into the sunset. Behind it, the air glowed and the Wraith appeared.

There were more than a dozen of them, several warriors

controlling half a dozen drones, plus the Queen, scarlet hair flaming over a suit of black leather, and a trio of warriors who seemed to be her personal escort. A fourth warrior stood beside Daniel Jackson, feeding hand to his chest.

O'Neill rose to his feet, P90 slung but ready, and adjusted the brim of his cap. "Hi there! Glad you could make it."

"O'Neill." The queen rolled the word on her tongue as though she were examining its taste. "As you see, I have kept my part of our agreement."

"And so have I." O'Neill waved behind him, and Teal'c prodded the young queen to her feet. At his side, Carter did the same with Will, and together they marched the two Wraith forward, the young queen snarling aloud.

The older queen bared teeth herself at the sight. "Release them, and I will release Daniel Jackson."

"Why don't we do it the other way round?" O'Neill asked. "Send Daniel across, and I'll let your people go."

To Teal'c's surprise, the queen laughed. "We could play that game all night. Look, there is distance between us. I will set your man walking, and you send my kin, and when each reaches their own, we will both retire."

"All right," O'Neill said. "Teal'c, Carter. Be ready." He looked back at the Wraith queen. "I'll count to three. On three they all start walking."

The queen inclined her head. "Agreed."

O'Neill held up one finger. "One. Two. Three."

Teal'c leveled his P90. "Begin walking."

The young queen snarled again, but did as she was told, the warrior trailing half a step behind. Across the field, the warrior gave Daniel a push, and he stumbled away into the grass. Teal'c heard the others cock their P90s, ready for whatever betrayal was to come, but Daniel and the released Wraith kept walking, silhouetted against the ring of the Stargate and the sun almost set behind it. Daniel passed the Wraith, ten yards between them, and Teal'c shifted position to keep the rest of the Wraith in his line of fire.

And then Daniel had passed the outermost of Sheppard's men, crouched motionless and hidden in the long grass, and O'Neill reached out to drag him in. A Dart screamed in the distance, and the Marines rose from their hiding places, P90s ready.

"Hold your fire," O'Neill shouted, and Sheppard echoed him.

The Dart flashed past, Culling beam shooting out only after it was well clear of the expedition. The Wraith on the ground disappeared, and a moment later the Dart had dwindled to a single bright point against the fading sky. Then that, too, was gone, and Teal'c allowed himself to relax at last.

"Daniel Jackson! Are you unharmed?"

"Fine, yeah." Daniel gave him an only slightly shaky smile.

"Well, obviously he wasn't all that appetizing," O'Neill said, and Carter laid a hand on Daniel's shoulder.

"Good to see you back."

"Thanks." Daniel looked at O'Neill. "The problem is, the Wraith do keep humans as — well, some of them seem to be sort of like pets."

"Wraith worshippers," Sheppard said. "That's what the Athosians call them — the Satedans, too. Needless to say, nobody much likes them."

"I'm glad nobody decided to keep you as a pet," O'Neill said, but the relief in his voice belied the sarcasm. "Let's get back to the city and make sure the Wraith have kept their word."

It was fully dark by the time they reached the other side of the lake, and a bonfire was burning in front of the mess hall, while various members of the expedition stood around it holding things on sticks over the flames. Jack frowned.

"Seems like it's a bit premature to end the evacuation, Major. We don't know that the Queen kept her word."

"Yeah." Sheppard lengthened his stride, and stopped abruptly as McKay came around the fire.

"Oh, there you are. The Wraith ship left orbit half an hour ago. It looks as though it jumped to hyperspace."

Sheppard relaxed visibly, and Jack couldn't help smiling just a little bit.

"You're sure?" he asked, and McKay bridled.

"Of course I'm sure! And anyway Dr. Anderson confirmed it from the other camp."

"Good enough for me," Jack said, and left him sputtering.

It was warm in the mess hall, plenty of lamps burning on the long tables, and the atmosphere was more relaxed than it had been since they'd arrived. Not that they'd solved their biggest problem, Jack thought, but at this point they were probably entitled to celebrate anything that wasn't a disaster. He accepted a cup of coffee from Dr. Kusanagi, glanced over his shoulder to be sure that the others were still there, still safe. It wasn't rational, he knew, but it was still good to see them there, Daniel and Teal'c talking about something by the food line, Carter arguing with McKay by the door.

"This is an unprecedented achievement." That was Teyla, appearing at his elbow so silently that she might as well have been beamed down from a Dart herself. "It is well to celebrate."

"But it's only temporary," Jack said. Perversely, he felt compelled to point out the problems now that she'd praised them.

"Yes. But that is more than anyone has gained from the Wraith in living memory."

"What will you — the Athosians — do?" Jack asked.

"It is not entirely decided. There are still many details to discuss. But — some of us will leave this world. It is a reasonable time for trading, in any case, and there will be many who will simply stay away that much longer, until they are sure it is safe to return. Others will go early to our winter grounds. We live more scattered there, and it will be harder for the Wraith to find us." She shrugged. "Of course, we will not have our full stores, and I fear it will be a lean season before we can move back to the gate fields again. If some of your people were willing to accompany us and share the labor, it might be easier."

"I expect Major Sheppard will want to keep the expedition

together," Jack said.

"And I am sure you will advise him to do so."

"If he asks. Yes."

Teyla smiled. "And then there are other worlds where we can live much as we do here. This would not be the first time that our people have left Athos for a generation, and come home again when the worst threat has passed."

It was hard to imagine living like that, Jack thought. On the one hand, the ever-present threat of the Wraith, monsters out of your worst nightmare who were capable of wiping out entire populations literally overnight. On the other, the Stargate, escape to other worlds — not worlds where the Wraith didn't come, there didn't seem to be any of those from what the Athosians said, but at least ones where the threat was less. "What are you going to do?"

"I do not yet know. It depends a great deal on what others do — Charrin, Halling, even the expedition." Her face changed, became abruptly serious. "But there is one thing that you must understand, General O'Neill. You — the expedition — must keep your promise. In five days, there must be no sign of any of you on Athos."

Jack felt a chill run down his spine. In five days, yeah, they could get people into shelter, find an alpha site and set up camp there. The SGC knew how to do that, and he was confident Sheppard could manage it. But five days wasn't nearly enough time to figure out how to use the ouroboros device to get them back to their proper timeline. That was asking too much even of Carter.

Teyla hurried on, as though she was trying to convince him. "There are many worlds where your people could live unnoticed. Or there are others, like Sateda, that would welcome them, and would be very glad to trade anything they had for the secrets of your rapid-fire weapons."

"The problem is that we — my team, not Major Sheppard's people — may need to stay in the city a little longer," Jack said.

"We're not from this timeline. We came here by mistake, and our first goal has to be to get back to our proper time."

"And can you not do that elsewhere?" Teyla tipped her head to one side.

"An Ancient device brought us here," Jack said bluntly. "We're going to need access to Ancient technology to get home. More than that — it looks as though there's a version of the device, or maybe a terminal, here in the city."

"I see." Teyla's face was grave.

"Problem?" Sheppard turned toward them, Daniel trailing in his wake.

"We were discussing what to do about getting us home," Jack said. He looked back at Teyla. "Look, I'm perfectly willing to go away for a while, either up into the hills where we can help out with your people, or to the alpha site with Major Sheppard, but we're going to need to come back here as soon as the Wraith are gone."

"But they will not just go away," Teyla said. "They will come and go and come again, not on any schedule, but as it strikes them. And if they find anyone in the city, then they will turn their full fury on this world, and destroy anyone who has chosen to stay. I am sorry, General O'Neill, but you are not worth that risk."

"Hang on," Sheppard said. "I don't quite see the problem."

"There's a version of the device that brought us here in the city," Jack said. "I'm not sure we can figure it out in five days."

"Ok." Sheppard nodded. "So you come on to the alpha site with us, and then come back when the Wraith are gone."

"But the Wraith will not be gone," Teyla said. "Not for a generation. You have already seen how persistent they can be, and this is nothing compared to what they will do if you break your word."

"All right," Sheppard said. "Obviously, we're not going to camp in the city, or anywhere too close to it, and we'll do everything we can to pass as ordinary Athosians. Will that make a difference?"

"Not enough of one," Teyla said. "And I am not prepared — we cannot afford — to run that great a risk for you, Major Sheppard."

She stalked away without waiting for an answer. Jack said, "Sorry about that, Major."

Sheppard bit his lip. "It was coming. We were going to have to have it out sometime, better now than later, I guess. You're sure this is the only place you're going to find one of these devices?"

"It's the only one we know of," Jack said. "Except for one in the Milky Way, and that's not exactly helpful under the circumstances."

"No, not so much." Sheppard rubbed his chin. "Maybe I can talk her into some kind of compromise."

"The trouble is, she's right," Daniel said. "Sorry, Jack. The Wraith — my impression is that the Wraith are just about willing to write us off as too much trouble to kill, but only as long as we disappear back to where we came from. And that's only because the Queen has overruled at least one of her advisors. If we keep working in Emege's ruins, eventually they're going to catch us at it, and then — well, from their perspective, they're going to have to do something about us."

"So what do you suggest instead, that we just give up?" Jack glared at Daniel, who returned the glare with interest.

"No, of course not. I'm thinking we do one of two things — better still, both of them. First, see if Sam can't figure out how to make the thing work in the five days we have left —"

"I'll loan you all the personnel I can, within reason," Sheppard said.

"Thanks," Jack muttered.

Daniel went on as though neither man had spoken. "And, second, see if we can't find the location of another device that we can gate to, and then try to get back home from there." He paused. "Of course, the problem with that is that Janus's devices are more likely to be in what used to be Ancient cities, which

I gather are taboo throughout Pegasus? Because the Wraith don't want anybody figuring out how to use any Ancient technology that might survive."

"Why wouldn't the lab be off on another world, like P6T-847?" Jack asked.

"Because that's a lab Janus built after the Ancients had returned from Pegasus," Daniel answered. "When he was in Pegasus, it looks as though he had the support of his fellow Ancients."

"So it was before he became a fruitcake," Jack said.

"He didn't —" Daniel stopped. "Yeah, pretty much. At least that's what it looks like." He paused again. "Also, to go back to what I was saying before, it looked to me as though the Wraith in this hive had spent some time exploring Emege themselves. At least one of their scientists was interested in and collected Ancient artifacts." He reached into his pocket. "One of which I helped myself to."

He produced a thin piece of lavender crystal, flatter than a lot of the ones Jack had seen before, but marked with the same familiar patterns. Daniel held it out and Jack took it, looked warily from the incised surface to Daniel. "Ok…"

"There," Daniel said, and pointed.

Jack turned the crystal to the light, and finally saw the snake gnawing on its own tail that was carved into the surface of the stone. "Oh. That's — interesting."

"Isn't it? I figured Sam would want to look at it."

Assuming he survived, assuming he escaped the Wraith ship. But that was Daniel for you, the perpetual optimist. Jack nodded. "Hey, Carter!"

She detached herself from a knot of scientists and came to join them. "Sir?"

"Daniel brought you a present," Jack said, and held it out.

Carter took it, her eyebrows rising almost comically. "Oh, wow. That's — that actually might be really useful. It looks a lot like the crystals in the device back on P6T-847."

"I thought it might help," Daniel said, with a grin.

"Any chance you could get that thing up and running in five days, Carter?" Jack said.

"I don't know. Remember, I haven't even seen it yet. Just Daniel's pictures. But — maybe? I can try."

"You can have whatever help we can give you, Colonel," Sheppard said. "The spare naquadah generator, Dr. McKay…"

"I'll stick with the generator, thanks, Major," Carter answered, and Daniel didn't bother to hide his grin.

"Right, then," Jack said. "You've got five days, Carter. And then things get a whole lot more complicated."

CHAPTER TWENTY-TWO

Interlude

THE QUEEN was still coldly furious, driving hive and men with equal rigor. The Young Queen was in disgrace, and had the sense to keep herself out of sight, huddling in her quarters with her Pallax and the young cleverman who was her half-brother. A rumor swept the hive that she would not be allowed to form her own hive, that her ship would be frozen or abandoned or given to another, and was just as quickly quashed by the Hivemaster. Spark retreated to his labyrinth of workshops in the stern of the ship, and the Consort sought refuge in Seeker's quarters and their endless game of towers.

I still think we should wipe them out, the Consort grumbled, and moved a stone to claim a cascade of forfeits.

And how would we do that? Seeker shifted a stone of his own, creating a block. The Consort frowned, moved another, won a second move, and shifted a scarlet round. Seeker smiled, played gray to block again. *We don't know how they came here — yes, they said they came by the Stargate, but as far as we know, that's impossible, too.*

And yet the Queen is sure he was telling the truth, the Consort answered. He checked his reserve, deployed three steel-blue cubes, and Seeker tilted his head to one side, considering. He moved more gray, then added a single magenta runner.

Which is another reason it would have been worth keeping one of them alive. Preferably Daniel Jackson, he was the most knowledgable.

The Consort refrained from rolling his eyes at that, and moved green. *Which we could not, under the circumstances.*

No. Seeker's tone was chastened, and he gave the Consort a look of apology. *No more could we.*

They're dangerous, the Consort said. *We can't afford to

leave them loose out there.*

I don't believe they can go home, Seeker said, slowly. *I do think Daniel Jackson was telling the truth when he said that they were sent on a possibly one-way mission, and I think that something has indeed gone wrong. They are trapped here, and we can hunt them down at our leisure.*

At our leisure? The Consort glared. *And how many of us will they kill in the process?*

More than any of us would like, I fear. But they cannot make those weapons they carry, and I doubt they can teach any of the other kine how to make them. We've not allowed anyone to advance far enough to make that jump. No, we're safe enough, in the long run. Seeker moved another gray sphere. *Forfeit, I believe.*

The Consort bared teeth in a silent snarl. *Double or nothing.*

If you're certain.

The Consort reached for the dice, slid half the set across the table, then tossed his own. Seeker smiled and threw, the antique bone cubes rattling across the stone. *Your luck is in,* he said.

The Consort smiled. The dice had fallen fairly well; he still lost men and position, but not as much as he might have. *Another round?*

Seeker was still collecting his winnings. *Why not?*

Before the Consort could respond, the communications globe in the center of the room chimed twice, and one of Seeker's assistants spoke from its depths. "Your pardon, Lord, but the zenana is summoned."

The Consort flinched in spite of himself and Seeker gave him a speaking look. "Very well," he said aloud, and returned the dice to their box. *Shall we?*

If we must.

The Queen seemed less angry than before, though there was still a sharp edge to her thoughts. Spark was there before them, sitting at her feet, a position that would have made the Consort snarl had the cleverman not been fiddling with some mechanical device. Seeker bowed, punctiliously correct as always, and the Queen raised a hand in a greeting that encompassed Seldom Seen as well, entering behind them.

My Queen, he said. *We are holding course as you directed.*

She nodded. *The question now is our next move. We gave them five days' grace, and after that…*

We must return, Spark said, without looking up from his device.

And we will not find the feral humans there, Seeker said.

We could seek out the Athosians, the Consort said, *find where the others have gone.*

A waste of time, Seeker answered. *Whatever the ferals tell them, it will be in their interest to do something else."

I don't think they're going to leave, Seldom Seen said. The others turned to look at him where he leaned on the back of one of the couches, and he shrugged. *There must be something there that they want, in the ruins of Emege, or they would have escaped through the Stargate after our first attacks.*

There's nothing there, the Consort said, but he looked at Seeker, and his tone was less certain than his words.

Or is there? Spark asked. *Seeker has an unhealthy interest in Ancient matters, after all…*

The Queen looked at Seeker, who bowed.

My interest in Ancient matters, as Spark puts it, has served us well in the past. But no matter. No, there is nothing extraordinary left in Emege that I know of. It is ruins and rubble, nothing more.

And yet the ferals remained, when all sense would have told them to go elsewhere, Seldom Seen said.

Seeker nodded. *It's logical, but I don't know what it would be.*

The question that arises, the Queen said, *is whether or not to wake my sisters. Is this threat enough? I am in two minds myself, and value your advice.*

I think they're deadly dangerous. It was Seldom Seen who

spoke first, to everyone's surprise. *And—I cannot believe I'm saying this—but, yes, I think you should wake the sleeping queens and track these ferals to their homeworld before they destroy us.*

The kine will not support us all if more hives are awakened, Seeker said.

And the hive that wakes the rest for less than good cause must sleep an extra cycle, the Queen said. *I am well aware of the agreements made among my sisters!*

I agree with the Hivemaster, Spark said. *We cannot afford to let them spread their technology any further.*

They cannot, Seeker said. *There aren't any other human worlds that can duplicate what they have, we've seen to that. They are too few to recreate their devices themselves, nor have they brought with them the tools to do so—I am sure of that from my conversations with Daniel Jackson. At worst, they will return to wherever it is they came from and not trouble us further. At best, they are trapped here, and we can eliminate them at our leisure.*

The Queen looked at her Consort. *And you?*

He was silent for a long moment. *I agree with Seeker.*

Well, of course you would, Spark snapped.

The Consort ignored him, his attention on the Queen. *And I also think it is too great a risk to wake the sleeping queens for something as yet unproven. That is a step that can be taken later, if it must be.*

The Queen reclined in her throne, considering the question. *We will wait,* she said at last. *In five days, Hivemaster, I would be in orbit over Athos. If they are gone, well and good. If not—we will decide whether to wake our sisters and exterminate them utterly.*

CHAPTER TWENTY-THREE
Janus's Device

SAM SAT back on her heels, studying the open pedestal of the ouroboros device. The interior had been well and truly shock-proofed — when the Wraith attacked the city or because the Wraith were going to attack the city? — and the remaining crystals were all intact. The problem was that about a third of the slots were still empty, and she had no idea where she was going to find suitable spares.

She'd already opened all the support consoles, and pulled out every crystal she thought might fit and that probably wasn't needed to power the system. It had been a good start, and she'd even managed to fill the biggest gaps, but now she was back to having to choose between taking crystals from the support consoles, and almost certainly compromising overall function, or cannibalizing crystals from the power plant McKay had discovered. And the latter had never been designed to work with this system.

The light shifted, and she looked up to see Daniel lowering himself down the ladder from the surface, an Athosian basket slung over one shoulder. She pushed herself to her feet and came out from behind the diamond barrier.

"You can't have found that many crystals," she said, and he shook his head.

"No. The rest of it's lunch."

She was hungry, she realized, and glanced at her watch to see that it was already past two. "Time flies."

"Yeah." Daniel set the basket on an intact console, lifted out a well-wrapped package — more crystals — and then a thermos and sandwiches. Sam reached for the crystals, but Daniel lifted a finger. "You might want to eat first."

Sam stopped. "Yeah, probably." She picked up the closest sandwich, peanut butter on heavy, yeasty Athosian bread, and took a cautious bite. It was good, better than she'd expected, and she poked at the wrapped package again. "Any luck?"

"Maybe?" Daniel took a swig of the lemon-scented tea. "I pulled everything that looked likely — Zelenka helped, before McKay pulled him off for something else. God knows what."

"They have a lot to do, too," Sam said. "I did figure out what that crystal you found was for. It's the key to the central console, the one that all the others connect through. Except there was already one in the pedestal."

"That's interesting," Daniel said. "That suggests that there is another chamber like this one somewhere out there."

Sam nodded. "And right now I'm just glad to have a spare. I'm pretty sure that as long as we have it, the thing's going to fire."

"Yeah, but will it work?" Daniel paused. "I wonder if Seeker knew what the crystal was — if that's why he took it."

"Do the Wraith know anything about Ancient technology?"

"I don't know," Daniel said. "That wasn't one of the things I thought to ask them."

"Yeah, I suppose not." Sam shook her head. "Anyway, it doesn't really matter. The main thing is to get this working."

"We've got three days left," Daniel answered.

"Counting today," Sam said. "I know." She stuffed the last of the sandwich into her mouth and began unwrapping the bubble wrap.

"What can I do to help?"

Sam glanced back at the open pedestal. If she couldn't find enough crystals, she was going to have to bypass the empty slots or somehow force the system to use crystals that didn't quite fit the parameters. She'd done both before, on other worlds, and it never quite worked the way she'd hoped. And she wasn't exactly eager to try it on one of Janus's devices. "Could you sort the crystals I've pulled? I need two things. First, if you find any like this one, those are the ones I really need. The color doesn't matter, it's the shape and the connector."

She held out a long slender blade, like a knife or a flattened quartz point, and Daniel took it, examining it carefully. "All right."

"And while you're looking for those, I need them sorted by size and approximate shape."

"Ok," Daniel said again. She realized she must have given him a doubtful look because he smiled. "Sam, I may not know what all of them are, but I can sort artifacts. I'll take care of it."

Sam nodded. "Sorry. It's just—"

"We're cutting things close," Daniel said. "I know."

"Yeah," Sam said, and turned back to the device chamber.

At least some of the layout was familiar from the installation on P7F-260, even if this was definitely an earlier version of the system. She had already identified the power connections, and the point where she could attach a naquadah generator to jump-start the system. Next up was figuring out the configuration of the main control panel, and then, with any luck, she'd be in a position to identify the targeting device. She hadn't been all that concerned with it back on P6T-847, since they hadn't planned to go anywhere, but this time she wanted to try to get them home. If she could just figure out how to direct the subspace energy, maybe she could figure out a way to shift them across the dimensions, just like that Ancient mirror had done… She felt in her pocket for a borrowed screwdriver and began to pry the panels loose.

The light had faded from the opening at the top of the ladder by the time she finished tracing the first round of circuits, and she struggled to hold a flashlight in her teeth while she pulled out a bracket to examine the fittings.

"Sam?" Daniel took the flashlight out of her mouth and trained it on the bracket. "We should be heading back."

"I want to stay a little longer."

"The light's bad," Daniel pointed out. "I'd move the second worklight in here, but I don't think it would do much good. Besides, you need to sleep sometime."

"Sleep's overrated," Sam said, but pushed herself out from

under the console and sat up. She glanced at her watch, and was startled to see that it was past seven.

Daniel nodded, and held out his hand to help her up. "We'll start fresh in the morning."

By the end of the next day, Sam had identified most of the differences between the installation on P6T-847 and this version of the device, but she was still short of useable crystals. She could see how to bypass the least important, but the others would have to handle an increased load, and there was no way to guarantee they could stand it. She said as much to Jack when he and Teal'c climbed down to see how things were going, bringing two more flashlights and a thermos of actual coffee. Sam took a cup gratefully, wrapping her hands around the plastic. It got cold after dark on Athos.

"So does that mean we can use it, or we can't?" Jack asked.

"It means I don't know," Sam said. "I can start it up, and I think it will run, but I don't know if the crystals will short out before we get where we're going."

"Does that mean we would be trapped in transit?" Teal'c asked. "Or killed?"

"Both are possible," Sam answered. "I think the latter is more likely."

"Oh, well, that's a comfort," Jack said.

"Yes, sir."

"But it could work," Daniel said. "Did you figure out if it has a DHD equivalent?"

"I did," Sam said. "And, no, it doesn't. It looks as though these chambers — or this chamber, anyway — was designed to go to a single, central hub. And before you ask, no, I don't know where the hub was meant to be."

"Does it still exist?" Jack asked. "More important, can we tell if it doesn't before we turn the thing on?"

"I've identified a set of what look like safeties," Sam answered, "and I think they will keep the system from firing if there's no locked-in destination."

"But if we're just going to a hub…" Daniel began.

Sam nodded. "I know. We're going to end up wherever this takes us. But, if it's the hub, then we should be able to program it to send us back to our own time. I think we'll have a better chance of doing it there than we would in a secondary device like this." She squared her shoulders. "Sir, if we're going to try this, we need to do it before Major Sheppard and his people leave Athos. That way, they won't lose a generator, and if something goes wrong, there's a chance McKay can get us out of it."

"I'd rather trust you," Daniel muttered.

"So would I," Sam answered. "But McKay is good."

Jack nodded. "I'll talk to Sheppard. I know they're starting to send people through to the alpha site at dawn, but I imagine he can spare us McKay and Zelenka for an hour or two."

As far as Jack could tell, everything was ready. Cables snaked across the installation's floor, powering the last of the expedition's work lights and ready to switch on the ouroboros device. McKay and Zelenka were bickering in the outer chamber, laptops open on two separate consoles, and in the inner chamber, Carter had her head literally inside the central console. She pulled herself out as he watched, and took a crystal that Daniel held out to her.

"Ok," she called. "I'm inserting the key stone."

"Yes, ok," McKay answered. "Ok, is it in?"

"Yes."

"Nothing's happening."

"Well, it's not supposed to," Carter said. "Not yet."

"I show a change in the background power flow," Zelenka said, and McKay abandoned his laptop to look over the other man's shoulder.

"Ok, that's interesting."

"Problem?" Jack asked, and McKay glared at him.

"Not so far."

"Sir?" Carter came to the opening in the diamond partition. "I think we're ready."

As ready as we're going to be, anyway. Jack swallowed the words, and looked at Sheppard.

"You heard Colonel Carter."

"Yes, sir." Sheppard bit his lip. "Look, sir, wouldn't it make more sense to come through to the alpha site with the expedition? We can give the Wraith a week or two to check things out while we get set up and Colonel Carter has more time to work out how the thing works — maybe even find some more replacement crystals. Dex says he thinks there are a number of them in museums on his homeworld. It's only a quick trip through the gate."

"If this doesn't work, we'll end up doing exactly that," Jack said. "But trying it now is the least risk to everyone. You know that, Major."

"Yes, sir," Sheppard said again. He paused. "It doesn't mean I like it."

"You don't have to," Jack said, with a grin. "Hell, I'm not sure I like it. But it's what we've got." He held out his hand and Sheppard took it, startled at first, and then with a grin of his own.

"Good luck, General," he said, and stepped back with a salute.

Jack returned it, more moved than he would have expected, and walked into the inner chamber. Teal'c shoved the chamber door closed behind them, and Jack took a breath. "Ok, Carter. Let's start her up."

"Yes, sir." She moved to take her place at the central console. "Ok, I'm connecting the generator."

Daniel was already at the secondary console, frowning over half a dozen screens that suddenly ran with Ancient lettering, while Teal'c waited beside Carter, his expression as impassive as ever. Jack felt something rumble beneath his feet, against his skin, too deep for hearing.

The radio crackled, and McKay's voice came through, cutting over a hiss of static. "The circuit is open. The power's flowing as predicted. Everything's smooth on this end."

"Everything reads good here," Daniel said.

"I am getting a backflow warning," Zelenka announced.

"Nothing," Daniel began. "Oh. No, wait, it's showing up here, too."

"More power, McKay," Carter said.

"That is exactly the wrong thing to do," McKay said.

"Direct subspace tap," Carter said. "Different rules."

"Fine. Increasing power." McKay moved to another console, touching keys.

"That's fixed it," Daniel said.

"Seventy percent charged," Carter said.

The hairs on Jack's arms lifted in the electric air. This was where it had all started to go wrong the first time.

"Seventy-five percent," Carter said. "Eighty. Eighty-five, eighty-eight—"

There was a crack and a puff of smoke from the central console. Carter flung back a cover, and Jack flinched from the sight of the tray of crystals bathed in weird blue-purple light.

"Crap," Carter said. "I can't—there's nothing I can do about them." Another crystal shattered. "Daniel! What's it doing?"

"Everything still looks good here," Daniel answered. "I show ninety-two percent."

"Ninety-five," Carter said. Two more crystals exploded.

"Hey!" Jack said.

"We have to let it run, sir," Carter answered. "And hope enough of them hold." She looked back at her screen. "Ninety-six percent."

On the back wall of the chamber, the snake's eyes were glowing again. A ball of golden light formed behind its head, began to move slowly around the curve of its body.

"Ninety-seven."

Another crystal shattered, but the light kept moving.

"Ninety-eight."

Two more crystals blew in quick succession, and this time the light seemed to falter, not quite to eleven o'clock.

"Sam," Daniel said. "I'm starting to see stress —"

"Ninety-nine," Carter said. "Come on, hold together…"

The light was moving again, almost to the snake's mouth, blue-white and painfully bright. Jack caught a last glimpse of Sheppard behind the glass, shading his eyes, McKay further back, his mouth open, Zelenka still busy at his console. And then there was a flat snap, concussive as a door slamming, and the chamber vanished.

Daniel lifted his head, wincing as he adjusted his glasses. The ouroboros device had worked, all right; he was in another chamber remarkably similar to the one on Atlantis, a smudged and blackened ouroboros on the wall above him. And he was unharmed, and so apparently were the others, dragging themselves back to consciousness around him.

"You know," Jack said, peevishly, "only Janus would think that it was a good idea for a transport system to knock you out on the way."

"Indeed," Teal'c said.

Daniel sat up, studying the room again. It really was a lot like the one on Atlantis, smooth, pearl-gray walls, the shallow platform beneath the damaged ouroboros, the tall doors in the corner of the room. He looked at the ouroboros again, trying to remember the pattern of the marks before. "Sam…"

"Yeah, I know." She lurched to her feet, wincing a little. "Sir, I think we may be back on Atlantis."

"Underwater? Turning things on just by being here?" Jack looked even less pleased than before.

"It's possible, sir."

"Assume we are," Jack said. "What do we do?"

"We need to find someplace to access the city's systems," Sam said, her voice grim. "As soon as possible."

Teal'c cocked his head to one side. "The transport chamber? It was not far from here."

Sam nodded, already moving toward the door. "I wish

there were something closer, but we can't waste time looking."

Jack waved his hand at the door's sensors and it slid back. "Let's go."

Even knowing where they were going, it seemed to take forever to get to the heavy doors and the transport chamber that lay behind them. Sam went instantly to the console, slinging off her borrowed pack.

"Everything's already initialized," she reported. "I think we are back where we started."

"That's not very helpful," Jack said. He was staying well away from any sensors, trying not to touch anything that might become active.

Daniel moved to join her, frowning at the screen. "This says everything's stable —"

"Yeah." Sam nodded, her hands busy on the controls. "It looks as though we didn't turn too many things on yet, and I think — yes, that's got it. I've told the city not to activate anything automatically. It should only bring systems on line in response to a direct command."

Daniel touched keys, hunting through the status screens for information on the shield. "Ok, the shield is still holding, and covers what looks like the entire city. Power levels are low, but steady. I don't see any big draw anywhere except the shield."

"Can we dial out of here if we have to?" Jack asked.

Sam nodded. "Yes. Anyplace in Pegasus."

"Well, that's something." He hooked his hands in his belt. "If there's a problem, we dial the alpha site. Everyone got that address?"

Sam and Daniel nodded. Teal'c said, "Yes, O'Neill."

"Ok." Jack looked around the city as though he had a personal grudge against it, which Daniel had to admit was not entirely unreasonable. "So why the hell are we back here, Carter?"

"That's a good question, sir." Sam was poking at the controls again, but shook her head. "I think that's better answered from the control room."

Daniel glanced at the transport chamber. "Do we want to turn that on?"

"No," Sam said. "We walk."

It took almost two hours to make the trek from the transport chamber — which proved to be two levels below what Jack insisted on calling the deck — to the control room. The climb into the tower seemed interminable, and Daniel's legs were burning by the time they finally reached the gate room floor. It was still dimly lit, the light that came through the long windows blued by the glass and the weight of the water overhead. The broken pieces of the champagne bottle lay where he had dropped them, final proof that this was indeed the same Atlantis they had reached before.

Sam climbed to the control room, moving from console to console until she found the one she wanted. She touched keys, and a few small lights came on, driving back the shadows. "That's all I dare do right now," she called.

It was better than nothing, Daniel thought. He followed her up the stairs, trying to make sense of the various consoles, and after a moment Jack and Teal'c followed as well.

"Any ideas?" Jack asked, after a moment.

Sam settled herself in front of what seemed to be a master control board, and called up a search routine. She plugged in Janus's name and squinted at the rapidly flashing lines of type. "Right now, I'm working from the hypothesis that this timeline's Janus designed the ouroboros system to go between Atlantis and various outlying stations — you couldn't go from one station to another, the way you can with the Stargates. If you want to use ouroboros to get from one world to another, you have to go through the hub here on Atlantis."

"It doesn't seem like the installation on P6T-847 was set up that way," Daniel said.

"It wasn't," Sam answered. "There were controls for entering a destination using a variation on the gate addresses. But we never entered an address."

"But this isn't even our timeline," Jack said. "Why didn't it just send us to our Atlantis?"

"I'm not sure," Sam said. "Right now, I'm going with the theory that it has something to do with tapping directly into subspace energy. Subspace — well, theoretically it's outside normal spacetime, so it's not part of any timeline, or, more properly, it's potentially part of all possible timelines —"

"Carter," Jack said.

"Sorry, sir. Essentially, I think this is probably the only Atlantis that's set up as a hub, but because it's tied into subspace through Janus's experimental power system, any ouroboros in any timeline that fires without having a destination set ends up here."

"So if we'd entered a destination, we'd have gone there?" Jack said. "In our own timeline."

"Assuming it still existed," Sam answered. "The thing I'm hoping is that the ouroboros has other similarities to the Stargate system, and that it keeps the most recent addresses in memory somewhere. If it does, we may be able to get back home — well, to P6T-847, anyway."

"But the power requirements," Daniel began, and Sam gave a little shrug.

"The ouroboros seems to be powered entirely separately from the rest of the city. We should be able to start the subspace tap without drawing more than the ZPMs can handle."

Jack nodded. "What's your next move, Carter?"

"Well, once I'm sure power consumption is safe and stable here," Sam answered, "I want to go back to the ouroboros chamber and see if it's intact and if it's preserved the original address."

"Jack should go with you," Daniel said. "In case there are things that need to be initialized. Teal'c and I can stay here and monitor the systems."

Sam nodded. "That would be a help."

"I don't like us splitting up," Jack said.

"I'm not crazy about it either, sir," Sam said. "But Daniel's right, there may be things attached to the ouroboros that will only respond to the ATA gene. And somebody does need to watch the power consumption here."

"Are you sure you want to trust me around Ancient stuff?" Jack asked.

"I've told the system not to activate anything unless it's done directly through the consoles," Sam answered. "That should hold it. If the city does try to bring anything on line, Daniel can stop it here, at this screen. And the sooner we can find a way to dial out, the more stable the situation will be."

Jack studied the screen. For all his disclaimers, Daniel thought, the man was no fool when it came to Ancient technology. He hated the stuff, but he understood it well enough. "All right, Carter. We'll do it your way." He looked at Daniel. "We'll stay in radio contact. Let us know immediately if there are any problems."

"Don't worry about that," Daniel said, and slid into a chair in front of the console.

There were controls in the ouroboros room after all, hidden behind almost invisible panels. They didn't respond to the ATA gene, and it took both her and Jack to lever them open, but the panels and displays they revealed were at least familiar. They weren't identical to the ones on P6T-847 — that would have been too easy — but there were enough similarities that she was able to find the basic diagnostic and run that.

And there it stuck. The program ran through its first seven steps and then crashed, without even achieving an error message. Sam ran it a third time, shook her head as the same flashing error-abort message appeared. "It's as though the system isn't on-line at all."

Jack peered over her shoulder. "But it has to be, right, or we couldn't have come through it?"

His voice trailed off, as doubtful-sounding as she felt, and she typed another inquiry string. Characters flashed, filling the screen and scrolling off, and she waited for them to finish before scrolling back, picking her way through the unfamiliar words. It seemed to be saying that the — annunciator? emitter? — couldn't speak without the reed, but she thought that probably meant there was something missing from the outgoing circuit. It certainly looked as though the diagnostic checked the outgoing system first. Sam scrolled through the rest of the display, seeing nothing else helpful, and looked around the room again. "All right, it says that there's something wrong with the emitter, and that should mean we need to open up the main control console. Except it's hidden, too."

"If you were an Ancient mad scientist, where would you put it?"

"Janus wasn't a mad scientist."

Jack gave her a crooked smile, and Sam grimaced.

"Well, ok, maybe he was. But that's not the point." She turned through a full circle, frowning. "Well, if he put the secondary consoles in the wall — maybe under the floor?"

At first glance, it seemed unmarked, but a closer look revealed a web of slightly darker lines woven through the warm brown surface. And some of them seemed to mark out a shape that matched the control console.

"Maybe here?" she said, and went to one knee beside the most likely set of markings.

"Nice going, Carter." Jack crouched beside her.

Seen up close, some of the marks looked like Ancient letters, spelling out the command to push, and she spread her hands to fit her fingers into the gaps between the letters. For a moment, nothing happened, and she looked over her shoulder. "Sir?"

Jack spread his hands, fitted them into the spaces where her fingers had been. The floor shivered and split, the console rising with a shriek of unoiled metal.

"Nice," Jack said again.

Sam touched her radio. "Daniel. We've opened up the control console. Any problems with the power?"

"Not here." Daniel's answer was reassuringly prompt. "Everything's steady."

"Good. Thanks." She stood back to study the console. All its indicators were dark, except for a single pinpoint of red glowing from the center of the upper arch. Probably that meant there was power, but it wasn't getting past some primary blockage — maybe a burnt-out crystal. She found the access hatch and pried it loose, pulling out the tray of crystals.

"That doesn't look good," Jack said.

"Not so much." Sam bent over the tray. On second glance, most of the smaller crystals seemed to be intact, though some of them showed scorch marks; she pulled and reseated them, and their sockets seemed to be undamaged. There were half a dozen larger crystals that showed signs of stress. The first she pulled had a hairline fracture running the full length of the shaft. The others were all in better shape, but they showed faint scarring and a couple had chips taken out of their long edges. At least the central crystal, the one that she was guessing was analogous to the master control crystal on a DHD, was intact and in place, but there was an empty socket beside it, and even at first glance she could see that the other circuits fed through it. "Damn."

"Looks like something's missing," Jack said.

Sam nodded. There was something familiar about the socket, though — the shape and size matched the key crystal Daniel had taken from the Wraith hive. She reached into her pack, carefully unwrapped the long shape.

"That's the thing Daniel found?" Jack moved closer.

"Yes, sir." Sam checked the socket and the connectors, decided they were close enough, and carefully eased the key crystal into place. It didn't quite fit, almost as though it was a slightly different model, but she wiggled it in until she had full contact. More lights sprang to life on the main console, and she straightened, looking at them. Power was flowing now, though the whole system was still on standby, and she slid the tray back into place. The lights flickered, but steadied. "Let me run the diagnostic now —"

"Sam!" Daniel's voice crackled from the radio. "Sam, I'm getting a cascade of systems trying to engage. I'm shutting them down as fast as I can, but I can't seem to get them to stop."

Sam grabbed for the tray, hauled it open again. Nothing seemed to be happening, but she pulled the key crystal anyway, stood back to check the console. The new lights vanished, replaced by the single red light, but nothing else happened. "Did that make any difference?"

"No. Not at all. It's speeding up."

"We need to get back there," Jack said.

"I know!" It was more than an hour away, even if they ran, and that was too long —

"The transport chamber," Jack said. "Come on, Carter!"

"But the power —"

"Doesn't matter if the shield collapses."

He was right, she knew, and hurried after him. "Daniel! Can you cut power to everything except the shield?"

"Sam, I can't cut power to anything! It just keeps coming back on."

"Keep trying!"

"Carter!" Jack was already at the transport chamber door. "Let's go."

"Sir, if Daniel kills the power while we're in transit —"

"We're dead. I know. But I don't think he's going to, and I want you up there now."

He was right. All around them, lights were flickering on, then off again, then back on, a pattern that in its own way was worse than a steady power drain. "Yes, sir," she said, and stepped into the chamber with him.

Jack closed his eyes, and there was a weird shiver of not-movement. The door slid open on the gateroom floor.

"Daniel!" Sam shouted, and started for the control room.

"Any progress?"

"No, not really." Daniel didn't look up from the console, a bad sign. "Oh, crap."

In the distance an alarm began to sound.

CHAPTER TWENTY-FOUR
Return

THE CITY shuddered under Teal'c's feet, its alarms a rising crescendo around him. Colonel Carter scrambled up to the control room level, slammed herself into a chair at Daniel's side.

"Oh, this is so not good."

Teal'c looked at O'Neill, whose face was tight with strain.

"Did you have to use the transport chamber?" Daniel demanded. "That turned on about six systems all at once."

"Yes, we did," Carter said. Her hands flew across the board. "Damn it, the shield's shutting down."

That must be the new alarm, Teal'c thought, the one whose strident note cut through all the others. That was what the ultimate disaster alarms always sounded like, ear-splitting, discordant, impossible to miss. He couldn't help looking around the gateroom, at the walls of colored glass bound only with thin strips of metal. If the shield failed, those windows would never hold back the water.

"Come on, Carter," O'Neill said, but too quietly for her to hear. The city shuddered again, metal creaking far beneath them.

"All right," Carter said. "Daniel, keep trying to divert power back to the shield. I — there has to be some kind of fail-safe."

"It's not working," Daniel said.

"Keep trying."

"Carter…" O'Neill's voice trailed off, drowned by the echoing alarms.

"We've lost the outer pads," Daniel said. "The shield's collapsing, I can't hold it."

The city groaned, a grinding metallic sound as though it strained against some enormous pressure. On the edges of the city, windows were shattering, water flooding corridors and towers, walls collapsing. It would happen here soon enough,

Teal'c knew. The shield would fail and all the beautiful glass would shatter, shards and water falling together in a killing wave, sweeping away even the Stargate.

"Dial the alpha site," O'Neill ordered.

"We can't," Daniel said. "There's not enough power."

"Carter!"

"I'm trying, sir." She was typing frantically, her eyes darting from screen to screen. "Wait, wait — Daniel, is this —"

"<u>Ancoram tollere</u> — to release —"

"Hang on!" Carter hit a final sequence of keys.

The city moaned again, metal snapping somewhere, and Carter squeezed her eyes shut. Teal'c caught the nearest stanchion as the floor lurched beneath him, the city swaying as though caught in a sudden current. Metal ground on metal, kept grinding, a long wail like a thousand raw-throated ghosts. The light behind the windows changed, grew brighter as the floor lurched again, wobbling as though an earthquake rocked them.

"We're moving!" Carter's voice cracked.

"We're rising," Daniel answered. He clung to the console's edge as the city shook again. "The shield's holding —"

There was new light outside the windows, true sunlight, and the rippling reflection of water sheeting down the outside of the tower. Teal'c turned as the last of the water rolled away and behind him, behind the consoles, the windows showed clear sky and Atlantis floating on the surface of an unknown sea. Water still poured from her roofs and walkways, but she was alive and safe for now.

"The shield's gone," Daniel said. "Sam, you did it!"

"Good job, Carter," O'Neill said, and Teal'c nodded.

"Indeed."

"We're on the surface," Carter said, reading from her console. "There's — well, not plenty of power, but without the shield to maintain, there's enough."

"Long-range sensors are coming online," Daniel said. "Do you want me to shut them down?"

Carter made a face, studying the readings. "Let's make sure there's nothing out there."

"Ok." Daniel peered at his screens. "I'm not seeing anything. It looks like we're clear."

O'Neill nodded. "Good news. Ok, Carter, what just happened?"

Teal'c released his grip on the railing. "I, too, am curious."

"Well." For once, Carter looked flustered, her eyes still wide, one hand caressing the edge of the console. "The city was underwater, and something had to be keeping it there — putting aside all the other factors, there was enough atmosphere trapped inside the shield to make the city buoyant. The city wasn't using any power to hold itself in place — there wasn't any to spare, and anyway, if there had been, that would have been sacrificed to keep the shield up. So there had to be some kind of mechanical anchor holding the city down, and — I released it."

"In the nick of time," O'Neill said.

"Yes, sir." Carter looked embarrassed. "Sorry, sir."

"Joking, Carter." O'Neill looked around, the sunlight pouring in through the colored glass, spreading patterns across the floor and walls. "So what have we got?"

"Looks like one Ancient city fully intact," Daniel said. "A little low on power —"

"A lot low on power," Carter said. "We certainly can't dial Earth from here, even if we were in the right timeline. And I'm not sure about the shield. I think maybe it could be raised, but I don't know how long it would last. Everything else, though — Daniel's right, everything else seems to be working."

Suddenly it seemed more important to be out in the air, to feel their escape in the air on his skin rather than to hear them discussing it. Teal'c pushed cautiously at what looked like a door, and it slid back, admitting a puff of warm, salt-smelling air. He stepped through onto the balcony.

The sky was clear, cloudless, the deep clear blue of a world with no industries to speak of. He tipped his head back, feeling the sun on his face and arms, looking up into an expanse empty enough to dazzle. It was warm, tropical, and all around him was Atlantis and her towers, riding steady on the breast of the ocean. He could hear water running in the distance, see a few thin, glittering streams where it still ran off roofs and overhangs. Below him the deck was already drying, and in the distance, sky and sea met in an endless, empty horizon.

"Makes you wonder what our guys found," O'Neill said quietly.

Teal'c turned, unsurprised at the other man's stealth. O'Neill had always been able to move silently when he chose. "Indeed."

"Is our Atlantis at the bottom of the ocean? Were they short on power, too? Did they get away through the gate, and are there Wraith out there chasing them?"

"We will find out," Teal'c said.

O'Neill shot him a glance that was for one instant naked in its concern. And then O'Neill looked away, familiar mask falling back into place. "Daniel's in there arguing with himself about whether all Atlantises have to have sunk. Carter's getting ready to dial the alpha site."

"Ah," Teal'c said, and O'Neill nodded.

"No reason they can't move back in now that we've solved their little problem for them. And it's a hell of a lot safer than bouncing around Pegasus trying to dodge the Wraith."

"Let us inform them," Teal'c said, and pushed open the door that led to the control room.

The Stargate lit again, the unstable plume collapsing to form the familiar rippling puddle. Sheppard emerged from the wormhole, looking around with a startled expression. McKay and Teyla followed him, both of them open-mouthed, and Jack couldn't help grinning.

"Welcome to Atlantis, Major!"

"Thank you, sir," Sheppard said, still looking around as though he couldn't believe it.

"We're not underwater!" McKay said. "How'd you do that?"

"It is beautiful," Teyla said. "Truly this is the city of the Ancestors."

"Carter figured out how to fix the problem," Jack said, to McKay — he figured he could afford to indulge himself just a little.

Sheppard shook his head in disbelief, but he was smiling. "Damn. It'd take us a couple of days to move everything through from the alpha site, but —" He shook his head again. "No sign of the Wraith? Any other hostiles?"

"The long range sensors are all clear," Carter answered. "They're capable of reaching well beyond the limits of this system, too. And Daniel says that there's a landmass about forty miles due east of here. Sensors don't show any lifesigns above the size of a bird. So you're good. For the moment, anyway."

"What about the shield?" Sheppard asked.

"You can run it for a few minutes," Carter answered. "After that, it'll drain the ZPMs."

"Not so good." Sheppard looked around again, unable to keep from grinning. "Still, if the Wraith don't know we're here..."

"And if you can find another power source," Jack said. "Another ZPM would be nice."

"We know they're out there," Sheppard answered.

Teyla nodded. "I have seen such things for trade, though I do not know if they would function, and also in museums on certain more advanced worlds. I believe the Satedans might be able to help you, though they will drive a hard bargain."

"We can bargain," Sheppard said. "And even without another ZPM, there's enough power to run everything except the shields. Right, McKay?"

"Right." McKay was looking at Carter's laptop, barely raised his head.

Sheppard looked at Teyla. "Your people would be welcome to take shelter here, at least until you're sure the Wraith have abandoned Athos. There's plenty of room."

Teyla smiled at that, a genuine smile that made her younger than she was. Or maybe she really was that young, Jack thought. Sometimes it was hard to tell any more.

"Yes, I do not believe that you are lacking in space, Major Sheppard. And I will gladly convey your offer to Halling and the rest of the council."

"I was thinking especially the kids," Sheppard said, and she nodded.

"That was in my mind also."

Jack could imagine them all too clearly, the gateroom and the soaring halls alive with a pack of kids. As it should be, as it had been once, and the thought was complicated enough that he shook it aside. "In the meantime, Major, we still need to get back to our own timeline."

"Whatever we can do, sir," Sheppard said, and Carter looked up from the laptop.

"Could I borrow Dr. McKay, Major? I have some ideas about the ouroboros that he might be able to help me with."

"He's all yours," Sheppard said.

"What have you got in mind, Carter?" Jack asked.

"Well, sir, I want to try to run that diagnostic with the key crystal in place," Carter said. "If the system is functional, then I want to check the master control crystal and see if it has the coordinates that we came from still stored in it —"

"No, no, no," McKay said. "There's no reason it would."

"Actually, when I was examining the system, it looked as though it was set up to reflect and record the various points of origin," Carter said.

Jack tuned out the argument, knowing Carter was going to win. He was suddenly dead tired, as though the weight of the city itself had come crashing down on him. And this was exactly why it had been time for him to get out of the field, no matter how hard it had been to settle down behind a desk. Yeah, he could still do it — he'd just proved that, no question — but it was a lot harder than it had been eight years ago. One last hurrah: yeah, if – *when* — Carter got them home, he'd stay in Cheyenne Mountain and manage things. At least for a while.

"Ok, Carter," he said, interrupting McKay mid-stream. "What do you need to make this work?"

Sam regarded the results of the most recent diagnostic with a certain satisfaction. With the key crystal in place, the system proclaimed itself complete, and, despite the warnings that flickered at the edge of the screen, she was reasonably confident it would function.

"You need to replace those broken crystals," McKay said. "If you don't — you're just asking for it to blow up in your face."

"We don't have any replacements," Sam said. "I mean, yes, if we had them, absolutely, but we don't."

"We could take them from the ouroboros on Athos," McKay said.

"I don't think that's a good idea."

"Look, what are the odds that the Wraith are going to show up at the exact moment we're in the city? We go through, we get the crystals, we gate back before anyone's the wiser."

Sam shook her head. "The way our luck is running, the Wraith will be waiting for us. First let's see if the return path is intact, otherwise we're going to have to do some pretty fancy calculations."

"It probably won't be," McKay said, but stepped out of her way.

Sam adjusted her probe, touched it carefully to the master control crystal. Yes, there was an energy signature stored within it, though it was faint enough that she suspected McKay might be right, and the residual effect wasn't intentional. But at least it was present. She touched keys on her laptop, increasing the sensitivity, and this time the probe connected immediately. She copied the signature, frowning at the unfamiliar pattern, and McKay came to look over her shoulder.

"Well, it's definitely not a normal pattern. I've pulled buffer patterns before, and this one's different. Are you sure it's an address?"

"If it isn't, I don't know what it is," Sam answered. "And you wouldn't expect it to look like a normal address if it's actually reaching outside the timeline."

"I suppose." McKay tilted his head. "How are you going to enter it into the system?"

"I was hoping to just reverse it," Sam said.

"That's not going to work," McKay said. "At least, I'm pretty sure it won't. I think you're going to need to run a Marsden transform on it to turn it into an address the system can work with."

"I'm not sure that's going to work, either," Sam said. "This isn't a gate address we're talking about, it's an entirely different form."

McKay didn't contradict her, which she supposed constituted agreement. "So your theory is that this is designed as a hub, and it's the connection through subspace that brought you here."

"Yes." Sam rubbed her cheek as a new idea struck her. "Not Marsden, but Wakefield. The Lowe-Wakefield theorem."

"Yes." McKay reached for his own laptop. "Yes, we can use that to define the general parameters of the problem as it relates to the subspace generator, and then we can plug in the reading you got—"

"After we translate it to coordinates using Lowe-Wakefield—"

"And that should let the system jump across timelines," McKay finished triumphantly.

Sam grinned at him, for all that they had hours of calculations ahead of them. "Exactly. We're just about done."

It took almost six hours to finish, even using the city's computers, and by that time it was dark and Sam was exhausted. The rest of SG-1 had claimed a suite of rooms in the tower one level below the gateroom, and she rolled herself into her sleeping bag, too tired to do more than wolf down the last of the power bars.

Sunlight woke her, the pink light of a spectacular sunrise, all of the eastern horizon pink and gold beneath a shell of cloud.

Jack was awake already, though Teal'c and Daniel were still asleep, and she rose quietly to come stand beside him at the window. The city glowed in the early light, a thousand reflections gleaming from glass and steel and stone, and the edge of the sun lifted above the sea, almost too bright to bear.

"It's beautiful," she said softly, and Jack nodded.

"It is. And abandoned all this time."

"It's hard to believe we finally found it." Sam paused. "Well, some form of it. Is Atlantis like this in our timeline, I wonder?"

"Daniel thinks so," Jack said. "It matches descriptions he's read or something, I wasn't entirely clear. He'd like to stay — well, if it was our Atlantis."

Sam nodded. "I'm almost ready. The system's almost ready, I mean. We should be able to try it today."

"Good job, Carter." Jack smiled. "It's probably time we were getting home."

It was noon before everything was finished. Daniel gave the city's towers a last regretful look before taking the transport chamber down to the lower levels. The door of the ouroboros chamber stood open, though there was now a console jutting up in the middle of the floor, and Sam and McKay were arguing across its top. Jack was leaning against the wall, trying to look bored, while Sheppard and Teal'c stood to one side, Sheppard looking faintly awkward as usual.

"I think we can tap this power source once you're gone," McKay was saying, "which will more than make up for the ZPMs. And all it takes is the boost from one naquadah generator, of which we have plenty."

"I don't think it's going to be that straightforward," Sam said. "Working directly with subspace is tricky."

"Oh, please, you don't think I can control it?"

"I think you're likely to blow up a sun or something," Sam said frankly, and Sheppard's frown deepened.

"How likely is that, Colonel?" he asked.

"Not very," McKay snapped. "And you might ask me, since I'm your head of sciences."

"That's why I'm asking Colonel Carter," Sheppard retorted.

"It's possible," Sam said, to Sheppard. "But – Dr. McKay does know what he's doing."

"I'll talk to Zelenka, too," Sheppard said, with a quick grin.

"Zelenka!" McKay's voice scaled upward. "What does he know about subspatial theory that I don't?"

"He has a lot more common sense," Sheppard said. "Are you ready, Colonel? General O'Neill?"

"Are we, Carter?" Jack asked.

"Yes, sir." She closed her laptop and handed it to McKay, who looked momentarily stricken.

"Maybe we should go over those calculations one more time," he began, and Sam shook her head.

"We're ready. And I think you and Major Sheppard should leave the chamber. Anything in here is going to get transported with us."

For a moment, Daniel wished he could have spent more time with the Ancient database — if he hadn't slept the night before, maybe, or if anyway he'd just stayed awake a little longer. There was so much here, so much that he hadn't had time to skim, never mind study… But this wasn't Atlantis, not his Atlantis, the Atlantis that was real to him. There was no guarantee that anything he learned here would be true in their version of the Pegasus Galaxy.

"Good luck, General, Colonel," Sheppard said. "Gentlemen."

"Thank you, Major," Jack answered, and Sam echoed him.

McKay started to say something, advice or complaint, not from the tone of it good wishes, and Sheppard pushed him out the door. The door slid shut behind him.

"All right, kids," Jack said. "Ready to go home?"

"Ready, sir." Sam bent over the console. "I'm starting the system now."

Daniel braced himself, but nothing happened. "Sam?"

"It's working." She eyed the console warily. "The connection is now open, and power is building."

"Should we take up any particular position?" Teal'c asked.

"Besides duck and cover?" Jack asked. Teal'c gave him a questioning look, and Jack sighed. "Never mind."

"Indeed."

"We shouldn't need to," Sam said. "Everything in the room should go." She looked at the console again. "Seventy-five percent."

"The eyes are glowing," Daniel said.

"Which is a good sign, right?" Jack said.

"Evidently," Teal'c said.

"Eighty-five percent," Sam said.

The ball of light formed, began to make its way around the snake's body, glowing white-hot, bright enough to leave green trails across Daniel's vision. Teal'c shaded his eyes, and Jack ducked his head a little, grimacing.

"Ninety percent," Sam said. "Ninety-five, ninety-eight —"

Another flat crack, like lightning, and abruptly they were stumbling off the edge of the platform in an installation like the one they'd started from. Daniel tripped and went to his knees, hauled himself up to see only familiar faces. Bill Lee, Nick Perry, Joe Periera — they were back on P6T-847, and in their own proper time.

"You did it, Sam," he said.

Jack nodded. "Nice work, Carter."

"Thank you, sir," Sam said, and Teal'c nodded.

"Indeed."

The nearest technicians were pulling back the door, and Lee shoved his way past to be first into the chamber. "General O'Neill! Colonel Carter! Thank God you're all right. What happened?"

"We went on a little trip," Jack said. "Apparently the — what did you call them, cut-outs? They didn't work."

"Well, um — no." Lee ducked his head, visibly embarrassed.

"What happened on this end?" Sam asked.

"Well." Lee blinked hard. "When the system wouldn't shut down, and you ordered everyone out — there was a flash of light and you disappeared."

"Did the ouroboros do anything?" Sam asked. "Say where we'd gone, anything like that?"

"Not that we've been able to find out," Lee answered. "We were just starting to try to get some decent diagnostics when the snake's eyes started to glow again. So we cleared the chamber and, bam! There you were. Back."

"Wait a minute," Jack said. "What do you mean, you were just starting to run diagnostics?"

"Well, first we wanted to be sure you weren't going to just, you know, reappear," Lee said. "And then we wanted to be sure we weren't going to disturb any important settings." He stopped, looking hurt. "You've only been gone about ten minutes, General."

"Ten minutes," Jack said, his voice flat. "Not to us, Dr. Lee."

Sam said, "It's kind of a long story."

"Be that as it may," Jack said, "we are not going to do any more fooling around with this thing until we have a lot better understanding of how and why we ended up in an alternate timeline. Got that?"

Lee looked as though he wanted to object, but he was quelled by Jack's lifted eyebrow.

"We're shutting this down now," Jack said. "Carter, I want you to find that key crystal and remove it. I want to be very sure nobody else gets sent off to some random location. Once again, Janus's stuff turns out to be more trouble than it's worth."

Daniel looked over his shoulder at the golden ouroboros set into the wall. It looked utterly innocuous, like some purely decorative object, and he shook his head. "Do you think this has any connection with what's happening to our expedition? Have they had to abandon the city? Fight the Wraith?"

"We cannot know," Teal'c said, and Daniel thought there

was a note of sadness in his voice. "Perhaps they found Atlantis intact, or perhaps they were able to raise it —"

"Teal'c was right the first time," Sam said. "There's no way to know. Not until we can find some way to contact them."

"But this isn't it," Jack said, and she sighed.

"No, sir. I'm afraid not."

"We'll find a way," Jack said. "But for now — it's time to go home."

ABOUT THE AUTHOR

Melissa Scott is from Little Rock, Arkansas, and studied history at Harvard College and Brandeis University, where she earned her PhD in the Comparative History program.

She is the author of more than twenty science fiction and fantasy novels, and has won Lambda Literary Awards for *Trouble and Her Friends*, *Shadow Man*, and *Point of Dreams*, the last written with her late partner, Lisa A. Barnett.

She has also won Spectrum Awards for *Shadow Man* and again in 2010 for the short story "The Rocky Side of the Sky" (*Periphery*, Lethe Press) as well as the John W. Campbell Award for Best New Writer.

Her most recent novel, *Steel Blues*, written with Jo Graham, was published by Crossroad Press in early 2013, and her next novel, *Death By Silver*, written with Amy Griswold, will be out from Lethe Press in the spring of 2013.

She can be found on LiveJournal at mescott.livejournal.com

STARGATE SG·1.

STARGATE ATLANTIS

Original novels based on the hit TV shows **STARGATE SG-1** and **STARGATE ATLANTIS**

Available as e-books from leading online retailers

Paperback editions available from Amazon and IngramSpark

If you liked this book, please tell your friends and leave a review on a bookstore website. Thanks!

STARGATE SG-1 is a trademark of Metro-Goldwyn-Mayer Studios Inc. ©1997-2020 MGM Television Entertainment Inc. and MGM Global Holdings Inc. All Rights Reserved.
STARGATE ATLANTIS is a trademark of Metro-Goldwyn-Mayer Studios Inc. ©2004-2020 MGM Global Holdings Inc. All Rights Reserved.
METRO-GOLDWYN-MAYER is a trademark of Metro-Goldwyn-Mayer Lion Corp. © 2020 Metro-Goldwyn-Mayer Studios Inc. All Rights Reserved.

www.ingramcontent.com/pod-product-compliance
Lightning Source LLC
Chambersburg PA
CBHW011159190726
48286CB00009B/2845